THE TIME GUARDIANS OF GERATICA AND GERATICAI

By Anne Hampton

Anne Hampton was born in Bristol in 1971. She writes stories with strong female characters, though not with an anti-man agenda. She approaches adult themes from a sexually dominant woman's perspective – reversing the traditional male/female roles in the bedroom. Her books do not really fit into a specific genre, but encompass such themes as science fantasy, politics, romance / adult and thrilling mystery.

The events of the first two volumes of this book, cover the period from Alexandra Radcliffe's birth, to just prior to her final year at Charterhouse, and can be seen as a prequel to the first chronicle in the original 'Geratica' series...

<u>VOLUME 1</u>

PART 1

CHAPTER 1

Geratica Summer 4995

On the third day of the twenty-ninth week of the Geratican year 4995, Linda Radcliffe was sat up in bed in a private room of Greenacres maternity hospital. In her arms was her newly born daughter.

It had been a remarkably comfortable birth. She was not a woman to be overly concerned by the process, but even taking into account the experiences related to her by others who had been through a relatively smooth labour, she felt that she'd been blessed by some kind of good fortune.

Whether this event would be repeated was a question not quite yet definitely decided in Linda's mind. She was a highly ambitious woman in her career at the court of Queen Beatrice in the Royal Palace of Geratica, and there could be some important moves to make in the next few years. With her husband continuing to work as a miner, a nanny would very shortly need to be employed to enable her to return to work, as was often customary. But Linda still intended to be very much involved in the girl's upbringing. Having another child might divide into two the level of attention and devotion which she wished to give, resulting in each being the poorer for it. Linda was determined that her daughter would develop to become the best she could possibly be. She had been an only child herself and did not consider that she had lost out in any way because of it. Once Alexandra reached a certain age, she would probably begin to dispense with the nanny's services.

The door opened, and a nurse entered, followed closely by a man.

"Your husband is here, Mrs Radcliffe," said the nurse.

"Hello Robert," said Linda.

Robert hurried over to the bed and gazed at his daughter for the first time.

"She's beautiful," he said, looking back at his wife with a beaming smile. "Just like her mother!"

Linda smiled back. "Thank you, sweetheart."

"Have you thought about what we will call her?" asked Robert.

"Indeed, I have been," replied Linda. "And my mind is beginning to settle on Alexandra. I should like to do that, as a tribute to the princess. That will be a great honour and a privilege for her to bear as she goes through her life. I'm sure that you agree?"

"I certainly can't think of any reason why I shouldn't," said Robert. "I think that's a wonderful idea."

"Right. Alexandra it is then," affirmed Linda, without a second more of hesitation.

Her husband deferred to her. It had always been the way between men and women of their world, throughout their recorded history. It was sometimes defined as "the authority of the skirt," or "the rule of a woman's skirt." This was a highly symbolic garment on Geratica, and traditionally the woman wearing it was asserting her power, and the man respected and obeyed it, though certainly not always without discussion and it was not even unheard of for an occasional exchange of views to take place between them. But Linda had a particularly dominant personality and was very conservative in her view of the way their relationship should be. Robert was naturally submissive to his wife's wishes – sometimes even more so than the average man - mainly because he believed that as a woman, she knew better than him, and partly because he needed her. Linda had realised this quite soon after getting to know him and decided that he was exactly the sort of man she wanted. Since their engagement and subsequent marriage, she had never changed her opinion.

According to Geratican custom, Linda had drawn up the terms of their marriage contract and as reflected her personality and beliefs, it was an extremely rigid and tight arrangement where he as the husband was totally subservient to her authority as the wife. Further, she as the wife possessed her husband absolutely and should the man ever be unfaithful to her, she reserved the right to horsewhip him.

Since ancient times it had always been the right of a Geratican woman to discipline her husband for insubordination or infidelity, or even her fiancé for backing out of a contract for marriage or engagement after signing it - though such occasions were now rare, and attitudes were changing. The second of Linda's terms had caused the town clerk who witnessed their ceremony to flush slightly when she read it, but it was also considered customary for a man to accept his future wife's terms without condition. Robert had happily signed the contract and he and Linda were duly married.

The union of marriage was a serious institution on Geratica. Infidelity was far less common here than on Geraticai. Nevertheless, there were always a minority of women who tried to have it both ways – strictly forbidding their husbands from being unfaithful, whilst secretly taking a lover themselves. Linda had strongly assured Robert that she was not one of those. Although she was most certainly a natural Geratican woman and even after marriage would always find other men attractive and sexually desirable, her husband was definitely the man she loved more than any other and her feelings for him in bed were in accordance.

Linda looked adoringly at Alexandra, feeling a great surge of joy, love, and passion. She was indeed a beautiful baby, and her mother had no doubt that she would grow into a very attractive woman. Already as she looked into her eyes, she could feel a tremendous natural bond between them.

CHAPTER 2

It wasn't long before Alexandra was brought home.

Home was The Grange, in the hamlet of Elmsbrook, on the outskirts of Greenacres. Linda had brought the house for herself and Robert, a year before Alexandra's birth. It was a very quiet and secluded area, ideal for Linda to escape to from the stresses of her work at court, and would be a peaceful haven for Alexandra to grow up in. The house was spacious, and set in an acre of land, with gardens at the back and front, and an orchard. A long gravel driveway led up to it from the entrance.

At the end of the hamlet drive there was a smaller house with a smart timber roof called The Lodge, where an elderly lady, Mrs Hilda Travers, currently resided.

The hamlet was built within a private wood – Elmsbrook - which ran in a semi-circle around the back of it, surrounding both houses. There were entrances to the wood, to a side of each house. A river ran through part of the wood.

Linda's mother, Agatha Radcliffe, a retired railway company owner, came to visit one afternoon and see her granddaughter for the first time. Her father, Godfrey, had been suffering from senility for a couple of years now, and was in a care home. They had been somewhat older than was average when their only daughter was born. Linda was now twenty-nine, Agatha seventy-eight and Christopher eighty. Agatha still lived at the house where Linda had grown up, in Manscombe, thirty miles to the north of Greeenacres.

"She certainly seems to take after you, Linda," remarked Agatha, sitting in the parlour chair that she usually occupied when at The Grange. "Come here child, and let Grandmother take a closer look at you."

She held out her arms expectantly, and Linda carried Alexandra over to her. Agatha brushed her hand over her granddaughter's

head, which was beginning to sprout a similar blonde hair to Linda's. She looked into her blue eyes. For a moment it seemed that Alexandra might begin to cry, but then her grandmother soothed her, and she began to murmur happily.

"Now. You be a good girl for your mother, Alexandra," said Agatha in a faintly stern way. She held up her finger. "Otherwise, if I come here and find you misbehaving, I may have to discipline you myself."

Linda bristled slightly but tried to remain civil.

"Yes, thank you, Mother. Alexandra is of course still but a few days old! But I can assure you that I have no intention of *allowing* her to misbehave, and *I* shall do the disciplining. *I* am the mistress of this house!"

"Indeed, you are – and very much so, I'm sure!" retorted Agatha. "I wouldn't expect anything less, and I applaud you for it. But be that as it may, as the senior female of the Radcliffe family, I do have the right to apply my own corrective methods if I feel they are absolutely necessary. You know that is the way it has always traditionally been. And of course if any woman has a child under her charge and care, whether permanently or temporarily, no matter what relation she may be to that child – mother, aunt, grandmother, godmother, guardian, schoolmistress, policewoman etc, or simply family friend – then the child is her responsibility, and that woman has the right to do discipline the child in whatever way she sees fit, for as long as those circumstances endure. I can assure *you* Linda, that it would only be as a last resort. I have no intention of being an interfering grandmother."

"I'm very glad to hear it, Mother," said Linda. "I will not tolerate that, and I hope you will truly honour the pledge."

"You have my word, of course, Linda," Agatha assured her. "I know, more than anybody, that to take such a stance would only be likely to create friction between us."

"Quite," replied Linda. "You are of course technically correct in your assertion about this right, but I hope that it will never become necessary for you to exercise it – and I strongly intend to ensure that you never *do* feel required to do so!"

"I don't expect that I will, Linda," said Agatha. "I am sorry. I didn't intend to cause you any annoyance. We have always, in general, got along quite well – notwithstanding the odd hiccup, now and again."

Sat on the sofa listening to the pair, Robert sighed inwardly. Both his wife and mother-in-law were very strong women, used to getting their way, but he thought that Linda was possibly even more indomitable than her mother. He had always suspected that his mother-in-law knew in her heart, that when the crunch came this was the case. It was true that there were rarely any serious disagreements between them, and Linda respected and revered her mother as her elder, which was part of Geratican tradition, but at the same time she was very much a woman with her own ideas – which she rarely conceded were wrong. He had also never met anyone who was such a natural leader and it had been what had made him fall in love with her. Her dominant personality, together with her beautiful looks had overwhelmed him from the moment they had met. He was a man of slightly less than average male height, but had always considered himself fortunate that his taller, long blonde-haired wife was most attracted to men shorter than herself. She could be quite imposing, particularly when she was asserting her authority with her hands upon her hips, but he never really minded. Courting together he had always liked being in her arms as they walked. Men liked to be held by women and gripped by their powerful legs, from which they were not strong enough to escape, but Robert particularly liked the feeling of protection that Linda gave him. When she made love to him, her entire body smothering him, and he looked up into her blue eyes, he was always taken to ecstasy.

Of course, being a 'mongrel' of their race, Robert had no parents of his own. His existence – and that of all those who had preceded him – remained a mystery to everybody. He had suddenly

appeared in the town of Rushmore as a boy, and was drawn towards an elderly woman, Fanny, who was another of his kind and had somehow anticipated his arrival (as generally seemed to be the case on such occurrences, though they were by then happening seldomly). She had taken him in, and he had found work as a miner. He had eventually met Linda, and it was shortly after Fanny died that they had married. He was now believed to be the last of his kind on their world. Children born of a union between a mongrel and a non-mongrel were half-mongrels and Alexandra Radcliffe would now be the last of those.

Robert cleared his throat lightly, before attempting to intervene and lighten the atmosphere.

"Hmm. Well, why don't we concentrate on what brought us here together today in the first place? To celebrate that we have a new addition to our family!"

"Yes. Why *don't* we?" asked Linda. "I think that's a very good idea."

She crossed the parlour to the sideboard and took out some glasses.

A moment later they were all sipping at sherry.

"Now," began Linda. "I should like to propose a toast. *To Alexandra Radcliffe!*"

"*To Alexandra Radcliffe!*" said Agatha and Robert together with Linda, and they all raised their glasses...

***

A short time later, Alexandra was introduced to a Mrs Mabel Tork, who Linda had arranged to become nanny to her at The Grange, whilst she and Robert were at work during the day.

Linda's return to court as Chief Administration Officer, was now imminent...

CHAPTER 3

Geratica Autumn 4995

Janet Dobson, Court Administrator to Queen Beatrice V, sat in the office of Princess Alexandra's personal aide, Lady Priscilla Horsecroft. It was late in the day, and she was looking forward to finishing work and going home.

The two women were each studying copies of a report written by Linda Radcliffe.

Janet finished reading and put down the document in front of her. She looked across at Lady Horsecroft.

"Well, I can't say that this comes as much of a surprise to me. Those of us in the court administration department have always known of Linda's ambitiousness."

"Damn it, the woman's got some nerve though!" replied Priscilla. "The job hasn't been formally advertised yet. I've not even officially confirmed that I'm going. And already the little upstart is putting herself forward as my replacement!"

"I'm not sure that even I would dare to call Linda Radcliffe a 'little upstart,' Priscilla!" exclaimed Janet. "And certainly not the women over there in our main office. She runs it like clockwork. It can't be denied that she's highly efficient in her job."

"Which she appears to want to continue doing," said Lady Horsecroft. "This is a proposal without precedent. That she should combine her role in that office, with the position of Personal Aide to Princess Alexandra. Who does she think she is? That's not for her to decide. It's a matter for you. Surely it cannot be possible anyhow? I mean, something would have to give somewhere. If you ask me, she would end up not being able to give the fullest

attention to either post, with the result that both will be compromised."

"Will you have another drink?" she continued. "I think I need another brandy."

Janet glanced at her watch.

"OK yes, perhaps I've time for another small sherry before I make tracks."

She ran her fingers across her chin, as Priscilla did the honours.

"I'm not so sure you know. She's made it very clear in her report, how she thinks it can work, and if anybody *can* do it, then she's the one! Though I concur that this could be seen as rather jumping the gun."

"You're saying that we might agree to her suggestion?"

"Well, obviously the first thing that needs to happen is for you to confirm that you're definitely retiring. Between you and me, I think we know that you are. And I also think that Linda and the other palace staff are assuming it to be the case. After you've made it official, then Linda can apply for the job when it becomes available. If she's successful, then we can decide on this proposal then."

"There are a couple of other matters to consider though, Janet." remarked Priscilla. "The established palace custom of recent Geratican history, is for Court Administration staff to run the affairs of state outside of it, and conduct parliamentary business, and take responsibility for the domestic and catering staff inside of it, whilst staying apart from the personal affairs of the family. Generally, the latter is dealt with by those connected with the nobility, and the former by 'commoners.' We all know that it was agreed in 4941, that your position should always be held by one of those, to help demonstrate the link between the crown and the people. And you of course have overall authority over the entire

Palace staff. Linda Radcliffe would be breaking with tradition by doing this, which somewhat surprises me given what I've heard about most of her views. It's bad enough that it's now been decided to subject our people to the 'interview process.' Until now, we've always dealt with these matters between ourselves, regardless of what the administration department has done in more recent years. I obviously have no issue with commoners in principle – having married one myself."

When Priscilla was a young woman, her late mother, Lady Alison Horesecroft, had expected her to a marry another member of the nobility, as was customary. Her idea of a suitable suitor for her eldest daughter, was Lord Victor Charnwell. But Priscilla had instead fallen in love with one of the stable lads on the Charnwell estate, Vincent Hart, and insisted that she wished to wed him. This had caused considerable friction in the family. Alison had not been impressed at all, saying that Victor was from a most respected family – his mother, Lady Joy Charnwell, was a personal friend of hers – and why should Priscilla ignore centuries of tradition? Her daughter had countered that Victor was just as respectable in her own eyes.

Alison had initially threatened to cut Priscilla off from due inheritance should she go ahead and defy her. Lord Barney Horsecroft had loyally supported his wife, though he did have some sympathy for his daughter. Priscilla had refused to back down and told her mother that she'd proposed in the traditional fashion, Vincent had accepted, and now she'd drawn up a marriage contract. They would marry with or without her mother's blessing – and if her mother wouldn't accept it then they'd simply go their own way and not have anything more to do with either the Horsecroft or Charnwell estates. Eventually Alison had come round, not wishing to have such a breach with her daughter – though the union had certainly not been conventional for the times, and a few eyebrows were raised in noble circles. But Priscilla had never regretted her decision and the union had resulted in three children – Crispin, Belinda and Tara. Belinda as the eldest daughter was the current heir to the Horsecroft estate. In the latter

years of her life, Lady Alison Horsecroft had fully accepted Vincent as a member of the family.

"As I said, we'll cross that bridge if we come to it," replied Janet. "And I'm afraid that you'll all just have to live with my decision to introduce interviews to select the right people, just as many other organisations now do. But you said that there were a couple of things?"

Priscilla shifted in her chair.

"Um. Yes. The other matter is somewhat more delicate. One of the princess's ladies-in-waiting, Lady Ginny Smallbridge, is quite friendly with me and I rather think she fancies that she'll get my job once I've left."

"I hope you haven't told her that it'll be a formality?" asked Janet.

"Oh no. Of course not. Well, not in so many words, anyhow. But there's no doubt that she wants it, and she'll be outraged if Linda Radcliffe, coming from where she is, gets given it ahead of her."

"No-one is saying that she definitely will!" exclaimed Janet, with a sigh. "Both women will have to be interviewed – and anybody else who might be interested, for that matter. Then the decision is for *us* to make – not Lady Smallbridge *or* Linda Radcliffe."

Lady Horsefield looked dubious.

"I still think that Ginny is going to expect to get the job. She'll say that she has the more relevant experience. But you're right. I must make my intentions known officially, as soon as possible. It's true. I *will* be retiring at the end of the year."

CHAPTER 4

The Buntingham Club, a mile away from the royal palace of Geratica, was serving lunch to its usual exclusive clientele of members, mainly from women of high standing who worked in the centre of Avermore, enjoying its delicacies during their hour (officially at least, although it could sometimes be a little longer) of relaxation.

At a table in one corner, two figures sat opposite each other - Lady Horsecroft, and another woman of around 40 years of age.

"That blasted woman!" fumed Lady Ginny Smallbridge, as she gulped back another swig of her wine glass, between rather large mouthfuls of food. "What does *she* know of our work? Radcliffe's an interfering busybody that much *I* know! I've spent years personally serving the princess. There's hardly anybody who knows her better than me. Now that it's going to be made public knowledge this afternoon that you're going, I'm the natural successor to you. I shouldn't have to be interviewed for the position. It's so undignified! Whoever heard of anything so ridiculous? But then you tell me that Linda Radcliffe..."

"Alright Ginny. For goodness sake calm down!" urged Priscilla. "Try and show a bit of decorum. The speed that you're shovelling your food in and tipping back the wine, you'll be going back to the palace with indigestion – or worse. Then what will Princess Alexandra think? Is that really how her potential future personal aide should be presenting herself after she's been out to lunch for an hour?"

Lady Smallbridge took in a deep breath.

"I'm sorry. But surely you must see this from my point of view. Not content with running that office over there, albeit underneath Janet Dobson's overall charge, she's now proposing to *in parallel* with that, take over the management of the princess's affairs as well! It's just typical of her trying to show off about how efficient

she is. In the name of Divinity, she'd be ruling us personal courtiers with a rod of iron, you mark my words. And I've no doubt that she's got her eyes set on the biggest job of all in the palace staff – Court Administrator!"

"I agree that Linda Radcliffe is being incredibly bold with that part of her suggestion, Ginny," said Priscilla. "I said as much to Janet, yesterday. But she did point out that it wasn't certain she'd be allowed to do it, even if she does get my position – which she has to apply for, just like you. I don't like that last part any more than you, but there's nothing we can do about it. It was Janet's decision to bring that method in. It seems to be the way things are done in most places now – and since the Palace administers the laws, we cannot be seen not to take the medicine we prescribe.

"But there could be a number of scenarios. If Linda should get it, you never know she might need to choose between both jobs and decide to stay put. Then another candidate might take the position instead. Or she could become the princess's personal aide and have to lose her current job. She might feel that her move had backfired on her then, depending on who took her place at the administration department."

"That will be no consolation to me!" remarked Ginny, ruefully.

"Well, if *you* get the job, then of course none of those other possible outcomes apply," pointed out Priscilla. "That's the one thing that can be in your control. But you obviously can't expect me to simply say that it's automatically yours. If you don't – well maybe you might become the queen's personal aide, soon. Hettie Danvers won't be around forever."

"Ha. Linda Radcliffe probably thinks she can do that as well, and hold all three jobs simultaneously!" retorted Ginny sarcastically.

Both women exchanged similar glances...

***

The phone on Linda's desk rang. It was Janet.

"Linda. Could you pop into my office for a moment? There's something I want to tell you."

"Of course," Linda replied. "I'll come at once."

"I'm just off for a quick meeting with Janet," she told a couple of her junior members of staff, as she headed for the door.

She had an idea what this might be about. After knocking on the door, she entered the Court Administrator's office.

"How is young Alexandra coming along?" asked Janet, after Linda was seated.

"Very well, thank you. The nanny says that she's actually a very sweet baby, who hardly causes any bother at all, and she generally sleeps through the night."

"That's good then. I sometimes wonder whether you were born lucky, Linda," continued Janet. "Many mothers experience all manner of difficulties with their babies when they're first born – sleepless nights and the rest – but you, so far you seem have been spared the lot. After apparently achieving an almost flawless delivery at birth too!"

Linda looked at her.

"Born lucky? I'm not sure what you mean. I can assure you I've had my struggles at times like everybody else, and what I might have achieved has been through darned hard work!"

Janet chuckled.

"It's alright Linda, I didn't mean to belittle you at all. I was just pulling your leg really, because I think a lot of women do rather

envy you. But I'd be the first to say that you fully deserve what you have. In fact, what you *might* potentially achieve in the future, is what I want to talk to you about."

Linda's heart fluttered with excitement, as Janet poured a cup of coffee for each of them.

"Lady Horsecroft has officially announced today that she will retire at the end of the year. This obviously means that her position will become vacant, and I know that you have expressed an interest. I've read your report, and your assessment of the workload and staffing situation. Last evening, I took a copy over to Lady Horsecroft's office, and she perused it too. It ruffled a few of her feathers, I can tell you. In Geratica's name, Linda! No one but you would dare to be so presumptuous, though I'm not going to put you down over it. You're entitled to make your observations, as long as you remember that the final decision is not yours to make on this particular matter. In any case, Lady Horsecroft expressed some reservations about whether you could really do both jobs together, though I will tell you, I informed her that *should you be successful in your application*, I believed that you might. But whether I will allow it, we shall have to wait and see. It will require some thought. It's been difficult enough in the first place, getting that side of the palace staff to accept the same selection process for jobs as we do.

"Also, for this position it has always been customary for a personal courtier to perform the duties. Again, you're breaking with convention in applying, being a member of this department. That surprised Lady Horsecroft too, and I can't deny I was also not expecting it!"

Linda's patience began to snap.

"Might I say a few words of my own?" she asked.

"As always. Please do."

"It doesn't surprise me that Lady Horsecroft doubts the ability of a member of our department to perform the duties of a personal aide

as well as their own. That has always been the view here, even though the theory doesn't really bear close scrutiny, as my report indicates. Good gracious me, I have a secretary working for me in our department. I think I know what they do! As most people are aware, I have the greatest respect for our nobility, but on this issue, I must say confidentially, that the likes of Lady Horsecroft often slightly exaggerate the amount of day-to-day work that is actually entailed in that position over there. A certain element of thumb twiddling and clock watching goes on, which most certainly does *not* occur in the administration department. And we always have to consider the court's finances, as shown in my cost analysis."

"Well obviously, but I would also have to assess the feasibility of the arrangement myself, first," declared Janet. "Lady Horsecroft thinks that in general you have assessed the job quite well, but she insists that there are one or two other things to consider – though she is not specific. A personal aide to the queen or princess is a little more than merely an ordinary secretary. To suggest that they sometimes 'twiddle their thumbs' is a serious allegation Linda, and one that I hope you will not repeat outside of my office!"

Janet saw Linda's fist clench, and then there was a thump as she smacked the edge of the desk and exploded.

"Blast it Janet! I tell you this for the last time. I know that job as well as I do my own. I've studied and researched it fully. Of course, I would not be so foolish as to make brash, undiplomatic comments about that side of the palace staff in a public capacity, and I think that my report is fair minded and objective. But we are in a private meeting, and with respect *you* are simply repeating the same rhetoric that has always been said before. I have even met with the princess herself on a number of occasions, and she has evidence that backs up my claims."

Linda fixed Janet with a look, as she prepared to reveal her hand.

"I believe that she is very keen to see me in the position. She has said as much to me."

Janet's eyes widened.

"Has she indeed? That you are acquainted with Princess Alexandra, I am of course aware – though not to what extent. When exactly did she express this sentiment? She is after all, just fourteen."

"I suppose it could be said that she has gradually come to the view over the past half year or so," replied Linda. "If you recall, there was one occasion when the princess was the guest of honour at the Sackville Estate, and you were due to attend also, but had to withdraw at the last moment for personal reasons, and I took your place. We were sat next to each other at dinner – Lady Horsefield was on the other side of her - and got talking. I have always been very impressed with what I see in her. She shows a maturity beyond her years. I think that she will one day be a fine queen. And – without wishing to boast – I believe that she gained a respect for me. Since then we have had several informal and off the record chats here at the palace – though discreetly, so as to avoid gossip."

"I see," said Janet. Suddenly, she could see the coming situation potentially becoming even more awkward than she'd anticipated and coughed nervously. "I'm not doubting what you say at all Linda. But it has also been brought to my knowledge that one of the princess's ladies-in-waiting, Lady Smallbridge, believes that *she* is the most experienced and best suited person to replace Lady Horsefield. The current personal aide describes their relationship as 'friendly' and *she* believes that Lady Smallbridge fully expects to be allowed to succeed her."

Linda showed no surprise at this news, almost it seemed to Janet, as if she was already aware of it.

"Lady Smallbridge is, I am sure, a very competent lady-in-waiting. But she cannot just assume this role to be hers for the taking, purely through ingratiating herself with the princess's favour and without having to face competition, just as I do not. Princess Alexandra feels that as she approaches adulthood in just two years' time, she will need someone to advise her and guide her towards it.

Much as she appreciates Lady Smallbridge's good intentions, the princess does believe that I have the better all round knowledge and ability to do that. Again, no one realises more than me that our department normally does not specifically play a part in the family's personal affairs within the palace, but perhaps it is time to review the policy as time passes by. I may be very much a traditionalist at heart, but I also know that nothing can ever be achieved without any change at all."

Janet regarded Linda for a moment. Contrary to her earlier pretension of modesty, she *was* a woman not afraid to occasionally be rather boastful, which when coupled with the forcefulness of her personality could sometimes annoy people. But Janet was sure that Linda wouldn't be making these assertions about the princess's opinion of her, if she didn't broadly believe they were correct. She was indeed highly educated and full of ideas, and after leaving Castra University with language and law degrees, she had come to work at the palace, starting as Janet's deputy when Frances Rackham was Court Administrator and she had been Chief Administration Officer. Linda had obtained various financial qualifications whilst in that post. Eventually, Frances had retired, and Janet and Linda had each been promoted to their current positions. The new chief administration officer had vigorously imposed her will and authority over the main office.

"I assume that the princess is aware of what you are proposing in your report?" she asked.

"Of course. And she approves," replied Linda. "It will be beneficial to her to have someone with a close interest in her affairs, who works here. I can keep her informed of any business that might be useful for her to know."

"I imagine it is a fairly safe guess that, when a time comes that I am no longer in *this* post, you will be almost certainly be putting yourself forward as a replacement?" enquired Janet, studying Linda's reactions.

There was only the briefest of pauses, and Linda's manner did not appear to change in her response.

"You've asked a direct question, therefore I will give a direct answer. I will indeed put myself forward, and doubtless there may be a couple of others who will do the same. And as we are currently having a private conversation inside your office and not *outside* of it, I see no reason not to say that I believe I will be able to demonstrate why I am the best woman for the job."

"And perhaps you'll eventually end up being the court administrator to Q*ueen* Alexandra!" remarked Janet, dryly.

"I am certain that our present queen has many years on the throne yet," said Linda, with a laugh. "By the time the princess succeeds her, I am sure that *I* will no longer be here at Court. And don't forget that at one time, it could be considered treasonable to even talk of the possibility of the queen dying!"

Janet smiled.

"I suppose that would be one of the changes you'd hope to make as Court Administrator? To put that law back on the statute books?"

"Ha!" snorted Linda. "I may be a traditionalist, but that would be taking us in a very bad direction. It is good that we – at least on Geratica – live in more enlightened times."

"Well, anyhow. We must be getting back to our work Linda," said Janet, as she finished her coffee. "The job will be advertised from tomorrow. I shall allow it to be available to all palace staff, as well as externally. Since I am letting you apply for it, I can't really deny the rest of the administration department the same opportunity – though again, I've no doubt that some of those on the other side of the palace won't be happy. But the decision on your specific proposal will not be made until I know if you will be doing the job, Linda. Until then – may the best woman win!"

Linda nodded and raised her cup in acknowledgement.

CHAPTER 5

As it turned out, there were four candidates – Linda Radclffe, Lady Ginny Smallbridge, and two from outside of the Royal Palace of Geratica. All were interviewed by Janet Dobson and Lady Priscilla Horsecroft, and it eventually came down to a straight choice between Linda and Ginny.

Janet and Priscilla met shortly afterwards to make the decision.

"What are your thoughts, Priscilla?" asked Janet, as they studied their notes.

"I think it's obvious that both of them could be good in the position. I would have a slight preference for Ginny, but then I suppose that's only natural as she's 'one of my own,' so to speak. I imagine that you feel in a similar way about Linda?"

"Well, I'm genuinely trying to fair to each of them. There's no doubt that Ginny has served the princess well, over the years, and could do this job competently. But I also know that Linda has vast experience of the type of work, and it can't be denied that her report does prove the merits of her proposal. I'm sorry, but I have to concede that she *would* be capable of combining the two posts, Priscilla, and it would also be beneficial to the court. Whether such an arrangement could always be the case, is a matter for another day. In addition of course, she also appears to have the backing of the princess herself."

"So, it sounds as if you're leaning towards her then," observed Priscilla. "I cannot disagree that Linda is a highly capable and efficient woman. I must say that prior to this, I hadn't realised how close her relationship with the princess had become. The final decision will obviously be yours, and I won't fight it – I won't be here much longer anyhow, so it won't directly concern me then. But Ginny certainly will not be happy if Linda gets it, and as a friend of hers I'm sure that we'll still see each other socially."

Janet laid down her folder and looked at Priscilla.

"I must say that I think Linda is my preference, when all is said and done. But we must both broadly agree."

"I *will* agree," confirmed Priscilla, sighing as she thought of the lashings of Ginny's tongue. "Let's put it like that. And I won't say you're wrong. I can imagine what some of the reactions will be to the news, over on that side of the palace, though – and not just from Ginny!"

"Well, I'm afraid they'll just have to accept it," replied Janet. "To quote Linda herself, 'Nothing can ever be achieved without any change at all.' I'm sure that they will, even if it takes time for some people. In actual fact, despite Linda's fearsome reputation, once people really know her, they often come to respect her, and even sometimes to rather like her. So now we must inform the candidates of the news."

***

The two external candidates were contacted by post, whilst Linda and Ginny were told in person. The panel decided that Janet would tell Linda, and the less easy task of informing Ginny would be dealt with by Priscilla.

Linda was naturally delighted, and even more so when Janet confirmed that she would allow her to combine the role with her existing one at the court administration department. She requested that she remain based at the administration department whilst performing both, and this was also accepted.

Ginny's reaction came as no surprise, either.

"Radcliffe's as crafty as a fox on my estate! So, she's been having secret unofficial meetings with the princess, has she? She managed to keep *that* very quiet. Skulking around in quiet corners of the

palace. I ask you! Is that entirely appropriate behaviour for a junior courtier aspiring to greater things? Imagine the scandalous rumours that Princess Alexandra might have been drawn into, if we'd known about that before now. It's obvious that getting into her favour, got Linda the job!"

"No it was *not*, Ginny and don't you dare start telling the rest of the staff that!" retorted Priscilla, her face grimacing at the thought. "Linda clearly demonstrated beyond all question, that she was more than capable of fulfilling the duties of the position. I'm being completely honest with you. I merely seek to tell *you*, as a friend, of the events, so you can see that there was an extra factor to take into account, when we made the decision – and ultimately it was Janet who had the final say."

"Linda Radcliffe's an empire builder, *that's* beyond all question!" snapped Ginny. "She'll be running this whole place one day, I'm sure of it. But you needn't worry about me saying anything. I believe that princess Alexandra is being led astray by Linda, but she clearly prefers that woman rather than me to look after her affairs. Therefore, I feel that my position here is intolerable, and I have no option but to offer my resignation."

Priscilla gaped.

"Oh Ginny, no. Please. There's no need for that!"

"I'm sorry but I've made up my mind," said Ginny. "I don't like the way things have been going here recently, and this is the last straw. You'll have my letter confirming it, tomorrow. I bear you no personal animosity Priscilla, and we will remain friends. But for now, I don't want to say any more, and if you'll excuse me, I'll return to complete my duties."

With that, she got up and walked out of the room, leaving Priscilla still in a state of shock.

***

Linda celebrated gaining the position a short time later, by going out to dinner with Robert at a restaurant in Greenacres, leaving Mabel to babysit for Alexandra that evening.

Ginny duly did resign and dealt with her frustration in her own way. Taking her favourite horse, Lightning, from the stables, she rode it hard around the Smallbridge estate. Driving the animal faster and faster, she sailed over gates, fences and hedgerows, at times reaching quite dangerous speeds. But Ginny was an experienced and accomplished horsewoman, and never did Lightning show any sign of discomfort at the feats commanded of her, nor the rider ever become in serious danger of falling from the saddle. As she rode, Lady Smallbridge cursed Linda Radcliffe. When finally she brought Lightning to a stop, Ginny felt her temper much improved, but even in her calmer and more rational state of mind, she vowed that if ever there was an opportunity to cause Linda some difficulty, then she would get even with her...

PART 2

CHAPTER 6

Geraticai Autumn 3945

Doctor Charmaine Read completed her examination of the patient lying in an enormous bed before her and looked up with some trepidation.

"I am afraid that the situation is grave, Ma'am," she said. "We physicians have truly done all we can, and if there was another way it would surely be taken, but I am afraid there can be only one conclusion from my findings. I respectfully and regretfully ask you to prepare yourself for the worst, probably in the next two or three days."

Princess Mary held back a lump in her throat, then ran a hand quickly across her dark hair as she nodded.

"It's alright, Doctor. Read. You can rest assured that the court will recognise that you undertook your best efforts to save my mother. We must all accept the inevitable. Queen Margaret will shortly die."

She glanced across the queen's bedchamber, to her lady chancellor.

"Lady Hamilton, we must begin to make preparations. It seems likely that, barring a miracle, I will be called upon to succeed my mother as queen very soon. I must have a meeting with my sister, and you will be present. See to it please."

"As you wish, Ma'am," replied Lady Helen Hamilton, and left the chamber.

"Continue to do what you can, Doctor Read," sighed Princess Mary as she looked back at her mother lying in a coma. "Let me know the moment that there is any more news."

"Of course, Ma'am," said the doctor.

***

An hour later, Princess Mary and Helen were seated around the table of the princess's study, in the Royal Palace of Geraticai. A third seat was occupied by the princess's sister.

"Victoria," began Mary, "The news is not good. The health of our dear mother is now in terminal decline, and rapidly so. We have been advised to prepare for the worst. It may come any day now."

"I should have liked to have been to see her myself," said Victoria. "We've obviously known for some time that she is very ill. I have always been closer to her than you – I think you will accept that. You were always closest to Father, before he died. Our dear mother? That's the first time I've heard you express such a warm endearment towards her!"

"I feel the distress at our probable imminent loss, just as much as you do!" protested Mary. "I will admit that Mother and I have had some occasional differences..."

"Occasional? Pah! Anyhow. Is the good doctor absolutely sure? I mean, can we be *certain* that she won't pull through? She's as strong as an ox, you know – in the finest tradition of our glorious royal lineage."

"We do believe that Doctor Read knows what she's talking about," replied the lady chancellor. "And one only has to look at Her Majesty lying there unconscious, to see that her life is swiftly draining away. Therefore events must be put in place, following the traditional procedure in the event of a monarch's death on Geraticai. As the heir to the throne, Princess Mary will obviously be declared the new queen, and the realm shall be informed. Then Her Majesty must be crowned as soon as possible, and there will be a week of official mourning. Queen Margaret will lie in state in

Arista Town Hall for that period and the people will be able to pay their respects. Then she will receive an official State Funeral."

"Very well then," replied Victoria. Although she maintained calmness on the outside, Mary could tell that inside her composure was cracking. "As the queen's youngest daughter, I really *would* like to see my mother, to pay my own respects. Surely I may be permitted that?"

"Of course you can," confirmed Mary. "There's no question about that, as you must surely realise. I would never dream of stopping you. You are my sister after all, even if you haven't always got along with me."

"Hmm. Well don't try to shift all the blame for that upon *me!*" said Victoria, hotly. "But enough. I shall go and see Mother, right away."

***

Princess Victoria stared at the queen's body, motionless, save the rise and fall of her chest as her breath wheezed, with a feeling of grief that she'd never experienced before. Her mother was only forty two, and herself not sixteen until early in the new year. She was so young to be about to die of whatever the disease was that availed her – cancer was the official diagnosis, as had been the case with her father Prince Rupert.

"I will not neglect your memory, Mother," she murmured softly, with tears in her eyes. "I won't let my sister change the ways of our world!"

A few minutes later the princess left the royal bedchamber, and went outside of the main palace building. Crossing the courtyard, she entered the Geraticaian Security Centre.

CHAPTER 7

The commander of Geraticaian Security – the headquarters of which were part of Her Majesty's court - was working in her office. Fiona – like Robert on Geratica, who she of course didn't yet know – was a mongrel who had arrived as a girl in Arista, the principal city of Spanda, and initially survived by herself and then under the guardianship of another mongrel, Hayley, before being recruited and trained by the security service to be an agent soon afterwards. She too was the last of her kind on Geraticai. Being a mongrel, she was the only one who could travel safely through the void and as a female with knowledge of constructing transportation capsules, had begun by making secret spying missions to Geratica, on behalf of the Geraticaian court.

Back on Geraticai Fiona then moved upwards through the ranks of the security service. She had at one point played a role in persuading a noblewoman, Lady Selina Ranscombe, that Queen Margaret – before the death from a sudden heart attack of her own husband, Prince Gregory - should be enabled to have a discreet affair with *her* husband, Lord Desmond – a man twenty years younger than Lady Selina. Lady Ranscombe had been offered a confidential sum of money and a seat on the queen's High Council as an inducement, which she had eventually accepted until her retirement.

During the earlier part of her career, Fiona had occasionally even secretly worked outside of the law, as an independent, professional assassin – to earn extra money on top of her official salary.

Fiona had gradually accumulated power, wealth and property – though she still craved for more. Her current position also gave her a seat on the High Council, and she was acquainted with senior members of Geraticai's army.

The phone rang on her desk.

"Yes?" she asked.

"I'm sorry to disturb you Commander, but Her Royal Highness, the Princess Victoria is here wishing to speak with you," said her ensign.

Then Fiona heard the princess's impatient voice say, "Oh never mind with all that faff!" and the door immediately opened as she came bursting in. "Fiona!" she barked, slamming it shut behind her, "I demand that you help me."

Fiona put down her pen and gave her a benevolent look. She was used to hearing the young princess's 'demands,' and dealing with them as appropriately as possible.

"How can I be of service, Your Royal Highness?" she asked, smoothly.

"You are aware that the queen is expected to die very soon?" enquired Princess Victoria.

"I am, Ma'am. Sadly, it is news that I think we have all been desperately hoping not to hear but have just recently been reluctantly expecting."

"Not *too* recently, I hope, Commander!" replied the princess, coldly. "Quite apart from the implication that my mother was not fully capable of recovering from any illness she might suffer, to suggest that the queen might be going to die before it is absolutely certain, is treason. It could mean that the person expressing such a view *wishes* our monarch to die, so that they – or another – might usurp her position. But only those of genuine royal blood can succeed to the throne. And you know that I believe in no concessions for punishing the crime of treason."

"Yes Ma'am, and I most definitely never believed that the queen's death was a foregone conclusion until just today," said Fiona, though it was not really true. But she was perfectly prepared to lie, whilst convincing the princess that she was sincere – if it meant

that she would live. It was a policy which she would maintain throughout her life.

"But this means that my sister will shortly be due to be crowned." continued Princess Victoria. "As you of all people know, Fiona, I despise Mary and disagree fundamentally and absolutely with her stated intention for Geraticai during her reign. I hate her so much that I feel no regret whatsoever in declaring that I wish her to be put out of the way. Permanently!"

"Put out of the way, Ma'am?" Fiona shifted slightly in her chair, but otherwise showed no noticeable reaction, and her tone was equally expressionless.

"To be blunt Fiona, I wish my sister to perish in some way, before my mother leaves our world, so that I may take the throne in her place, and rule as I know that the queen would wish. And I wish you to personally arrange it for me."

"You mean assassinate her, Ma'am?" Fiona had been anticipating that Princess Victoria would desire to make some kind of move against her elder sister, ever since it had become likely that she would become queen far sooner than had been previously anticipated. Knowing the girl as she indeed did, it had crossed her mind that the princess would propose going as far as this. Even so, her apparent iron conviction still came as a shock.

"Could my words have any other meaning?" asked Princess Victoria.

"No Ma'am. I understand you perfectly," replied Fiona. "If I might just offer my counsel though? You are still not quite sixteen. After what you desire happened, then until you were of age to inherit the throne, the court would have to appoint someone as Regent, to rule on your behalf. Could you not wait just a few more weeks until your birthday in the new year? Then you can reign in your own right. And there is always a *chance* that the queen will survive until then, anyhow."

"No Fiona. Both Mary and yourself have indicated that you believe Queen Margaret will die at any time now, and I am forced to agree. I have visited her myself. Once that happens, my sister will immediately be declared queen, and once crowned will begin her reforming ways at once. I cannot afford to wait. I want her taken out of the equation, right away."

"But who will we appoint as Regent, Ma'am?" asked Fiona. "And could the deed not at least be done during the week of the official week of mourning for the queen, before Princess Mary's coronation is due to take place?"

"Fiona, are you questioning me?" demanded Princess Victoria. "Remember that I am a princess of Geraticai. You will obey my commands! I *have* to be Queen." She stamped her foot on the office floor as she said it. "And it *must* be now!" she continued, stamping it again. "*You* will be my regent, Fiona. Once I am declared Queen, we shall ensure that Lady Hamilton is arrested, and declare you as Lady Chancellor. When I am finally crowned in just a few weeks' time, as much of the court's coffers as you can dream of will immediately become available to you. I shall pay you far more than any of your predecessors. I give you my word on that. And after becoming Lady Chancellor, you shall declare yourself as my regent."

The princess moved across to Fiona's desk and placed her hands upon it. Leaning imposingly across it, she pushed her face into Fiona's.

"Now *will* you do what I ask of you?" She banged the desk hard with her fist as she shouted. Then her voice changed to a lower, more menacing tone. "Or do I have to have you killed? I don't want to. You've been a great ally and mentor to me. And you could provide good service to me as Lady Chancellor. You will find my rewards very satisfying – as long as you are totally loyal. But I could have you killed very easily – or even do it myself!" With one hand she removed a small knife that she always kept securely sheathed within her many layers of skirt and waved it threateningly before the commander's face.

Fiona breathed in and out deeply. She had grown accustomed to Princess Victoria's temper. It could sometimes be particularly nasty, as seemed to be in evidence now, and her tantrums when she was finding it difficult - or was unable – to get her way, had turned the palace upside down on many occasions. As far as Fiona was concerned, the girl was certainly a spoilt brat who could probably do with a spanking or two, but Queen Margaret had always rather regarded her as the favourite daughter and indulged her every whim. Unfortunately, this couldn't alter the fact that the lesser favourite princess was supposed to be destined to inherit the throne on her mother's death, by virtue of being the eldest. Whilst working within the palace complex, Fiona had got to know Princess Victoria, and had some sympathy with her feelings. They were actually kindred spirits in some ways as it turned out – both being greedy and selfish, caring little for others so long as their own pleasures were satisfied, and could be somewhat impatient. Fiona though, did have the cooler temper, and she often sought to calm and - so far as she could – control the young princess, to discourage her from being too over–rash, especially in her terrible jealousies and disagreements with her sister.

However, this time it seemed that Princess Victoria's determination had reached a level of intensity not seen before. She often terrified the palace staff with her bullying, although Fiona was rarely so troubled and knew how to fight back in subtle ways that would not get herself into trouble. She knew that the princess was indeed becoming powerful in her own right, but even so she exaggerated just how much when she threatened to 'have her killed'. Apart from the fact that she still hadn't quite reached womanhood, Fiona was the tool that she normally used to enable her to get what she wanted. It wouldn't be so easy for Princess Victoria to find a similar tool elsewhere to assist her in the same fashion. Fiona was certain that she *would* be prepared to personally kill someone, as previous queens and princesses had occasionally done in Geraticaian history. But the present commander of Geraticaian Security was, she felt, too valuable for the princess to truly wish to dispose of – at least for the foreseeable future.

"Please Ma'am. Put your knife away," she said gently, raising her hand in a pacifying manner. "I haven't said that I won't do it. Far from it, in fact. As much money as I can dream of, you say?"

Princess Victoria smiled wolfishly, as Fiona looked at her. She could tell that they were both thinking of the same things. Fiona would not be able to resist the temptation of the rewards yielded from complying with her.

"I guarantee it," she replied. "Imagine the wealth, power, and indulgences that will come our way, if we can play our cards right. We can build an alliance between us like no other. Though remember that I will be the monarch. You will work for me. But this is your chance to be a queen maker!"

"Very well, Ma'am," declared Fiona. "Leave the fate of Princess Mary to me."

Princess Victoria's heart raced, and she was unable to conceal both her excitement and glee.

"Excellent!" she grinned. "But make sure to do it quickly. Time is very short!"

CHAPTER 8

The following morning at the palace, in the royal family's private dining room, the two princesses were finishing breakfast. Some servants were clearing away dishes to be taken to the kitchens.

"I think that I shall go and visit our mother again, before I begin my work preparing for the tragic event that we know is to come," announced Princess Mary. "Will you join me Sister, or do you have any other plans for the day?"

"In fact, I am due to go riding very shortly," said Princess Victoria. "Lady Rosemere will be arriving soon. I must leave myself now, to get ready. But I shall see the queen later and pay my..." She paused as she saw her sister suddenly wince slightly and then frown. "...Are you alright Mary?" she asked.

"It's funny, this toast seems to have a strange taste to it. I'm only just beginning to discern it as I finish eating. I could swear the bread was off!" She took another sip of coffee, to try and wash away the discomfort.

"Oh?" Princess Victoria raised her eyebrows. "Mine seemed to be fine. If you think that yours was bad, you should find out who the baker was and punish her! But that of course is for you to decide. You *are* the heir apparent, after all! Well, I must now take my leave of you, for the reasons I explained just now. Goodbye Sister."

"Goodbye Victoria," replied Princess Mary, as she left.

***

Princess Victoria was on her way to the stables. Once she had collected her horse, she was meeting Lady Rosemere in the grounds just outside of the Palace.

Suddenly one of Princess Mary's ladies-in-waiting came rushing up to her.

"Please Your Royal Highness. You must come quickly. There is an emergency inside the palace!"

"Is it the queen?"

"No. It is Princess Mary, Ma'am. She has suddenly become gravely ill!"

Princess Victoria's mind raced. Suddenly she remembered her sister's comments about the bread that she'd been served at breakfast. It might have been pure coincidence, but surely it must be likely that Fiona had made good on her promise of the previous day and was behind this sudden turn of events. She felt a thrill rush through her, though this time she took deliberate care not to show it.

"Where is she?" asked Princess Victoria.

"In the queen's bedchamber Ma'am. The princess was visiting her when she was suddenly overcome by a terrible choking fit and was violently sick."

"I will come at once," confirmed the younger sister.

***

As they entered the palace, Princess Victoria saw one of her own ladies-in-waiting in the main lobby.

"Your Royal Highness. I was on my way to find you myself," said the woman, seeing that one of Princess Mary's own court had already done so. "Lady Hamilton is at the bedchamber now."

"Never mind about that, Lady Verncombe," snapped princess Victoria. "Please go out and find Lady Rosemere. Tell her that I will be delayed, and indeed we may have to postpone our riding expedition."

"At once, Ma'am."

Princess Victoria was already sweeping away down the corridor. The queen's personal physicians would obviously be tending to her in the bedchamber. She desperately hoped that if Fiona *had* poisoned her sister in some way, then they would not be able to save her in time.

Upon arrival she soon found out if her hopes had been realised. Princess Mary lay on the floor, blood trickling down her chin from her open mouth, and staining her gown. Her eyes stared out blankly and her body was still. Lady Hamilton and Doctor Read were with her.

"Your Royal Highness," each said, curtseying.

Doctor Read looked at Princess Victoria, her face ashen.

"I am sorry Ma'am, but there was no warning. It happened so suddenly and with such speed and ferocity, that there was nothing we could do to save her. I regret to inform you that Princess Mary has passed away! The one good thing was that just before it happened, Her Majesty briefly came out of her coma and glimpsed her one more time. By the time the princess had died, she had slipped back into unconsciousness again."

"This is a great tragedy for our world!" exclaimed Princess Victoria. She would now have to put on a show of shock at the event, and display some feelings of deep sorrow and regret, which would be entirely false since she possessed neither of those things at the death of the heir to the throne. Most people at the palace were aware that the two princesses had not been close, but all the same she would surely now become queen, and they had at least been sisters. And obviously her role in orchestrating the murder of

Princess Mary must never be officially known. If it ever was, or there was a serious danger that it might, then she would have to somehow deflect the blame onto Fiona and she would die. Of that much, Princess Victoria was already decided.

"Do we know exactly what happened?" she enquired.

"We cannot be totally certain at the moment, Ma'am," replied Doctor Read. "But it was almost certainly a poison of some kind. Her reactions and the symptoms bore all the hallmarks of that."

"Then my sister was assassinated!" declared the princess. "And the murderer may be within these very walls!"

"With your permission Ma'am, I shall immediately begin conducting an official investigation" said Lady Helen Hamilton.

"Well of course you have my permission, Lady Chancellor," retorted Princess Victoria, trusting that Fiona had covered her tracks sufficiently well, and had made some kind of cover plan to ensure that they were not exposed. "Do not ask such idiotic questions!"

"I am sorry, Ma'am," replied Helen. "Please forgive my foolishness."

However, there was suddenly a hive of activity around Queen Margaret's bed.

"What's the matter?" demanded the princess.

"I am rather afraid that Her Majesty's condition is deteriorating rapidly Your Royal Highness," said Doctor Read, sombrely. "It may have been that seeing what happened to Princess Mary when she came round, was too much for her. She is slipping away. I am sorry."

Princess Victoria stepped forward towards the bed. Around it, instruments and monitors checking on the queen's condition

hummed and beeped wildly. The princess reached out and touched her hand. Everybody was silent. For a brief moment, Queen Margaret's head tilted slightly and it appeared she might be going to regain consciousness once again. But then the queen gave a deep rasping sound as she tried to take another breath, before her head slipped back the other way, and her whole body went limp. The monitor above her head displayed a continuous long line, and registered a long, low tone. Doctor Read made a final check. There was no doubt. She turned back to Princess Victoria.

"I am very sorry, Ma'am. Her Majesty has passed away."

There was another brief period of silence as everybody took in the news. The princess felt some tears prickling behind her eyes, before composing herself. Then Helen cleared her throat nervously and spoke.

"On behalf of Her late Majesty's court, may I offer my sincere condolences to you Ma'am."

"Thank you, Lady Chancellor," acknowledged Princess Victoria.

"There is one formality which we must immediately deal with though Ma'am," continued Lady Hamilton. "The matter of the succession. Until this morning it was to be your sister, Princess Mary. However, you have today of course also had the added misfortune and distress of suffering her death also. Our deepest sympathies go to you for that loss too. This means that the inheritance must fall to you. You are though not quite sixteen, and consequently cannot reign on your own. It will only be a matter of weeks, but it is still our custom and law. This will mean that a regent must be appointed. As lady chancellor, I would be happy to take on the role, if others were agreeable. You would normally be crowned soon after the late queen's State Funeral, however in this instance it couldn't be until your sixteenth birthday at the earliest."

"Therefore," continued Helen, "it is my duty to officially declare you as the queen of Geraticai. Long live the new queen!"

"Long live the new queen!" agreed everybody present.

Queen Victoria inclined her head. She felt a ripple of excitement inside.

"I shall call an emergency meeting of the High Council, and discuss the issue of a regent," declared Lady Hamilton.

It was at that moment that the bedchamber door opened, and Fiona burst in with some security guards.

"Helen Hamilton, Lady Chancellor of Geraticai, you are hereby under arrest!" she barked.

Lady Hamilton jumped and her eyes bulged wide in consternation.

"Commander, have you gone mad?" she cried. "What in the name of the Divine Being is the meaning of this? On what charge?"

"That you did administer a poison and applied it to Princess Mary's breakfast this morning."

"What? That's a complete lie! How dare you come barging in here and make such an outrageous allegation, Fiona. You are getting above yourself!"

"I have evidence to support my case, Lady Chancellor," declared Fiona. "A maid reported me that when some fresh bread was delivered this morning, you intercepted the van and told the driver that there needed to be an inspection. You conducted this 'inspection' yourself, and she saw you secretly sprinkle something over one of the loaves. She further states that you then specifically ordered the kitchen staff to serve that loaf as slices of toast for Princess Mary at breakfast."

"Oh? And who is this maid?" demanded Helen. "She is making up a completely fictional story!"

"I am protecting her identity." replied Fiona. "But there is more to say. Security have now also conducted an investigation – of your private quarters. And we have found this." She held up a small bottle.

"What is that?" asked Queen Victoria.

"It is a bottle of bysnic, Your Royal Highness. A poisonous substance of Geraticaian origin, as I am sure you are aware!"

"My sister commented on the strange taste of her toast, this morning!" exclaimed the queen. "She remarked that it seemed 'off.' Clearly, we now know the reason. You were right to take this action, Commander. Escort Lady Hamilton to a detention cell!"

"Guards!" said Fiona, looking around. "You have your orders. Take her away."

"Ma'am, I beg of you. This is absurd!" protested Helen, as she was bound by the security guards. "I know nothing whatsoever of these events. They are a concoction of falsehoods! Please Ma'am!" She bore an aghast look as she was taken out of the bedchamber.

"Ma'am. Under the circumstances, I believe that I should take the role of the lady chancellor in transferring the royal seal from Queen Margaret to yourself."

"Of course. Go ahead Commander."

Fiona quickly went to the body of the late queen, and with reverence removed the ring from her finger. Then she walked back, and the princess held out her hand, struggling not to let her excitement show. Fiona gently placed the seal on her finger.

"Long live Queen Victoria!" she announced and curtseyed. Everyone else in the chamber followed her example.

Then Fiona glanced around to one of the other guards still present.

"Sergeant. Ensure that no news of the events of this morning, nor Queen Victoria's succession to the throne are known to the public yet. I want no one to be permitted to leave the palace or be granted entry until I say so. Understood?"

"Perfectly, Commander!" obeyed the sergeant.

"Doctor Read. I am in no doubt that the late Princess Mary was poisoned. You will perform a post- mortem on her body, to establish the exact substance used."

"As you wish, Commander," replied the doctor.

"We will leave you and your physicians to complete your duties, Doctor Read," said Queen Victoria, glancing at the group of women still attending to the corpse of her mother. "Fiona, come with me."

She quickly led the way out of the chamber, and shortly afterwards they were alone in the throne room.

"Excellent work Fiona!" said the queen, smiling broadly. "I presume that you orchestrated this little affair?"

"Affirmative Ma'am," replied Fiona. "There was indeed an inspection of the bakery van when it delivered the bread to the Palace this morning. My guards commandeered the vehicle, and I conducted it myself! After ensuring that I was alone, I administered the poison. It's existence in the bread was barely traceable, but its effects would be deadly."

"You are certain that there were no witnesses?"

"Absolutely certain, Ma'am. The kitchen maid was indeed fictional. However it is true that the staff were told to serve that particular loaf of bread to your sister. I succeeded in bribing the head palace cook to order the instruction on the grounds that it was the best in quality. She was slightly surprised but did not ask too many

questions. Now that this deed is done, I will ensure that she is stopped from talking."

Queen Victoria nodded. Geraticaian society, corruption, and temptation, were heavily intertwined, and always had been. Most Geraticaians – and the women especially, as they were the sex who ran their world absolutely – were involved in the system at some level, no matter what their class or background. Money was the prime instrument of inducement. Few could resist the thought of what advantages and pleasures they might gain from it, and this was often entirely what drove them. It was so strongly present in their minds that any other was given much less consideration, regardless of ethics or morality. Sometimes this could bring people to do unpleasant things to achieve their desires. The degree to which they were driven, and the lengths that they were prepared to go, did vary from person to person, and the better off tended to be the ones who did best. Queen Victoria and Fiona were amongst the most extreme of their race.

The queen was determined that in her reign, she would behave in the way that most had done before her, as was – in her view – the monarch's divine right by birth, which had always been the time honoured tradition. The only other being more worthy was the Divine Being herself. She was going to indulge in all the entrapments of power – another thing that Geraticaians often greedily sought – and she knew that Fiona would be happy to help her, in order to fulfil her own ambitions. Queen Victoria had no intention of implementing any of the more liberal reforms of Geraticaian society that her sister had been planning, and certainly expected men to know their place. As soon as she was crowned, all Geraticaian people had to be subservient to her – and men most of all.

"Ma'am, we must now move fast," continued Fiona. "I will serve an immediate and urgent summons to the High Council. It must meet this very morning, before any news of today's events spreads beyond the palace. It will be informed of Queen Margaret's death and Princess Mary's murder, that the evidence points unequivocally towards Lady Hamilton's guilt, and that I have taken

her place as lady chancellor. I will then declare myself as Regent until you are sixteen at the beginning of next year. Lady Hamiltion will be executed, and Geraticaian Security will assume all command until you are crowned. Anybody who objects shall be imprisoned for treason. Also, I believe that it would be prudent to immediately kill the head palace cook, and for the bakery van driver to be traced and disposed of too."

The queen's tongue ran hungrily around her lips, and she placed her hands on her hips.

"So, I shall be Queen in my own right, in a few weeks! I will follow your guidance as my regent until then, and I believe that you should commence the plan just outlined, without delay. I trust you like my own mother, Fiona. But that said, I am *almost* sixteen already. It is only a matter of weeks. I would not have you do anything that I fundamentally disapprove of, and I insist on being involved in all *c*ourt decisions, until I am crowned – after which *my* decisions will be rule. For a start, I wish to attend the High Council meeting. They must be made aware of what is expected of them!"

"As you wish, Ma'am," replied Fiona. The young queen is already flexing her muscles, she mused to herself.

CHAPTER 9

"Thank you all for responding to my summons at such short notice, My Ladies," said Fiona. "I have the gravest possible news to inform you of."

The members of the High Council were in their meeting room at the palace.

"Why have *you* called this meeting, Commander Fiona?" demanded a member, Lady Fornsby. "Why didn't the lady chancellor do so?" She looked around. "Where *is* Lady Hamilton?"

"I will come to that in a moment," replied Fiona. "First, it is with the deepest sorrow that I must announce the death of Queen Margaret, this morning. She had obviously been very unwell for some time."

There was a brief silence, and then there were many expressions of regret from the assembled group.

"There is however further dreadful news. Princess Mary, who as we all knew was the late queen's heir, has this very same morning been murdered!"

This time there were gasps of horror from the Council members.

"*Murdered?* How?" asked a second member, Lady Crowhurst.

"She was poisoned. She became ill directly after eating her breakfast this morning. We have incontrovertible evidence that bysnic was applied to the bread that she ate, and that the lady chancellor herself was the administrator. That is why she is not here, and I have called this meeting in her place. She has been detained by Geraticaian Security on a charge of murdering the heir to the Geraticaian throne. She is likely to be executed soon."

"What? Surely there must be a trial to prove her guilt first?" cried a third member, Lady Jefferies. "I cannot believe that Lady Hamilton would have done such a thing. What would her motive be?"

Fiona ignored her. As far as Queen Victoria and herself were concerned, there would be no trial.

"With this unfortunate event having taken place, the crown must therefore now pass to the next in line of succession. My Ladies, I can confirm that the royal seal has now been passed to the finger of Princess Mary's sister." She nodded to a guard stationed by the door of the room, who turned and opened it. "Her Majesty, Queen Victoria!"

The queen swept into the room, flanked by her personal guards. All the members of the High Council abruptly stood up with surprise, before chorusing, "Your Majesty!" and curtseying. She raised her hand, both in acknowledgement, and in order that every member clearly saw the royal seal upon her finger. Then she went and stood beside Fiona's chair.

"Members of the High Council, I am honoured and humbled to become the queen of Geraticai," she announced. "Naturally, I wish things would have been otherwise, and I bitterly mourn the loss of my beloved sister. I hope that her murderer will be suitably punished. But we are nevertheless in the tragic situation that we find ourselves, and I pledge to serve my queendom and its people as best that I can, in the same tradition as my dear mother who I shall miss greatly, and the rest of my ancestors. Fiona is now to become my new lady chancellor."

"*Fiona* the lady chancellor, Ma'am?" asked Lady Fornsby. "With respect, is she necessarily the best qualified for the position?"

The queen's eyes flashed a hint of fire, as impatience stirred inside of her. "Fiona *will* be My Lady Chancellor!" she asserted firmly, stamping her foot.

Fiona winced slightly inside. Queen Victoria's habit of stamping her foot to emphasise her point, or to forcefully demand her will to be followed when she was frustrated, could be embarrassing to witness and considered impetuous, when it came from a divine monarch of Geraticai. It was one thing that she must gently try to encourage the queen to curb, during the brief time that she had as her regent.

"Ma'am. Again, I mean no disrespect, but if I could just point out that you are not quite yet of age to reign in your own right, despite being the undisputed monarch. Under the circumstances, since you have no other adult family of noble blood, then the Council will have to appoint a regent to act on your behalf. Surely then *she* can appoint the lady chancellor?"

"Fiona has already suggested herself as Regent, and I have agreed to it," replied the queen.

Lady Fornsby's head reeled across to Fiona, and then back to Queen Victoria.

"Fiona has designated herself as Regent, Ma'am? But the Council must decide collectively on the matter. And she is not of noble blood! She is a mongrel, with no family history."

"There is actually no rule to say that the whole Council must decide on this, Lady Fornsby," declared Fiona. "This particular situation rarely occurs. And despite my non-noble blood, the queen and myself are in complete agreement that I am the best person to guide her through the short weeks leading up to her Coronation on the day of her sixteenth birthday in the first week of next year. The subject is closed."

"Well I'm sorry, but I really must protest!" began Lady Fornsby, but Queen Victoria paced around the table to her chair.

"Lady Fornsby you appear to not fully appreciate the absolute divinity of the Geraticaian monarch. Under my reign there will be nothing less than total loyalty from *all* of my subjects. Fiona shares

many of my views and believes that she will be able to govern on my behalf until I am fully of age. I trust her like a second mother and will happily follow her. My subjects will do likewise. But I will soon indeed be an adult, anyhow. The regency period will be short – *very* short! Which is more than can be said for your tiresome and endlessly dissenting tongue, Lady Fornsby! But I can do something about that. I will not tolerate hearing any more from it!"

Suddenly, her hand flew out from within her vast layers of skirt where had been hidden her knife. Gripping Lady Fornsby's face tightly with her other arm, she drove the blade into the Council member's mouth with a neat thrust. Lady Fornsby had no time to react, so swift had been the queen's motion, other than to convulse briefly in shock, and then collapse in her killer's arms, throat cut. Queen Victoria gently eased the body face down over the table, still sat in its chair.

There was a stunned silence. "In the name of Divinity!" breathed Lady Jefferies, with horror. The queen stepped to her, placed her hand lightly on her shoulder, eyes as cold as ice, and spoke menacingly into her ear – but not so quiet that all others present would not hear.

"Yes, My Lady? Do you have something you wish to say regarding Divinity? You question whether I have the divine right, given to me at birth by the Divine Being herself, to rule Geraticai as I see fit? Do you too, agree with Lady Fornsby?" She raised her blood soaked knife to the woman's neck.

Lady Jefferies shivered with fear. "No Ma'am I do not. You are of course the absolute monarch of Geraticai, and I will always obey you. Fiona shall be Lady Chancellor and your regent, until you are sixteen, early next year."

Queen Victoria smiled, and patted her on the back. Then she pointed at Lady Crowhurst.

"My Lady, you too have sometimes caused me trouble and offence. This court now wishes you gone."

Lady Crowhurst looked at the queen in shock.

"You are *banished*, Lady Crowhurst!" affirmed Queen Victoria. "Go immediately, before I sentence you to the same fate as Lady Fornsby! Guards, escort her from this place!"

Two did as they were ordered. Then the queen returned to Fiona, who motioned for the rest of the guards to move in closer, with their weapons raised.

"This is now the official court position. If any member of the High Council wishes to object, then do so now and my guards will escort them to a cell in the Detention Centre. The charge will be treason. If any member agrees, then she should now say, 'Yes, My Lady Chancellor' What do you say, members?"

It barely took more than a few seconds for each of them to look around anxiously at one another and realise in the hopeless expression of the look returned, that they had little choice.

"Yes, My Lady Chancellor!" was the unanimous response.

"Thank you, members. That concludes our meeting," declared Fiona.

***

And so, began the reign of Queen Victoria. The head palace cook and the delivery driver both immediately disappeared, and were never seen again. The post-mortem into Princess Mary found evidence of bysnic in her blood and the new lady chancellor, Fiona, declared the previous guilty of murder, and ordered her execution - which on Geraticai meant beheading. Fiona as Regent, oversaw proceedings for the double State Funeral of Queen Margaret and

Princess Mary, the service of which was carried out by the mayor of Arista in its Crematorium. Their ashes were laid to rest beside Prince Rupert's.

As Regent – though with the young queen's close involvement - Fiona began a purge of all those who she thought might make trouble. Several people were found guilty of treason with little or no trial and were executed. Queen Victoria insisted on witnessing their deaths. Fiona seized many of their estates and sold them to the court – taking a hefty cut for herself, by permission of the queen. One she was allowed to keep as a country retreat of her own.

Then on the fourth day of the first week of the year 3946, Queen Victoria's sixteenth birthday, her official Coronation took place at a lavish ceremony, in Arista Town Hall. She was now free to reign as Geraticai's monarch, in her own right. In her acceptance speech she vowed to reign in the same manner as all her ancestors had done on Geraticai, and also to continue the policy of closely monitoring Geratica – the inferior later copy of their own true world created by the Divine Being, whose presence they all felt in their minds – and treating it with disparagement and suspicion.

The queen further declared that all her subjects would now be required to swear an oath of loyalty and obedience to their monarch.

Victoria kept her word, and Fiona was able to procure a hefty salary for herself from the court's Treasury. Nobody dared refuse it. She was on her way towards becoming one of the wealthiest women on Geraticai...

PART 3

CHAPTER 10

Plumas, Geraticai Winter 3948

At the dead of night, a boat carefully navigated its way into Sea Birds Bay. It was known as *"Francis"* though all signs of its name had been blacked out to avoid detection. Once it reached the shore, the captain ordered her crew to securely drop anchor. Then they waited.

A moment later, the light of a lantern outside flashed three times. Captain Keira Crawford stepped out of the cabin and gave a return signal with her hand. A group led by a tall, thin woman, then began boarding the vessel.

"Captain Crawford," said the leader, Tilda Morris. "Thank Divinity that you made it here safely! The waters are particularly rough tonight."

"The rocks surrounding this cove have always been treacherous," replied the captain, "but not impossible to pass through. The *Francis* has never let us down yet! He is a fine ship. The *Arthur* is not far behind and will reach here presently. Well now, we have the cargo aboard. The sooner that we can unload it and receive payment from you, the sooner we can be on our way again. Come this way and I'll show it to you."

Tilda nodded and signalled for the boarders to follow. Keira unlocked the door to the hold. Inside there were numerous crates, stacked up and fastened securely in place for protection during their journey from the other side of Geraticai. She picked up a knife, and began to open some of them up, revealing beverages, narcotics, foodstuffs, herbs, spices, clothes and more.

"Damn the queen!" snarled Tilda, as she inspected it. "For all this to be rationed or banned, and the only way that most of us can get

what we need is though the black market. I bet *she's* getting all of it and more! And the nobs around her."

"Be careful not to be so frank and open when you're speaking ill of the queen!" cautioned the captain. "You never know just who might be listening. You should be amongst friends here, but she has spies in many places, working for her lady chancellor, Fiona. It could cost you your head!"

"Alright, I know," replied Tilda. "And it's always been the way. But our new young queen seems to be even worse than most!"

"Anyhow, I trust that this all meets with your satisfaction?" asked Captain Crawford.

Tilda looked longingly at the goods. She couldn't wait to get her hands on them. A drop of saliva became visible on the edge of her lips as her mouth watered. There were a band of her contemporaries waiting on the beach to help unload the cargo from the boat without being seen, and then divide it between them. The same would be done in the case of the *Arnold*. As the best educated, and able to read and write, it was her job to buy the stock. Bur already Tilda was thinking about how she could try and get the biggest share. She'd done it before.

"It is," she confirmed. "Let's get started.

After spending a moment haggling over the price, Tilda handed over the cash and hurried back onto the deck. At a brief signal from her, the rest of their party appeared and clambered on board. In the hold, Captain Crawford opened all the crates and her crew joined the others in shifting the cargo out to the beach. It didn't take long. Tilda's group all had a lustful look in their eyes as they worked, through a combination of their natural greedy desires and the desperation of their poverty stricken lives. Once all was complete, Tilda paid Keira on the boat.

Suddenly in the distance, there came the sound of a terrible crash. Captain Crawford looked up sharply and traced the direction from

which it had come with her eyes. It was swiftly followed by another, as people's cries began to be heard.

"Oh no. Please no, merciful Divine Being!" breathed the captain.

One of her crew came racing up. "Captain. The *Arthur* has struck the rocks!" she cried.

Keira rushed to the side rail. "Hush woman. We mustn't be detected! Tell the crew to embark immediately. We must leave quickly and do what we can to save anyone from the *Arthur* as we pass back through the cove before the authorities get there. Mrs Morris you must get those goods out of sight!"

"Aye Captain!" replied the woman, and she and Tilda hurried off.

In a couple of moments, the crew of the *Francis* were aboard, and the anchor raised. They raced as fast as they could towards the mouth of the cove. Up ahead through the stormy sea, they could see the wreckage. The boat had been sliced in two, and its bow was sinking. A small dinghy containing four crew members was desperately battling to stay afloat, and there were bodies in the water. To their horror they began to witness the sight of them being smashed against the surrounding rocks by the waves. Gradually the *Francis* drew nearer to the *Arthur* and the dinghy was alongside it.

Then a loud foghorn blasted out, and the scene was engulfed in light. The noise of the crash had alerted the coastguard, and a rescue boat was coming, accompanied by another. Captain Crawford recognised its design. She knew with sickening certainty who its occupants would be.

The *Francis* was still struggling to completely connect with the dinghy, as the waves continued to storm. The crew couldn't quite reach those on board to help them to safety. The other two boats were bearing down on them. Though the lashing wind and rain almost drowned it out, a woman's stern voice from the second

could just be heard. "Crew of the *Francis*, this is a Geraticaian Fleet Command ship. Prepare to be boarded!"

Keira could see the more powerful rescue ship beginning its operation as it gained on them. Some of its crew were attaching ropes to the dinghy, in order to winch it upwards to safety. The *Francis* could do nothing more for the survivors from the *Arthur*, now. They must make their own escape. The last thing that they wanted was to fall into the hands of the Command ship.

"About turn. Hard to starboard, Ensign!" she shouted.

"Aye Captain!"

The *Francis* edged forward to the exit of the cove, hoping to navigate the rocks and escape into the open sea. But they were too late. The dark black imposing figure of the Command ship blocked their path.

"Abort your course and prepare to be boarded, or we shall open fire!" came the woman's voice again.

A moment later it was beside the *Francis*, and a group of officers came steaming over the side rail and onto the deck, weapons raised. Commander Smart bounded over to where Captain Crawford stood. "Captain. You and your crew are all under arrest on a charge of smuggling illegal goods!" she declared.

The crew of the *Francis* were heavily outnumbered. Quickly they were overpowered and the ship eventually left the cove under the control of the Geraticaian Fleet.

***

Meanwhile, back on the shore, a squadron of Geraticaian Security guards raced to intercept the group who were trying to get their newly acquired goods away from the beach.

"Run quickly!" warned Tilda. "Everybody for themselves!"

But it was too late. At an order from their commanding officer, the guards opened fire. Before anybody could escape, all were massacred...

CHAPTER 11

Spanda, Geraticai Summer 3948

Queen Victoria was reclining on a lounger in one of the gardens outside of her palace, enjoying the sunshine. It was a warm day and after lunch she had changed into a simple summer frock, rather than the more formal attire that she wore when working on court affairs. Her fair hair slipped idly down her neck.

The queen's mind drifted away. She had now become a woman and was beginning to consider her future, particularly in the light of her position as monarch of Geraticai. Her hormonal desires were becoming more and more developed and pronounced, and she wanted to act upon them. To put it bluntly, she was now impatient to have sex, and the queen had grown accustomed during the first two and a half years of her outright reign, to getting what she wanted immediately. Fiona was an extremely efficient fixer. In any case, she would need to marry at some point, primarily with a regard to the succession. Queen Victoria's virgin geratis grew thick and hard, as it extended from her vagina. She ran her finger lightly over it through her dress and felt a tingle shoot through her thighs. She shifted position on the lounger so that she was lay on her stomach, and the feeling of her geratis pressing down beneath her made her legs twitch. The queen closed her eyes, and the vision of her perfect man came to mind. What she would do with him! And the pleasure she would feel. Queen Victoria was certain that as a monarch, she would be able to make love to a man like no other woman. It was as natural to her, as it was that night followed day. She was now breathing heavily with excitement, and she groaned softly as her geratis emitted small drops of blue fluid into her pants.

"Um. Excuse me, Your Majesty." A voice suddenly brought the queen back to reality and made her swear under her breath.

"Oh, Fiona!" she replied wearily, slowly twisting herself onto her side to face the lady chancellor. "I thought we'd agreed that business was finished for the day, after this morning?"

Fiona quickly surveyed Queen Victoria, before replying. The shape of her solid long geratis was plain to see through the thin fabric of her dress, and for once she wasn't wearing layers of skirts. But it was obvious that she was extremely well endowed – even more so than herself – and sometimes even those could not disguise the queen's erection when she was particularly aroused. Not that she seemed to mind. On the contrary, she liked to boast about it. As the reigning monarch of Geraticai it more than compensated for her rather short stature.

"Ma'am. I am afraid that there has been a spot of bother over in Plumas," she began. "Two ships belonging to the merchant navy were involved in a smuggling operation at Sea Birds Bay. One of them delivered a consignment of contraband to a group of peasant folk, in return for payment. The other was lost on the rocks, in a storm around the mouth of the cove. It is obviously winter at the moment, on that side of the world, across the Nibulus Ocean. Some survivors were picked up from a dinghy, and the crew of the first ship was apprehended before they could escape. They are all now in custody, here in Arista. The peasants were shot."

"*What?*" exclaimed Queen Victoria, scrambling off the lounger. "How dare they? How many more times will this happen? And to use two of the navy's ships. How did that happen? Did they steal them?"

"It seems that the two crews were officers of the navy, Ma'am, including the two captains. They took the two ships on an unscheduled trip from Darrow in Nerva, to Sea Birds Bay. Both had their nameplates blacked out, and each had a cache of goods inside their holds."

Fiona now had a vast network of spies working for her, who were able to quickly report back on any activity declared illegal by the

Geraticaian court, or anybody or group who might possibly be plotting dissent against the monarch.

"Smuggling rationed or illegal goods to unauthorised persons is strictly forbidden in our law," asserted the queen. "I may still be a young woman who has only been on the throne for two years, but even I know that! I believe that people are trying to take advantage of me. I will not have it! I want those responsible to be put to death. Do you hear?"

"Loud and clear, Ma'am," replied Fiona. "But before that happens, I believe that we should question the captain of the first ship, the *'Francis'*. The other captain perished. The port of Darrow has a private trading relationship with the court. We have evidence that the goods were obtained with the compliance of the authorities. I cannot be certain, but the lady mayor of Nerva, Raquel Black, may have been involved. As Your Majesty knows, Mrs Black used to be an officer in the security force like me. If she is guilty then she too must be punished."

Queen Victoria scowled. "I want *all* the traitors brought to justice! Let my will be done, Fiona."

"Of course, Ma'am."

"One other thing," continued the queen, as Fiona began to curtsey before turning away. "I have been giving some thought to the question of a husband."

You don't say, thought Fiona, as she noted the bulge still visible inside the sovereign's dress. "Indeed Ma'am?" she asked.

"Yes. Now that I am Queen, I want to settle the issue of an heir to the throne as soon as possible. And frankly, now that I am a woman, I simply want to *have* a man – if you understand my meaning, Fiona? Maybe even more than one! I know of eligible noblemen who might be suitable. Let them be made available for me to sample, lady chancellor. Then I shall make my selection."

"Marriage and the succession are indeed of paramount importance, Ma'am," replied Fiona. "But perhaps Your Majesty wishes to sow her wild oats beforehand?"

Queen Victoria smiled. "As many as possible, in the tradition of my predecessors! And *should* I become with child, from a man who I nevertheless do not wish to marry, then I will of course have the brat terminated. But now that Geraticai has developed birth control methods, the risk of that happening has reduced in any case. I am the queen of Geraticai and I, of course, have the biggest geratis. I want to use it."

"Naturally, Ma'am," said her lady chancellor.

In fact, Fiona couldn't be sure, though this assertion about her womanhood wasn't something anybody dared challenge. It certainly was very long when fully extended – almost reaching the queen's knee.

Fiona herself had never been all that interested in romance, but she loved sex and was a regular secret visitor of brothels. She could perfectly well understand the young queen's longings. As long as she was discreet about it, in her position.

"And it will be bigger than any puny queen's on Geratica!" added Queen Victoria.

"I would point out, Ma'am," said Fiona, "that there will be a summer ball at the palace in a couple of weeks' time, which several noble families will be attending. Your Majesty's eye may be free to rove, then."

"Excellent," replied the queen. "And now, please go and deal with those traitors!"

***

In Nerva, a group of security guards suddenly rushed into the office where Raquel Black was working.

"Lady Mayor Black, you are under arrest," said their commanding officer.

"Oh? And on what charge?" demanded Raquel.

"You will find out in due course," replied the officer. "For now, you must accompany us to Spanda."

"I really must protest. I have done nothing wrong!" said Raquel, as she was chained. But it was no use, and she was led away.

At the same time, a similar arrest was made of the Darrow harbour mistress, Milly Square.

CHAPTER 12

Keira Crawford screamed as the peal of horse whips lashed against her bare skin for a twentieth time, whilst she lay strapped to the table of the interrogation room in the detention centre, within the complex of the royal palace.

"For the umpteenth time, Mrs Crawford," said Fiona, coldly. "I simply want you to tell me who it was that authorised the shipment that you transported from Nerva to Plumas. Was it the mayor of Nerva? If you tell me, then it might be possible for your sentence to be commuted to life imprisonment."

"I swear to you, I don't know, My Lady!" rasped the captain. "All that my crew were told was to simply pick up the goods from Darrow and take them to Sea Birds Bay. The harbour mistress gave us permission to leave."

"And she swears that the document signed 'Ann Smith' which appears to authorise the shipment, was sent to her, and she doesn't know who that person is," said Fiona.

"Nor do I, My Lady!" insisted Captain Crawford, desperately.

At a signal from Fiona, the three women brandishing the whips cracked them again, and once more Keira cried out. Then there was a repeat. Followed by another.

Fiona held up her hand to indicate a pause. One of the women, of a large build and muscular frame, who had got her job largely due to the immense strength in her arms, was particularly enjoying her work and couldn't resist getting in another thrashing before complying with the order.

"Rogers, I told you to stop!" snapped Fiona. "If you disobey me again it will be you on the table next time!"

"I am sorry, My Lady," replied Pam Rogers. "Oh! I was so near to committing my next strike, that I couldn't stop myself before you said so."

"Pah!" snorted Fiona. The woman was all brawn and no brain.

She was getting nowhere and becoming increasingly exasperated. The captain *might* be telling the truth. If not then either the woman was exceptionally strong willed, or a very good liar. Or possibly both. Most people eventually cracked under the torture of the horse whips if they were trying not to confess to a crime that the court said they had committed, or they were holding back information. They simply wanted the pain to cease. Sometimes the offer of a lighter sentence in return for information was enough to loosen their tongue. But at present the lady chancellor simply couldn't be sure of her prisoner.

"You are still adamant about this?" she asked Keira.

"I am, My Lady!"

"Very well Mrs Crawford. I shall return later, after making more enquiries. But bear in mind that you are facing the prospect of losing your head very soon, in your current position."

"Take the prisoner back to her cell, guards!" Fiona ordered, as she rose and stalked firmly out of the room without another word, her black gown swirling about as she left.

***

A short time later the lady mayor of Nerva, Raquel Black, was visited in her cell by the lady chancellor of Geraticai.

"Raquel, the papers authorising the shipment of the cargo must have been signed by somebody," Fiona was saying. "This woman, Ann Smith. No one has ever heard of her. I believe that she does

not exist, and that her signature is a forgery, using disguised handwriting. The question is by whose hand was it written? Captain Crawford swears that she doesn't know and that her crew simply picked up the goods to be transported. Assuming that she is genuine in this assertion, that does not of course absolve them of their crime in Plumas. But there must be others, or at least someone, who knew of the operation, and they are guilty of the same. There are a couple of people who I think the court might reasonably suspect. And you are one of them, Lady Mayor."

Raquel's body tensed. "Fiona – er – My Lady, I also respectfully swear that I know nothing of this. I have never been responsible for the shipment of contraband goods to Plumas. Aside from normal, official business, Darrow has the exclusive personal trading relationship with Her Majesty."

"Yes, yes," replied Fiona, glancing swiftly towards the guard posted at the door. She didn't want that subject talked about too openly. It was top secret information that the court of Geraticai received its own supplies of contraband in discreet locations along the coast of Spanda, from the other three regions. They were generally the best quality of everything. The goods were syphoned off from the regular shipments and given directly to Queen Victoria.

She thought for a moment. Raquel was an old acquaintance of hers, and five and a half years older. They had both been officers in the security force previously, and their relationship had been reasonably cordial. There had however been a rivalry developed between the two of them. Trouble had brewed when Fiona had become the organisation's head instead of her, then promptly demoted her when an indiscretion with a married male private had come to light.

Raquel and the private had been together in the canteen of their section headquarters, one day. Knowing that Raquel fancied him and wasn't happy at the moment, the man (who wasn't happy in his marriage) had played the role of seducer and come on strong to her. He'd boldly asked his superior officer if she'd like to sleep

with him that night, and if so, he'd happily go to her home if she invited him. His wife was away until the following afternoon, therefore she wouldn't miss him. Raquel had not been able to resist such temptation, and that evening, had taken the man to her bedroom and made love to him. But unfortunately for them both, one of Fiona's spies had observed them during the course of their liaison and informed her boss and his wife (blackmailing the latter in the process, as a price for not making the affair public knowledge). Fiona had dismissed the private from the security service, and his wife had horsewhipped him for being unfaithful.

After Fiona had taken the opportunity to demote the officer and remove her as a potential rival, Raquel had left the service in a huff and embarked on an alternative career, culminating in her becoming Lady Mayor of Nerva. Fiona still respected her and considered her a supporter of the monarch, but she was also suspicious that the lady mayor might be using her position for corruptive purposes, just like many others, including possibly fiddling the books to cherry pick her own small share of the queen's contraband. The lady chancellor had never been able to prove anything though.

"Well, everybody is saying that they know nothing," she continued. "But someone must know *something*. And the court *will* find out the answer that it seeks!"

"Are you going to put me to the whips?" asked Raquel.

"If necessary, yes, but I would not wish to. The captain of the *Francis* is currently undergoing sessions in the interrogation room. If these prove fruitless, then others must follow."

"I know. I've heard her. The sound of a woman's scream travels far in this centre."

"That is the general idea, as you well know, Lady Mayor Black," replied Fiona, coldly.

"Well, you will get nothing from me either, My Lady," asserted Raquel.

Fiona's eyebrows rose. "We shall have to see about that, won't we?"

CHAPTER 13

The following day, Fiona entered Captain Crawford's cell.

"I am told that you wish to see me, Captain," she said. "Does this mean that you have suddenly remembered some kind of information, and that you wish to pass it on to me?"

"I've been thinking about what you said before, about the possibility of my sentence being more lenient, should I supply a certain fact, My Lady."

Fiona inclined her head. "Go ahead."

"Do you swear that this will happen?" demanded the captain.

"You have my word that such an action will be to your favour."

Keira took a deep breath. "The one whose signature appeared as 'Ann Smith,' was in fact Milly Square."

Fiona looked at her searchingly. "Can I be certain that you are telling the truth? Only yesterday you were telling me that you knew nothing of who was behind the operation."

"You have given me your word, Lady Chancellor. Now I am giving you mine in return. You asked me for the information, and I have given it to you. I can do no more than that."

Fiona continued to study her. "Do you swear on the life of Her Majesty? Remember that to lie after undertaking such an oath is treason!"

"I do, My Lady!" replied Captain Crawford.

"Say the words specifically!" insisted the lady chancellor.

"I swear on the life of Her Majesty, that Milly Square signed the order fraudulently in the guise of the mythical Ann Smith, My Lady."

It was at least a breakthrough, Fiona decided. It was all she had, and possibly the only lead that she would ever gain. She was under a lot of pressure from the queen to secure a conviction, and her own patience was wearing thin.

She walked over to where Keira sat. "Well thank you for this. I am sure that it will prove most useful, captain!" she declared.

Then, standing behind her she pulled out a piece of shawl from her gown pocket. In a rapid movement she thrust it tight around the captain's neck and twisted it violently. Caught off guard, Captain Crawford reached up with her hands and tried desperately to force Fiona's grip to release, but the lady chancellor was too strong. Gradually she choked, and a few seconds later had been strangled to death.

"Dispose of this woman's body immediately!" she ordered to the cell guard, as she left.

"Yes, My Lady," obeyed the woman. Though the guard officially paid no attention to what might be being said during an interview with a prisoner and concentrated on their own job of security, she couldn't help but note that her boss, the lady chancellor of Geraticai, had gone back on her word...

***

Next, Fiona went to Milly's cell.

"Miss Milly Square, harbour mistress of Darrow, Nerva, we have evidence that you are guilty of authorising a shipment of contraband goods to Sea Birds Bay in Plumas," she announced. "You are to be executed immediately!"

"What? No, My Lady!" Milly leapt from the bed upon which she had been lying. "That's not true. I knew nothing of it. What 'evidence' can you possibly have?"

"Captain Crawford has confirmed to me that the person in question was you. I have formed the view that she is telling the truth. That is all there is to be said."

"But I challenge her assertions, My Lady!" cried Milly, desperately. "Show me the signature. I will not be able to replicate it, I swear. My handwriting will bear no relation. That will prove that it was not mine!"

"No, it will not," declared Fiona. "An expert in the art of disguised handwriting could simply hide any such evidence further."

"It is her word against mine, My Lady!" protested the harbour mistress. "I should get a fair trial to contest her claim. Let her repeat it in a court of law!"

"Her Majesty has little time for things like that," replied Fiona. "And unfortunately, the good captain suffered a misfortune just after giving me the information. She is no longer here to speak for herself. I am sorry Miss Square, but *her majesty's court* finds you guilty, and now you must pay the price. Take her away, guards!"

Milly looked at her in horror as she realised her impending doom. "No please, My Lady!" she shrieked, as she was bound. She screamed as she was led out of the cell.

Fiona needed to be able to report a positive outcome to Queen Victoria, regarding the investigation – and quickly. She couldn't afford to hang around. The queen was fast assuming the role of a dictator, with the greatest of ease. And it appeared that Raquel Black was in the clear...

***

...She was given the news a short time later.

"So, you are free to go," confirmed Fiona.

"Thank you, Lady Chancellor," said Raquel. "And please pass a message on to the queen, that the next delivery made through Nerva's special trading relationship with her, will be *particularly* special!"

Fiona nodded to her in acknowledgement.

As she left the detention centre, the lady mayor of Nerva puffed out her cheeks. "That was a close one!" she thought to herself. She'd thought that she was a certainty to visit the interrogation room and suffer the pain of multiple whip lashings on her bare skin – and maybe even found guilty of authorising the smuggling operation. Luckily for her, it appeared that Captain Crawford had been tempted by the lady chancellor's false offer of leniency in return for any information she had – probably in part to stop the torture of the whips. She had lied – Raquel was certain that she hadn't really known - and luckily chosen to make Milly Square the scapegoat, rather than her. It had been Raquel's hand that had signed the papers as Ann Smith...

The lady mayor of Nerva had got away with it this time, but she knew that she would have to be very careful for a while, and maybe take some action back at home to make absolutely sure that all traces of her involvement in the operation were wiped out. The queen and her lady chancellor would be furious if they ever found out that they'd been double-crossed. Her head would surely also roll...

***

A week later a bumper consignment of contraband cargo was secretly delivered to a hidden cove in the coastal town of Marbleston in Spanda.

The collection and transportation of the goods to the royal palace in Arista, was on this occasion, personally supervised by the lady chancellor...

CHAPTER 14

It was a warm late summer evening at the royal palace of Geraticai, and the queen's summer ball was in full swing. The doors of the large conservatory were open to allow air in, and inside the ballroom, as a band played in the corner, Queen Victoria was busy dancing with as many men as she could. As she led them around the floor, they could all sense her sexual arousal. When she held some of them close, they could also feel it.

The queen also played cards with some of the women. Using a stacked deck, she fraudulently won money off them. There was little that the women could do but remark upon their monarch's apparent skill, though one, Lady Wera Smethurst, at one point found it difficult to completely hide the scepticism from her face as Queen Victoria's hand miraculously won again. The queen eyed her.

"Lady Smethurst. I trust that all is well?"

All of a sudden, Fiona seemed to advance from nowhere to Wera's side as she sat on her chair, so that she was almost up against her. Lady Smethurst gulped.

"Oh yes! There is no problem at all, Ma'am!" she replied, forcing a nervous smile.

Queen Victoria nodded, and the game continued.

Later, the queen was sat with Fiona on a comfortable chair, watching proceedings. She felt particularly attracted to a dark-haired man of medium height, by the name of Lord Edward Harkworth. A couple of years older than her, she was aware that he was in a similar position to herself, having lost his own parents at a young age. Currently he lived with his sister, Lady Nicola Harkworth, who was herself unmarried.

Queen Victoria's mouth watered and her eyes gazed with desire at him. The lord noticed and smiled back. The queen lost her breath as she sipped at her glass of wine, and she shifted in her chair as her geratis extended. Then she made a decision.

"Fiona," she demanded. "How much longer does this function have to continue?"

"It is due to last another hour, Ma'am," replied the lady chancellor. She looked at her enquiringly. "Would I be correct in thinking that her majesty is starting to feel a little bored?"

"Bored? No, I wouldn't use that particular word. Perhaps you would care to think of another, my lady chancellor?"

Fiona considered for a couple of seconds. "Tired then perhaps, Ma'am?"

The queen smirked. "Yes. Oh yes, that would indeed be a word I would choose!" She fidgeted and made a motion of yawning, her hand raised before her mouth. "I think that I shall retire for the night. I shall bid my guests farewell. But Fiona, please ask Lord Harkworth to remain at the palace and not travel home immediately. I would have him brought to my bedchamber."

Fiona looked at Queen Victoria. After momentarily being caught by surprise, she felt that she didn't need to ask what the queen's intentions were. "Very good, Ma'am," she nodded.

The queen snapped her fingers and signalled for one of her ladies-in-waiting. "I am going to bed," she informed her, as Fiona left. "Please escort me as I make my withdrawal from this company."

The lady also looked slightly surprised but was immediately compliant. "Of course, Your Majesty." she replied.

***

The ladies of the royal bedchamber were dressing the queen in the night attire that she desired. It was obvious to them, due to its erotic nature, what the queen's plans were for the evening. They were always under strict instructions never to divulge any of the activities that they might be aware of happening in the chamber, with anybody outside, and most particularly if they involved someone who – as had frequently been the case throughout Geraticaian history – was not betrothed to the queen.

When she was finally prepared, Queen Victoria pressed a button on the wall. The door opened and Fiona entered the chamber.

"Your Majesty. Lord Edward Harkworth is here to see you, as requested."

"Thank you, Fiona. Good evening, Lord Harkworth," replied the queen.

Lord Harkworth's eyes nearly popped out of his head as he viewed her standing before him, her hand upon her hip. Through the waist length split of her black nightdress, Queen Victoria's geratis hung like a trunk. Lace elbow length gloves adorned her arms, and similar stockings her legs. Her fair hair clung to her neck.

Quickly he regained his composure and bowed. "Good evening, Your Majesty."

The queen nodded and looked about. "Leave us. All of you," she ordered.

The ladies began to file out. Fiona lingered for a moment.

"That includes you, Lady Chancellor!" The two women exchanged brief glances.

"Very good, Ma'am," said Fiona, with a hint of a smile, and went away. She presumed that the next time she saw the queen, she would have made herself truly a woman.

"Did you enjoy this evening, Lord Harkworth?" asked Queen Victoria.

"I did Ma'am," he replied. "As usual your company was divine. I confess that this meeting here is unexpected, though."

Queen Victoria smiled and walked to the bed.

"Take a seat, Lord Harkworth." She indicated the place by patting a spot with the palm of her hand. "And if I may, I shall now simply address you as Edward."

"As you wish, Ma'am," said the lord, as he complied.

The queen knelt upon his knees, then squatting down she wrapped her thighs around him. Lord Edward felt his legs locked inside of hers.

"Edward," she said softly, but firmly. "I think that you must realise the reason for your summons to the bedchamber this evening?"

Lord Harkworth flustered. "Oh! Oh well, of course I would never presume to be certain of Your Majesty's intention, but I am her most humble and loyal servant, and will serve her in whatever way she desires."

"Hmm. Good answer, Edward!" smiled Queen Victoria. She reached out, slipped his dinner jacket off, and began loosening his bow tie and unbuttoning his shirt. Her geratis thickened and lengthened further, slithering all over Edward's thigh. He took in a deep breath as he felt its power. The queen felt a wave of sexual energy tingle in her thighs like never before and had to battle to stay calm, but finally she managed to hide the excitement from her voice as she went on. "I trust that you also understand the importance of discretion over matters of this kind?"

"Of course, Ma'am." It had been an open secret throughout history, that most Geraticaian queens were not virgins when they married

and some had even taken at least one lover, if not more, outside of that union. But hardly ever had vague rumours become more hardened fact, leading to a potential scandal. Those who knew for certain, turned a blind eye. There was one infamous case when a lady of the bedchamber had been exceptionally careless with her tongue and paid for it with her life. In years gone by, if a queen had become pregnant by a man who was not her husband, then it had usually been announced that she was ill during the duration of her confinement and she was not seen in public. Once it was born the baby was declared a bastard and packed off elsewhere. No one would ever speak of it in relation to her. As far as the lord knew, Queen Victoria was yet to sleep with a man, but he couldn't be sure. It was highly likely that he was to be one of several that the queen would fancy and use to satisfy her sexual lust, before deciding to settle down. Until she did marry, her liaisons would be strictly unofficial.

Meanwhile, Queen Victoria had removed all of the lord's clothing. She licked her lips as she viewed his naked body and her geratis throbbed almost out of control. She pushed him back on the bed and crouched forward above him. "I am the queen of Geraticai, and you are my subject. You will let me have my way with you!" she commanded. "And it *will* be my way!"

Lord Edward's genus had inflated considerably and his heart beat fast with excitement. Queen Victoria was an attractive young woman, and quite apart from the fact that no man was ever in a position to refuse the advances of his queen, without incurring her wrath – or worse – he truly wanted her to have him. She had the longest geratis he had ever seen, and he couldn't wait to have it inside of him. Besides, to have slept with the queen – that was still an honour that came to only a few Geraticaian noblemen. He could live with that memory for the rest of his life, regardless of whatever else came or didn't come of it.

"I am yours to have according to your desire, Ma'am!" he replied, breathlessly.

Queen Victoria's geratis extended as far as it possibly could outside of a man's vagina. Unable to wait any longer, she laid down over him and her geratis swept inside of Lord Edward, as it had been aching to do all evening. It raced across his wall and finding its target, wrapped itself around his genus. The queen let out a deep sigh, which became a faint moan of pleasure, as she felt a man's sexual organ for the first time. Her heart thundered against the lord's chest. He was not himself a virgin but could sense that he was indeed Queen Victoria's first. The knowledge aroused him even more.

With Lord Edward's body now finally open and available to her, the queen's geratis thickened inside of him. She kissed his lips deeply, as her legs and arms tightened around his body and pulled it up towards her own. Now he gave a sigh of pleasure. Her lips moved hungrily down his neck and onto his chest, and her geratis widened to fill his entire vagina, and throbbed against his walls. It ground against his genus on the most sensitive spot, as she continued to squeeze him tight and kiss his body all over. The feeling was even better than Queen Victoria had ever dreamed.

Lord Edward was in ecstasy too, and with his genus ballooning to its full erectness, held on to the queen's body atop of him, and let her take control. Her desire grew stronger and stronger, as she urged her geratis on to give her the orgasm that she sought. Just before the moment when she could tell instinctively that she must be about to come at last, Lord Edward's genus exploded and he came himself, with a scream. As his semen trickled through the pores of her geratis, towards her own vagina, Queen Victoria finally went over the threshold and orgasmed, shooting a huge stream of blue fluid all over the walls of his vagina, as she squealed loudly. The cries of both of them blended together and the lord closed his eyes with pleasure as he felt every part of his body nourished by the queen's hot juice.

When it was over, Queen Victoria rolled off Lord Edward for a moment, and as she lay panting hard on the pillow next to him, glanced across the bed. A thought was forming in her mind, and she wanted to make a decision. She felt a fondness for him, partly

through knowing that he was in similar circumstances to herself – even if he had not, as she had done, had his own sister murdered. It perhaps gave them a bond of sorts, which the queen rarely felt with others – male or female – her mother and Fiona being exceptions. She had been distantly acquainted with him before on occasions, and when he was with women he had always seemed to have the sufficient submissive qualities that a Geraticaian queen traditionally expected from her prince consort, which was particularly vital to her. It might be the nearest she would ever come to truly loving a man, and Queen Victoria had no romantic notions whatsoever about that subject. The act of marriage was for her, primarily a tool to produce issue, in order to establish, or make plans for, an heir, and the sexual intercourse that came from it, purely for her own pleasure, to satisfy her considerable appetite. However the queen found herself feeling the most intense longings for Lord Harkworth, and she did want to marry as soon as possible. He was a suitor, and there was certainly no other man who she fancied more.

"Did I please you, Edward?" she asked, as her breath returned to normal.

"Oh yes. Definitely, Ma'am!" he replied, hoarsely. He was being truthful, though he thought that no man would have ever had the nerve to tell his queen that she hadn't. At the moment the question of whether making love to him had given Queen Victoria pleasure, was more prominent in his mind. But he didn't feel it was quite his place to ask that – at least not yet. However, the queen then gave him the answer, anyhow.

"You pleased me too, Edward. I shall have more presently!" She smiled for a moment, then reached out and cupped his chin in her hand, so that she could hold his gaze.

"Now, I have a few more questions, which I want you to be completely honest with me in answering. If, after this evening, I take a certain course of action, but then I subsequently find out that you have lied, then your life will be in the balance. Do you understand my meaning?"

Lord Edward's breath was also returning. However, now his heart began to beat faster again as he looked back and wondered nervously what the queen could be going to ask him. "I do indeed, Ma'am," he replied. "I am most certain of it in my mind!"

"Very well. My first question is this. Are you a genuinely free and single man, Edward? And if so, can you give me an assurance that you are not in any kind of relationship – intimate or otherwise – with any other woman?"

He forced himself to remain calm, before replying in as confident a voice as possible. "The answer is, yes to both questions, Ma'am."

Queen Victoria kept her eyes fixed on him. "Has there ever been anybody significant? Anyone at all who I should know about?"

Lord Edward flushed again. "Um. Well I was for a time intimately involved with Lady Jefferies, Ma'am. As you know, she is married. She had no intention of leaving her husband, and eventually decided to end the affair. That is all there is to it. Your Majesty can be assured that I am not in any form of relationship with another."

"And she is considerably older!" observed the queen. "Lady Jefferies, eh?" she chuckled. "You naughty boy, Edward! Well, you've given me your assurance and I will trust you as a nobleman. I am sure that dear Lady Jefferies would not wish to come between us. She has been most particularly loyal since a certain *conversation* that we had, at the meeting of the High Council that took place immediately after I became queen."

"Good," she continued. "Well then, I shall now come straight to the point. I have a proposal for you, Edward. I intend to marry soon, with a long term view of establishing my heir. I am attracted to you, and I have a certain feeling for you. To be blunt, I wish for you to become my husband, and prince consort. What do you say?"

Lord Harkworth gaped. Even for a monarch this was an incredibly fast and bold move to make. "Er. Well, Ma'am. I must say that the speed of this has come as something of a shock! I am of course truly honoured that you have asked me."

"Well naturally. I should hope that you are!" retorted the queen. "But as I said before. I am the queen and you are my subject. It is the custom that my wishes are complied with, and I demand that the custom be maintained. Therefore, think carefully before answering my next question. Do you accept my proposal of marriage?"

Lord Edward thought for a moment longer. He had never known the queen well but had met her when she had been a princess. At that time, no one had ever envisaged that she would succeed her mother as monarch. As well as finding her attractive, her company had generally appeared pleasant enough to him – though her reputation for having a nasty temper if she couldn't always get what she wanted, was well known to everybody, and he was occasionally slightly frightened of her.

To be the queen's husband! He couldn't help but feel a tremor of excitement. The honour and patronage that might come to his small noble family! They would certainly be pleased and wish to become members of royalty. It might not be all plain sailing, but it was true – no Geraticaian nobleman had ever dared refuse such an offer from his monarch, throughout history. He shifted nervously, but then addressed Queen Victoria directly.

"I accept with great pleasure, and without reservation, Ma'am."

"Then we are agreed then!" said the queen, giving one of her sweetest smiles. "I expect the terms to be a formality, but I will state them, nevertheless. Firstly, you as prince consort will know your place, and accept my rules and conditions. You will obey me. It is your duty as a man to do so, and I reserve the right to punish you myself, if you defy me or step out of line. Such a punishment will be severe indeed. Naturally, you will not be involved in any court business, except for some time that I intend to set aside for us

on a daily basis, to go about the process of producing my heir. Nor will you intrude into the affairs of women in general.

"Secondly, you will never be unfaithful to me. Sometimes under the strain of the burdens of her duties as monarch, a queen may – or may not - have her extra needs, which she has every right to satisfy. This will be her own private affair. But her husband must be absolutely loyal and true. I trust that I do not have to explain the penalty for an act of adultery by a prince consort, towards his queen?"

The lord breathed deeply. The first term was natural enough for any Geraticaian man – even to some of those of noble blood, who like himself had received a small cursory amount of education from their families. No man was ever formally educated on Geraticai and they were the subservient sex. It was not uncommon for a woman to punish a man.

The second was obvious, but theoretically at least *could* be the one to potentially cause a problem if he was not very careful – even though he was under no illusions about what the queen meant by the penalty. That would be execution, for certain. He assumed that Queen Victoria might well seek pleasures elsewhere. But Lord Edward himself had always had a roaming eye and found it difficult to resist a beautiful woman – especially if she came on at him with all of her charms. Lady Jefferies had been the last to have taken him to bed. But truthfully, there had been several others who he had gone with before that. There were still some others who he would have liked to have given his body to. But he would obviously have to try and curb that side of his nature, from now on.

"I will naturally accept whatever terms you see fit to set, Ma'am," he replied.

"Right," asserted the queen. "I shall instruct my lady chancellor to draw up a contract for our marriage terms and begin preparations for our wedding!"

"Do I scare you, Edward?" she continued, running her fingers lightly across Lord Harkworth's cheek. Without waiting for a reply, she moved in close to him, trapped his thighs inside of hers, and whispered forcefully into his ear.

*"It's alright, Edward! There's no shame in admitting it. You **should** feel fear. It's only natural, given who I now am, and my divine right to govern as all of my ancestors have done. It gives me great **power**, Edward! Power over all my subjects – and **I** am not afraid to use it. I **love** the feeling that it gives me, and what I can get by applying it!"*

She moved her hand down over Lord Harkworth's chest and stomach, as she spoke, and grazed his thighs with her fingers. He shivered.

*"Woe be tied **anybody** or **anything** that gets in **my** way and denies me **my** will, now that **I** am queen, Edward! **I** know what **I** want, and how **I** want it, and **I** am going to have it exactly as **I** want it. But you and I have known each other for a long time. You already know that **don't** you Edward? I am sure that **you** will never be a part of something that frustrates my desire. **Will** you Edward?"*

Lord Harkworth felt himself being bullied as he heard her words, spoken deceptively softly, but laced with menace.

"No, Ma'am!" he managed to gasp back, in a whisper of his own.

Queen Victoria leant right across him, wrapped her arms around his shoulders, and continued.

"Just be a good, traditional, submissive prince consort for your queen – the way that I have always observed you to be with a woman – and we will have no problems. You are mine, Lord Edward Harkworth, and I am pleased about it. Do not give me any reason to think otherwise! Are you pleased to be mine?"

"Yes, Ma'am!" whispered Lord Edward, as he looked up at her, still feeling cold shivers down his spine.

The queen's voice remained soft, but the hard edge became replaced with seductiveness.

"Good. Well, now that we've got that out of the way, let us pick up where we left off a few minutes ago!"

She launched herself upon Lord Edward's body again, and made love to him a further three times...

***

Immediately after Lord Harkworth had left the bedchamber, Queen Victoria was dressed by her ladies in her regular night attire and donned a dressing gown. She summoned Fiona, who was surprised by the news that the queen gave her.

"But did Your Majesty not say that she wished to sow as many wild oats as possible, before settling down?" she asked. "This is all very sudden!"

"I did indeed. And I still will, before my marriage. But the lord is most suitable, and I wish for things to be made official as soon as possible. Once that happens, I intend to spend a portion of my working time with my consort, on a daily basis with a view to providing issue. This will be regarded as official court business. See to it that my marriage contract and ceremony are organised and administered quickly, My Lady Chancellor."

"Of course, Ma'am," replied Fiona. The young queen was acting highly impulsively as usual. Sometimes her whims seemed to change almost every day. There was likely to be a lot of lust governing her decision, though she had detected Queen Victoria's interest in the man as a person, before. Fiona hoped that she wasn't making a mistake, but the decision had clearly been made. No one would challenge it now – not even her.

She coughed lightly. "I trust that Your Majesty found her first taste of carnal activity satisfactory?" Being as close to the queen as Fiona was, she felt able to discuss such a private matter with her.

Queen Victoria smiled slyly as she replied. "Most satisfactory, thank you, Fiona!"

CHAPTER 15

Fiona arranged for the queen to marry Lord Edward Harkworth on 3/12/49, in the same hall that her Coronation had taken place in. They each signed a marriage contract along the lines that Queen Victoria had outlined before, in her proposal to the lord. Trumpets sounded and music played, as those present expressed their rejoicing. Afterwards the queen and Prince Edward were paraded around Arista in an open top carriage, and the people dutifully cheered in celebration.

In the weeks leading up to the ceremony, Queen Victoria had in fact "sewn some wild oats" with three other noblemen, all of whom attended the wedding, and were sworn to secrecy about their one brief sexual liaison with the reigning monarch of Geraticai.

PART 4

CHAPTER 16

Geratica Autumn 4999

Queen Beatrix was holidaying in one of her other royal palaces, in Volva.

This morning a royal hunting party was leaving the palace to embark upon an expedition around the surrounding countryside.

The queen's personal aide, Hettie Danvers was there at the palace. Several noblewomen and men were riding with her. Lady Horsecroft was amongst them.

"It looks like a good day for it, Priscilla," remarked Queen Beatrix. It was a chilly day, but the ground was not too hard. There was a hint of mist in the air, but it wasn't raining.

"Yes Ma'am," replied Lady Horsecroft. "I think that we should get a good morning's worth of sport and be back in time for lunch."

In the yard, grooms were waiting with horses for the party to mount. Alongside, barked the pack of hunting hounds that would accompany them.

Suddenly, a horn sounded, signalling the start of the hunt.

"Right, ladies and gentlemen. Follow me!" cried the queen, and urged her horse, Prancer, forward. A moment later, everybody was cantering away towards the open countryside...

***

The morning did indeed go well. The queen seemed on exceptionally good form as mistress to her hounds and had caught several foxes.

In the distance came the sound of barking. Queen Beatrix sensed that they might have smelt more prey.

"Onwards!" she commanded, raising her arm to indicate the way forward. Prancer galloped ahead. She was still well in the lead when something happened. The horse seemed to catch her hoof on a divot in the ground and tripped. The queen had sped off very fast and was caught off guard. As Prancer stumbled, she was thrown violently from the saddle and flew through the air. She landed with a sickening crunch on the ground, several metres away.

A gasp went around the group of hunters.

"Ma'am!" shouted Priscilla. As she caught up with Prancer, she dismounted and raced across to where the queen lay. The full horror of what had taken place became immediately apparent to her. The ground might have been reasonably soft, making it easier going for the horses, but at the speed that queen Beatrix had been travelling, the impact of the heavy fall had been catastrophic. Her skull was broken, and blood poured from it copiously...

CHAPTER 17

Back in Castra, at the Royal Palace, Linda's extension rang. It was Hettie Danvers.

In the early autumn of 4998, Janet Dobson had retired and – as had been widely expected by the rest of the staff – Linda had been appointed the new court administrator to Queen Beatrix. As was now standard practice, the post had been advertised both internally and externally, but Linda had still proved to be the strongest and most suitable candidate.

"Mrs Radcliffe," said Hettie, her voice betraying signs of stress. "I have the most dreadful news. You will not believe it. The queen is dead!"

"What?" gasped Linda, immediately springing bolt upright in her chair. For a moment, her mouth hung open as she took in Hettie's words. "But how?"

"Her Majesty and some guests staying at the palace in Volva were out hunting this morning, Mrs Radcliffe," replied Hetttie. "I was with them. It appears that her horse somehow tripped and she was thrown to the ground. She seems to have fallen head first and sustained a fracture to her skull. The impact was immediate, and she was killed instantly."

"Oh, my goodness. How awful!" breathed Linda. "In the name of Geratica!"

For a few seconds she was so stunned by what had happened that she could only express her horror. Then Linda's mind cleared, and she began to take control, as she realised the momentous event which it was now going to be her responsibility to deal with.

"This is obviously terrible! I must make immediate plans to have the queen's body brought back here, and then sadly her funeral will need to be arranged. This also of course, means that Princess

Alexandra will now become queen. Hettie, you are to ensure that this news is not shared to anybody who doesn't already know, until the princess has been informed, and I have released a statement to the media. I want complete secrecy from everybody. Is that clear?"

"Of course, Mrs Radcliffe," replied Hettie.

Linda put down the phone, gulped down the rest of her coffee, and hurried out of the office. She quickly walked down the palace corridors to Princess Alexandra's private rooms.

After being promoted to Court Administrator, Linda had suggested combining the role with that of the princess's personal aide, as she had been latterly as Chief Administration Officer, but Queen Beatrix had insisted that with her new responsibilities she must allow somebody else to be in charge of the princess's personal day to day affairs, and Linda had accepted the wisdom. As a result, Glenda Purves had been appointed from outside of the palace.

Linda knocked on Glenda's office door, went inside and closed it firmly behind her.

Is the princess here?" she asked, quickly.

"She is, Mrs Radcliffe," replied Glenda. All of the palace staff now addressed her thus. "She is in her parlour. Her luncheon is due to be served in half an hour."

Linda looked through an adjoining door to the kitchen, and could see the cook busy at the stove, apron on and sleeves rolled up. She went over and shut it.

"Glenda, I am afraid that I have some tragic news, which unfortunately Princess Alexandra needs to be told."

Linda informed Glenda of what had happened.

"Oh, good grief, Mrs Radcliffe!" cried the aide.

"The princess must be informed without delay," said Linda. "To lose her mother in such a way and then suddenly have the full responsibility of a monarch thrust upon her so unexpectedly soon, will be both a dreadful shock – not to say a disaster for her – and an immense burden. Only the week before last, she was celebrating her eighteenth birthday!"

"I agree, Mrs Radcliffe. We will go to see her straight away," replied Glenda.

"I don't say this to in any way undermine you, Glenda," said Linda, "But if I could suggest that it might be best for me to break this particular news to her myself, alone. She and I always had a very close working relationship – few palace staff know her better than I do - and I suspect that she might need a few moments of comforting and for composing herself, before doing anything more."

"Oh yes. As you wish, Mrs Radcliffe," agreed Glenda.

"This news is to be kept strictly private until I've finished speaking with the princess," said Linda. "On your head be it, if it should become anything else before then."

Glenda gulped.

"I understand, Mrs Radcliffe," she assured her.

"Good," said Linda. "Right, well I shall go and see her now."

She hurried through to the main corridor of the princess's quarters. At the parlour, she once again knocked on the door which was open. Princess Alexandra was sat on the sofa, reading.

"Your Royal Highness," said Linda, curtseying. "I wonder if I might have a private word with you?"

"Of course." She nodded to her lady-in-waiting, who was also present. "Leave us please, Bertha."

"Lady Donaldson," cut in Linda, as she turned away. "I do not want the princess and I to be disturbed until further notice, *by anyone at all*. That is an order. If anybody disregards it there will be severe consequences. Is that clear? Close the door behind you, as you leave."

Bertha Donaldson's eyes widened slightly. But she knew the court administrator well enough, and especially by her tone, to know that she was serious.

"Perfectly clear, Mrs Radcliffe," she replied, and quickly scuttled out of the room. The door closed.

"Linda!" exclaimed Princess Alexandra. "Take a seat. What's all this about?"

"Thank you, Ma'am." Linda sat on the parlour chair opposite the princess. She took a deep breath.

"I'm sorry, Ma'am," she continued, as gently as possible, "But there's no easy way for me to tell you this. I must urge Your Highness to try and be brave, for I have the most tragic news for you. I am afraid that your mother – Her Majesty the queen – has died this morning."

The princess froze with shock and stared at Linda in bewilderment. "Died? What do you mean? How?"

Linda explained what had happened. Princess Alexandra put her hand to her mouth to try and contain a sob. As she continued to search Linda's face, her eyes filled with tears. Linda quickly moved over to the sofa and sat beside her.

She opened her arms. "Oh, I know, Ma'am. It's terrible!" she said soothingly, cradling the still young princess. For a couple of minutes Princess Alexandra wept, as Linda did her best to console her. Then she grew on some strength deep within her and wiping away a tear, faced her former personal aide.

"Did she suffer at all?"

"I believe not, Ma'am," replied Linda. "If there is any blessing that can come from this tragedy, it is that your mother appears to have died instantly, without pain. It is likely that she never even had any real chance to react. Her last memory would have been tumbling off her horse. Unfortunately, Prancer was too badly injured and there was nothing that could be done for her. She was put to sleep. At least she too did not suffer any further agonies."

Princess Alexandra sighed heavily. "It just seems so unbelievable that one moment she was in the fullness of life, and then the next she was no more! She was an experienced horsewoman, after all. It is a royal family tradition."

"We are all deeply shocked, Ma'am," said Linda. "There will be a need to formally conduct an inquiry, but it is unfortunately likely to have been simply a tragic accident. I am sure of that. And it goes without saying that Glenda and myself offer our sincere condolences. At the moment we are the only two who know, apart from those at the palace in Volva, who will naturally stay silent until an official announcement is made."

"Thank you. Both of you," said the princess.

"Ma'am. I am afraid that alongside your natural grieving process there will, as you probably appreciate, be certain urgent matters to attend to at court, now. You will become our queen. With Your Highness's position, I will start making the necessary arrangements, once you feel able to devote your attention to them."

"Of course. Go ahead," agreed Princess Alexandra. "But Linda. You have been a solid supporter of me, as I have grown from girl to woman princess, and I was greatly honoured when you named your daughter after me. Now that it seems that I must inherit the crown so early in my adult life, I shall need your help and advice more than ever as queen of Geratica. Now I am alone. My father,

Prince Peter of course died of a fever when I was two, therefore I have no memory of him, and I was my mother's only issue."

Linda nodded. "You can be assured that I will do my very best, Ma'am, and be determined that your reign will be a long and successful one. I shall be at your side, always. I lost my father two years ago, therefore I have some idea of the grief felt at the loss of a parent, but obviously it was not in such circumstances as this."

"I know that I can rely upon you, Linda," replied the princess.

***

Linda straight away made arrangements for the late queen's body to be flown back to Castra. She also confirmed that there would need to be a brief questioning of those who witnessed her accident. But this was likely to be a formality. Meanwhile she drafted a statement for the press and radio. Shortly afterwards she went to Parliament House and made an urgent address to inform MPs what had happened. Simultaneously the statement was released to the media.

Both the parliament and the people of Geratica were stunned and aghast at the news. After a minute's silence in respectful memory of Queen Beatrix, the court administrator assured parliament that it appeared to have been a tragic accident, and that the queen had died instantly, without pain. Once her body had been returned to Castra, and a brief formal inquiry had taken place, her State Funeral would be held as soon as all those likely to attend could be invited. As soon as possible after that, a Coronation ceremony would take place for the new queen. The whole process would be conducted swiftly, given the importance of maintaining the presence of a queen on the throne of Geratica.

***

Early that evening, the royal seal of office was presented to the princess, and she was officially declared Queen Alexandra of Geratica...

CHAPTER 18

After an inquiry confirmed that there were no suspicious circumstances surrounding Queen Beatrix's death, her funeral took place two weeks later. Her body laid in state for a week, and thousands of Geraticans came to pay their respects.

The State Funeral was naturally a sombre affair, and Queen Alexandra wore a black mourning veil with a matching flowing dress to Avermore Crematorium. The hearse was driven from the royal palace, through the town centre, where crowds of people had gathered to pay their last respects. A massed throng lined the road outside the crematorium whilst the ceremony took place. Geratican radio broadcast it live. As was traditional, the town clerk conducted the service.

Later, the late queen's ashes were buried in a plot, at a private ceremony within the royal palace's own cemetery.

It was decided that the personal aide to the late Queen Beatrix, Hettie Danvers, would continue her role in support of the new queen, and Glenda Purves left.

By contrast, a week later, the mood of the Coronation was more joyous, and Queen Alexandra was cheered as she travelled in a horse drawn carriage to Avermore Town Hall, accompanied by Linda, and her ladies-in-waiting. She wore the formal white gown and long gloves of the Geratican head of State. There was a huge crowd gathered outside in the city square, and trumpets blasted as she entered. Choir girls sang songs of glory and devotion, and the ceremony, following centuries of formal tradition, eventually came to a climax with the lady mayor of Castra placing the crown upon the queen's head.

After it was over, Queen Alexandra returned in the carriage to the palace, where a short time later she appeared on the balcony to wave to the cheering onlookers, alongside Linda. Then they went back inside, where a sumptuous lunch awaited them in the state

dining room. A musical band with a group of singers entertained them as they ate.

The entire event was again broadcast by Geratican radio.

***

Although people travelling between the two parallel worlds of Geratica and Geraticai had been considered impossible for many years – apart from mongrels – they were still able to scan for significant events that happened in each other's territory. Geraticai was particularly keen to observe the goings on in Geratica, believing – erroneously – that they were an inferior copy to their own true version of the world. Many a Geraticaian queen had cursed them as an imposter and expressed a wish to be rid of them. Queen Victoria was certainly no exception. Their security force was very interested in the information that they could pick up in relation to Queen Alexandra's Coronation ceremony. Geraticai's only remaining mongrel – Fiona – was busy with Court duties and Queen Victoria did not wish to spare her. Therefore she didn't visit Geratica to witness it.

PART 5

CHAPTER 19

Geratica Winter 5000

On 1/2/00, Linda left her office at the palace and walked down the corridors towards Queen Alexandra's rooms. She had a meeting with her at 10.00 am. After waiting in the lobby outside for a moment, she was led into the queen's study by Hettie.

"Linda Radcliffe is here to see you, Ma'am."

"Your Majesty," said Linda, curtseying low, as she believed befitted the respect that a subject should feel for their monarch.

"Good morning, Linda" said Queen Alexandra. "I trust that you had a pleasant weekend?"

"Very, thank you, Ma'am," replied Linda, sitting down in front of the desk.

A buzzing noise came from Hettie's office, which led off from the study. "It sounds like your guest has arrived, Ma'am," she observed.

"Ah, good. That means we can get started right away. Show her in please, Hettie and then get the three of us some refreshment."

"Of course, Ma'am." Hettie slipped lightly away.

"How is my namesake?" asked the queen, whilst they waited.

Linda smiled. "Alexandra is fine, Ma'am. She will be finishing introductory school this summer in Greenacres and starting at the elementary school in the autumn. She is already showing promise, despite being rather a shy and one might even say timid girl. Nor is she the most physically strong. But I am proud of her."

"And do you think that she might follow in your footsteps at Charterhouse? She can start there in the prep school at seven, in two years' time, at middle school level."

"I would like her too, I will admit, Ma'am," said Linda. "We shall see."

A second later, Hettie returned. "Professor Chloe Piper, Ma'am."

"Good morning, Miss Piper. The court welcomes you!" said Queen Alexandra, rising with a smile.

Chloe curtseyed. "Your Majesty. Thank you for inviting me."

"Take a seat, please." The queen indicated a chair next to Linda. "You may know my court administrator, Linda Radcliffe. Will you take some refreshment with us?"

"Oh. Yes please," replied the professor. A white coffee with two sugars please."

The queen glanced at Hettie, who nodded and withdrew again.

"Right," said the queen. "Let us begin. The reason for this meeting is to discuss crime and punishment. Specifically, what is currently the most severe and final punishment for a crime in the queendom of Geratica. The death penalty. Whilst of course we accept that some crimes are so serious that the maximum possible sentence should be imposed upon those who commit them, the court administrator and myself are both nevertheless not entirely convinced that "capital punishment' as the death penalty is sometimes known, is necessarily the right way to go about it. Although we are both conservative minded people – very much so in some areas, in fact – it must be said that we are not always comfortable with bearing the responsibility for authorising the killing of Geratican people, regardless of the atrocity of their crime. I know that you have done a lot of research on this subject at Castra university, Professor Piper. I asked if you would prepare a

report for us and give us your conclusions. I presume that you have done so?"

"I have, Ma'am," confirmed Chloe. She opened her briefcase and pulled out a folder.

"Good. Then please proceed," said the queen.

From the folder the professor handed the two other women copies of the report. Placing another before her on the desk, she began.

"Ma'am, our research, which has been conducted over the past decade, indicates that although murder is still relatively rare in Geratica when compared to the overall crime rate, it has nonetheless been increasing slightly, year by year. The cause could be explained by a variety of factors – economic, social, or even a general lowering of moral standards. But whatever the reason, the argument that capital punishment is necessarily a significant deterrent for people not to commit the crime is beginning to lose its validity."

Hettie returned with the refreshments, the queen and Linda having their usual black coffee.

"Therefore, the question of whether the punishment should continue, might be worth evaluating," continued Professor Piper. "There are those who feel that we do not have the moral right to decide that a particular Geratican should die, regardless of how horrendous their crime might have been. Of course, that often comes down to how the individuals tasked with making that decision, feel about the issue. Moreover, several of those who work at the gallows, within the tower of Avermore, have become increasingly uncomfortable about administering the final execution, feeling that has become barbaric in this day and age."

"I have witnessed the punishment myself, and if I am honest, I felt similar unease," remarked Linda. "The court's own records concur with the research undertaken by your learned establishment, which I of course attended a few years ago. And since the start of the

queen's reign, I have had to asked her to sign the death warrants of more people during those few weeks, than any of her predecessors did in the corresponding period of theirs. That makes it debatable at best, as to whether it truly acts as a deterrent. I must say that I too am of the opinion, that we shouldn't assume we have the authority to send someone to their death. In reality it can be seen as simply a way of legitimising another kind of murder, which makes us no better in our 'morality,' than they are. Those who say that the person 'deserves it,' or that someone who takes a life should automatically forfeit their own, are often seeking pure vengeance – despite what they may say in denial - which is not acceptable as a principle in law. There are also times when a murderer shows genuine remorse for what they have done. And after all of that, you also have the possibility of a mistake made, and an innocent person getting executed for a crime they did not commit. We must acknowledge that this has happened in the past, and it obviously leads to animosity from those relatives left behind towards the court, however deeply we express our regret."

Chloe finished a sip of her coffee.

"You will notice that my report also concludes that in several cases, the perpetrator believes that they will not get found out when they commit cold blooded murder, despite the fact that a vast majority of similar criminals have done previously. They are sure that they are committing 'the perfect crime.' If someone is that sure that they won't be caught - or even in some extreme cases, that they feel within their own mind justified in their action – then the notion of a 'deterrent' becomes irrelevant to them. Some will simply do it, no matter what."

The queen studied Professor Piper's report on her desk. It set out the case for her findings, supplemented by various charts and figures, and statements from a couple of experts in this particular field with the same opinion. She put down her cup and saucer and arched her fingers under her chin, as she considered things in her mind.

"Thank you, Professor Piper," she said. "I note that you acknowledge that there are some others who take a different view on this, and we have in fact, over the past few weeks consulted with a number of people with relevant knowledge of this subject. The majority consensus seems to support the conclusion of your report, but to be as balanced as possible we must say there are a couple whose opinion is in the opposite direction, basically arguing – at times forcibly – that the death penalty still does act as a deterrent to others, and as Linda has observed, suggested that someone who commits a murder should be executed, no matter what. As I said earlier, I think that Linda and myself are broadly sympathetic to your report's findings." She flexed her arms about herself, her fastened blouse sleeves rising slightly over her wrists. "The one thing that I do *not* want, is to appear to be weak or soft on murder, particularly during the early period of my reign. It is clearly the most serious of crimes and still needs to be dealt with severely. Life sentences must be given by the criminal courts."

"I totally agree, Ma'am," said Linda. "I would suggest a system of parole should be followed, as happens with other crimes, but the criteria for considering any possible early release must be of the strictest kind. Under the new legislation that I would prepare in any bill put before parliament proposing the abolition of capital punishment, I envisage that a vast majority of such people would never leave prison. The public would have no rational reason to fear anything from the minority who did."

After some more discussion, Queen Alexandra thanked Professor Piper for coming, and dismissed her. Then she turned to her court administrator. "So, Linda. What would your advice be, now that we have heard all the evidence?"

"Well Ma'am, this is always the busiest time of year for the court, with your queendom's annual budget to be calculated and drafted before being presented to parliament. With regard to a proposal for abolishing capital punishment, I recommend that we proceed with the reform. My department has obviously been preparing statistics on the subject for some weeks now and I can begin the rough sketch of a bill immediately, but this is quite a major piece of

legislation, so we will need a bit of time. Perhaps we could aim for a time shortly after the budget to introduce it? I also anticipate that there will be some stiff opposition from several MPs in the house. It will be highly contentious, and we can by no means be certain that it will pass – even after three readings. But I believe it is possible and we must at least try. *Sometimes* you have to be radical in order to achieve change, even if it isn't universally welcome - and it proves to be the correct decision in the end."

The queen pursed her lips. "I am very firm that I want this reform to be implemented, Linda. Let parliament be in no doubt as to my determination in that. I will visit the house personally to offer my support to you, if there are any major difficulties."

"Thank you, Ma'am. I would appreciate that," replied Linda. She looked at the queen. Parliament was completely free to throw out any piece of legislation that it disagreed with, but in general most bills were ultimately passed. The will of the monarch and her court, who decided on policy, usually carried the day. If any highly significant legislation failed to get through parliament, it caused a crisis. So far in their history though, those moments had been rare, and eventually resolved peacefully. Geratican queens ruled as absolute monarchs, but unlike in Geraticai, where there wasn't even any such thing as a parliament, they were not dictators. The people were completely free – though the governance by their queen was strict.

Queen Alexandra was a warm natured, friendly young woman, with an empathetic quality that her court administrator planned to sell to the Geratican people. When the queen was on official engagements throughout Geratica, Linda had recently initiated a new tradition whereby if appropriate, she gave 'walkabouts', meeting the subjects of her realm. The court administrator marshalled these events with a firm hand, and they had proved extremely popular.

But Queen Alexandra was also quietly assertive and had already proved it on occasions during this early stage of her reign, when she felt particularly strongly about something. She made sure that

her subjects were in no doubt about who was in charge of 'her' queendom.

"Very well. That's settled then," said the queen. "I shall let you begin drawing up the bill to be put before parliament, Linda."

"Of course, Ma'am," said Linda. "Just one other unrelated subject. Can we definitively clarify the position over the eventual establishment of your heir to the throne?"

Queen Alexandra sat back in her chair and looked thoughtfully at her court administrator.

"Very well, Linda. I think you know that I regard all aspects of my reign to be important. Eventually securing an heir is obviously of crucial importance to Geratica, but I am still a young woman of eighteen, and as far as marriage is concerned, I want to be more mature before I make a decision. It has to be the *right* man for me and my queendom, and I will not be rushed. It will not be in the foreseeable future – possibly several years ahead. And I am also clear that I intend to be a virgin until then. But in the meantime, with you at my side I want to make Geratica stronger and more prosperous than it has ever been before, and to be regarded as a worthy monarch. I see that as my duty. I am sure you don't mind me saying, Linda, that you are a highly ambitious court administrator. I am an ambitious queen for my queendom. If the unthinkable should occur, and I die without ever producing an heir, then another solution to the issue of an heir will have to be sought. It would not be *entirely* without precedent in our history. I do have a very distant relative, the daughter of a male cousin, several times removed, who in theory would be the next in line, in that situation. I believe that she is of a similar age to me. Now. Does that satisfy you?"

Linda took a deep breath. "Quite, Ma'am. I completely concur with your wish not to rush into marriage before finding the right man. As you know, I was much the same age as you when I first proposed engagement to be married to a man, and he subsequently broke the contract – under some pressure from his mother, I might

add. It caused great anguish and embarrassment at the time, as it is usually accepted a man complies with a woman when she proposes an engagement with him and obviously completely against all custom for him to walk away from the contract that she has drawn up and they have agreed upon. I was furious and felt humiliated that such a thing should happen to *me*, and as was my right I administered a horsewhipping before releasing him from the engagement, but I now look back and realise that we were too young. It is the only mistake that I have ever made in my life."

The queen's lips ever so slightly twitched as she tried not to laugh at her court administrator's boastfulness, which those who knew her well were used to. Fortunately, she never minded, and took it as part of Linda's charm, as her court administrator often seemed to genuinely believe the assertions that she made about herself. She didn't always say the things purely for effect.

Despite Queen Alexandra's efforts Linda noticed her reaction, fleeting though it might have been. Displaying a level of confidence that the queen never saw in any of her other subjects, she simply looked her squarely in the eye and raised her eyebrows enquiringly, before continuing.

"It is obviously part of my role to advise you, so that *you* might not make mistakes, Ma'am. Fortunately, I was quickly able to start a relationship with Robert and I was twenty- two when we married. He is the love of my life. And you are certainly correct about ambition. I am - both for my own career, and for you as monarch. I know how you desire for your queendom to be run, and I will do my best to make you one of the greatest queens that Geratica has ever had – if not *the* greatest. Together our combined ambition will make your queendom prosper, and there are other priorities to focus on besides any future marriage.

"The only thing that I should say, is that *were* the worst to come to the worst, and you had no heir when you passed away, then the lineage to your relation is *extremely* distant. Most in Geratica are unaware that it even exists. Do you know her name?"

Queen Alexandra's brow furrowed. "Um. No, I must admit that I don't recall it at the moment."

"Hmm," said Linda. She wondered if the queen had ever known it. "Obviously, Ma'am, a direct descendent is the most ideal, given the importance of securing a new queen on the throne after her predecessor has died, as quickly as possible. But it would not be impossible to arrange the current alternative. I confess that in this day and age, I am not sure if we can totally believe the prophecy which states that the Divine Being at the core of our planet would abandon us and let our world be destroyed, simply because we did not have a queen, but few of us are minded to actually put it to the test!"

"I am inclined to agree with you up to a point, Linda," replied the queen. "But as a member of the royal family, Geratica's traditions have been drilled into me since birth, and this has always been the most important one. Geratica can rest assured that I would never willingly risk Geratica's very existence – however extraordinary it might seem – by not ensuring that there was at least somebody to take my place on the throne when I died!"

"I am sure that we are all glad to hear that, Ma'am!" remarked Linda. "And I too am of course a staunch supporter of Geratica's most important traditions."

CHAPTER 20

Next day, Linda called a meeting of her staff. There was some surprise at this, as the regular weekly one that she chaired regarding the processing of court business, and other general issues, had only taken place the day before. However, Linda wanted to specifically update them on the new proposed legislation that she and queen Alexandra were planning. She was entitling it the 'Penalty For Murder Reform' bill.'

"Now I began working on this yesterday, both in my office and at home, and have briefly outlined the details. I have copies for you all to read." She passed two sheets of A4 paper around to everybody seated at the meeting room table. "As you will see, the maximum penalty for murder will be amended from execution to life imprisonment. But there is a lot of specific detail still to be put on the bill, which as usual everybody in the department will have a role working on, before I take the responsibility for writing the final document."

There was a silence in the room as each of the women read Linda's briefing.

"Mrs Radciffe," began Ruth Spearman, now Linda's successor as chief administration officer. "I think it's fair to say we all had an idea that something was being planned, after all of the information and statistics we've been asked to produce and the records we've pulled out, relating to this subject. I confess to being a little surprised by the proposal that we now read. Um, can we assume that this is primarily Her Majesty's wish which she insists upon, and that you have been tasked with trying to implement it – possibly against your own will?"

Linda shot an angry look across the table. "No, you may *not* assume that, Ruth!" she snapped. "My views are always in an adviser's capacity only to the queen, and secondary to hers. But as it so happens, we are at one on this issue."

"I wasn't trying to be impertinent, Mrs Radcliffe," replied Ruth, regretting that she had been quite so frank. "But I simply would have expected you not to be supportive of this, knowing you as I – and indeed all of us – do."

"*I* don't support it!" remarked another member of the group, Debra Cross. "I don't see why we should reform the policy at all."

"Yes well, I shouldn't need to remind you all that your job is simply to assist in preparing new legislation for parliament's scrutiny," said Linda. "And just to be clear, I will not tolerate anybody refusing to pull their weight to the best of their ability, purely because they do not agree with a specific bill. I regard that as a disciplinary offence. We are administrators of court policy. The queen has the final say, with input and advice from me. Now, can we please get on?"

The court administration department went on to discuss their individual roles.

"Right," asserted Linda when they had finished. "The next few weeks are going to be very busy for us. As usual, the annual budget will need to be prepared, and I shall deliver it to parliament on 2/7/00. But in addition to the court's other business, this will be another major piece of legislation. So, *all* hands to the pump, please!"

Then she softened her expression, and her tone became lighter. "As I said yesterday though, I have been impressed with the way the department has begun during the new reign of Queen Alexandra, and Janet Dobson's retirement. You are all highly capable workers, and I am sure that court administration will rise to and surmount the challenges that are about to come."

***

Afterwards, everybody was filing out of the meeting room to return to their office.

"Ruth," said Linda. "A quick word with you in my office, please."

She shut the door – with her name and title on it - after Ruth, when they arrived. "Take a seat."

Once sitting at her own behind the desk, she looked sternly at the chief administration officer.

"I'm not going to let what you said in that meeting pass without further comment from me. It isn't your place to cast aspersion upon my views over court policy in front of everybody in a meeting like that. Particularly when it comes from somebody in the position that you now hold. I'm surprised at you. I accept that gossip will go on out there in the main office – though I tried to keep it to a minimum when I was there – but I don't want to hear it in an official department meeting. Understood?"

Ruth looked at her and flushed. "Yes, Mrs Radcliffe. I did apologise. But with respect, do you not think you may be overreacting a little?" She generally got on well with her boss, but she was annoyed by this, and wanted to fight her corner slightly more than she would do normally. In Ruth's opinion, Linda didn't like people who stood up to her too much. Most were likely to get flattened by her domineering personality.

"Never mind that," replied Linda, impatiently. "I just want you to take the point, and also confirm to you strongly that I genuinely share Her Majesty's desire for this bill to be passed and implemented successfully."

Ruth nodded. Over the years the equivalent women in Linda's position at court had always been closely involved with deciding on policy with their monarch. Most queens relied upon them quite heavily for advice and tended to allow them a substantial input. It was them who drafted the bills – including the crucial annual budget – though nothing was ever presented to parliament without

a queen's express approval. Sometimes she would request a policy be implemented herself. Her will was of great importance, and some had proved more 'hands on' than others.

There certainly was debate behind the scenes at court about what the working relationship between Queen Alexandra and "Mrs Radcliffe," was really like. Everybody knew that they were relatively close. The queen appeared to have a clear vision for what her reign would be like, but at the same time, Linda obviously had strong ideas of her own to put forward as advice. Was the queen accepting virtually all that her court administrator said, and allowing her to formulate policy almost at her own will? If as some speculated, this was the case, then Linda could now be very much 'the power behind the throne'. If Linda was in favour of this latest reform – and it appeared she was – then had she persuaded Queen Alexandra, rather than the opposite way around that Ruth had initially thought? Or were they both genuinely of the same opinion, as Linda insisted?

Ruth suspected that Linda was indeed becoming a powerful figure in the queendom. There was no question that Queen Alexandra's overall approval was still of paramount importance, but Linda had been a major influence on her since she was heir to the throne, and she was still young. The queen was strong willed and determined, but someone as clever, capable, and ambitious as Linda couldn't fail to make a significant impact on her. The likelihood was that their views on many subjects were broadly the same, and that in the areas where Linda had the greatest expertise – such as in handling the queendom's finances – Queen Alexandra was happy to trust her judgement.

"I do take your point and I understand, Mrs Radcliffe," she replied. "I'm sorry if I spoke out of turn."

"Good," replied Linda. "Well. Let us get back to work, and say no more about it, then."

CHAPTER 21

In the weeks leading up to the budget, there was the usual steady but slightly fraught atmosphere amongst the staff of the court administration department. Last year, the knowledge that it was the first one to be delivered with Mrs Radcliffe in charge, had added to the tension, and this year it would be the first of Queen Alexandra's reign.

Linda had always been a hard task mistress, and demanded great detail in the information processed, that would form the basis for calculating the precise value of the queedom's finances, down to the last dorken. The daily postbags were heavy with correspondence, files were checked, and records pored over. As figures were painstakingly checked, everybody was conscious of the importance of accuracy, and acutely aware of Mrs Radcliffe's intolerance of mistakes.

Gradually, with Linda leading, all the complexities of forecast projections for the year ahead, balance of payments, wages, and taxation levels were worked out, until finally she was able to pull all of the information together and begin drafting the budget for the 5000-5001 Geratican year. Fortunately, there were no serious problems, though one woman did feel the lashing of Mrs Radcliffe's tongue over a "schoolgirl error."

Whilst all of this was going on, the details of the 'Penalty For Murder Reform' bill began to be pieced together. Linda had her weekly meeting with the privy council members to discuss court business. There were a few dissenters to the bill, but the council was nowadays a largely symbolic institution, with no real power, and it accepted the will of the Queen.

CHAPTER 22

On 1/7/00, Linda was busy in her office making the final touches to her speech regarding the budget that she would present to parliament the next afternoon. She had just returned from lunching out when she was interrupted by the phone.

"Blast it!" she muttered to herself. It would be her secretary, Kara Pringle, who filtered all of her calls. She'd made it clear that she wanted no calls today, unless it was something extremely urgent.

"Yes?" she asked, propping the receiver under her chin as she answered the call, so that she could continue writing a vital piece of text.

"I'm sorry to disturb you, Mrs Radcliffe," said Kara, sensing the irritation in her boss's voice. "But I have a reporter from the Geratican Times on the line. She wants to speak with you."

Linda tutted impatiently. "Tell them that I will not be releasing any details about the budget before I present it to parliament tomorrow. I'm not talking to any journalist about it until after then, Katie."

"That doesn't seem to be what she's so interested in, Mrs Radcliffe. She says it's about your forthcoming bill proposing to abolish capital punishment. That's why I thought I should let you know."

Linda dropped her pen on the desk and clasped the receiver more firmly. "What?" she said. "How does she know about that? We never announce any new legislation that we put before parliament, to anybody beforehand. It's confidential!"

"I know, Mrs Radcliffe," replied her secretary. "What shall I tell her?"

"Oh, you'd better put her through," said Linda. "Which reporter is it?"

"Sian Walton, Mrs Radcliffe."

"Right." Linda knew the woman slightly. She'd spoken to her before. But her mind was still reeling. Clearly, somebody who was aware of the research being done, both by and on the court's behalf, had spoken to the press. There was no other explanation. But who?

"Good morning, Mrs Walton. How can I help you?" she asked, as the line connected.

"Good morning, Mrs Radcliffe. And a Happy New Year to you too!" replied Sian. "Is it true that Her Majesty's court is to introduce a bill to parliament, proposing the abolition of capital punishment?"

"I don't know how you came by that information." Linda's tone was even. "The court considers a wide range of issues, which may or may not result in new legislation being put to parliament, but it does not discuss them outside of the palace."

"But is *this* a piece of legislation that is going to be introduced?" asked the reporter.

"I'm sorry Sian, but such matters are confidential to the queen and her court, until such a time that parliament might be called upon to scrutinise a particular bill – if indeed they ever end up doing so. You know that as well as I do, as a political correspondent."

"Can I take it that it is at least being considered then?" pressed Sian.

Linda took a deep intake of breath. Darned journalists! They would never let go when they thought that they were on to something. Breathing out, she tried not to let her exasperation be too evident.

"Well you obviously believe that it is, or you wouldn't be asking me about this. May I ask what evidence you have? Has somebody categorically told you?" Now it was her turn to try and get an answer. She very much wanted to know.

"Someone who used to work at Her Majesty's court heard a rumour and contacted my editor at the Times," replied Sian. "She assigned me to the story."

Linda's eyes widened, and she quickly considered what might have happened. Could it be true? Someone who knew that a bill might be being prepared, or even worked on it, had told someone else who was familiar with the court?

"Oh? And who might that be?" she asked.

"With respect, Mrs Radcliffe, I note that you haven't answered *my* question. Can you confirm that the court are considering abolishing the death penalty? Is it Her Majesty's wish?"

"I am sorry," said Linda, firmly, "but all I can say is that the court considers and consults on many issues, and decides in conjunction with Her Majesty on whether any new legislation is appropriate and should be put before parliament, or not. We do not discuss it beforehand with anybody, and you cannot expect me to make an exception with you."

"Well, all that *I* will say then, is that there is someone who may have a score to settle with a certain member of Her Majesty's court," suggested Sian, slyly. "I think that you will find out soon enough, anyhow! If that's all that you have to say on this matter, then I'll say good day to you, Mrs Radcliffe."

"Good day, Mrs Walton," replied Linda.

With the call ended, she immediately contacted Hettie Danvers and requested an urgent meeting in the queen's study...

***

"How in the name of Geratica did this get out?" demanded Queen Alexandra. "Confidentiality is usually strictly observed and respected in court matters. We rarely have instances like this, when the press are tipped off about a bill that we are yet to introduce to parliament. And this could be a potentially contentious piece of legislation!"

"No, Ma'am, and the timing could not be worse, with the budget being presented tomorrow," agreed Linda. "In fact, I rather suspect that it may be no coincidence, if it is indeed somebody who bears malice, and is familiar with the affairs of Your Majesty's court. They will probably seek to cause maximum disruption to the general order of our business, at a moment when we have the most on our plate. I don't know who that might be, but dear Mrs Walton did seem to suggest that we might find out in a short while. Naturally, I would not be drawn on whether her story was true. But the bill was due to be introduced to parliament for a first reading on day 4 of this week, and to finally be put to a vote on the first of next. The Geratican Times will want to print something. Normally they are a newspaper that I favour, but I don't like the court's business being leaked before it even reaches parliament! We shall have to take some action."

The queen glanced at the clock on her wall. "Is the main lunch time news bulletin about to be broadcast on the radio?"

Linda checked her watch, "It should be, at 1.00 pm, ma'am."

"Well why don't we tune in to it?" suggested Queen Alexandra. "I sometimes do, to find out what they're saying is happening in my queendom!"

"An excellent idea, Ma'am," replied her court administrator, as she pulled a portable set out of the bottom drawer of the desk and switched it on.

The item that concerned them turned out to be the main headline. Linda groaned as she listened.

"I might have known. Lady Smallbridge! Well, I suppose she's waited long enough. I would imagine that it's *me* who she wishes to settle a score with!"

In an interview for the bulletin, Ginny Smallbridge said that she 'had it on good authority' that Her Majesty's court was about to introduce a bill to parliament, which if passed would abolish capital punishment. She was sure that many people were unaware that the court had been seriously considering this and questioned whether a majority of the public would be in favour. Later, she also suggested that Queen Alexandra might be being "overly influenced," by her court administrator.

"That is surely a serious allegation to make against Her Majesty, Lady Smallbridge!" exclaimed the interviewer, sounding shocked and perhaps a little nervous that such a statement had been made live on Geratican radio.

"I mean no disrespect whatsoever to Her Majesty," replied Ginny. "I used to work at court, as lady-in-waiting to the then Princess Alexandra, and always believed that she would eventually become a great monarch – though like everybody, I never would have expected it to happen so soon and in such tragic circumstances. But we all knew the current court administrator, 'Mrs Radcliffe' even when she was a junior clerk in their little administration office. She was highly ambitious and gradually taking over the running of things. She had the princess's private ear, even when she was still a girl. In this position she will be ruling the roost at the palace, there can be no doubt about that. What Mrs Radcliffe says, will go, and you can be sure that court policy will be heavily dominated by her views."

Once this item was finished, the bulletin moved on to some speculation over the next day's budget, which 'Mrs Radcliffe' would be introducing. Linda listened to some of the comments with interest. Everybody would have to wait until tomorrow to hear the details.

Queen Alexandra turned off the radio. "Damn her!" she exploded, hitting the desk with her fist. "Damn and blast her impertinence and disloyalty to the court that she always claimed to serve so well! How dare she speak like that to the media about our business and the way that we conduct it at the palace?"

She got up out of her chair and stalked about, her face red with fury. Linda had never seen her so angry, and opened her mouth to say something, but the queen held up a hand to silence her.

"I hope that I will prove to be a just, kind, and fair-minded monarch, but the queen of Geratica has always been respected as the ruler. I will not have my authority being brought into question. When I know what I want for my queendom there must be no underestimation of my will, either by the court or the people. That has always been our traditional way. But equally, I will not have your reputation slandered. The woman in your position has always played a crucial role in formulating policy. Any queen who thought that she didn't need to draw heavily on their expertise and advice when it came to the technicality of court business, would be a foolish one indeed. In the name of divinity, how many would have the necessary qualification and ability to set a yearly budget? You have the forcefulness of personality and abundant knowledge and skills to be a particularly effective court administrator, and I trust your judgement implicitly. I will have all of my queendom most strongly made aware of that fact!"

She stopped pacing and closing her eyes she took a deep intake of breath to compose herself, and then returned behind her desk.

"I'm sorry, Linda. I don't often lose my temper, but I do feel that this is a deep betrayal by one of our own – and somebody who previously worked so closely for me in my private quarters."

"That's alright, Ma'am," said Linda. "I wouldn't take it too personally. As I said earlier, I think it is me that she seeks vengeance upon. A junior clerk, indeed! I'm as incensed by this as you are.""

"I want us to act swiftly," asserted the queen. "I'm sure that I can rely on your judgement to steer us through, but my one order to you is to summon Ginny Smallbridge to the palace this very afternoon and find out exactly what she knows."

"Certainly, Ma'am," replied her court administrator. We need to find out exactly who it was that told her of the preparation of the bill. I will question her on that, but I think that I had better speak with my department too, without delay. I sincerely hope that none of my staff were responsible, but it cannot be ruled out as a possibility. With regards to the bill itself, we should put out a general statement from the palace to the media, along the lines of what I told the newspaper earlier. But once that is done, I recommend that we proceed with its presentation as planned. We should demonstrate firstly our determination to implement the reform, and secondly to Lady Smallbridge plus whoever else has been involved in this leak, that they will not obstruct us."

"Agreed," said Queen Alexandra. "And Linda. Please make it very clear to Ginny that the queen is not pleased. In addition to the information that the court seeks, I wish to receive an apology from her in writing, within the next week. Let her leave the palace in no doubt as to how the queen feels about this."

"With pleasure, Ma'am!" Linda inclined her head.

***

Back in her office, Linda immediately made arrangements for Ginny Smallbridge to be found and escorted to the palace for an interview with her. Next, she contacted the palace press office, and dictated a statement for them to release to the media without delay.

Then she phoned through to the main office, and instructed Ruth to bring everybody to the meeting room immediately...

CHAPTER 23

Linda sat at the head of the table, wearing a white blouse and black neck-bow, beneath a black waistcoat. Her sleeves were rolled up as she looked around at each of the women.

"A very serious situation has developed," she began sternly. "*Someone* has informed Lady Ginny Smallbridge - who most of you will remember, once worked at the palace as Queen Alexandra's lady-in-waiting, whilst she was still the princess – of the fact that we are about to introduce the 'Penalty For Murder Reform' bill. I found out when a journalist from the Geratican Times phoned this morning. I did not confirm it, and simply told her that many policies are considered at court that may or may not be put before parliament, and neither would I tell her if this was one of them, as we *never* discuss them outside of the palace, beyond those who we sometimes consult for extra research. It is confidential information, and I cannot state enough how angry the queen is that this has been breached. I don't know if any of you are aware, but it was the lead story on the lunch time news, when we would have expected the media to be talking more about tomorrow's budget.

"As we all know, this has the potential to be a very tricky bill for us to pass through parliament, and this is the last thing that we wanted. A statement has been released by the palace, similar to what I told the Times, but the queen and I are still determined to proceed as planned. Unfortunately, there will now inevitably already have been some negative discussion beforehand, though, which will make it an even more uphill task.

"Lady Smallbridge has been summoned for an interview with me to discuss how she came to know about this. She will also learn of the queen's displeasure. Now, I can only think that she was either told by one of those that was consulted when we were collecting information for the bill, or someone within the palace - which would appear to suggest someone in this room. So, I must ask this.

Does anybody have any idea who it might be? The queen and I wish to know, and let there be no mistake, I *will* find out! If it is someone outside, then they will also be summoned and rebuked for their indiscretion. If it proves to be one you, then the harshest of disciplinary action will be taken."

Linda spread her palms outwards to invite anybody wishing to speak to do so, then folded her arms and waited.

There was a lengthy pause as all the women looked at each other. Eventually Ruth Spearman spoke up.

"We did know that the newspaper journalist phoned this morning, Mrs Radcliffe. Kara told us it at lunch time. Speaking for myself, that was the first I knew of any of this – and I was concerned, as it should never happen. No sooner were we were back in the office, then you summoned us in here."

"That is correct. I did say thus, Mrs Radcliffe," said Kara. She would normally have been taking the minutes, but Linda had told her that this meeting was strictly off the record. "I hope I didn't say something that I shouldn't have at that stage?"

"Well. Since we are on the subject of confidentiality, then strictly speaking you shouldn't be gossiping in the rest room about my phone calls, Katie!" remarked Linda. "Perhaps I need to redistribute a copy of the court's code of conduct to you all regarding this." She sighed. "However, I appreciate that things like that will always go on, particularly in my absence, so we will overlook it. I am sorry. It's just a bad time for that to come up, as I am furious that this breach has occurred, and I am not directly accusing anybody here of doing it, unless I have evidence, or receive a confession. Does anybody else have anything to say?"

There was another even longer silence, and this time there didn't seem to be anybody willing to break it. Linda tapped her foot lightly on the floor. She finally lost patience.

"Very well. If that's the way it is, then we're all busy, so we'd best get back to work. But don't think that you've heard the last of this, whether someone from this department was involved or not. I intend to get to the bottom of it. Lady Smallbridge will be brought here soon for questioning. I shall speak to you all again later. That will be all."

She got up and marched out of the room. Soon everybody else followed.

***

Ginny had been brought into the court administration department by the court security officers and was now being questioned by Linda in the interview room.

"I don't see why I shouldn't have told the media what I'd discovered, *Mrs* Radcliffe," she was saying. "They have a right to know if the court is planning something as outrageous as this. You've brought it on yourself."

Linda's temper soared. "How dare you? To think that you of all people, who were a lady-in-waiting here at the palace, would say that! It isn't for you to determine what is right and what is wrong. The queen and her court decide on policy."

"You mean that the court administrator does, Mrs Radcliffe."

"You know very well how things work at the palace, Lady Smallbridge," snapped Linda, "even if you never were part of this department. I am not going to get drawn into an argument with you over that. Her Majesty has specifically asked me to convey her displeasure at what you have done. She thinks that you need reminding who reigns in her queendom. You may have insisted that you meant her no disrespect, but that is exactly how she reads your actions. She will not tolerate court confidentiality being breached in this way. I suspect that part of this is to gain a measure

of revenge over me, after you were overlooked for a position here."

Ginny smirked faintly. "Possibly. It's taken a long time, but patience comes to those who wait, as they say. It's been worth it, even just to see your face, Mrs Radcliffe!"

"Vengeance is not an excuse for this!" fumed Linda, her eyes flashing fire.

"That's not all that this is about though, Mrs Radcliffe. I genuinely cannot believe that Her Majesty's court would pander to such soft liberal twaddle. I wouldn't need to read this new bill to know that I totally disagree with it. I strongly support the death penalty and would be quite prepared to hang the scoundrels myself! I say that a lot of people agree with me."

"I haven't said that the court is planning such a bill."

"Ha! That's not what I've heard I'm afraid, Mrs Radcliffe." Lady Smallbridge looked at her. "I'm surprised that you're going along with it, I must admit. But I suppose one can never completely be sure of what another thinks about a particular subject. So, what happened? Did you twist the queen's arm to get her to agree?"

"Lady Smallbridge that is *enough*!" shouted Linda, thumping her fist on the desk. "You have been officially summoned here to answer for your indiscretion and to help us with further enquiries. You do not seem to appreciate your position. You are currently out of favour with the court – in disgrace, even. I would have thought that someone of your noble birth would be ashamed of that."

"I know exactly what my position is, Mrs Radcliffe. This is what can sometimes happen if someone steps a little too far out of line in the queen's judgement. That's what the phrase, 'Conveying the queen's displeasure,' signifies. I am being quietly warned. And you're relishing the opportunity to talk down to me. *You* are a lowly commoner, *Mrs Radcliffe*, who has no right to talk to *me* in such a way! Admit it!"

Linda's eyes narrowed. She had a deep respect for the nobility, but this lady gave them a bad name.

"That is irrelevant, as are the other views and observations that you've expressed. But the court demands an answer to another question. Since you claim to have heard that there is a bill planned for presentation to parliament, then who was it that informed you? Was it somebody from inside the palace, or outside?"

Ginny smirked openly this time, as she answered. "Inside, Mrs Radcliffe."

Linda's heart fluttered. "Are you saying that it was somebody from within this department?"

"Within *your* department, Mrs Radcliffe!"

There was a brief silence. "Well?" demanded Linda. "I will have a name please!" She was waiting with baited breath. Could it be true? Someone in the administration department had betrayed the court?

"Sorry, Mrs Radcliffe. That's confidential!" Ginny chuckled to herself.

Now Linda completely lost her temper.

"Don't play games with me, trying to be clever! You won't win. You've made an allegation against this department. If you are being truthful, then the court must know the full details." She pointed her finger. "But if you're just stirring things up further..."

"It is the truth," interrupted Ginny. "But I am saying no more!"

"Damn it, Lady Smallbridge. You will!" Linda's patience was almost exhausted. She glanced at the clock. She still had work to do on her budget speech for tomorrow, though it would probably be continued at home tonight. Later in the afternoon she had to go

over to Parliament House. She couldn't afford to stay here for the rest of the day.

"I must also tell you that Queen Alexandra requests a written apology from you, within the next week."

Ginny scowled. She'd been half expecting that. A letter of apology was a standard way of showing penance for offending the queen.

"Very well. I shall do so, Mrs Radcliffe," she said, with some reluctance.

"Then all that remains is for you to give me the name of your informer," said Linda. "Supply it, and the court will have no further need of your presence here and release you from your summons. If not, then it reserves the right to detain you here until you do."

"What?" Lady Smallbridge stared at her. "You haven't the power to do that! I've not committed a crime. Nothing like that has happened at court for years! There are no facilities for keeping me at the palace indefinitely, and you certainly can't throw me into the tower, as they might have done in days of old!"

Linda looked back at her, impassively. Ginny was quite right, of course. But the court administrator was gambling that if she detained her at the palace for long enough, then the lady might start to get impatient to be gone and cooperate. She would hold her until the end of the palace working day – which was stretching the rules slightly, but not actually breaking them. After that she would have to release her, though she wouldn't tell Ginny that at the moment. In the meantime she decided that it might be worth questioning her staff more closely. If one of them was indeed the culprit, then perhaps she could extract a confession from them, regardless of whether the lady chose to expose them. Ginny might still leave the court having not answered the crucial question, but it was worth a try, and Linda was determined to sort this out.

"We shall see, Lady Smallbridge," she replied. "You will of course not go to the tower, but neither will you leave this room!"

She went and opened the door. Outside was Sergeant Starkey of court security, with another officer.

"Sergeant Starkey," she ordered. "Lady Smallbridge will be staying here until she provides the court with another piece of information. Please advise my secretary to tell my staff that the interview room will be occupied for the rest of the day. She should also ensure that she is supplied with sufficient refreshment. No one is to enter. Post an officer in here and outside. Inform me if she wishes to answer the court's question."

"Very good, Mrs Radcliffe!" obeyed the sergeant, and left.

"I am due at parliament later, Lady Smallbrige," continued the court administrator. "For now, I have work to do in my office. If you decide to answer the question, then let the sergeant know and I will return. Good afternoon!"

She left Ginny sat at the table. A female guard now stood in the room with her, whist a male was outside the door.

***

Linda returned to her office and phoned through to Ruth, asking her to come in. She told her of Lady Smallbridge's revelation.

"She seems determined to defy my attempts to prise out of her the specific detail. If what she *has* said is true, then this is very serious. You know what will ultimately happen, Ruth. Her majesty will expect it, and I will not hesitate to follow court procedure because I am unequivocal that it should be. I know what you said earlier, but I must just ask you this for the record. You are certain that you know nothing more?"

"Positive, Mrs Radcliffe," replied the chief administration officer.

"Right," said Linda. "Well my next step will be to start questioning all the staff individually in my office, without delay. I might have some very vague suspicions of one or two of them, but I shall keep an open mind. Send in Debra first please, Ruth."

Her deputy drew in a deep breath and released it. "As you wish, Mrs Radcliffe."

***

Once she'd been made aware of the propose for her unexpected meeting with her boss, Debra was indignant.

"Why have you called me in first, Mrs Radcliffe?" she demanded. "Does that mean that you suspect me? It could have been any one of us. That's if Smallbridge isn't just making it up to cause more trouble!"

"Um, Lady Smallbridge to you, Debra!" Linda admonished her. "She may have shown a degree of disloyalty to her majesty, but the court will still at least show respect and address her by her correct title. But no. I do not have any hard evidence that this leak was perpetrated by you – though you did express your disapproval for this particular bill, rather more strongly than the other department members. You are not being accused. But somebody had to be first. I am not doing this in any specific order."

This wasn't strictly true. Actually, Debra Cross had been the first person Linda had thought of, given what she had said previously. But after her, the court administrator really was at a loss.

"Sorry, Mrs Radcliffe," replied Debra. "But I insist most strongly that I would never break the court's code of conduct regarding the confidentiality of its business."

After a couple more questions, Linda excused her. She gradually did the same with the other women, intensely studying their reactions to her probing. In general, Linda considered herself quite good at determining whether someone was concealing information.

Halfway through the process, the next person on her list was Sally Bolt, the junior office clerk, who had only been at the palace for about a year. She called Ruth and asked for her to be sent in.

"Sally isn't here, Mrs Radcliffe," said her deputy. "She complained of feeling unwell and has asked to go home. I was going to inform you and ask whether you'd give permission, when you were next free. Meanwhile, I've taken her to see Freda."

Freda was the name of the palace nurse. She was in charge of the medical needs of everybody at the palace.

"Really?" asked Linda. "She showed no signs of illness at the start of the afternoon. What ailment does she complain of?"

"A splitting headache, Mrs Radcliife."

Linda narrowed her eyes a fraction as she thought.

"Hmm," she said. "Right. I will go over to see her for myself. Say nothing more to the office until I return."

Leaving the administration department, she quickly made her way to Vera's medical room. Her mind was pondering. She found the nurse, dressed in her royal blue uniform gown, sitting with Sally.

"What seems to be the problem, Nurse Morrison?" she asked.

"Sally has a headache and is complaining of feeling a bit giddy, Mrs Radcliffe," replied Freda. I don't think that it's too serious, but maybe she needs some rest."

"Right," replied Linda. "If I could have a moment alone with Sally, please?"

The nurse glanced across at her. "Oh. Well of course, if that's what you wish, Mrs Radcliffe. I'll be just adjacent, in my office." She went out through an adjoining door.

Linda stepped forward a pace and folded her arms, regarding Sally enquiringly. The clerk looked uncomfortable.

"Mrs Radcliffe, please. With the deepest respect to you, I don't feel that I'm up to talking with anybody at the moment."

"I will try to be brief," said Linda. "When did you first start to feel ill? You seemed in good health at the department meeting after lunch."

"I didn't feel quite right this morning, but it did suddenly worsen in the afternoon, Mrs Radcliffe," replied Sally.

"Well, I don't want to suggest that you aren't genuinely ill," continued Linda. "It might be pure coincidence that you've been struck down like this at the very time when I've been conducting this investigation. But you have to see how it could appear to me. Unless of course, there is something else."

She paused to let her last sentence hang in the air for a moment. Sally shifted on the couch.

"I don't know what you mean, Mrs Radcliffe."

"What I *mean* girl, is that Lady Smallbridge has told me she was informed of the preparation of the afore mentioned bill by a member of our department. If this is true, then I must find out who that person was. Do you know anything about it?"

"No, Mrs Radcliffe. I do not," declared the clerk, her eyes darting towards the wall.

"Look at me, Sally," said Linda. She sensed tension. "Think very carefully!" As their eyes met, she probed fiercely to try and detect the possibility of something being hidden.

Sally flinched. "Please stop, Mrs Radcliffe!" she begged. "You're making me feel even more unwell!"

Linda continued to study her. That could explain her reaction of course. But she still felt that she might at last be on the right track.

Suddenly, there was a knock at the door, forcing Linda to break her concentration. Vera appeared and opened it, to reveal sergeant Starkey.

"Sorry to disturb you, Nurse Morrison," she said. "Could I speak with Mrs Radcliffe outside please?"

"Alright, Sergeant Starkey. I'll come," declared Linda.

"Lady Smallbridge has indicated that she is now willing to give you the answer to your question, Mrs Radcliffe," said the sergeant, after the court administrator closed the door.

Now Linda's heart leapt.

"Excellent!" she replied. "Wait here a moment, and then I shall go to see her."

Linda went back into the medical room.

"Right then Sally. I have just been told that Lady Smallbridge is now willing to tell me who her mystery informant was. I shall go and hear what she has to say."

The clerk started with shock.

"Lady Smallbridge said that she wouldn't..." Sally broke off, a look of horror beginning to cover her face, as she realised her mistake.

"What was that?" Linda had begun to turn away, but now she rounded on her. "Lady Smallbridge said what exactly?"

The clerk looked at her desperately.

"Come on girl. I think you'd better tell me everything now," pressed her boss. "You've already said too much to continue with this lie."

Sally gave a groan. "I know Lady Smallbridge a little, as my aunt is the butler at her estate, Mrs Radcliffe. She offered me some money, if I would give her some information about any business of the palace that she could reveal to the press. Preferably something controversial. I initially refused, but she said that if I did, my aunt's future employment would come into question. So, when this came up, I told her. I didn't know then what her personal view was on the subject, but it wasn't through any personal desire to make a point about it that I did so. I was thinking of my aunt. I am certain that the lady would have dismissed her. She did promise me though, that she would never reveal who her informant was. But then Lady Smallbridge was summoned to the palace to be told of the queen's disapproval, and she appeared to have told you that it was one in our department. When it became clear that you were questioning everybody individually, I panicked and tried to get permission to get sent home sick from work before you could speak with me!"

Linda looked at her coldly. "And the money? Were you not thinking of that also? How much did she offer you? Has the sum been paid?"

"1,000 geros, Mrs Radcliffe," Sally was sniffing slightly with emotion. "And yes, I admit, the payment has taken place. My husband and I only recently moved into our own home. The money would come in useful to me, but I do not use that as an excuse." She dabbed her nose with her handkerchief. "Oh please, Mrs Radcliffe. What will happen now?"

"That is correct, the usefulness of the money to you is indeed irrelevant, young woman," asserted Linda. "You effectively accepted a bribe. That makes what you have done even worse. You have been foolish in the extreme, Sally. How dare you presume that you have the right to disclose such a matter to *anybody*? As to what happens now, I am afraid that there is only one option. Even though you say that you were concerned for the future employment of your aunt, which is obviously laudable, the court cannot treat the betrayal of its confidential business or internal affairs, as anything other than gross misconduct. Sally Bolt, you are dismissed from the services of Her Majesty's court, with immediate effect."

Sally began to break down.

"Pull yourself together!" Linda chided her. "You are supposed to be a woman, not a man or child! I do feel for your position, and realise that you probably regret what you've done, but it's a little too late for that now. The deed is done, and that being the case, now that the court is aware, it cannot shirk from the responsibility of what must be done in response."

She walked to the door and opened it.

"Sergeant Starkey, please escort Mrs Bolt from the palace, immediately! Have her collect her personal belongings and go."

The sergeant quickly became alert. "At once, Mrs Radcliffe!" She turned to Sally. "This way please, Mrs Bolt."

Trying to show as much composure as possible, Sally followed her out of the medical room.

***

Ginny was slightly disappointed when Linda told her that Sally had already confessed to being the informant, before she could tell her

personally, back in the interview room. However, she was now free to go, and confirmed once again that she would write a letter of apology to Queen Alexandra for her disrespect, within the next week. Linda hoped that she had finally seen the last of her. She phoned Hettie and asked her to pass on the latest news to the queen. She had an appointment with her tomorrow morning, and there wasn't time today to request another.

Shortly before four o'clock she left her desk for the day and walked the brief distance from the palace, up the Royal Avenue to Parliament Square. There in the chamber of Parliament House, for more than an hour she went about overseeing the progress of the court's legislation, liaising with the leader of the house, Anna Prowse. The members were debating and then voting on a number of the bills that they had been reading since being introduced to the house. the previous week. Linda stood at the dispatch box and argued the case herself for a couple of them. Fortunately, after the drama of her afternoon at the palace, things went relatively smoothly and there were no major problems.

Finally, with her day's work done, she left Parliament House, went to her car parked outside of the back entrance of the palace, and drove home.

Despite her apparent success in finding out the informant of the bill to Ginny Smallbridge, Linda was still highly annoyed. That a member of her own administration department would betray the confidentiality of the court's business. She would crack the whip down particularly strongly in the coming few days. As far as the court administrator was concerned, this was never going to happen again.

CHAPTER 24

Linda arrived back at The Grange, a few minutes before six o'clock. In the future it was likely that she would sometimes work rather later, but at the moment she was determined that with her daughter at the age she was, Alexandra would get as much time with her mother as possible in the evenings. Nanny Tork fetched her from school and looked after her until Linda came home.

Robert's working day as a miner at Rushmore, finished at five o'clock, and after cleaning up and changing he then travelled the ten miles home on the company bus. It meant that he was usually back in Greenacres by six o'clock. They all had their main meal at lunch time, so Linda prepared supper for them all in the evening.

When the bus stopped at the depot, Robert, as usual, got off and swiftly made his way to Elmsbrook Firstly, his wife decreed that half past six was their family supper time, and she was a stickler for punctuality. He had to be home and then ready to eat, by the time it was on the table. Her rule was clear, and the lashing of her tongue could be severe if he broke it. But secondly, he always longed to be reunited with Linda after the day's work. By this time, it was usually very strong. He loved his wife deeply.

Letting himself into The Grange, he went straight towards the kitchen. In the breakfast room that immediately preceded it, Alexandra was sat on the floor playing with a toy. She leapt up in delight upon seeing saw him. "Good evening, Father!" she said.

"Good evening, little one!" he replied, smiling. As he picked her up and kissed her, Linda's voice came from the adjoining kitchen door.

"Well done, Alexandra. That is the correct way to address someone."

Her daughter beamed proudly, as Robert put her down again.

Linda bounded boldly forward and swept him into her arms. He melted submissively in the way that she always liked. There was nothing like a compliant man who let her do what she wanted with him – that in her opinion was how a man should ideally be – and her husband had always been one of them.

"Good evening, my little man," she said, softly. She kissed his lips affectionately. Two inches shorter than her, Linda had always liked smaller men. Christopher – from her broken off earlier engagement – had been of similar height. Being as dominant a woman as she was, it simply felt most natural to her that her ideal man might be shorter. In her heels she could indeed tower above her husband. His stature, looks and submissiveness made him irresistible to her and she loved him more than any other man in the world.

"Good evening, my love," Robert replied. His wife moved her leg slightly so that her thigh wrapped around his and pushing forward against him firmly kissed his mouth three more times, her embrace tightening ever more with each one, giving him all the love that she felt. He sighed heavily at the pleasure she gave him. Linda's thighs tingled and her geratis grew aroused as she thought of her husband in bed later. Robert felt it through her skirt, prodding against his thigh. His genus responded with natural attraction. For a brief moment they smiled at each other, reading their sexual thoughts. Before Alexandra's birth, it had occasionally even been known for Linda to make love to her husband as soon as they were both home from work.

Robert had never forgotten the first kisses that Linda had ever given him, after a date at the cinema. It was a romantic film based on a classic Geratican love story, with light love scenes which appealed to the traditional Geratican female and male tendencies, whereby a woman was strong and a man when it came down to it most naturally needed her to protect him, ultimately finding solace within the powerful embrace of her legs in times of crisis or fear. In common with most of the other men watching he had wished he could be the handsome male character who was the object of the beautiful leading lady's desire, and Linda like the rest of the women had been aroused as she identified with the lady's passion.

Robert had instinctively reached for Linda's hand when the man appeared most in need, which greatly thrilled her. Some women at the back had leaned across to become intimate with their husbands or boyfriends as the film ran. Linda was not one of those, but later outside in a quiet spot with nobody else around, pinned against a wall, he had been smothered by her tall body, locked between her thighs and caressed passionately. Linda's tongue had boldly entered his lightly open mouth, and the feeling of it licking his own had taken his breath away and sent his genus wild. Her pleasure in loving him had been obvious too, and he had felt the hardness of her erect geratis against him.

"How was your day?" asked Linda, as she released her husband.

"Fine. Just routine, really. And yours?"

Linda breathed in deeply. "Not one of the best starts to a week as a matter of fact, dear. You probably won't have heard any of the news at lunch time. I'll talk to you about it over supper. It will only be ten more minutes, so lay the table and be ready please."

"Of course, my love," replied Robert, in subservience.

In the dining room, he opened a drawer and took out some plates and cutlery. Alexandra happily helped him to arrange it all in their places at the table.

A few minutes later, they were all sat down and ready to eat. Laid before Linda on the table, was a stick. It was present at all meal times as a warning to Alexandra from her mother not to misbehave at the table – something she would not tolerate. Alexandra had occasionally experienced a couple of strokes of it on the palm of her hand.

As they ate, Linda told Robert a little of what had been reported on the news that day.

"But is it true that the court is proposing this?" he asked. "I know what your personal opinion is on the death penalty and I agree with it, but does Her Majesty also?"

"I'm not going to say anything more than I have to everybody else, Robert," said Linda. "Even as my nearest and dearest, I can't discuss a matter like this. I do sometimes talk about more general, everyday things that happen at the palace within my department, but as you know, even then it's always in confidence. But the reason that I'm mentioning today's events is just to warn you of what you might expect in the next couple of days. Because of what's been in the media – and I listened to the radio news at six o'clock – I believe that several of your fellow workers will be quizzing you to try and find out more information, given that they know who you're married to. Some might think that there must be something in the story, and that the court is hiding something. But you must try to stay calm and simply tell anybody who should ask that you don't know any more than they do, which is true after all. Nothing more than that. If you have any personal opinion, then keep it to yourself. If they enquire as to whether you've spoken to me about it, you can say that I've only told you what's been in the news. Is that understood?"

"Well, yes love. I don't suppose it'll be too difficult to keep my mouth shut about something confidential, when I don't know the details myself!" Robert chuckled. "Sometimes the men do ask me the odd question and think that my wife must tell me about everything at court, but I have to disappoint them."

"Alexandra! Elbows off the table when you are eating, please!" ordered Linda, suddenly. Her daughter jumped, glanced anxiously at the stick for a brief second, and then swiftly upwards to her mother.

"Sorry mother!" she said, immediately.

Linda looked her in the eyes. "Alright. Just remember your table manners."

Then she returned her attention to Robert.

"That is exactly my point, darling," said Linda. "Tomorrow, your workmates should be disappointed again."

"Of course, Linda," replied Robert.

"Good. Right, there's one other thing to tell you," continued his wife. "I've found out that there is a vacancy at one of the new rigs that are being set up in the Geranda ocean by Geratican Oil. Early this morning, I made arrangements for you to go over to it for a brief chat with somebody about it."

Robert stopped eating momentarily. "Oh. I see," he replied. This was something that the two of them had been discussing for a while. Linda was keen for him to move out of the mining industry and start working in the newly developing market of oil production. She saw this as a major new source of energy which could compliment that which had been extracted from under the Geratican surface for several centuries, and had used her position at court to drive through the policy of exploiting it.

"We've talked about this, Robert. I know that it's something different from what you've always done, but you've got the skills to do it. And the job will be better paid. Oil is going to become a valuable commodity in the coming years."

"So, I'd be drilling for oil at sea, rather than mining for minerals underground," said Robert. "I suppose it wouldn't be any harder for me." During the time that his wife had been pushing the subject, he had first come around to giving it consideration, then to the fact that Linda might be right. He usually did, and mostly didn't take long to accept her judgement. It was usually made fairly clear to him that he should – either as a result of realising she was right after a brief conversation, or simply being told that it was so.

"When is the interview?" he asked.

"On day 5 of this week," said Linda. "The manager's name is Daisy Hollis. And you shouldn't have a problem. I've been given permission to accompany you. The woman will ask you a couple of questions, but no more than that. Men's job interviews generally don't require anything more. I shall also be able to speak on your behalf as a woman, which as you know often happens. I'm confident that you'll get the job."

They had finished eating now, as her husband took in this other piece of news.

"As I said before. I obviously can't swim. I never did get on very well with those lessons you got me take, after we were married. I hope that there'd be no danger of me falling off the rig!"

"No, darling," said Linda. "I' m assured that you shouldn't need to actually come into any direct contact with the sea, in your specific job. I want you to do this."

"And it will mean me being away on weekly shifts, so I won't be here as much," mused Robert.

"Yes. You'll be working one week and then at home the next. But being halfway across to the other side of the world, you won't be coming home in the evenings. You'll stay on the rig."

"You're sure that you won't mind?"

"Darling, I shall miss you terribly!" admitted his wife. "But it's only every other week, and I can also see the benefit. In any case, when you do come home after finishing a shift, then I'm sure we'll make the most of it. It'll make your time back here all the more special. I won't be able to wait for that first night when we're reunited!"

For a moment Linda's geratis twitched, and her thighs tingled. She got up, walked behind her husband's chair, and slipped her arms around his shoulders. Then she whispered into his ear. "*I shall*

want you *so* much, **my little man!** *I 'll make love to you like never before!"*

Robert smiled. "Hmm. Lucky me!"

"As always!" declared his wife. "But anyhow. We are agreed that this is the right thing to do, and we'll fly over for you to meet Mrs Hollis at the end of the week?"

"I'd better start preparing for it," said Robert, in response.

"Then that's settled then," said Linda. "It will be on rig number two, specifically. I'll make arrangements for us to be flown over, and you must be sure to book the day off, Robert."

"OK, Linda," replied Robert. "I take it that you will, too?"

"I already have done."

Robert stared at her. "Oh, right. So, you already knew that we'd be going, before you came home and told me tonight?"

Linda looked back at him, impassively. "Husband, if you'd really insisted that you didn't want to do the job, then I would have given you strong words of instruction, otherwise. In the end if you were still unwilling to do as I asked, then I would have made my instruction an order. And you know that there are always consequences for disregarding one of those from me in our marriage. But as it happens, I was confident that you'd agree in any case, regardless."

"Hmm. Yes. Of course, dear!" Robert smiled.

Linda nodded and then skirted back around the table. "Right. Supper over. Time to wash up."

***

After she and her husband had cleared away, Linda sat with Alexandra in the parlour and listened as she demonstrated her reading skills. Her daughter was progressing extremely well at school and had impressed her mistresses. Linda had given her a short book which was quite advanced for a girl of her age, yet she read it aloud very easily, delighting her mother immensely. Linda had been told that she wasn't very confident in reading aloud at school, which didn't surprise her very much, as it was obvious that Alexandra was a shy girl, but she was sure that er daughter would soon gain confidence.

Soon afterwards Alexandra said goodnight to her father, and Linda took her upstairs to bed. Now   her mother read one of her bedtime stories, and Alexandra held Linda's as she lay in her bed listening and sucking her thumb. Gradually she began to feel sleepy. Finishing the book, Linda opened a musical box which played a pretty, soothing tune. Then she leant over and gently slipped her arms around her daughter's shoulders, stroked her hair and spoke soft words of loving into her ear. As Alexandra gazed into her mother's eyes, she felt so secure and protected that she fully relaxed and drifted off to sleep, her thumb still in her mouth.

Downstairs, directly below Alexandra's bedroom, Linda then did some final preparation of her budget speech for the next day, in her study. It was quite common for her to bring work home from the palace. Then she went to the parlour to join Robert, and they sat together on the sofa listening to some music, and sipping coffee and port. Soon Linda pulled her husband close in her arms and shifted to wind her legs around his. A woman's legs were stronger, and once locked inside of them a man could not break free from their grip. It also meant that women could run faster. A man's upper body was stronger than a woman's though. Wrapped in his wife's strong thighs, and with no wish to escape, Robert laid his head on her shoulder. She smiled and kissed his cheek.

They sat like that for a while, Linda beginning to become sexually aroused. Robert looked up lovingly at her, and she saw the need in his eyes. Her mouth moved to rest over his, and she kissed him

again. She was thrilled to experience the familiar feeling of her husband's body melting into hers, just the way she liked it.

Robert was always happy to play the role of seducer to his wife, which he knew turned her on even more. The look on his face became sexy and Linda's geratis bulged and strained inside her skirt. His hand instinctively moved down and lightly touched it. Linda exhaled deeply in pleasure. She pushed Robert backwards onto the sofa and laid over him. His already erect genus ballooned almost to the maximum, and she could sense his breath shortening as she held and kissed him. Her heart began to beat fast. They both knew what was to come in a few minutes, and Linda couldn't wait any longer.

"Time for bed, I think!" she said, after glancing over to the grandmother clock. It was a quarter to ten, and they normally retired on the hour.

Robert stood up.

"*Make yourself available to me, husband!*" said Linda, huskily.

He smiled and replied softly, "*Of course! It is my duty and my pleasure to do so, for my wife!*"

At these moments Robert always remembered their wedding night. His wife had literally swept him off his feet and placed his body down on the bed before making love to him for half the night. When the first orgasm had ripped through his body the incredible feeling of ecstasy had been so intense that he had thrashed about uncontrollably and needed to hold on tight to Linda's body until he had fully come. He had continued to be grateful of having her to cling to ever since. Robert had been a virgin but Linda had previously once slept with Christopher. At the time this had been frowned upon, but the urges had been so strong that this had been one time that the normally deeply traditional Linda had strayed from convention – though she had naturally taken full precautions and it was not a widely known fact. When their engagement had abruptly ended shortly afterwards, the fact that they had briefly

shared such intimacy had made things even more painful. But all the same, Linda did not regret it and was actually quite pleased that sex before marriage was becoming more accepted.

As Robert went upstairs, Linda locked up for the night, prepared for the next day and turned out the lights. Then she followed.

Her husband was in bed ready and waiting for him when she entered the bedroom, as she always wanted him to be. The sight of his gorgeous naked body displayed invitingly to her ignited a huge wave of sexual energy deep inside. Her thighs tingled and she licked her lips. She quickly undressed and readied herself for the night in the ensuite bathroom. As she came back out, Robert looked at her longingly, and spread himself in a submissive position.

"Take me! I'm yours!" he whispered.

Linda became so aroused that she almost ran to her side of the queen size bed. Climbing on to it she crouched on all fours in an aggressive fashion for a second, devouring Robert. She licked her lips like a hungry tiger again before prancing across to his side, her geratis briefly grazing the sheet and staining it with a drop of blue fluid as she did so. She launched herself upon him, locking his legs inside of hers and engulfing his smaller body. Linda murmured at the pleasure she felt in going down over him and having his whole body beneath her. As she kissed his lips hungrily, she squeezed him in her arms and held his legs in a vice like grip inside her thighs. Linda pressed herself dominantly into Robert, until it seemed to him, not only was her geratis inside of his vagina, but that their two bodies were becoming one. It was always like this.

*"I love you so much, **my little man!**"* breathed Linda, looking into his eyes, and running a hand through his dark hair. *"And I'm going to have you!"* Robert held on to his wife, and sank submissively into the bed beneath his wife, as she took control. She kissed his neck and shoulders and squeezed him tight. *"I'm going to give you **all** my loving,"* she whispered. *"I'll make you feel ecstasy. No other woman can make love like I can!"*

Robert felt Linda's geratis draped across his genus, beginning to grind against the most sensitive spot as her passion intensified, making him gasp. She squeezed her thighs inwardly, making the tightness even stronger, and he moaned with pleasure. As her kisses continued across his chest, she ran her a finger lightly down his body.

"Oh, my love, you know I'll need you forever!" murmured Robert. *"Do what you want. Make love to me!"*

Linda's geratis thickened so much that it throbbed against his vagina walls. A natural Geratican woman, she liked nothing more than making love to a man. Robert sighed deeply as he felt her grow fully erect inside of him. As so often before, in his ecstasy he wondered if there was enough room, so completely did she seem to fill him.

*"Look into my eyes, **my little man!**"* urged his wife. As they met, her strong gaze made clear to him her dominant desire. Linda saw the natural submissive reaction in Robert, that she loved so much. He felt the beat of his wife's heart pounding against his chest as she thrust deep into him and kissed his lips again. Her tongue easily found its way into his mouth and hungrily licked his. She gripped him in an even bigger embrace and crushed his legs inside of her thighs. Her geratis ground his genus. His own heart raced. He was on the brink.

Linda breathed heavily as she thrust again and again, ever more deeply into her husband's body, letting out intermittent moans of pleasure at the feeling it gave her. She knew that Robert was about to come, but she was close too, and her geratis released a small burst of juice against his vagina wall which he felt nourish his veins. Robert felt as if his wife was completely inside of him, and he had to submit to her. Her geratis thrust again against his genus. Totally dominated, it burst, and he came long and hard, making him squeal, and the feeling of his semen slipping through her geratis pores finally sent Linda over the edge. She cried out as a

huge orgasm caused her to shoot a much larger quantity of fluid all around her husband's vagina. He oozed with pleasure.

Linda's passion was still strong. Half an hour after going to bed, she had made love to her husband three times and come herself four.

In her bedroom along the passage, Alexandra had slept through the sounds of their cries of passion, undisturbed.

CHAPTER 25

Next morning, Nanny Tork arrived before Linda left for work. She would be taking Alexandra to school, a little later.

Linda drove Robert to the bus depot, on her way out of Greenacres. They kissed goodbye, and he wished her luck before he got out. Today would be Linda's most important since becoming court administrator, introducing the court's annual budget to the parliament. She hugged and kissed him a final time (causing an effect on them both which would remain in their memories all day, and keep then in mind of each other), and then they parted and she headed off for Avermore.

Robert did find his journey to the pit a little different from normal. Generally quite a quiet man, he usually spent the time in peace and reflection, before the rigours of the day ahead. However, today he was besieged on the bus by some of the men, who wanted to try and find out some more about the news they had heard the night before. He suspected that one or two had been pushed to do so by their wives or girlfriends. It wasn't difficult sticking to the line that Linda had told him – and not just because of the trouble he knew that he knew he'd be in if he said something he shouldn't – as he genuinely had no information to give, though in his own mind he thought it likely that what Lady Smallbridge had said was true.

"Robert can't say anything, or his wife'll put 'im over her knee and give 'im the cane!" remarked the man sitting next to him, with a smirk, as the bus passed a mill. There were several chortles. He often took some ribbing from the men due to their perspective of his marriage to the court administrator of Geratica, given her domineering reputation. Though they didn't know the affectionate nickname that Linda had for him, he was in fact sometimes thought of as "the little man" by them when he went home to his wife at night – in more ways than one. He usually took it in good fun, and they weren't *always* that far wrong in any case – he did as he was told. But he was sure that very few indeed, if any of them, had a radically different relationship with their own wife or girlfriend,

even if the partner did not have such a forceful personality as Linda's.

"Sorry. I honestly don't know any more," he insisted.

Some of the men exchanged glances. They were convinced that the court administrator must share *some* things with her husband.

***

At the palace, Linda had an eleven o'clock meeting with the queen to show her the completed final draft off the budget speech. They also talked about Lady Smallbridge and Sally Bolt.

"I shall await Ginny's letter with interest and take great pleasure in reading her apology when I receive it," asserted Queen Alexandra. "As for Sally, I cannot help but feel sorry for her, I must admit. She has been a silly girl, but I appreciate her circumstances. Perhaps the court could find a way to show some leniency."

Linda looked at her in surprise. "Are you saying that we should take her back, Ma'am? With respect, I do not think that would be a wise thing to do. If we do that for one member of the court's staff, then there is a danger that others will feel encouraged to leak information about our business to an outside source. Especially if they are offered payment for it. I only dismissed her yesterday, and it will undermine what I said – that the court regards the matter as gross misconduct!"

"I certainly have no wish to undermine you, Linda," replied the queen. "I totally agree that she cannot remain at court. But Lady Smallbridge has behaved disgracefully. She previously left the palace in a huff because she didn't become my personal aide, and now it appears that she threatened to dismiss Sally's aunt from her own employment if the girl didn't comply with her demand."

"She also accepted 1,000 geros, Ma'am!" remarked Linda. "At the very least she could have refused that."

"Yes, I know, and that made things worse." said Queen Alexandra. "But this what I propose that we do. You should summon Mrs Bolt back to the palace and reaffirm that the queen will not have her at court, but recognises the personal position that she was in. Therefore, she will be pardoned and allowed to offer her resignation, rather than face dismissal, which will allow her to leave with a reference from us, making no mention of this incident. My *conditions* will be, *one* that she too pens a letter of apology to me, and *two* that she pays the money that Ginny gave her directly to the court's treasury. I will not have somebody formerly in my court, seen to profit financially from this kind of indiscretion. If she needs to pay in weekly instalments, rather than in a lump sum, then that will be acceptable."

Linda considered. "I am still a little wary of showing any compromise over this Ma'am. I too sympathise with her over the position of her aunt, as I told her yesterday. But even so, if I had my way, that would not justify disloyalty to the court."

The queen smiled. It wasn't often that she overruled her court administrator, but she was going to on this occasion.

"You usually do get your way in most of your life do you not, Linda?"

Linda gave a slight incline of her head, in acknowledgement, without replying.

"But you must surely empathise with Sally's predicament, leaving aside the money for a moment?" continued Queen Alexandra. "Nobody wants someone from their own family dismissed for no good reason! Think also on this. From what you say, she freely volunteered that Ginny offered her payment for the information. She didn't have to. If she had kept quiet, we might never have known about that side of this. I am sorry but I've made up my mind about this, Linda. My proposal is an order!"

Linda sighed inwardly. The queen quite obviously was one of the very few women in Geratica whose will she had to bend to if it was imposed upon her. She had no difficulty in accepting that. As she further reflected on the matter, Linda had to admit that what Queen Alexandra said made sense.

"You are probably right, Ma'am" she declared. "We should always be fair as well as firm in matters such s these. I like to think that I usually am – *in most of my life!*"

Queen Alexandra laughed. "Very good Linda! I am sure that you are. Right then. Summon Sally to be brought to the palace and tell her my proposal. But make it clear that she has been fortunate to receive this generosity, so I advise her to accept my terms. I cannot imagine why she would not, if she doesn't want to be dismissed and without a reference to give any new employer."

"As you wish, Ma'am," replied Linda.

"I trust that your budget speech will be ready for this afternoon?" enquired the queen.

"Of course, Ma'am,' confirmed Linda. "And during it I shall be making our announcement concerning the new mining operations."

"Excellent,' replied Queen Alexandra.

***

At two o'clock, dressed in a royal blue suit with a matching bow, Linda took to the despatch box in the chamber of Parliament House to deliver the court's budget. There was a hushed silence as the MPs listened.

The court administrator declared that the economy was in reasonably good shape, but now with a new monarch on the throne,

with her permission she intended to take the opportunity to implement some changes. She felt that the court's current level of spending could not be maintained, without borrowing considerably more. She strongly believed in balancing the books, therefore building up too much debt was to be avoided, and pledged to allow Geratica's private enterprise to thrive further, in order to create greater wealth in the economy, which she maintained would enable less public spending and for personal taxation to be cut for everybody as a consequence. She believed in enabling people to be aspirational. Linda also announced that the court planned to open two more mining platforms in the Geranda ocean this autumn. After she had delivered the usual forecasting for the year ahead, and complex taxation and spending details, Linda commended the bill to the house, and sat down.

There had been speculation in the media beforehand that Mrs Radcliffe might be slightly tougher in her approach to the economy than the previous court administrator, now that a new queen had recently been crowned. These reforms weren't universally popular in the house and there were a few lively questions asked of her by some of the members. But ultimately the bill was passed into law by the vote that followed, and most of the newspapers gave it a cautious welcome.

***

The next day, 3/7/00, Sally Bolt was brought into the palace. She looked white as a sheet, wondering what had happened now.

"You don't need to look quite so worried, Mrs Bolt!" Linda told her in the court administration meeting room. "You aren't in any more trouble." She went on to explain the queen's offer.

Although Sally still would no longer be employed at court, she was nevertheless relieved to discover that she was now not to be dismissed, but allowed to resign. Linda also assured her that she could see no reason why her reference wouldn't be a good one,

given her previous good record. It was a blow to the former clerk that she was going to have to pay the 1,000 geros given to her by Lady Smallbridge directly to the court. She didn't have the means to do so in full at the moment, having already spent a proportion of it on the house that she'd recently brought. Linda told her that she could arrange to pay in instalments if necessary – but it was the price that she must accept for her indiscretion, in addition to writing a letter of apology. The queen was particularly anxious for her to understand that she was fortunate to be given this opportunity to resign, rather than be dismissed, and strongly advised her to accept her conditions. This Sally did, and also asked Linda to pass on her gratitude to Queen Alexandra.

***

In the afternoon, Queen Alexandra made her weekly appearance at parliament, where she formally announced the bills that had been read and passed into law by the house over the previous week. As was customary, she also spent a few minutes answering any questions that MPs had about the queendom's affairs. Although her court administrator was chiefly responsible for the business of the court, the queen was always closely involved, through regular meetings. She spoke as its head, with background support from the administrator who sat behind her during the session.

Today, they were anticipating a question relating to the news from the beginning of the week, that had been broken by Ginny Smallbridge. Sure enough, one of the MPs asked whether there was any truth in the rumour that the court was preparing to introduce a bill to parliament, which would propose abolishing the death penalty.

With the obvious exception of the budget, it wasn't the custom of the court to disclose any business before it was introduced for a first reading, but since there had been so much speculation over this particular bill in the media, and it was imminent, Queen Alexandra and Linda had decided that they would have make an

exception this time, or they would look ridiculous when it happened. The queen confirmed that a 'Penalty For Murder Reform' bill was indeed to be introduced to parliament for a first reading, tomorrow. It would be debated and voted upon on 1/8/00...

***

Afterwards, Linda paid a visit to the Geratican Scientific Research Centre, where she was updated on the latest intelligence, based on their scanning of Geraticaian activity. She was always vocal in her view that Geratica should be vigilant in this activity, given what it knew of the belligerent attitude of many on that world towards them – especially their monarchs.

Happily, from what was reported to her, there seemed no undue cause for alarm. She would inform Queen Alexandra tomorrow.

***

On 5/7/00, Robert had his "chat," with Daisy Hollis. They flew in a Geratican Oil Company helicopter specially chartered by Linda, from a helipad in Avermore, across the Geranda Ocean to the rig. There were currently five rigs in all – two in their own northern hemisphere, and three in the southern – though several more were planned. There were also a number of refineries situated in all four regions of Geratica. They approached number two rig fifteen minutes before noon, local time, and the pilot set them down on the platform.

They stepped out of the helicopter, and were met by a burly looking man, who led them through the wind into the main cabin area. The man knocked on a door and opened it.

"Robert Radcliffe is here to see you, Daisy," he announced. "And his wife, er, Mrs Linda Radcliffe."

"Good morning, Robert! Good morning, Linda!" Daisy greeted them. "Come into my office and sit down."

Linda glanced at her husband with an urging look.

"Thank you, Mrs Hollis," he replied, and they followed.

"I trust that you had a good journey?" enquired the manager.

"Yes, it was fine. No problem at all, Mrs Hollis," said Linda.

"Please. We are all on first name terms here. Call me Daisy!"

After ensuring that Robert and Linda had refreshments, she began the interview. As Linda had predicted, she only asked him a couple of basic questions, largely related to his general fitness and what his general duties currently were as a miner. She felt that he would be someone who could soon learn "on the job." For what he'd be required to do, not being able to swim wouldn't be a problem. But Linda also spoke at length about her husband's skills, dedication and willingness to work, and drew from her briefcase a glowing reference which she'd obtained from his manager at the pit, regarding his performance.

After about ten minutes, Daisy pronounced the interview over, and confirmed that Robert was suitable for the job. She offered it to him at once. He looked at Linda, who nodded. He accepted it.

Daisy produced an employment contract for signature and handed it to Robert, but wasn't surprised when he passed it to Linda. A lot of working men were only semi-literate, if they were at all, and consequently contracts were usually handled and signed by women – very often wives or partners, or sometimes other representatives. Robert had some basic grasp of literacy, taught informally to him by Fanny, but even so he let Linda study the document, which she did most thoroughly. He was actually quite competent in writing his name, but when his wife was finally satisfied, she signed it herself without a word of discussion between them. He had never

signed anything in his life. Robert deferred to her always, and she regarded it as a woman's role to perform all such related responsibilities. At that time most women took the traditional Geratican view, that it was not necessary for men to be formally educated. What little some did pick up, was generally from their mothers within the domestic home. As a mongrel, Robert had no known parents, and his relationship with Linda was *extremely* traditional. The dominance of her personality meant that she naturally took control of everything – even more so than many other women. She expected her husband to generally be submissive to the way that she ran the home.

Linda also agreed with Daisy that Robert would start at the rig on 1/12/00, after the Radcliffe family had returned from a two week holiday in Utipides.

Afterwards, Daisy showed Robert around the rig, to see where he would be working and what roughly he would be doing, and also where he would eat and sleep during his shifts.

It was the first time that Robert had ever been on an oil rig, but not so Linda. After the field had been discovered on the bed of the Geranda ocean by geologists from Dumas, the oil company had been formed and the rigs constructed. The formal opening of the oil field had taken place before she had become Court Administrator, and Queen Beatrix had visited number one rig to do the honours, accompanied by Janet Dobson – much to Linda's envy. But as soon as she had succeeded to the position, she had taken the first opportunity that came to travel over to not only that rig, but number two as well. As a result, she had become acquainted with their managers, including Daisy Hollis.

Then, Linda and Robert bid their farewells to Daisy, who remarked that she looked forward to seeing Robert on the first day of week twelve. They climbed back aboard the helicopter and were flown back to Castra and Avermore.

Robert's presence on the rig accompanied by "Mrs Radcliffe," had led most to presume that he was in line for the vacant job. Upon

hearing that Robert Radcliffe would indeed be starting work there soon, there were dark mutterings from a couple of them that his wife might have pulled a few strings. Daisy firmly told them all that Robert had been a first class candidate and he deserved to get the job. She was adamant that everybody would like and appreciate him once he'd settled in. What his wife did was none of their business, and there was nothing anybody could do about it, anyhow. Everybody was entitled to their opinion, but Daisy warned that if anybody gave him a hard time due to personal resentment, then she would sack them...

CHAPTER 26

At four o'clock on 1/8/00, Linda was at parliament, as the 'Penalty For Murder - Reform' bill began to be debated after its first reading by MPs. Outside Parliament House there was small and relatively peaceful protest from people who had heard about the proposed legislation and opposed it – still a highly unusual occurrence at this time in Geratica's history. Lady Ginny Smallbridge had sent her letter of apology to Queen Alexandra, and had thought it wisest to stay away. As a Geratican noblewoman she didn't wish to fall *too* far out of favour with the queen. The court had also received a similar one from Sally Bolt.

As expected, there was a hot debate over the matter, and Linda went to the dispatch box to defend the bill as MPs asked questions and gave their opinions.

"Why should we care about what happens to a murderer?" demanded one MP. "Hang them and be done with them, I say!"

"I am the first to say that their crime is despicable and of the highest order," declared the court administrator. "It deserves, and as far as I am concerned it will always receive, the most severe of penalties from our law courts. But we are entering the sixth millennium of Geratica's history, and there comes a time when we have to stop acting as savages and behave more humanely. Many of those who are ultimately responsible for administering the final outcome, do not wish for the practice to continue."

"I will happily take their place!" shouted another MP. There were shouts of agreement from several others.

"Perhaps if you had to witness the hanging process yourself on a number of occasions, then you might begin to feel differently," said Linda. "I regard myself as very conservative in my views on law and order. I believe strongly in corporal punishment for children in the home and at school, and horse whippings for the most serious of juvenile crimes – as court administrator I will

never flinch from carrying out my duty in relation to the latter. But I have witnessed the execution of a prisoner, and I have to tell you that even *I* was not comfortable with it! That might surprise many of you, but that is how it is."

"Would the court not agree that if someone takes a life, then they should pay for it with their own?" was the question asked next.

"No, we would not," replied Linda. "I am sorry but no matter how serious the offence, Her Majesty's court no longer believes that it can be justified for the state to take someone's life. It merely legitimises murder of a different kind, making the state no more morally better than they are."

"The difference is that a murderer has taken an innocent life, but that the state is taking a guilty one!" said an MP sat not far away from the dispatch box. "The court should remember who the victim is in these cases!"

Linda looked across at her. "The court does not forget, and the offender must still be punished by spending the rest of their life in prison. But you cannot have it both ways. If, as most of us strongly believe, it is wrong for an individual to take a life, then the state must abide by the same rule in its response to that wrong. That goes to the crux of the matter. Once you understand and accept that, then all the other arguments for, become irrelevant. Two wrongs do not make a right, and however terribly hard that it must be to face the loss of a beloved one in this way, eventually the hard fact has to be faced. The 'victim' cannot be brought back, and those left behind have to move on with their own lives. No one is suggesting that they should be required to have much sympathy for the offender, but there is such a thing as forgiveness. They are still a person.

"And furthermore, for any other crime, we would not say that doing the same thing to them was appropriate, fair, or even justifiable punishment. Why should our attitude towards this one in particular, be any different?"

The previous speaker stood up again. "So, does the court believe that there are no circumstances in which a murderer might bring their fate upon themselves – primarily that by committing the act they have forfeited their right to be treated fairly, and in that situation those 'left behind' are entitled to say the murderer deserves to be hung?"

"We do believe that such a person must accept their fate when a court of law passes a prison sentence – just as they should for any other crime," remarked Linda. "But the rest of what you say is an attempt to justify vengeance -   and that is not acceptable in law, however tempting it might be to practice it, in order to make ourselves feel better. Speaking personally, I will not for one moment stand here and pretend that I have never sought such a thing in my own life after a defeat or humiliation of some kind. But we are talking about the taking of a life, and that is a slightly more serious matter. For the record, we also do not believe that so called 'vigilantism' is acceptable. It must be left to the authorities to do their job."

"The death penalty acts as a deterrent to others who might consider committing such a crime," commented another member.

"As this bill makes clear, that assertion has been found to be false over the past decade," retorted Linda. "Geratica is a predominantly peaceful world and murder is still relatively rare – from what we know of Geraticai, it is more common there. But the number of murders has been increasing for several years, and the court's records show that no other monarch had to sign as many death warrants as Queen Alexandra was called upon to, during the first quarter year of their reign. It is often a mistake to believe that many people who commit murder, think with the same rationality as others do. Often the offenders truly believe that *they* will get away with this sort of crime, despite the fact that previously, a vast majority of people have not. Some can even rationalise and justify the act in their own minds and will be determined to do it, no matter what. The so called 'deterrent' factor then becomes less and less valid. As well as using information from or own records, Her Majesty's court has consulted widely – though confidentially - in

our research on these matters and received reports from both sides of the argument. The bill states our conclusions, and the reason why we are proposing this reform."

"Even if just one person is deterred, then surely it is worthwhile?" asked the same member.

"For every one of those, there will be several others who won't be," countered the court administrator. "But basically, in all of this I come back to my earlier point. The court does not believe that it or anybody else has the right to order a person to be put to death, regardless of the circumstances, and that being the case, there is little else to say. We have though attempted to put a compelling body of evidence into the bill, to back up our belief. It is now for parliament to decide if it agrees. The queen is very much of the opinion that it should be passed, though."

"You also stated earlier, that rather than a murderer being hung, they would spend the rest of their lives in prison," said another MP. "And yet the bill does make provision for some to be freed on parole. How do we know that they will not repeat the same offence?"

"We already have a parole system for prisoners, which works very well," remarked Linda. "The board will closely examine any prisoner who becomes eligible for possible early release. They will only allow that if they are certain that the prisoner no longer poses any threat to the public. And the court is proposing that such a consideration will not be granted until they have served at least three quarters of their sentence, which is quite a number of years. For at least as long as I am court administrator, I anticipate that this will be the case."

"The board can never be *absolutely* certain of a murderer never killing again though, can they?" asked a member across the chamber, in the front row directly opposite Linda.

Linda raised her eyebrows a fraction. "Well, Miss Lucas, it is difficult to be *absolutely* certain about many things. I believe that I

will leave the palace tonight and arrive home safely, but I cannot be *absolutely* certain that I will not be killed in a car crash, along the way! The chances of it happening are – I hope – so slim that it isn't worth my worrying about. I am sure that the public need not unduly worry about the possibility of a murderer repeating their crime, under the court's new proposals. And it should be pointed out that murder in Geratica is still relatively rare, compared with other crimes."

"Would the court administrator be prepared to 'forgive' an offender who murdered one of her own family?" asked an MP, at the back of the chamber, behind Linda.

"I would find it very difficult, I am sure," replied Linda with a sigh. "Anybody would. Let us be honest about that. But I hope that after a period of time, I would not find it *impossible*."

Some snorts and derogatory mutterings greeted this last remark. Linda rounded on them angrily, before speaker Lesley Reeves intervened with a shout of "Order!"

"There are occasions when someone who commits a murder experiences genuine remorse," continued Linda. "Such a sentiment should not *always* be dismissed."

Despite there being several questions raised in opposition to the court's bill, there were also a number of members who spoke in its favour.

One such woman stood up. "Does the court agree with me that under the current system, if someone is hung for the crime of murder, but is subsequently proved innocent, it represents a major miscarriage of justice?" she asked.

"The court does agree," said Linda. "There have been such occasions in the past, and we have had to acknowledge that a mistake has been made. Tragically of course, the person cannot be brought back, and it is terribly hard to have to face any relatives or friends who are left behind and obviously dreadfully upset and

angry. Often it can lead to legal action, resulting in compensation having to be paid."

Another member commented that though she would support the bill, she thought that if the death penalty was abolished for murder, the main detail which would have to be agreed was the parole system – exactly who should ever become eligible for early release, and how long they should serve before they were entitled it.

"Can the court clarify the position of Petra Watt?" enquired an MP.

"On day 5 of last week, Miss Watt was found guilty at Liverton Crown Court, of murdering her lover by poison, after he rejected her proposal of marriage," replied Linda. "It appears that she felt that if she could not have him, then no other woman would either. She used a substance which she thought would be undetected, resulting in the cause of death being determined as natural causes, but unfortunately for her, the post-mortem investigation discovered traces of it in his blood. The jury concluded that it was indeed Miss Watt who administered the poison. She has been sentenced to death. However, due to the fact that this bill is currently being considered by parliament, the queen has personally intervened to defer the event until after a decision has been made by members on it becoming law. Indeed there are a small number of others in a similar position, but the sensational nature of her case as depicted in the media has made people focus on it. Obviously, if this bill is not passed today, then it will get amended and read again, and a further time should it be necessary. If the bill does become law, then the woman's sentence will be commuted to life imprisonment. But if parliament should decide to defy the will of Her Majesty and her court, then we will have to withdraw the bill and consider whether to begin drawing up another from scratch. In that scenario, regrettably it is likely that she will hang. Therefore, it could be said that whether she and the others live or die, is dependent upon parliament's acceptance or rejection of the 'Penalty For Murder Reform' bill."

After more debate, finally, Speaker Reeves asked the house to state its final opinion of the bill.

"And so, to the matter of the 'Penalty For Murder - Reform' bill. All those who say aye, say 'aye!'" There were several shouts. "All those who say no, say 'nay!'" More shouts were heard.

As there was clearly a substantive favour for both viewpoints, the speaker then shouted, "Division! Clear the lobbies!" The members left their seats in the chamber and filed out to vote.

Fifteen minutes later, they returned. The tellers lined up in front of the speaker's chair.

"What say you?" asked Lesley.

Their spokeswoman read out the result. "The ayes, 94. The noes, 106."

A murmur slipped across the benches of the chamber. She handed the result to the speaker.

"The ayes, 94. The noes, 106," confirmed Speaker Reeves. "The noes have it!"

Linda wasn't entirely surprised with the outcome, given the contentiousness of the issue. She stepped back up to the despatch box.

"The court acknowledges parliament's view on this matter. We will now make any amendments that we deem necessary, and then the bill will be read again."

***

The next day, Linda met with Queen Alexandra and they discussed the court's position.

"I am still determined that this bill will be passed!" asserted the queen.

"I think that the court expected that we would have some difficulty though, Ma'am," replied Linda. "But the numbers are actually not too bad. Assuming that the ninety four members who voted for it will do so again on the second reading, then in theory we would only need to persuade at least seven who voted against to change their minds after the second reading."

"I shall attend parliament myself when it votes a second time," said Queen Alexandra, and Linda saw cold steel in her eyes. "If any gentle persuasion is required, then it will be administered by me! Do you have any suggestions as to what amendments to the current legislation we might make in order to get a majority vote in support of us?"

"Possibly, Ma'am. If we were to increase the minimum sentence that an offender had to serve, before they could be considered for parole – perhaps to 85% - whilst also giving an even firmer assurance that the parole board would only consider those offenders who it was as sure as possible would never repeat the offence, then I think that we might be hopeful. I can make an enquiry of one or two people about it over the phone, and all being well get a new draft of the bill drawn up today and tomorrow. We should aim to start the second reading in the latter part of this week, so that it can be voted on in early week nine. In weeks ten and eleven parliament is in recess, therefore it would be best to get this bill through by then, particularly in the light of there being offenders due to be executed. If we require a third reading then normally the vote would not take place until the next session of parliament, though we can in certain circumstances rush the bill through to get one earlier, which would probably mean it taking place at the end of next week."

"Do that, Linda," ordered the queen. "I want parliament to vote on a second reading of this bill on the first day of next week, and I shall be very much in attendance!"

CHAPTER 27

Queen Alexandra wrapped her arms around the man's shoulders and took him down onto the bed. She ran her fingers through his neat fair hair and covered his whole perfect body in kisses. Her medium length red hair brushed against his smooth skin, as she moved about him, and touched it with her fingers She squeezed him inside of her thighs. Her geratis was thrusting against his genus. She was pleasing him greatly and he was about to come...

Abruptly the queen awoke. The vividness of the erotic dream had ignited intense sexual arousal deep within her. Instinctively, she reached up for a pillow from the royal bed and held it tight, kissing it as she would a man as she lay on her stomach. Her geratis emitted a drop of fluid as it pressed deep into the sheet beneath her, making her gasp heavily.

Eventually she returned the pillow to its former place and laid still for a while. It wasn't uncommon for her to feel such lust. She was still a young queen and a natural Geratican woman, with desires like any other. She had suitors and most were handsome, but as she had made clear to her court administrator before, she was in no hurry to rush into marriage for the foreseeable future. There were other matters of state and court business to attend to. Today, 1/9/00, she was attending parliament as promised, as it debated a second draft of the 'Penalty For Murder Reform' bill. It had been amended in the way that Linda had suggested, and MPs had begun reading it on 4/8/00.

***

At four o'clock, Queen Alexandra appeared in the chamber and sat at the throne as the debate unfolded. She wore a royal blue skirt and matching starched blouse. Midway through, as a couple of members voiced objections, she indicated to the speaker that she wished to intervene.

"Her Majesty will speak!" barked Speaker Reeves.

"Thank you, Madam Speaker.," replied the queen, rising from the throne. "I certainly *will* speak my mind!" She began to stalk aggressively about the centre of the chamber, looking assertively around at all of the members, her hands upon her hips.

"Ladies it is my will that this bill be passed!" she declared. As she circled about, her flaming red hair flowing from her shoulders, she lifted her leg and bent her knee, so that the hem of her skirt hoisted up in the direction of the members. The skirt was the symbol of female authority and she was asserting the power of the monarch. "Defy me if you choose, but I *shall* ultimately bring about this reform through my court. I will have us move into the sixth millennium! If we regard ourselves as an enlightened society, then we must begin to demonstrate it through our actions."

Before the debate was finished, Queen Alexandra spoke twice more. At the end there was once again a division and the MPs went to the lobbies and voted.

"What say you?" asked Lesley.

"The ayes, 104. The noes, 96," answered the spokeswoman for the tellers.

Speaker Reeves took the document from her and read the result for herself. Then she confirmed it.

"The ayes, 104. The noes, 96. The bill is passed!"

Linda breathed a sigh of relief. It was an exact reversal of the first vote. Some of the members looked less than happy, though. But the queen was pleased. She thanked parliament for the decision that it had made.

"All rise for Her Majesty!" called the speaker. Everybody in parliament stood as she left the chamber.

***

Queen Alexandra and Linda were in good spirits the next day.

"I am convinced that we have done the right thing," said the queen.

"Morally, I think we are correct, Ma'am," agreed Linda.

"No more of having to sign these gruesome death warrants!" added Queen Alexandra.

Petra Watt and the other offenders were spared the death penalty and were sentenced to life imprisonment instead.

CHAPTER 28

A short time later there was due the annual Town Guild dinner in the centre of Greenaces. The presidency of the town guild rotated between the members each year. Last year it had been Linda's honour. This time it was held by Cathy Webber, a post mistress.

Linda wanted herself and Robert to be in attendance, but unfortunately the night of the proposed date clashed with a vital appointment which she had to keep at court. There was urgent business to attend to with the queen and Linda was going to have to work overtime. She had rung Cathy from her study at The Grange and enquired as to whether there could be a chance of the dinner being rearranged.

After some toing and froing between them, Cathy was becoming rather put out.

"Well, I'm sorry but this really is too bad Mrs Radcliffe. The organising of the dinner has been going on for some time and all the guests notified. It's a little too late in the day to change everything now. And not wishing to take anything away your position in Geratican society and your good work at Her Majesty's court, to change things just for you at the best of times might cause a bit of resentment. I mean, with the greatest possible respect Mrs Radcliffe, some women in the town question whether you should even be a member of the guild, since although you've now lived here for a few years, you've never actually worked in Greenacres."

Linda pursed her lips in exasperation.

"Perhaps those women should remember that as well as being Her Majesty's court administrator, I also supply a very large contribution to the guild's funds, out of my own personal pocket each year! The Radcliffe family contributes to the town in our own way, just as much as its businesses do. And Her Majesty's court works to help enhance their businesses."

"Oh yes, Mrs Radcliffe, and we are all very grateful," replied Cathy. "But I still don't think that I can do anything to help the situation which you now complain of."

Now Linda sighed.

"Very well then. I do appreciate that it might seem rather a lot to ask. Robert and I will just have to miss the event this year."

"Well. Of course, just because you are unable to make it, there would no reason why your husband couldn't still come. I understand that Jane Atherton is enquiring if anybody knows of an available man who might be able to accompany her for the evening. Then at least your family name would be represented."

"In the name of Geratica, I wouldn't hear of such a thing!" exclaimed Linda. "Robert is my husband and outside of work, rarely goes anywhere without me. He needs me with him and that is the way I think it should be. A man's place is behind his wife. I will not have him with another woman!"

"Then the alternative would be for him to come alone," suggested Cathy.

"A man!" exploded Linda. "Go to a function alone? Whoever thought of such a preposterous notion!"

"Hmm. Well admittedly it's not something which most people would expect at present, but times are changing, and you never know what might begin to become more acceptable soon enough."

"Pah!" spat Linda. "If I had a gero for every time somebody told me that times are changing. Those times will have to overcome me first if they ever *are* to come at all! To be absolutely clear, I shall never allow my husband to do the thing you suggest. A man needs his wife there with him to lead, and furthermore I don't want him to be at the whim or the mercy of another. I know what some women can be like when a man is alone. I won't have him possibly being led astray. Robert has been warned of what will happen to

him, should he be unfaithful to me. I am not saying that I think he would, but even so I would never give such an opportunity a chance, however unlikely it might be to come to pass."

"Mrs Atherton is a happily married woman, Mrs Radcliffe!" said Cathy, with a slight trace of indignation in her voice. "The only reason that her own husband is not attending is due to the fact that he is currently in hospital for a minor, routine operation. I am sure that she would have none of the intentions which you suggest."

"That might be so, but nevertheless my husband is mine," asserted Linda. "I make no apologies for being possessive of him as a wife. That is as it should be."

"I know that you are very strongly traditionally minded woman, Mrs Radcliffe - "

"As I hope are all the others in the guild!" interrupted Linda. "I would have it made aware that Her Majesty's court believes most strongly in those traditional Geratican values and customs and expects its subjects to conform to them."

"I think that we are all of a broadly traditional mind," replied Cathy.

"Yes, well as far as my husband is concerned, I just want to declare – lest there be any doubt about it in a any quarter of Greenacres or anywhere at all in Geratica - that if any woman should dare try to come between him and me, then they will wish they hadn't. I am the court administrator and as such I can ensure that certain retributive actions are taken."

Now Cathy became truly angry.

"Mrs Radcliffe are you threatening the guild members? Again, with respect, I do not believe that you alone have such power to act upon a personal matter through Her Majesty's court. You are not the queen and I am sure she would not see fit to involve herself in it!"

"Maybe not directly," said Linda. "But do not underestimate my relationship with Her Majesty."

Cathy's eyes widened at her end of the line. Then Linda sighed again and softened slightly.

"I am sorry. It certainly is not my wish or intention to threaten anybody and I should not bring the court into it. But let me just say this. It is generally my experience that any woman or man who gets on the wrong side of me, usually finds it a somewhat uncomfortable place to be, and decides that they desire to do anything which might enable them to cross over to the other as quickly as possible. Sometimes that desire becomes an urgent one."

Even though she was as polite as possible at the end of the call, after putting down the receiver   Cathy cursed Mrs Radcliffe. How dare she talk to her in such a manner? Whether she was the court administrator or not (although she had to have a care about that). Mrs Radcliffe was quite the most domineering and overbearing woman that it was possible to meet and a very possessive wife.

***

It didn't take long for Linda's words to spread around Greenacres, aided initially by the lips of Cathy.

As it turned out, once Queen Alexandra became aware of her court administrator's problem, she proved to be quite accommodating and urged Linda to arrange affairs so that their business was concluded at the palace in time for her to still attend the dinner with Robert. Although they had to arrive a little late, Linda was able to come home and change before taking her husband to Greenacres Guild Hall.

She and Cathy were on slightly better terms than when they had last spoken on the phone (although the gown which Linda had chosen to wear was extremely stylish and Cathy felt that she as president might be seen to have been rather upstaged). Linda proved popular amongst the guests. Despite her reputation she was usually quite good company – provided that such company stayed on the right side of her.

CHAPTER 29

On 3/29/5000, the occasion of Alexandra's fifth birthday, Linda took her to court for the first time, where she had her first glimpse of the Geratican Royal Palace in Avernore and first formal introduction to the queen.

Alexandra was greatly in awe of her surroundings as Linda shepherded her around the palace. She saw the State Ballroom, State Dining Room, and all the other main features. She was fascinated by many of the pictures and portraits that hung in many of the rooms.

With her mother's arm around her she was admitted into the queen's presence. Alexandra was an extremely shy Geratican girl and after Linda had curtseyed and made her formal greeting, she stood behind her skirt, feeling quite nervous. Linda gently but firmly pushed her daughter forward.

Then Alexandra took a deep breath and curtseyed low to the queen. She managed to execute it perfectly, in the manner which her mother had taught her at The Grange.

"Your Majesty," she said.

The queen smiled broadly.

"Good afternoon, Alexandra! It's good to meet you properly, at last. When I saw you first, you were still a baby!"

"My daughter is indeed beginning to grow up, Ma'am," said Linda.

"I believe that you'll be going to elementary school in the Autumn, Miss Radcliffe," added Queen Alexandra.

Alexandra smiled and nodded. She looked up at her mother, standing tall beside her. The queen was obviously the most respected figure on Geratica. But beyond Court, Gertatican

children were traditionally brought up to respect and obey their mothers, and Queen Alexandra knew that Miss Radcliffe particularly looked to Mrs Radcliffe for instruction and guidance and was quickly learning the lesson of obedience.

It had been quite an effort for Alexandra to do as she had and despite some gentle coaxing from the queen and her mother, she could not be persuaded to say much more.

"Well, at least she has made a start in public life!" remarked Linda.

"I have little doubt that we shall see each other more times in the future, Alexandra," declared the queen.

Afterwards, Linda warmly congratulated her young daughter.

"Well done, my darling. You did as you were expected and have behaved well today as I told you to. You've done well and I'm proud of you. I shall give you a treat as reward."

Alexandra glowed happily, but pushed against her mother's body. She still felt a little intimidated by everybody around her.

"I want to stay close to you, Mother," she said.
.

"And so you shall, sweetheart," replied Linda, and tightened her grip around Alexandra. She lowered her face to kiss her daughter, who gazed up adoringly into her eyes. Their bond was growing stronger by the day.

Later, back at The Grange, Alexandra's treat was her favourite dinner.

PART 6

CHAPTER 30

Spanda, Geraticai Spring 3950

Queen Victoria rolled off Prince Edward, after making love to him in her queen- sized bed of the royal bedchamber.

It was mid-afternoon and the queen was due back in the throne room for another meeting with her lady chancellor, shortly.

She glanced across at her husband, as they both lay recovering from what had just happened. They had been married for just over a year, and still there was no sign of her becoming "with child." That was the official purpose of the queen's presence in bed with her prince consort at this time of each day – apart from the desire to satisfy her voracious sexual appetite. She badly wanted to secure for herself an heir. Never a patient woman, she was becoming increasingly exasperated at the lack of progress.

Added to that word occasionally reached her ear that the prince was showing an interest in some of the women who worked at the palace, though she had no solid evidence that he had been technically unfaithful.

Her relationship with her husband – who she had never *truly* loved - was becoming extremely strained.

"What are these rumours I hear about you trying to be friendly with my head parlour maid, dear Edward?" she suddenly asked, coldly.

The prince jumped and rolled to face his queen.

"What?" he asked. "I don't know what you mean. Oh, in the name of Geraticai, not again! How many more times do I have to tell you that these are just malicious lies?"

"Hmph! These stories come to me far too regularly to be pure lies," said the queen.

"Who is saying such things this time?" asked Prince Edward. The royal bedchamber was the one place where he did not have to address his wife in her formal capacity.

"The head parlour maid!"

The prince's eyes widened slightly, and Queen Victoria saw a flash of guilt in them.

"Alright. I admit that we talked together. But nothing happened. I swear on it!"

"I heard that you tried to do a bit more than talk," said the queen, menacingly. Her temper flared.

"Right!" she seethed. Reaching down over the edge of her side of the bed, she picked something up from underneath. Prince Edward froze when he saw what it was.

"Victoria! Please, not that!"

"Lie down on your front!" ordered the queen. When the prince didn't move, Queen Victoria bounded across the bedclothes and gripped hold of him.

"I said lie down!" she barked and pushed him onto the sheets. Then she trapped him inside of her thighs.

"I'll teach you to play around behind my back!" The queen raised her arm. "How dare you!"

She thrashed his naked skin with her horse whip, and he cried out.

"If there's any repeat of this, then I'll give you a whipping you'll never forget!" She raised her arm and brought it down again hard, making her husband squeal. "You are mine and no one else's. And

if you should ever *sleep* with another woman, I hope that you still remember what will happen!"

She whipped him a third time. "What will happen, dear Edward?" she demanded.

He winced. "I will lose my head!"

"Correct!"

The prince exhaled heavily and made an effort to calm himself. "With respect, Victoria, I get so bored during the day. I have little to do."

"Bored? Little to do?" asked the queen, incredulously. "You're a cheeky brat to use that excuse, for what you *have* just done! You are a mere man. But a man who is my prince consort! It is not necessary for you to have anything to do, apart from providing me with an heir. Being my prince consort is enough, and you should be proud of your position!"

"Oh, I am, Victoria! I am!" replied Prince Edward, desperately.

"Well anyhow. *I* have something to do right now," Queen Victoria told him. "I have a meeting with the lady chancellor. I cannot stay in here all day. You know why it is that I *am* here, during daytime hours. You are keeping me waiting in your duty, dear Edward! I shall see you later."

The prince was playing a dangerous game. The queen was coming to the conclusion that once he finally delivered her heir, then she would get Fiona to dispose of him.

CHAPTER 31

A few minutes later, the queen met with the lady chancellor. What they were due to discuss was another major problem that she faced.

"Ma'am. I am afraid that the situation is now disastrous," said Fiona. "This morning Lady Brimmington succumbed to the fever and died, leaving the prince consort and your majesty as the only members of the nobility left! I am truly sorry."

Queen Victoria looked dumbfounded. "I still cannot believe what has happened in the last year!" she exclaimed. "For the whole of our class of Geraticaians to be wiped out in such a short space of time. It's not possible! Execute Geraticai's chief physician, Evette Grant!"

"As you wish, Ma'am," replied Fiona. "But you will of course remember that there has been some kind of deadly disease – doctors now consider it a plague – infecting the whole of the Geraticaian population for about a year and a half. It seems to have originated in some of the poorest areas and spread. A number of the nobility class used to visit areas where it was common, for various reasons. I know for a fact that some of them used to visit brothels and prostitutes. It seems likely that they picked up the disease from their contact with these areas - though I wouldn't suggest that it *only* came from the afore mentioned. It was widespread. Then those noble people spread the disease amongst themselves. Some doctors think that the nobility's immune system was not strong enough to deal with it, and that consequently their symptoms developed at a much faster rate than for others. And there were fewer nobles than common people. Perhaps the prince consort and your majesty were able to escape the disease due to spending most of your time in the palace and not being exposed so heavily to it. There have been many deaths throughout Geraticai as a whole though, including unfortunately some of the doctors who tried to treat the sufferers. However, the situation does now seem to be being brought more under control. The epidemic has been

halted, at least, and a vaccine has been created which it is expected will act as an antidote to the virus."

"Well that's something then, at least," remarked the queen.

"Hmm. Yes, Ma'am," replied the lady chancellor. She knew that queen Victoria's lavish lifestyle and personal greed had effectively bankrupted Geraticai, and her high taxation of the people and rationing of their goods had left them in deep poverty. Much of the healthcare given to the poor was vastly inferior to that provided for the queen. It was a system that by and large had been in place throughout Geraticai's existence, but queen Victoria was one of the more exceptionally corrupt monarchs. As lady chancellor, Fiona tried to manage the queendom's finances as best she could, but the queen was never going to change course. She believed that she had a divine right to reign in such a way, as had always been traditional. Not that her lady chancellor had ever complained. She had become very wealthy and powerful in the queendom, and as far as Fiona was concerned, as long as she was one of the rich, she cared little for the poor. She had also throughout her life, spent a lot of her time in gambling institutions where she had often increased her wealth, whilst at the same time taking advantage of their backroom facilities to meet prostitutes (though since the outbreak of the recent disease, she had decided to refrain from that, knowing where many of the men originated from).

Queen Victoria was also a brutal tyrant, ruthlessly suppressing dissent with the aid of her lady chancellor. On her behalf, Fiona had ordered the execution of more people than any of her predecessors. Some confessed under the torture of the whips. All forms of communication were secretly monitored. Fiona loyally followed her mistress's orders, regardless of what her personal views were, whilst being paid handsomely to do so. She was feared almost as much as the monarch. And she valued her own life above anybody else's. Despite their closeness, and her fondness for the queen, Fiona was very much aware that even she could be dispensed with.

"This only makes it even more important that I am delivered an heir by my cursed husband!" continued Queen Victoria. "It is now also vital that he provides me with a girl. A boy cannot inherit my throne and must be married off to somebody else who will subsequently become heir. But she must be of noble blood, and there is now nobody left. Any son of mine cannot possibly become involved in marriage with a commoner. It goes against all tradition and even at the best of times they are totally unsuitable. I mean no disrespect, My Lady Chancellor!"

"None taken, Ma'am," replied Fiona. "Although you gave me the position, and I carry the title, I am not a noblewoman as my predecessors were."

"He would be risking catching some terrible infection, too," said the queen. "Nor could I risk a liaison with a commoner either, for the same reason. The situation is clear. My prince consort *must* deliver me an heir soon. I do not know what the problem is, bit I cannot wait forever. If I cannot be delivered an heir, then there we will be a major crisis and a solution will have to be found."

"Indeed, Ma'am," agreed the lady chancellor. Fiona knew that such a scenario would pose a huge problem under Queen Victoria's conditions. At present, neither she or the rest of the court could think of what the solution might be...

VOLUME 2

PART 7

CHAPTER 32

Castra, Geratica Autumn 5005

On 1/32/05, Alexandra Radcliffe walked through the gates of Charterhouse College, in Buckmore.

Today was the first day back after the fortnight's summer holiday, which for girls born at the time of year that she had been, meant the start of a new school year. But this was a significant year for Alexandra as, now aged ten, she had left Charterhouse Preparatory School and was starting at "The Big School."

She felt a sense of trepidation as she passed through the car park and approached the entrance of the main building. This would be a new chapter in her life. In four years' time she would be sitting her Certificate of Geratica examinations, and then - assuming she stayed on after she was fourteen - two years after that, the Advanced Certificate. Her mother had drummed into her the importance of working hard and gaining good qualifications in preparation for the future. She didn't want to let her down. In addition to that, she would now be in a new environment. A nervous girl, she remembered having been quite frightened on her first day in the prep school, aged seven, and although they were more fleeting ones, starting introductory and elementary school in Greenacres aged three and five, had not been enjoyable experiences, either.

In the car park, girls were unloading their luggage with the help of their parents. Many of Alexandra's contemporaries were boarders. She was a day pupil.

Alexandra swallowed hard and went through the door. All of the first year girls starting that term were to report to the assembly hall and be addressed by the headmistress. Along with a small group of others she was helpfully shown into the hall by one of the mistresses.

Most of the girls were already familiar with each other, having attended Charterhouse Preparatory College since the age of seven, but there were also two who were new to the establishment, coming from other primary schools throughout Geratica. They had all passed the examination – and their mothers were paying the entrance fee - to get there. Alexandra briefly greeted one of the girls who had been in her class previously in the prep school, Emma Thatcher. Glancing out of a side window she could see a lake. Grassy meadows ran beside its banks on either side. At the end of it, slightly too far away to be visible from this building, was the prep school.

At half past eight the headmistress, Elizabeth Spencer, flanked by two other women, strode on to the stage at the back of the hall and spoke to them all.

"Good morning girls, and welcome to Charterhouse College. I am Mrs Spencer, the headmistress. To my left and right are Mrs Baldwin and Mrs Dewhurst, the two housemistresses.

"Now, there should be twelve of you in all. Many of you will already know each other from Charterhouse Preparatory School, but to those who are completely new, I am sure that both mistresses and girls alike will do their best to help you settle in. It may seem a little daunting to you all, as you first enter the college campus, but it won't take you long to find your way about, and again your mistresses will help.

"There is great honour attached to attending such a prestigious school as Charterhouse College. We are the premier and most exclusive public school in Geratica, and you should be proud to be here. We expect girls to work hard and aspire to great things. A majority stay to Advanced Certificate level, and several of those go on to university. In fact, the biggest intake of students at both Castra and Orpington – the top two – normally comes from Charterhouse.

"We of course have rules here which should be followed, and the traditional methods of punishment will be employed if they are broken, just as they were in your previous schools. But I hope overall that you will be happy here."

Mrs Spencer held up a piece of paper that she had been carrying.

"I shall now tell you all which of the two form classes you have been assigned to. Gillian Spencer, Imelda Thomas, Rachel Cuthburn, Benita Davis, Melanie Patterson, and Alexandra Radcliffe, will all be under the charge of Miss Ford, who you all met at the door. You will live in Rovers House, headed by Mrs Baldwin. The other six of you will be with Mrs Hunt and live in Beavers House, headed by Mrs Dewhurst. They will now take you to your dormitories where you can unpack your personal belongings, and then show you to your form rooms. Alexandra you are just a day pupil, so you will now go straight to your form class with Miss Ford. Lessons will begin after the mid-morning break. That will be all from me, for now. I shall see you all again at lunch time which will be in the dining hall at 12.45pm. Have a good day."

Mrs Spencer stomped off across the stage and left through a back door. The boarders followed the housemistresses with their luggage, out of the hall and down a corridor from the lobby, where they disappeared through a side entrance towards the dormitory. Meanwhile, Miss Ford took Alexandra across the lobby and up a flight of stairs. At the top there was another corridor. Directly opposite the staircase was a room with the number '1' on it. Alexandra glanced down the corridor and could see several more numbered doors.

"This is our form room, Alexandra," said Miss Ford. "Room 1. Mrs Hunt's is in room 2, on the opposite side."

"Very good, Miss Ford," replied Alexandra, looking across.

The mistress opened the door, and they went inside.

"Sit yourself down and settle in before the others get here," she said.

"Thank you, Miss Ford," said Alexandra, showing the polite respect for authority that her mother had brought her up to display. She chose a desk at the front of the room. Pulling out the chair she took off her blazer and placed it on the back, then put her school bag down beneath the desk. As she sat down, she collected her thoughts.

Of the girls who were to be in the same form as her, Melanie Patterson was new. The rest had been in the prep school, so she knew them, but not that well as they'd all been in the other class, and she'd not had much to do with them. Gillian Spencer had something of a reputation though. She was Mrs Spencer's daughter. In the other form, Emma Thatcher and three of the others had been in the same class as she was in the prep school, a fifth girl had been in the other, and the final member was another new starter. It seemed that they had decided to put one new girl in each college class of six, and swap around one of the girls from the two former prep school classes of five. Emma was the person who she had been the closest to, though Alexandra was a very shy girl, who didn't enjoy mixing very much. She really preferred her own company.

Under the Geratican education system, a girl started her formal education at elementary school on the week following their third birthday (or if that be during a school holiday, the first of the new term). Their academic year subsequently began at the start of the term in which they'd first started. Alexandra's classmates in the prep school had been born in Autumn 4995, though she herself had been born in the last week of that year's summer term and had therefore of course been the eldest. She believed though, that Gillian Spencer had actually been born two days before her, so now the latter would have that distinction.

Everybody in the prep school had known of Gillian, and Alexandra's main contact with her had been in the dining hall. She

was scared and intimidated by her bullying nature and had always done her best to avoid her.

As she waited, Alexandra put her thumb in her mouth and briefly sucked it, before removing it with great alacrity. She could hear her mother's voice inside her head, sharply scolding her. Ever since she was a baby, Alexandra had enjoyed the habit, but now that she was ten her mother was determined to break her of it, saying that older girls didn't do that. Often she did it for relaxation, but also sometimes if she was feeling nervous it helped to sooth her. But her mother was becoming insistent that she stopped and starting to suggest that stronger measures might have to be taken if she didn't. She glanced over at Miss Ford, but the mistress's head was bowed as she intently read something on her desk and didn't seem to have noticed.

After a few moments, the door opened and the other girls came walking in, chatting to one another.

"Quiet!" ordered Miss Ford. "Show respect for a mistress when you enter her classroom! All of you quickly find a desk and sit down."

Gillian Spencer immediately headed for one of the ones at the back, and the rest took what came.

"Good morning girls," said the mistress, once everybody was settled. "I am Miss Ford."

"Good morning, Miss Ford!" the girls answered in unison.

"I am pleased to meet you all, and trust that we will get along together!" continued Miss Ford, breaking into a smile. "As Mrs Spencer told you, your lessons will begin after the mid-morning break. Before then, I will explain the daily procedures and general house rules of Charterhouse, as well as providing you with your timetable for lessons over the course of this term. But I will begin in the traditional manner, by calling the register. Please answer 'present,' when I say your name. It will also enable me to match

your faces to the names given to me on the list. At the front here of course must be Alexandra Radcliffe, as she was the only girl not required to visit the dormitory earlier, and at the back – er, well I believe it is Gillian Spencer..."

"I am the headmistress's daughter!" said Gillian, grandly.

As if we didn't know, thought Alexandra.

"Of course!" said Miss Ford. "Right. Cuthburn!"

"Present!" replied Rachel.

The rest of the girls' names were called in alphabetical order of their surnames, finishing with Imelda Thomas.

"Good!" said Miss Ford. She stood up and took off her black gown, draping it neatly over the back of her chair. Dressed in the Charterhouse mistress's uniform of a long black skirt, white blouse, and a neck-bow with the Charterhouse colours on it, she placed her hands on the desk.

"Right. Let's begin. Firstly, the form that you are in will be known as 1F, and will be based here in room 1. Those in the other form under Miss Hunt, will be 1H. They will be based in room 2, on the other side of the corridor. As you now know, there are two individual houses in the Charterhouse seniors – Rovers and Beavers. Half the girls are in one throughout their time here, and vice-versa. 1F is in Rovers and 1H in Beavers. Each house has its own base with a dormitory, prep room and recreation facilities, and is under the control of a housemistress – Mrs Baldwin in the case of Rovers, and Mrs Dewhurst at Beavers.

"Now, to the regular daily routine. As this is the first day back for a new term, the normal procedure does not start until break time. But from tomorrow, it starts for those of you who are boarding, at a quarter past seven in the dormitory, when you will rise, shower, and dress. Beds must be made before breakfast and will be inspected daily by your housemistress. The afore mentioned meal

will be served in the dining hall at eight o'clock, before the official school day begins at half past eight, when the day pupils are due, and registration takes place immediately. At a quarter to nine there is morning assembly with Mrs Spencer, followed by fifteen minutes of exercise in the yard at a quarter past nine, which she also supervises. Then at half past nine, lessons begin. There are a total of six periods, all of forty-five minutes in length. Some of your lessons during the week will be double periods. After the first two there is a mid-morning break at eleven o'clock, of fifteen minutes when time is your own, and then after the next two, lunch is in the dining hall at a quarter to one. This lasts for fifty-five minutes, before afternoon registration at twenty to two. The final two periods then follow from a quarter to two, meaning that the official curriculum is finished for the day at a quarter past three, when the day pupils are free to go home for the night, or the weekend – whichever the case may be.

"Then, from half past three until six o'clock there are extra-curricular activities for the boarders, though day pupils are welcome to stay and participate if they so choose. Half past six is supper time in the dining hall, followed at seven o'clock by prep back at your house base. I shall show you where the prep room is, a little later this morning, when I take you on a tour of the campus. Finally, at half past eight, girls return to their dormitories and lights go out an hour later.

"At weekends, there are no lessons but the times that you get up in the morning and go to bed at night, and when you take your meals, remain the same. The day pupils are obviously not here, but more extra-curricular activities are undertaken by the boarders."

"Does anybody have any questions about this so far?" she asked.

"Yeah," said Gillian. "What's for grub this lunch time? I hope it's better than that muck they served us in the prep school!"

"The menu for each day's meals appears on day 1 of every week, on the noticeboard outside the assembly hall," announced the mistress. "I shall show you that too, later. At lunch time there are

occasionally day pupils who do not eat the food served but instead their own packed lunches, if they eat their main meal of the day at home with their family in the evening – as would have been the case when you were in the prep school."

"Radcliffe goes home to her mummy's cooking, Miss Ford!" said Gillian, sneeringly. "She' a *Mummy's Girl!*"

Alexandra's cheeks flushed. This had always been a derogatory term used by some of the girls who boarded to reference day pupils, though it was beginning to go out of fashion now.

"Spencer!" growled Benita. "Miss Ford, Alexandra does take the lunch served by the college sometimes."

"Well. Why don't we ask her to speak for herself?" asked Gillian, sarcastically.

There was a pause. An unfortunate symptom of Alexandra's shyness and nervousness was a slight stammer. It had developed just after she'd begun at Greenacres Elementary School and her father had apparently died in Autumn 5000. Luckily, it had not been too severe, but it had been noticeable. With her mother's help she had more or less overcome it before starting at the prep school two years later, but occasionally there was a recurrence and she had suffered some taunts from a couple of her former classmates in the prep school. She hadn't spoken up about it, for fear of any possible reprisals, but eventually her mother had discovered the truth from her, after Nanny Tork had suspected that something was wrong. Linda Radcliffe had been furious, and in a letter to the prep school headmistress, Mrs Roz Moreton, demanded that one of the girls in particular, Sophie Brewster, be disciplined. Sophie had been duly caned in the assembly hall in front of the whole school and moved to the other class. Now that they had started in the main college, she was the other girl besides Alexandra who had been swapped form groups.

Alexandra hated speaking in class, and being in a company such as this, where she didn't know anybody very well, tended to heighten

her anxiety, she could still struggle to form her words. Gillian was trying to intimidate her. Remembering her mother's training in helping to overcome her impediment, she drew some strength from within, and steadied herself.

"I...I will be eating college dinner, today and tomorrow, Miss Ford," she said, finally.

"Excellent," said the mistress. "Girls, I am sure that we will all understand if there are sometimes domestic reasons why Alexandra isn't taking the lunch served by the college. Of course, her mother, Linda Radcliffe is a former pupil here, who was by the end also Head Girl."

Miss Ford intensely disliked the term that Gillian had used and wanted to admonish her for it. If it had come from one of the other girls she might have done so. But she was mindful that Gillian was indeed the headmistress's daughter, and Elizabeth Spencer had (unofficially) made it clear that none of the mistresses were to rebuke or discipline her in any way. She maintained that she alone would decide if that was ever necessary and would do it herself in private. A few eyebrows had been raised at this, and some disgruntlement expressed, but Elizabeth had been adamant and made a veiled (though not direct) threat to make things difficult for any mistress who took a harder line on her daughter in class than she wished. Most believed that she was at least sincere in this and knowing that Mrs Spencer currently had some solid backing from certain members of the college board in her position as headmistress, they were reluctantly complying. In fact there was even a rumour that Mrs Spencer had ordered the kitchen staff only to serve specific dishes that her daughter liked, as she had hated much of what had been provided for her in the prep school.

"Anyhow," she continued. "Moving on. As Mrs Spencer said in the assembly hall earlier, we do have rules which you must follow. You should be punctual in attending all your daily commitments, and you are strictly forbidden to leave the college during the week, with the obvious exception of day pupils at the end of the main school day. Boarders will find that there are opportunities to go

outside at weekends, should they choose to indulge in certain extra-curricular activities. Also, at the weekends, mufti clothes may be worn. But the college uniform must be always worn during the week.

"We also expect the highest of standards from our girls, and respect to be shown at all times. If a mistress comes into a room when you are there, you will immediately stand for her. Some may prefer you to wait outside a classroom before they arrive. All must be referred to formally, as 'Miss' or Mrs', followed by their last name. Traditional classroom discipline will be maintained, and once a mistress has closed the door the lesson will be conducted under her rules, at her own discretion. You will all I am sure by now, have noticed the cane on my desk. I would say that I am on the whole a tolerant and relatively liberal minded mistress, who will use her cane sparingly. During your time in the college, you will without doubt encounter some who are stricter. I could even go so far as to say that you might find my style more relaxed and flexible than most, as we go along."

She leant forward on her palms and looked around at all the girls before speaking again. "But a girl who believes that I would *never* give her due beating on the hand or bottom, is a very naive one indeed! Nor will it be *unknown* for me to raise my voice and administer a stern telling off! Now, do we all understand each other?"

"Yes Miss Ford!" chorused form 1F.

"Good," she replied. "Then I am sure that we need not dwell on the matter further, except to mention that any serious offences in the classroom will be referred to Mrs Baldwin and then if necessary, Mrs Spencer, as will any other particularly bad behaviour throughout the Charterhouse campus.

"And so we come to your timetable for lessons each week. Soon you will find that you will be able to remember them off by heart and won't need to refer to them anymore. You will see that it also gives the room numbers where each lesson will take place, and the

mistress teaching you. As far as Geratican language is concerned, you will have the pleasure of *my* instruction! For the first six weeks you will attend your lessons as 1F, and 1H will attend their own, but during week 36 there will be a series of tests for you to undertake. Based on the results from those, all girls in 1F and 1H will then be divided into two streams – 'A' and 'B' – for lessons, from week 38 onwards, though the basic form classes will still convene together at registration and continue to be members of the same house. In fact, the first period on day 3 of every week is a form period (sometimes known as a tutorial period), when any issues or events that may be currently taking place can be discussed."

Miss Ford picked up some pieces of paper and came out from behind her desk.

"I shall now hand out a copy of the timetable to each of you. If you study it, it should provide all the information you need, but if there are any questions or comments, then I am happy to hear them. Also provided is a small map which will hopefully help you to learn the layout of the campus and enable you to navigate your way around. As Mrs Spencer said earlier, it shouldn't take too long for you to pick things up, and most of you are already familiar with Charterhouse College through having been in the prep school, anyhow. Melanie, I know that you are completely new, but I am sure that if you follow the other girls you will have no major problems, either."

"Yes Miss Ford," replied Melanie.

She was feeling even more apprehensive than Alexandra. In truth, she was not a hugely self-confident girl either, and rather insecure. She liked other girls to think that she was 'hard,' even though she wasn't so much in reality, and often tried to ally herself with those who had the most aggressive personalities. She felt safer that way.

Melanie had been quite fortunate to get into Charterhouse College. Her mother, a shop assistant, had inherited quite a large sum of money which had eventually enabled her to be sent there. No

woman in her family had ever before been given such a school education as this college was reputed to provide. She felt that her background wasn't quite the same as many of the other girls, and she had never been the brightest of girls at her previous schools. In actual fact, she had never worked as hard as she should have done and been regarded by many of her mistresses as lazy. Despite that she had somehow just managed to scrape through the entrance examination for Charterhouse College. Her mother had urged her to work harder and take advantage of this opportunity that she now had, but unlike Alexandra, Melanie didn't like schoolwork and wasn't sure if she could be bothered.

She hadn't always been the best-behaved girl either, though she wasn't a major troublemaker. Sometimes it was mischief of her own making, but often she fell in with others. In some ways she saw coming to a boarding school such as this, as an 'opportunity' to possibly get into some scrapes whilst being many miles away from home.

Everybody began to read what their mistress had given them.

"Double maths! What a way to start!" exclaimed Imelda.

"They could have broken us in more gently!" agreed Rachel.

"Yes. Well, something has to be first," said Miss Ford. "Mathematics – to give the subject its full title – will indeed be your lesson after the mid-morning break, on day 1 of each week this term, lasting until lunch time.

"Completed prep should be placed in the personal pigeonhole of the relevant mistress, outside of the staff room, by the time which she specifies. Late or non-delivery will not be tolerated, unless there is a very good reason."

Mathematics was one of Alexandra's strongest subjects.

After more discussion and questions, Miss Ford checked the clock on the classroom wall, and announced that she would now take the girls on a tour of the campus, before break time at ten to eleven.

Outside it was still just warm enough to be without a coat on this early autumn day, though it would start to turn colder over the next couple of weeks. The girls walked about following their mistress, looking very smart in their fresh new uniforms.

Miss Ford introduced them to all the places that they would need to find over the course of a week, including the dining hall – and also, should they be interested - the college library, and the tuck shop. Not far behind them, 1H were being given the same guided tour by Mrs Hunt.

"The tuck shop supplies most things in the way of sweets and crisps," she declared. "Not everybody uses it, but it is popular. It's largely operated by some of the older girls themselves. It is open at morning break time, and again in the afternoon at the end of the main school day. You can queue up at either time. One thing which you should bear in mind is that the money will be coming out of your own personal allowances, as opposed to your main meals in the dining room which are automatically catered for as part of the fees that your mothers have paid the college to educate you here."

She finished the tour at Rovers House, where she showed them both the prep and recreation rooms.

"Alexandra. You obviously won't be very interested in the dormitories, as a day pupil, and you won't be here when the boarders are doing their prep in the evenings, but nevertheless you are a member of this house, and can therefore come in during the mid-morning break, or after your lunch in the dining room – or even after the main daily curriculum is completed in the afternoons – to visit the recreation room. If you so wish you can also go into the prep room and work."

"Thank you, Miss Ford," said Alexandra.

The mistress looked at her watch. "Alright then girls, that's it. Very soon you will hear the school bell which rings every time there is a new phase or period in the day, from when you wake up in the morning, to 'lights out' at night. If anybody wants to visit the tuck shop at break time, then take my advice and go over there now before the bell rings, so that you can be first in the queue. I hope that you have a good day, and will see you later back in room 1, at afternoon registration. You may wait for me inside, if I am not there first."

"Thank you, Miss Ford," said the girls as she left them.

"Well, let's go and pay the tuck shop a visit then." said Gillian.

Alexandra followed the others. The bell rang shortly before they arrived. After queuing up for a couple of moments, she brought a chocolate bar and began to eat it as she stood outside the shop and surveyed her surroundings. She would definitely be exploring the library. That was her sort of place. She loved books and already had quite a collection in her bedroom at The Grange. If she ever went to Rovers House, she would probably be in the prep room more than the recreation room.

She looked at her watch. Ten past eleven. In five minutes, the bell would be ringing again for the end of break and the start of 1F's first lesson. An hour and a half of mathematics did not in itself bother Alexandra at all. It was one of her favourite subjects – not that she really had any that she especially disliked. Looking at her map, it shouldn't be too hard to find, as it was in the same main block of the college, but on the corridor above that which contained their form room. The corridor could only be accessed by ascending a flight of stairs from the other end of the building, though. Alexandra decided to start walking, leaving the others who were deep in conversation. She remembered Miss Ford's words about punctuality, and it was something her mother had always been strict about at home. They would probably be given some grace whilst they were still new to the college, and finding their way about, but she suspected that normally the mistresses would deal with tardiness in much the same way as her mother – by usage

of the cane. Alexandra in general was a naturally obedient girl, but the rule of her mother's skirt was particularly strict, and if ever she did digress in some way, then it would result in a punishment - the severity of which depended upon the nature of the offence.

Emerging at the top of the stairs, Alexandra went along the corridor looking for the room. All of the classrooms were of similar type. She jumped slightly as the bell rang. Then halfway along, she found her destination.

Alexandra knocked on the door, and cautiously opened it. There was nobody inside – clearly their mistress hadn't arrived yet. She closed the door and decided to wait outside.

The rest of 1F were making their way up the stairs. Melanie had quickly concluded during their time with Miss Ford, that Gillian seemed to be the one who thought herself the boss and that she didn't think much of Alexandra. Gillian wasn't the kind of person that Melanie wanted to be on the wrong side of, and she hoped to gain from her protection. She was already trying to stick close to her.

"Where's Radcliffe?" asked Gillian, suddenly.

Benita looked about. "I don't know. She was with us just now at the tuck shop."

"Ha! Ha!" scoffed Gillian. "I bet the stupid girl's got herself lost already!"

She was disappointed to be proved wrong when they arrived at the classroom.

"You, *keener*, Alexandra!" she sneered. "Hoping to get into the mistress's good books by getting here early, were you?"

"I very much hope that *all* of you girls will be just as keen over the course of your time with me!" said a voice behind them.

Whirling around the girls saw their mathematics mistress, Mrs Willis. Tucked under the arm of her gown was her cane. She took it out and used it to clear a pathway for herself, through the group to the classroom door. Opening it, she looked back at the girls.

"Right 1F. Enter!"

The mistress waited as they all filed in, and then followed, closing the door behind her.

Having been first in the queue, Alexandra again selected a front desk and taking off her blazer once more, she unpacked what she would need for the lesson from her school bag, before sitting down.

Mrs Willis began by asking the girls to introduce themselves and whereabouts they were from. Alexandra had been warned by her mother that the mistresses would probably start their first lessons along such lines, so that they might get to know their pupils, therefore she was prepared. The mistress started with her and then worked her way towards Rachel who was at one of the back desks, alongside Imelda. To Alexandra's relief she managed to articulate herself adequately. Once again, Gillian boasted of her relationship with the headmistress.

Then Mrs Willis announced that she was setting them a short test to assess their capabilities as they began at the seniors. She handed them all a single sheet of paper. There were twenty short questions, and she gave them five minutes to answer them. Just before they began, Gillian, this time sat at one of the middle desks, quickly glanced around with a look of contempt at the other girls, determined – and indeed convinced – that she would be top.

When time was up, Mrs Willis gathered up the papers and spent a few moments marking them, assuring the girls that she could do this and keep an eye on them, concurrently. The mistress dared any girl who doubted it to put that to the test, as she commenced her task. During the silence which ensued, Gillian picked up an elastic band and flicked it at Benita who was sat in front of her.

"Spencer!" Benita turned around angrily in her chair to confront Gillian, as she flinched at the feeling of the band pinging against her wrist.

Gillian insisted on calling all the other girls by their surnames, feeling that it gave her an heir of superiority over them, and demanded they address her in kind.

"I'm sure you didn't mean to do that, Gillian," remarked Mrs Willis. "But perhaps you might apologise to Benita?" Inwardly the mistress winced at her own compulsion to make what she considered a grossly weak and inadequate response to such blatant indiscipline, which would have been quite different if it had been committed by any of the other girls. She itched to reprimand *this* girl and make her come to the front of the class for a caning on the hand, but refrained from doing so because of the headmistress's order.

"I'm sorry, Davis," said Gillian. "I didn't mean to hit you." Then she smirked. "I was aiming for Radcliffe!"

Alexandra glanced across the room in alarm. Gillian was sat back in her chair with her arms folded. Whereas the rest of the girls had their jumpers on, she was as usual just in her blouse sleeves, with them rolled halfway up her forearms.

Mrs Willis fumed at the cheek of the girl.

Melanie, sitting behind Alexandra, sniggered. "I'll get her for you, Spencer!" she said. She picked up a band of her own and stretched it. Rising from her chair, she stepped right in front of Alexandra and released it directly at her. Alexandra couldn't stop herself from emitting a small cry of fear. The elastic band caught her on the inside of her left elbow, which was exposed as she'd pushed up her own sleeves shortly after the commencement of the lesson.

"Ow!" she yelped, faintly.

Now Mrs Willis leapt to her feet.

"Right!" she shouted. "Miss Patterson. Come to the front of the class!"

After a momentary look of dismay, Melanie recovered and walked over to where the mistress stood with as much swagger as she could muster, a slight smirk upon her face.

Mrs Willis wagged her finger. "Take that smile off your face, Miss Patterson! What you just did was *highly* dangerous. You could easily take somebody's eye out. I will not have behaviour like that in my class!" She pointed to behind her desk. "Face the wall!"

"Yes Mrs Willis," said Melanie, as she complied.

The mistress picked up her cane and standing behind Melanie, delivered three strokes of it to the girl's bottom. Mrs Willis saw her buttocks naturally clench as she received the blows, and whilst her face was turned to the wall, she quietly smarted.

"Now, go and sit back down!"

"Yes Mrs Willis," replied Melanie. Though she couldn't resist the initial urge to rub her bottom, as she walked back to her chair with her back turned to the mistress, Melanie smiled slyly at Gillian. This was to be only the first time that she would be caned by a mistress at Charterhouse College.

"You must have very bad aim, Spencer!" exclaimed Benita, sarcastically.

Mrs Willis banged her cane on the edge of her desk. "Silence 1F! I will have no more discussion on the matter. I hope that what just happened to Melanie will serve as an example of my methods for dealing with misbehaviour in class. You will find that *many* other mistresses at Charterhouse College use the very same!"

She put down her cane and sat back down.

"We will waste no more time and return to the lesson. I demand *total* silence for a moment, whilst I finish my marking."

This time nobody challenged the mistress. Eventually, she gave the girls back their papers and they saw their marks out of twenty, together with their position in the class. Alexandra had got all the questions correct, Gillian nineteen and a half, Benita eighteen, Rachel fourteen, Imelda thirteen, and Melanie nine.

The results were broadly in line with what she expected from a class of girls just starting their education at Charterhouse College. Clearly some of them had done particularly well – Alexandra obviously could not have done any better. The Rovers house mistress was also head of the mathematics department and she had decided that Mrs Willis would be the mistress who taught the subject to the 'A' stream, after the 1F and 1H classes had been formally assessed and split according to their average academic abilities. Mrs Willis secretly cursed the fact that if maths was anything to go by, then based on these initial findings, Gillian would most likely be amongst that select group. Melanie was obviously currently at the other end of the scale. It remained to be seen if she would improve over the coming weeks.

The mistress told them that she would make a note of these preliminary results, and then moved on. She spent most of the rest of the lesson lecturing and writing on the blackboard as the class took notes. Alexandra began to settle down as she concentrated intently on Mrs Willis's teaching, her pen busily scribbling. Sometimes Mrs Willis would spring a sudden question on a girl about what she was learning. This was something Alexandra dreaded, but fortunately she was usually at her most confident in mathematics and when called upon gave a competent answer. She felt that she'd made a good start with the mistress's impromptu test.

Occasionally if she happened to move her head to the right, she could make out Gillian in the corner of her vision, though she tried to block her out. Alexandra could sense that she was furious at not having come first, especially as she had grown accustomed to normally being top of the class in the prep school. But Alexandra

had often been top of hers. In fact there had even been an occasion when after several lessons in which she'd finished an exercise well ahead of her classmates and then moved on to another before them, Sophie had suggested that she slow down and wait for the rest of them to catch up – though their mistress had overheard and rebuked her, saying that it was Alexandra's privilege to progress at her own pace, and Sophie should make more of an effort to quicken up if she didn't like it.

Now they were together in the same class for the first time. Alexandra felt a twinge of satisfaction in having beaten Gillian, though she would have to be very careful not to make it too obvious. Gillian was known to have a nasty temper when it was stirred. At the moment she wouldn't know for certain who had come first, as they all only knew their individual positions, but Alexandra was sure that she would seek to find out after the lesson.

Towards the end, Mrs Willis set the class some prep from their textbooks, based on what they'd been taught in the lesson. It was to be handed by lunchtime, the next day. There would be another period for this subject on day 4. Shortly afterwards the bell rang for lunch time...

***

In the dining hall, all the girls took their lunch together in one sitting. It was a large room consisting of seven long tables with benches on either side of them, arranged in rows, each with the capacity to sit up to twenty-six people. Two of them at the end nearest the entrance were reserved for the mistresses, and the rest were occupied by the pupils. In addition, there were half a dozen single tables situated around the walls of the hall.

As Alexandra walked into the hall, she could see that the single tables had already been taken by some of the older girls. She would have preferred one of those herself.

One of the mistresses was shepherding the newcomers to an area on one of the tables. She explained that by and large the girls tended to keep the same places in the dining hall each day. Gillian had positioned herself at the table's head, and Melanie was to her left. Alexandra saw Emma about to sit down and hopping over the bench grabbed a place to her left. Looking up the benches she saw the rest of 1F and 1H. She was relieved to see that Sophie was sat some distance away, also, and hoped that they could all indeed retain the same positions on a daily basis. It would mean that she could keep out of the way of the two girls who frightened her most.

"How's your morning been?" asked Emma.

"Not bad, I suppose," replied Alexandra. "Miss Ford seems quite nice. In mathematics, Mrs Willis gave us quite a tough lesson, but I think she's quite a good mistress. Melanie, the new girl in our form got the cane in it, though."

Emma looked at her in shock. "In the very first lesson? Why? What in the world did she do?"

"She flicked an elastic band at me. She stood right before my desk and hit me on the elbow! Gillian Spencer started it by flicking one at Benita Davis, and then she told Mrs Willis that she was sorry and had been aiming for me! Melanie then said that she'd get me for her."

"Goodness me! She doesn't sound like good news," exclaimed Emma. "I hope that we haven't got a new troublemaker at Charterhouse! Mrs Hunt seemed OK, and Miss Doolan who we had for maths."

Just then a gong sounded. Alexandra and Emma looked across the hall to where Mrs Spencer stood at the head of the first mistresses' table. Everybody went quiet and stood up.

"Lunch will now be served!" declared the headmistress.

A door at the back opened, and several kitchen staff entered one by one. They passed through the rows of tables, placing a plate of food before each girl, and then the same for the mistresses. A cup of water was also provided. Once they had finished and returned to the kitchen, Mrs Spencer glanced around at everybody present and then nodded. They all sat down and began to eat their main course.

A hubbub of noise soon engulfed the hall as the girls talked whilst tucking into their lunch. Alexandra didn't like the arrangement very much. She felt rather packed in like a sardine, and after a while there seemed to be such a din that she doubted she would be able to make herself heard, even if she wanted to indulge in a lot of conversation. The meal was perfectly fine, and Alexandra would never have dreamt of complaining, but she suspected that her mother could have made it even better. Whilst in the prep school she had seen Gillian on several occasions have the nerve to tell a mistress that her meal was terrible, and demand it be taken away and replaced with something she liked. Once, upon - as usual - having her call turned down, and being sternly rebuked for showing such ingratitude, she had lost her temper and nearly caused a riot in the dining hall. Mrs Moreton had given her 'six of the best,' as a result, but it did not seem to stop her from complaining.

There had even sometimes been food thrown about - usually if the mistresses attention appeared distracted for a moment. Alexandra had been shocked that some of the girls who she assumed had been brought up in much the same way as herself, would show such bad table manners. Behaviour like that at The Grange would, she knew, get her a beating.

A little later, Mrs Spencer sounded the gong again, and once more everybody rose. The kitchen staff came around and took the plates before another was provided. This was the dessert course. After they had all been served, the headmistress indicated for them to sit, and everybody began eating again.

When she had finished, Alexandra sat for a moment. Emma was now chatting to somebody to her right. Presently the headmistress

rang the gong again and announced that lunch in the dining room was over. They now had twenty-five minutes of their own time, before afternoon registration at 1.40 pm. Alexandra wanted to quickly get out of the hall and decided that she would go and look in at the library again. She swung her legs off the bench, got up and made her way out through the door, down the corridor and out of the building. It wasn't far. She could spend ten minutes or so there, before going back to the form room for registration.

The library certainly fitted with Charterhouse's reputation. Alexandra picked up and scanned through three books. Judging by this sample, as she quickly glanced up at some of the shelves, it contained a sumptuous array of information on a vast array of subjects. She was keen to devour as much of it as possible.

Mrs Lattimore, the librarian had just returned from lunch. Alexandra checked her watch again. It was nearly half past one.

"It's Alexandra Radcliffe, isn't it?" asked the librarian, walking over to her. "Linda Radcliffe's daughter?"

"Um. Yes, that's right, Mrs Lattimore," replied Alexandra. Unlike Gillian, she never liked to make too much of who her mother was, in case people thought that she owed her place in the college to the senior court administrator, who might also be thought to be trying to obtain preferential treatment for her from behind the scenes. This was completely untrue, but nevertheless Alexandra was always conscious that some of the girls might think it.

"It's good to see somebody on their first day at the college, show some early interest in the our books!" remarked Mrs Lattimore. Would you be interested in buying some library tickets?"

"Oh. Yes Mrs Lattimore. Thank you!"

"Come with me to the counter then," said the librarian, and Alexandra followed her. A couple of moments later she had purchased three tickets and with them borrowed all the books that she had just been perusing.

Then she left the library and returned to room 1, in good time for afternoon registration.

***

Once again Alexandra was first to reach the classroom. She went in and sat at the same desk as before. They would most likely soon settle into regular places.

The others gradually began to arrive. Gillian looked coldly at her.

"Where did you run off to so quickly, Radcliffe? Hiding away like a little mouse, were you?"

"Er, I went to library, Spencer," replied Alexandra.

Gillian made no further comment about that but continued straight on.

"Was it you who came top in that stupid maths test? It must have been as everybody else tells me that they finished below me!"

"I..I did, Spencer. Yes," said Alexandra, nervously.

"Well, I got nineteen and a half out of twenty," said Gillian. "So, you must have got full marks!"

"Well, yes. As a matter of fact I did, Spencer, but..."

"How in the name of Geratica did you manage that?" demanded Gillian. "You must have been given the questions in advance!"

"No. No, Spencer, I didn't!" protested Alexandra. She was stung by the suggestion, and her cheeks coloured.

"Why do you say that, Spencer?" asked Benita. "Could it actually be that you begrudge Alexandra her success?"

"Shut up, Davis!" replied Gillian, fiercely. "I don't begrudge anybody that, if they deserve it. I just can't believe Mouse could have managed it, that's all. Still, I suppose everybody gets lucky, once in a while!"

It was in fact mainly Gillian's temper doing her talking, and she wasn't being honest in answer to Benita's question either. She was still furious at only coming second, and to have just got one question wrong and then been pipped at the post by that one mark, made it even worse. Never yet had she managed to get *every* question right in a test. Deeper inside, Gillian realised that it was unlikely that Radcliffe had received any prior assistance. However, she was jealous of her success and vowed to get vengeance on her soon.

At exactly that moment Miss Ford arrived, and Gillian swiftly moved to a desk at the back of the room, as everybody stood up for her...

***

The first lesson after lunch was Geratican language. As Miss Ford had said earlier, she was their mistress for this subject, and this particular lesson took place in room 1, so they could obviously begin as soon as the bell rang for the next period.

Miss Ford tested the girls on their basic grammatical knowledge, by going around the class and asking questions from the textbook. She circled the group twice, starting with Melanie, who was sat at one of the back desks. On both occasions, Alexandra worked out in advance what question the mistress would be likely to ask her, based on her direction of travel, which helped her to prepare the answer. She was correct on each occasion – she understood the structure of Geratican language very well – but there was more pressure when the questions were asked in this way.

The mistress suddenly looked closely at one of the girls.

"Imelda! Are you chewing gum?" she demanded. "I'm sure you know the rule from your time in the prep school. We do not allow that in lessons. Come to the front and spit it out into the bin."

"Yes Miss Ford, I'm sorry,' said Imelda. She got up and walked over to the bin.

"Um, Miss Ford?" began Rachel.

"Just one moment, girl," replied the mistress. "Go on Imelda," she ordered. "And let's all hear the ping as it hits the bottom of the bin! Don't think that I'm not wise to the old schoolgirl's trick of leaning over as if to spit the gum out, but then not doing so once her mistress's attention is diverted elsewhere! Then return to your seat."

Miss Ford watched as Imelda did as she was bidden.

"Now Rachel. What is it?" asked the mistress.

"Er, nothing Miss Ford," said Rachel. "It doesn't matter now."

She'd been hoping to distract her mistress's attention in order for Imelda to perform the exact forementioned trick. Miss Ford eyed her suspiciously, but then allowed the moment to pass.

The mistress gave them more prep to do after this lesson, again to be handed in by lunchtime tomorrow. They had a double period of the subject on day 3, which would be in a different classroom.

The last lesson of this day's official curriculum was history. For this, the girls of 1F went out of the building to the humanities block. On the way, Benita spoke to Alexandra.

"Is it true that you got 100% in the maths test?" she exclaimed. "I thought I'd done well to get 90%!"

"Well, yes," Alexandra shrugged. Although she was naturally pleased, it hadn't occurred to her that she'd done anything particularly remarkable. It had just seemed that the questions were quite straight forward.

Benita still looked impressed. "Well done!" she said. Then she lowered her voice. "Don't worry about what Gillian says."

"Thanks!" said Alexandra, with a smile. The trouble was that she couldn't help but be bothered a little by Gillian. It was the way she was.

At the lesson, once again they were asked to introduce themselves to their mistress, Mrs Bannister, and once again Gillian added that she was the headmistress's daughter. Alexandra was already greatly interested in the subject, having read several books on it for pleasure. Once her mother had discovered her passion, she had encouraged this, and provided some of them herself. It was of course a vast subject, though. Alexandra enjoyed listening to their mistress, Mrs Bannister, give a lecture on a particular period, going back several centuries ago, as everybody took notes. She already had some knowledge of it, but it was all relatively new to the rest of the girls. Gillian appeared to hardly be interested at all and messed around considerably at the back of the room. Mrs Bannister was annoyed, but just about managed to curb her natural desire to discipline the girl, in order to toe the official line.

There would be a further period of this too, on day 5, when the mistress announced that prep would be given. At 3.15 pm the bell rang signalling the end of the official day. Everybody began packing up, and then the boarders were leaving to go back to Rovers House.

"Are you coming to the house with us, Radcliffe?" asked Gillian.

"No Spencer," replied Alexandra. "I've got a train to catch home, and I don't want to miss it."

"Pah! Mummy's girl!" retorted Gillian, as she turned and walked out of the room, with Melanie not far behind.

"See you tomorrow, Alexandra," said the rest of the girls, as they did the same.

Alexandra picked up her school bag and left the humanities block. Shortly afterwards she hurried out of the main entrance of Charterhouse College and started walking towards Buckmore train station. Her train was due at 3.40 pm, and she might actually have had a moment or two to spare for going to Rovers House, if she was quick, but in truth she was just glad to be able to go home as soon as she could. In any case, her mother always told her to make sure she was at the station in plenty of time before the train was due. By 3.30 pm she was in the waiting room...

CHAPTER 33

Five minutes later, Alexandra went out on to the platform at Buckmore station. The route she travelled on to and from Greenacres was a small branch line, which in fact was part of the railway once owned by her grandmother. With the season ticket that her mother brought her, she simply got on and off the train from either Greenacres or Buckmore, and showed her ticket to the guard en route.

The train arrived on time and Alexandra got into a carriage. She sat down on the seat that was always reserved for her with the ticket and flopped down gratefully, her school bag on her lap. She was relieved to have got her first day in the main college over with. Despite there only having been two thirds of the normal lessons, Alexandra still felt quite drained.

A whistle blew, and the train began to puff away. It was a twenty-five minute journey to Greenacres, taking in one stop in between. The guard soon appeared, and she checked Alexandra's ticket before moving on.

Until recently, a nanny, Mrs Felicity Tork, had been responsible for taking Alexandra to and from school and looking after her at the Grange until her mother came home from work. But early this year, with Alexandra soon to reach public school age, Linda had finally ended the arrangement with Nanny Tork, and now she travelled to school on her own in the mornings, after her mother had dropped her at the station, and then back again in the afternoons, before walking home. Then she took responsibility for herself until her mother arrived.

Alexandra opened her bag and took out one of the books from the library. She normally had a book of some kind with her to read on the journey. Looking forward to soon being home, she settled down to relax.

At 4.05 pm the train pulled into the station at the centre of Greenacres. She got off and began walking home.

***

About twenty minutes later Alexandra let herself into The Grange with her key. She went down the passage to the left of the hall, along the front of the house, into the study at the end, and put the post that she'd collected from their letterbox on her mother's desk. Then she took out what she needed for her prep from her school bag and put it on her desk. She took off her blazer and placed it on the back of her chair, then pulled up her sleeves before leaving the room and heading off down the opposite passage which led off to the right of the hall. Both passages had a window. At the end was the parlour door – an extremely spacious room which stretched right across the righthand side of the house. Then the passage turned left into another, at the end of which was the breakfast room and kitchen area, running in parallel with the rear of the parlour. Just before it, to the left was a small utility room, with an airing cupboard in it. She walked across the breakfast room and down a step into the kitchen, where she put the kettle on.

As Alexandra waited for it to boil, she took her cup from the cupboard to the workbench and placed some coffee granules in it. She glanced at the kitchen clock. Her mother would be phoning soon. She always did around this time, to check that she was home, and often to issue or reiterate instructions. At all times, her mother expected her to do everything that she asked, by the time she designated.

Alexandra made the coffee. Also, in a prominent position on the workbench was a short stick. There were actually a number of them, situated in various rooms of the house. If she had ever misbehaved or not done as she was told during her upbringing, then her mother had used whichever one was closest to hand to punish her. Alexandra could remember getting two strokes on the palm of her hand, at least once in many of them.

She had seldom ever misbehaved in public whilst out with her mother, but the punishment for this was to be given the belt, there and then. Alexandra had always been warned that it would be happen if she was naughty, and normally if her mother drew subtle but clear attention to the fact that she was beginning to remove the belt from a skirt she was wearing, it gave her warning to desist from whatever the mischief or nuisance was.

Alexandra took her coffee and went back to the study. Behind her mother's desk was the cane. This was used for more serious misconduct. It usually meant that she had grossly disobeyed her mother, either directly or indirectly, broken a house rule, or hadn't done something that she'd been ordered to. The punishment was generally a traditional Geratican one of six strokes on her bottom, and then some kind of penalty, sometimes lasting for a specific period of time. Alexandra had been given it on a small handful of occasions, but in fact when she listened to some of the girls who she was at school with talking about the lives they led both inside and outside of their own homes, she didn't seem to have had it as much as them.

The first thing that Alexandra did after sitting down, was to reach for her accounts book. Turning to the latest page, she carefully entered the details of the chocolate bar that she'd brought at the tuck shop and the library tickets, together with the amounts paid, and deducted them from the balance column. She was given a weekly allowance which she was allowed to spend as she wished, although her mother kept a strict control over it. Anything that Alexandra brought had to be explicitly written down and accounted for with any receipts she was given kept, and once a week her mother checked her book, and balanced it against the money in her personal petty cash box. Alexandra didn't really do a lot of personal shopping outside of her mother's presence, and what she spent at school was often her main outgoing anyhow, but she couldn't make a purchase without her knowledge. The one occasional exception that could be made, was if she brought a present of some kind for her mother, and hadn't given it to her by the time her book was checked, in which case she could simply

register it as 'present' and keep the receipt to herself until afterwards.

Then the phone did indeed ring. There were several extensions throughout The Grange. She got back up, glanced at the number on the display screen of the one on her mother's desk, which confirmed the caller's identity, and lifted the receiver.

"Good evening, Mother," she said.

"Good evening, darling," said Linda. "How was your first day?"

"It seemed to go alright, Mother," replied her daughter.

"There! What did I tell you? I said that you'd be fine, didn't I? I can't talk for long, because I'm about to leave for parliament. But what was your first lesson?"

"Maths, Mother. The mistress gave us a quick test in it, actually. I got full marks and came top."

In her office at the palace, Linda was delighted.

"Excellent. That *is* good news, sweetheart!" she said. "She must have been impressed by that."

"Hmm. But I didn't think it was very difficult, Mother."

"Well, I expect that it *was* quite basic, but you still were the only one to get everything right, so that's quite an achievement. I'm very pleased, darling, and you mustn't undersell yourself!"

"Thank you, Mother!" beamed Alexandra.

"What else did you have today?" asked Linda.

"Geratican language and history, Mother. A double period of science would have normally been first, but we didn't start lessons until after morning break time, as it was the start of term."

"I assume that they've given you some prep?"

"Yes. For mathematics and Geratican language, Mother."

"Right then, Alexandra," continued Linda, her tone becoming strict. "I've told you the drill that will be followed during these nights of the week. Do you understand what you're to do?"

"Yes, Mother," said Alexandra. "I'm to get straight on with my prep when I get home, as well as making sure that supper is prepared and anything else that you want me to do before you arrive, later."

"Good girl. I shall be home at around a quarter to eight, so supper will be at that time. And you are not to take your prep up to your bedroom. Is that clear? I'm not having you working whilst you listen to music or do anything else at the same time. That will distract you. You need quiet in order to be able to concentrate, just as your classrooms should be at school. I shall be very cross if I ever find out that you've done that."

"It is clear, Mother," replied Alexandra. "I'll do my prep at my desk in the study."

"That's what I shall be assuming will be happening when I'm not there, Alexandra!" declared Linda. "And you are also still strictly forbidden to leave the house for any reason after dusk. That will be a little later tonight, but the nights will be drawing in from now on, so it will soon mean from the time that you should be arriving home from school."

"Yes Mother. I understand," said her daughter, obediently. "Is there anything else that you want me to do tonight before you get here?

"No. That will be all until later," replied Linda. "Was there any post for me?"

"A little bit, Mother. It's on your desk."

"Alright," said Linda. "Well now I really must be going, but we'll talk more about your day at supper time. I'll see you then – with a big hug and kiss. I love you, darling!"

"I love you too, Mother. I'll be looking forward to your hug and kiss!"

"Goodbye then, sweetheart," said Linda.

"Goodbye, Mother," answered Alexandra, and hung up. Picking up her pen, she turned her attention to making a start on her prep...

***

She had only been working for a few minutes before the doorbell suddenly rang. Alexandra jumped in surprise, before realising who it would probably be. Peering out of the study window she saw Tom at the front porch door. She had been so engrossed in concentration that she hadn't seen him come down their drive. He had said that he might pop to see her this evening when she was home from Charterhouse. She hurried out to open the door.

"Hello, Tom."

"Hello, Alexandra," he replied. "How was it then?"

"Not too bad. Come on in, but I've got prep to do now in the evenings, and have to start it as soon as I'm home. And when Mother's working later, then I still have to get the supper ready for when she returns. She's already been on the phone to make sure that I fully understand the rules."

She closed the door.

"OK. Well, I won't stay long," said Tom.

"Come into the study," Alexandra urged him. "They've put me with most of the girls from the other prep school class for my form group, though they've moved Sophie to be back with Emma and the rest. There's one new girl with us, and a second in the other form class."

Tom knew about Sophie. Alexandra had eventually confided in him about what had been going on when she'd been taunted over her stammer. He'd been horrified by it and urged her to tell her mother. But Alexandra hadn't wanted to and had only eventually done so one night, after Nanny Tork had sensed something was wrong and told Mrs Radcliffe. She'd broken down in distress when her mother had questioned her.

"Well, at least they've made sure that Sophie's not in your – what you just said - class, so that's surely a good thing, isn't it?" he asked. Being a boy and not going to school, such things as 'form class' were a bit of a mystery to him. In common with some of his age, he had been helping out with very light duties at a local noblewoman's estate – in his case Lady Sackville's – for a few hours each week, since the age of seven.

"Form class," repeated Alexandra. "Definitely. But it's a pity we couldn't all have been kept as we were in the prep school."

Tom was her best friend. After the death of Mrs Travers at The Lodge, shortly before her grandmother, Fiona Clark had arrived just after the latter's funeral and brought the house. A few days after that Alexandra's father, who couldn't swim, had seemingly drowned after falling into the river that flowed through Elmsbrook wood and being swept away. Fiona had been with him at the time and had apparently been unable to do anything to save him, as it had all happened so fast. Not long after moving in, Fiona had started working at the Royal Palace. Then she had met Tom's father, Colin, quickly married him, and then moved them into The Lodge with her. Alexandra and Tom had both been five at the time, and as the only two children from the only two houses in their secluded hamlet, they had played and talked together regularly, and become close.

Upon the death of Linda's mother in the autumn of 5000, shortly before Robert's disappearance, she had inherited quite a large sum of money, which coupled with Linda's considerable salary gave her extra financial security and had enabled her to pay off the mortgage for The Grange.

After they'd chatted for a few more moments, Alexandra checked the study clock.

"Tom," she said. "You know I always like seeing you, but I'd really better be getting on. If Mother finds out that I've been wasting too much time before I start my prep, then I'll be in trouble."

"Of course. I know," replied Tom. "I need to go back home for my dinner, anyhow."

Alexandra was his best friend too, and he knew that her mother was very strict. But he also liked Mrs Radcliffe, and had a healthy respect for her, partly through the natural fact that she was a woman of more senior years and that was what boys like him were brought up to do, but also because he instinctively felt that she was wise and knew what was best for Alexandra.

"I'll probably see you again sometime in the week, and we'll meet up at the weekend," said Alexandra, as they parted at the front door.

***

Later, Alexandra finished her prep, and with some time to spare, left the study, followed the passage to her left leading to the cloakroom area and staircase (which had a communal lavatory beneath it). She went up the stairs which wound to the right, 180 degrees halfway. A window there, overlooked the side of the house. Alexandra crossed to her bedroom (one of five, all ensuite), situated directly above the study and left-hand passage downstairs,

where she listened to the news on the radio. She did indeed then listen to some of her music, whilst reading her current book, and also took the opportunity to suck her thumb as she did so. Nobody would see her now, and her mother wasn't around to tell her off about it, just at the moment. It had been quite a day and she still had more things to do, but as far as school was concerned, that was it. Alexandra looked around. Her mother inspected her room daily, to make sure that she had made her bed properly and it was tidy. She was sure that it would meet with her approval.

Her mother's 'mistress' bedroom was situated above the front end of the parlour, on the other side of the landing. A window was in between. Another small staircase led up to the loft in the roof. It had a window and her mother had installed a telescope in the room. They sometimes viewed the night sky together. There were three more spare rooms at the back of the house; one each to the left and right-hand sides and one in the centre.

Alexandra had begun to learn about cooking from her mother. She wasn't quite up to preparing a main meal yet – and certainly not she felt to the standards of her mother – but by a quarter to eight, she had made the supper that she'd been ordered to, as Linda arrived home.

In the breakfast room, Linda embraced and kissed her daughter, who gratefully received the affection. Alexandra returned the kiss, before her mother did it again, holding her tighter. Alexandra felt engulfed by her mother's tall body, and as she looked up into her eyes, the feeling made her give out a small ooze of pleasure. Linda smiled at her daughter's appreciation and couldn't resist planting another big kiss upon her lips before letting go.

"It smells like supper's ready," she said. "Is the dining room table laid?"

"Yes, Mother," replied Alexandra.

"Good girl."

A couple of minutes later they were sat down and eating in the dining room, the door of which was situated at the far end of the main hall. This room ran from beside the breakfast room and kitchen, along the rear left hand side of the house. There was in fact a door which connected it to the kitchen. It had a full-length window, overlooking the patio - which stretched right across the back of the house - and the main back garden of The Grange. Steps led down from the patio to the large garden, which had a gate at the bottom. Beyond that was their apple orchard.

As was still normal Linda had placed a stick on the table between them, though in truth it was now quite a considerable amount of time since she had used one to discipline her daughter at the meal table.

"Have you got on alright with your first prep?" asked Linda.

"Yes, Mother. It's finished," said her daughter. "There wasn't anything too difficult. Tom actually came just after you phoned. He just wanted to know how my first day in the main college had gone."

Linda eyed her. "I hope that you didn't go into the wood. I made it quite clear that you were to start working, and it wouldn't have been long until the light started to fade."

"No. No, Mother!" Alexandra assured her. "He was only here for a short while before he went back home for dinner, and I did tell him that I had to get on with my prep."

Linda beamed. "That's what I like to hear, darling! But your friendship with Tom is perfectly welcome, also. Right. Tell me more about today. How did they organise your form classes?"

"Sophie Brewster and I have been swapped over, and there's one new girl in each form, Mother," said Alexandra. "I'm not sure exactly why they've done that."

"Hmm, well," said Linda, thoughtfully. "At least they've kept that confounded Sophie Brewster away from you. I would have had *serious* words with your headmistress if they'd put you two back together! But I did wonder about this. It may well be that your headmistress and housemistresses feel that as you start at the main college, you should mix in the company of the girls who used to be in the other class to you in the prep school. After all you are the only day pupil in the two forms, and in the prep school all of those boarders were in the same dormitory, so they know each other quite well already. I can understand that.

"You can still in theory be involved in the extra-curricular activities after half past three, when you'd maybe meet those outside your form class, and one or two of those things *might* be beneficial to you, but I believe that you can still learn about the most relevant of them here at home with me.

"Also, in practice it would obviously mean you having to catch a later train back to Greenacres and arriving back home later than I would wish. I don't like you being out late, especially in the autumn and winter, and you need time to do your prep once you *are* home. I could come and collect you on my way home from work, but on certain nights that won't be possible, and even when I could, you'd still have less time here in the evening. I don't think it would necessarily be good for you to be seen being picked up from Charterhouse by your mother on too many occasions, either. I don't want to give the boarders more chance than is necessary to make an issue of the fact that you're a day pupil. It should be irrelevant, but I remember how it was – and I believe I know how it still is within some quarters.

"I have made it clear in a letter to your headmistress that I think it unlikely you will stay past the time when the main curriculum is finished for the day – unless there is something that you *really* wish to do, darling! I have always said that I believe you are a girl best suited to being able to come home at night rather than board, and on the whole I would also say that you should let Charterhouse take the lead role in your daily curricular studies, and allow your mother to guide you exclusively in all other matters!"

"Thank you, Mother. I will do that, then – particularly if you've already said that to Mrs Spencer," replied Alexandra. "I haven't found out what is specifically on offer as far as extra-curricular activities are concerned, but I would always prefer to come home as soon as the main day is over. Are you saying you think that could be part of the reason why I've been put in this form class?"

"I don't know but it might be, yes, sweetheart," said Linda.

Elizabeth Spencer had been the headmistress at Charterhouse for a year. Linda had met her on a number of occasions outside of it, but they hadn't warmed to each other, and there were a couple of things which they disagreed over, though that wasn't her daughter's concern. Now that Alexandra was in the main college, Linda was intending to try and get elected to the board of governors. She was hopeful of being successful, given that she was an old girl of the college and now the senior court administrator to Queen Alexandra – though it was unlikely that she would have the time to attend every one of their meetings.

"Which house does that put you in?" she asked.

"Rovers, Mother."

"Ah!" said Linda. "Quite the most superior one, I believe. I'm pleased that you've been put into this class now!"

Alexandra raised an eyebrow and smiled. "Oh, right. I presume that means that you were in Rovers House too, Mother?"

"You presume right, darling!"

"In a few weeks' time though, the two forms will be split into separate streams for lessons anyhow, Mother," pointed out Alexandra.

"True. But as you say, Alexandra, in a few weeks' time. On the subject of the lessons themselves, how did you find them?"

"I did find them very interesting, Mother," said Alexandra. "They were quite hard work – not that I mind that – but some of the methods the mistresses use, are quite exacting!"

She described what had happened in the three lessons, leaving out Melanie Patterson's misconduct towards her, and the problem that she'd faced with Gillian Spencer.

"It sounds like you've experienced a broad range of processes that mistresses can adopt to make sure that their girls are paying attention and understanding what they're being taught, darling," said Linda. "It's all part of daily life in the classroom – it always has been, and as far as I'm concerned it always should be. I don't think I need to tell you, Alexandra, that I will always be on the side of a strict mistress – so long as she is fair. I hope that you won't meet too many who are complete bitches, just for the sake of it!"

Alexandra giggled at her mother's choice of adjective. "Did you come across some of those back in your day, mother?" she asked.

Linda raised her eyebrows. "Alexandra, I may not be quite as young as one or two of your form class members' mothers, but it wasn't *that* long ago!" Her eyes twinkled, and her daughter could tell that she was only giving a mock scolding. "As a matter of fact, yes there were some – though I stress that they were very much in the minority, as I'm sure is still the case *in your* day."

"I know it's hard, darling," she continued, "but you just have to roll up your sleeves, concentrate intensely – which I know you can do – and get on with it."

"Yes, Mother," said Alexandra.

"By the way," said Linda. "I hope that you managed to refrain from sucking your thumb?"

"Um. Yes, Mother," replied Alexandra, though technically she knew that it wasn't a completely true answer to the question.

Linda sensed that there was something more. "Look at me, Alexandra," she ordered.

Her daughter did so, and immediately crumbled under the scrutiny of her gaze. "It was just a fleeting moment in the form class this morning, Mother, before the boarders arrived," she blurted out. Alexandra could rarely keep things from her. "I promise you I immediately remembered what you've told me before and stopped doing it. I'm sure that Miss Ford didn't even see it – she was busy reading something on her desk at the time."

"I *am* determined to stop this, Alexandra," said Linda. She reached for the stick and took her daughter's hand. Alexandra flinched, fearing that she was about to be beaten.

"Perhaps I will have to start giving you two strokes just here, every time that you do it," said her mother, resting the end of the short stick directly across her thumb.

"No. Please, Mother! I will try. I promise!" replied Alexandra.

Linda put down the stick and squeezed her daughter's hand from the outside. Alexandra instinctively squeezed back from the inside and felt her mother's fingers slip over hers. She worked her own inside of them and looked into her eyes. For a moment they communicated without spoken words in their own private way. They could articulate their deepest feelings silently and understand each other. Alexandra always assumed that other Geratican mothers and daughters sometimes did the same thing. But in fact, Linda had discovered the bond between them when Alexandra had still been quite young, and she knew of no other people with the same link. She thought it might be partly because they had a particularly close relationship – though others obviously did too. Linda had gradually developed the technique with her daughter, until they were able to converse without speaking to a remarkably high level, although it could never come close to replacing their standard communication of ordinary speech. It wasn't telepathy – they couldn't exactly read each other's thoughts, but words were

quite possible to discern. It helped give their relationship even greater intimacy, and also could occasionally come in useful if the pair of them ever wanted to communicate together without others knowing. For those reasons Linda had kept their apparently unique ability a closely guarded secret. Nobody else currently knew about it.

The tone of her voice became softer, as she spoke again in normal speech. "Darling, I do appreciate that you do it for comfort, and that when you feel anxious it can be a nervous habit, but I still repeat that women don't do that – and you're aiming to become one of those, when you leave Charterhouse. And if now that you're beginning to get older, the other girls start seeing you sucking your thumb, some of them will tease you. I'm not just being an overbearing mother here. I'm trying to help you – as I do in everything. I believe that you *will* try, but just bear in mind my warning. I'll use the stick if I have to – but *only* if I have to. Try not to give me cause. Do you promise not to do that?"

Alexandra squeezed her mother's hand back from the inside.

"I do, Mother," she said.

"Good," replied Linda. In fact, she had decided that having issued the warning she would let things settle for a while. If she caught her in the act then she might take further action, but otherwise she wouldn't enquire.

"Right. Well, now that we've both finished our supper, it's time to get washed up and cleared away," she asserted.

Alexandra dried as her mother washed up, and then put everything away.

"Take the rubbish and put it in the bin outside the door please, Alexandra."

"Yes, Mother," she obeyed. Removing the bag from the kitchen bin, she took it down the passages to the front door. The dustbin

was just outside their porch and she put it inside. There was a bit of a nip in the late evening air, and Alexandra hurried back inside and shut the door behind her.

After replacing the bag, she went into the study and began to prepare her school bag for the next day. Presently her mother came in with two cups of coffee.

Linda took a document from her briefcase and sat down at her desk to work on it.

"Your room is spick-and-span as usual, darling," she said. "Good girl. Now, I won't be long. I've just got something I must do before tomorrow. Then I'll join you in the parlour until bedtime."

"Very good, Mother," replied Alexandra.

"So, what lessons have you got tomorrow then?"

"Geography, Geratican literature, music and home economics, Mother."

"Quite a variety, then," noted Linda.

"Ancient Geratican and artistic studies are on day 3, Mother," added Alexandra.

As Linda worked, she could hear the sound of the piano coming from the parlour. Her daughter was very interested in Geratican classical music and developing quite a talent for playing it, though she lacked confidence. Linda was similarly inclined and keen to encourage her at home and to study it at Charterhouse. She had played a little herself since childhood and was of a reasonable standard. Alexandra's favourite Geratican composer was Philippa Barrington.

Shortly afterwards Alexandra was curled up beside her mother on the parlour sofa, with another cup of coffee, as they listened to some late night music on the radio. By the wall, the grandmother

clock ticked away. She was suddenly beginning to feel quite drowsy after the rigours of the day. She put her empty cup and saucer down on the table, sat back and rested her head on her mother's shoulder.

Linda glanced over and saw her daughter's eyes drooping. She tightened the grip of her arm that was wrapped around Alexandra's shoulders, and with her other one squeezed her waist. Alexandra's eyes opened slightly, and she smiled contentedly.

"I love you, Mother!" she murmured.

"Yes, And I love you too, my darling," replied Linda. "But I think it's time you were going to bed! You're looking tired."

Alexandra shot a look at the clock. "No, I'm alright, Mother," she said. "It's only a quarter to nine. I normally go up at nine o'clock, to be in bed at a quarter past!"

"Well tonight you're going to bed a quarter of an hour early, because you're tired, Alexandra. I'm telling you, and that's that!"

She squeezed her daughter again and kissed her. "Come on! You've had a good day today, and Mother's very pleased with you. She wants you to have another one tomorrow, so do as she says. Who knows best in this house?"

"You do, Mother!" said Alexandra, and hauled herself up.

"Good girl," said Linda. "I'll be up at a quarter past nine then, to say goodnight.

"Yes, Mother."

Alexandra went to her bedroom, undressed, and did her ablutions in her ensuite bathroom. Then by nine o'clock she was in bed. She was allowed to read for fifteen minutes before her mother put the light out and locked her in for the night. She set her alarm clock for the next morning, though her mother always unlocked the door and

came in shortly afterwards anyhow. Then she took her book from the bedside table and read a couple of pages. She had to concede that her mother was right though. She wouldn't be long going to sleep tonight. Outside she could hear the sound of the wind rustling through the trees of Elmsbrook wood.

By the time Linda arrived to say goodnight at a quarter past nine, Alexandra had put down the book and was laid on the pillow. Her mother lent over, lifted her gently in her arms so that she could hold her, and kissed her lips.

"Right. Good night, and sweet dreams, my sweetheart!" she said, softly. "I'm putting the light out now, and you know that means sleep. If it comes on again, it should only be if you need to go to your bathroom. Nothing more!"

"Yes, Mother!" replied Alexandra, sleepily.

"I love you, daring. Goodnight!" said Linda.

"I love you, Mother. Goodnight!" said her daughter.

Linda snapped out the light, went out of the bedroom and closed the door. Alexandra heard the sound of the key turn in the lock and her mother's footsteps going back down the stairs. She felt so tired that she knew she couldn't possibly have the energy to put the light on again and do something. But it was strictly forbidden, in any case. If her mother saw the light on after she'd turned it out, then Alexandra had to have a very good reason for it.

When she had been younger, Alexandra had occasionally secretly switched her bedside light back on to read her book, if she'd reached a particularly exciting or interesting point and she couldn't wait until the following day to read on – breaking her mother's rule. She'd felt confident that she would always hear her footsteps at the bottom of the stairs if she came up, and quickly put out the light before she saw it. However, one night she had been absorbed in a chapter, when suddenly before she'd known what was happening, to her horror the door had quickly unlocked, and her mother had

bounded into the room. In her panic, Alexandra had thrown her book towards the bedside table, but it had missed and landed on the floor just a millisecond before her mother had come in. She had tried to pretend that she'd just returned from the bathroom, but her mother had been instantly suspicious of the book on the floor, which had been neatly placed on the table as normal when she'd said goodnight – and that had only been a few minutes previously. A quick glance at her mother's ankles had revealed the main reason why Alexandra hadn't heard her footsteps coming up the stairs. She had happened to be in her stockinged feet.

Having immediately realised the truth, her mother had been outraged at her disobedience. She had demanded that Alexandra get up and put her dressing gown on, and then dragged her downstairs to the study. Alexandra had been severely reprimanded and given six strokes on her bottom with the big cane. Dressed only in her nightgown with her dressing gown over the top, the strokes had been particularly painful, and she had howled. Back in her bed, she had cried for several minutes. The following day, her mother had punished her by confiscating the book, and a number of other things from her bedroom for three days, and also warned her that from now onwards she would always be taking off her shoes whenever she came up the stairs in the period between Alexandra's lights out, and her own bedtime.

Alexandra didn't often commit offences that her mother deemed warranting of the cane as punishment, but when she did, neither daughter or mother ever forgot the incidents – and they were seldom repeated...

CHAPTER 34

At 7.15 am the following morning, Linda dove the car up to the security gate of Elmsbrook. Very tall and surrounded by a high wall, she had arranged for it to be installed for extra safety after the death of Robert. At the same time, Alexandra wheeled the dustbin from The Grange to outside of the gate, ready for it to be collected during the day. Then she got into the passenger seat of the car, and her mother drove away.

They were headed for Greenacres train station, where Linda would drop Alexandra off at around 7.25 am, on her way to work at the palace in Avermore.

"Right then, Alexandra," said Linda, as they approached the station. "What is it I've told you that you should always remember during your school day?"

"That I must work hard and not misbehave, Mother."

"And what will happen if you do misbehave?"

"I will be punished at school, and then again later at home, Mother."

"Correct. And I *will* be very likely to find out if you are naughty, Alexandra, even if it isn't straight away!" warned Linda. "You should always bear that in mind. I will not tolerate you misbehaving behind my back. So, what are you going to be today?"

"I am going to be a good girl, Mother," said her daughter, obediently. "I always am at school."

"You *usually* are, darling!" corrected Linda, as she brought the car to a stop. "I hope that you will be."

She was actually fairly confident about it. Alexandra wasn't a naughty girl by nature, and Linda had always made sure to check on her behaviour whenever she met the headmistress of the prep school. She demanded to be informed of any indiscretions – to an extent that even her daughter didn't fully know – and was very proud of the fact that it appeared Alexandra had always been by far the best behaved girl in her class, with an almost spotless record.

Linda unfastened her seat belt, shifted around in her seat and held out her arms. After Alexandra unfastened her own, she moved across into her mother's embrace. Swallowed up deep and kissed strongly, Alexandra gazed up into Linda's eyes once more, and felt the dominant force of her mother's love. She briefly murmured at the pleasure it gave her. Despite the strict lecture that she'd just received, which – in variations of words and forms – she was used to getting on a semi-regular basis, she wished that she could stay in her mother's protective arms all day long – a feeling that she was used to experiencing every school day morning. She gave a kiss back and then received a final one which made her tingle. Alexandra murmured again and heard her mother's own soft sigh from the pleasure she felt in giving it.

"I love you, darling!" said Linda. "Have a good day, and I'll speak to you this evening."

"I love you too, Mother! Speak to you then," replied Alexandra.

She got out of the car and shut the door. They waved to each other as Linda drove away.

Alexandra went into the station and walked to her platform. She always could very well believe that her mother would find out if she ever got into trouble at school. And it was true that she couldn't say she had *never* misbehaved. During her time in the prep school she had been caned just once – less than any of her contemporaries – and even then, she felt that it had been down to her own naïve stupidity.

One day during a lesson, she had noticed a grammatical error in a sentence from the textbook that she had been handed out and corrected it with her pen. She had actually thought that it was just that book, and not every one in publication. A couple of days later, the books had been handed out again, and one of the other girls who was in receipt of the same one had noticed the writing and queried it with their mistress, Miss Gates. The mistress had demanded to know who had 'defaced' the textbook, and having received no reply, had decided to check the handwriting with some of the girls' work which was on her desk. She had ascertained that it was Alexandra's and asked her to explain herself. Alexandra had nervously admitted that it was her who had written in the book, but insisted that she hadn't realised it had been wrong to do it – if she had, then she wouldn't have done so. Miss Gates had told her off and, though she had accepted her defence, given her a single stroke of the cane on the palm of her hand. Alexandra still remembered the embarrassment that had felt and the sting of the   stroke – though luckily the mistress had not beaten her as hard as she had seen her cane some of the other girls

Alexandra had hoped that would be the end of the matter, but in this she had not been so fortunate. Mrs Moreton had decreed that the textbook be replaced, and the bill for buying a new one had been sent to her mother, along with an explanation of what seemed to have happened. Her mother had been cross and told her that she'd been stupid. Quite apart from the fact that Linda was being asked to foot the bill (which was actually no real financial hardship to her), surely her daughter would not have done such a thing to a public library book, so why should a school textbook be any different? She had enquired of Alexandra which hand Miss Gates had caned, and on being informed that it was her right, immediately proceeded to do the same to her left. Alexandra had been made to write out, "I must not write inside any book," twenty times.

Linda had of course paid the bill, but - having found out from her daughter exactly what the error that she'd amended in the textbook had been - also pointed out to Mrs Moreton that Alexandra had shown an understanding of basic language which was perhaps

beyond her years, as she had been quite correct – though that didn't excuse her writing in the textbook, and she had been disciplined for it. But Linda knew that Alexandra was by no means the first girl to do such a thing (though for entirely different reasons). She could remember from her own time at Charterhouse, seeing a comment which was quite sarcastic and rude, that had been cheekily written by a girl in the back of an Ancient Geratican Language textbook, who clearly thought that particular subject unimportant. If Alexandra ever did that, then she should be severely dealt with by the college and most certainly would be by her mother.

In fact, the end result had been that the publishers were later contacted and the offending sentence reprinted - and the college received a free batch of new textbooks with the correct wording, so Linda felt that her daughter had indirectly done Charterhouse a favour...

Alexandra sat in the waiting room before her train arrived. Five minutes before it was due, she went out on to the platform in readiness. By 8.05am the train had delivered her to Buckmore and she was at Charterhouse by a quarter past eight. She went up to the form room to prepare for the other girls arrival at 8.30am, after their breakfast in the dining hall, and registration.

They had their first assembly in the hall at 8.45am with the headmistress, and then at a quarter past nine, they went into the yard directly outside of the hall for 'exercise' which amounted to them walking or sometimes jogging around the space for fifteen minutes, under Mrs Spencer's instruction. They were told that they must always wear their full uniforms for this, and that unless it was pouring with rain, overcoats should not be worn, even in winter. Aside from supposedly helping to keep them fit, Alexandra could see little point in this part of the daily routine, and was glad to get to the first period, and another forty-five minutes of maths.

As her mother had suggested, she pulled up her sleeves and prepared to give complete concentration to the day ahead.

CHAPTER 35

That same morning on Geraticai, a group of protesting workers had gathered in the town square of Arista in Spanda. At the head was their leader, a factory manager called Vera West.

Gradually, more workers began to gather and join them, and their shouts grew louder. Soon a platoon of soldiers arrived, alerted by the noise.

"Go back to work you women!" ordered their sergeant. "You're creating disorder."

"We demand better working conditions," replied Vera. "We will not return to our posts until our grievances are properly heard and dealt with!"

"I know you, Miss West," said the sergeant. "You've organised these protests before and been arrested for the trouble caused! Your 'grievances' have been heard already – on more than one occasion. Move on peacefully or we will force you!"

"No. We refuse!" retorted Vera.

The sergeant raised her gun, threateningly.

"In the name of Her Majesty Queen Victoria, I order you all to return to work, or we will open fire." She glanced around to her soldiers. "Platoon! Ready!"

All of the platoon raised their weapons.

There was a tense pause as the workers looked at each other. Vera cast her gaze over the soldiers. She sighed.

"Arrest me again then, and let these other women go. I don't believe that you can hold me for long, anyhow. There will be no more protest today, but it will only be a temporary pause – I guarantee you that!"

"We shall see about that," replied the sergeant. "Very well. Disperse immediately women or we *will* open fire on you! If I were you, I'd think twice before taking this kind of action again."

Two soldiers stepped forward and chained Vera's wrists.

"Don't take any notice of her!" she shouted as she was led away. "It's time we stopped being intimidated by Her Majesty's thugs!"

"Hold your tongue, subversive!" cried the sergeant.

A murmur went around the other workers as they reluctantly began to leave the square.

***

"That damn Vera West again!" fumed Queen Victoria when she was told of what had happened. "Keep her in custody. I've had just about enough of her. If there are any further protests tomorrow, then I order that the workers be shot on the spot!"

Daniella Sturridge, acting as lady chancellor whilst Fiona was away on her mission to Geratica, gulped slightly.

"Shoot them, Ma'am?" she asked, with a trace of trepidation.

"Yes!" replied the queen. "This type of action is happening far too much. The workers must know their place. See that my order is passed on!"

"Of course, Ma'am," said Daniella.

CHAPTER 36

Meanwhile back on Geratica at the Royal Palace, Queen Alexandra was holding a meeting with her two premier courtiers. One was Linda Radcliffe, now in the relatively newly created position of Senior Court Administrator. The other was Fiona Clark, Linda's neighbour at Elmsbrook, who in early 5001 had become Court Administrator, as Linda's deputy. Today was the queen's twenty-fourth birthday.

What Queen Alexandra and Linda didn't know of course, was that this new woman at the heart of their court was actually Fiona, the former lady chancellor of Geraticai, and a mongrel, who was now living a bogus life here on Geratica, as a Geraticaian spy and agent.

It was now five years since she had arrived and carried out the first part of Queen Victoria's desperate plan to establish an heir - abducting the Geratican mongrel, Robert Radcliffe, in order for his mind and body DNA to be surgically merged with the infertile and deceased Prince Edward – who she herself had murdered. Then she would conceive with him – in the absence of any suitable man on Geraticai. Fiona was remaining on Geratica to try and ensure that their Queen did not manage to marry and produce an heir of her own in the belief that if she ultimately died with her queendom in that position then that world would be destroyed. If necessary, she must take drastic action to prevent Queen Alexandra from doing so.

As it had turned out, Queen Alexandra appeared to be in no hurry to marry just yet, and in the meantime back on Geraticai, until the genetically altered prince did his duty and enabled Queen Victoria to conceive, then the queen wanted Fiona to proceed slowly in case there was a problem at their end. She wished to keep all her options open. Fiona made occasional visits back there in her transportation capsule which was secretly disguised within a bush in the wood at Elmsbrook, and unfortunately the queen's plan had indeed not yet progressed as she had hoped. She was still not pregnant, and now had certain other problems to deal with, in some rebellions within her queendom, which were keeping her army

busy and providing a distraction, as she needed to devote attention to them. Protestors were regularly detained by the authorities. Unlike Geratica which had always been predominantly peaceful and where there had never been a war, the same was not true of Geraticai where there had been the occasional internal dispute that a queen had settled by force.

Fiona did not anticipate returning to Geraticai at any time in the immediate future.

She had found it almost laughingly easy to settle into her new fictitious identity here on Geratica. Their security systems appeared to be very lax, as they had believed for some time that the threat of danger from Geraticai was minimal and in any case the Divine Being kept a force field around the two parallel worlds which should prevent any potential invasion from aliens elsewhere in the universe. She had been provided with a fake birth certificate (as Fiona Clark) when she left Geraticai, along with a certain amount of money (and Geraticaian currency had for a long time now been identical and indistinguishable from Geratican). But with no other checks made upon her identity or origin, she had been able to buy The Lodge at Elmsbrook and begin a career within the royal palace in Avermore, Castra, with no problem at all, after forging a reference from a fictitious former employer. The name of the person she had used was someone who she knew had owned a restaurant and just recently passed away. She also produced some false education certificates and claimed to have gone to a particular school (that she knew no longer existed) – though she'd never been to university.

Fiona often reflected gleefully how furious and dismayed Queen Alexandra and the somewhat domineering, controlling, and fastidious senior court administrator, 'Mrs Radcliffe' would be if she knew of how easy it had been – especially as it had also been Fiona who had deceived the latter into believing that her husband was dead, when in fact he was living as Queen Victoria's consort on Geraticai, albeit in a different guise as Prince Edward. (Indeed, in six years' time when her true identity was finally revealed,

Linda would react with very much those sentiments, and set about considerably tightening their security arrangements).

Having initially been head chef to Queen Alexandra, she had impressed the queen with her overall knowledge of court procedures. This had led to her rapidly being promoted to the position she now held. The queen had felt that it was high time Linda was given a deputy to her direct position who could relieve some of the burden of her responsibilities. Mrs Radcliffe not been entirely happy with the decision, telling Queen Alexandra that she did not feel the need for a deputy, and that all she needed was her secretary (now Veronica) to filter her phone calls, type the letters she dictated, and so on. There was already the chief administration officer, working in the main office of her department who had always been regarded as second to the court administrator. Fiona knew that she didn't like any loss of control over court affairs. But the queen had overruled her, saying that in Geratica's modern age when the court was busier than ever, she shouldn't be expected to manage her role alone. Therefore, Fiona had been given responsibility for the day to day running of Queen Alexandra's personal courtiers, domestic staff and caterers, and the palace receptionists, though Linda outranked her and still had overall charge of the entire royal palace staff. She was also an advisor to the queen in the same way that Linda was. Fiona had been given a new office opposite Linda's that had formerly been the interview room, and her own secretary, Carol, who now worked with Veronica.

Linda still very much retained the day-to-day running of her 'little empire' as she affectionately referred to the administration department. It frustrated and disappointed Fiona somewhat, that she didn't get as much day-to-day access to the very top level of Geratican court affairs as she would like (apart from if she should be filling in for Linda when she was absent). Fiona held a position with exactly the same title as Linda's had been before her arrival – yet since her promotion Linda still performed several of the same functions in that role as she had previously.

Linda had also begun a gradual process of bringing some non-nobility members into the palace to fill vacant positions of personal courtiers. Fiona had a place in parliament with Linda behind Queen Alexandra at her weekly address and could occasionally deputise for Linda in her other duties – though that was still largely the senior court administrator's job. She tried to take advantage of this role by gaining as much information as possible about the Geratican court and its intentions – and from time to time passing some of it back to Geraticai.

In another more recent modernising reform, the custom of 'conveying the queen's displeasure' to any of her subjects who might have shown too much disrespect for her authority, which had already been becoming more seldom, was now almost never practised at the palace, though they still retained the right to ask court security to bring people in to be questioned about a particular subject by the court administrators, in certain circumstances, which would take place in the meeting room of the administration department.

Soon after starting at the palace Fiona had met Colin Ryder who had been making a grocery delivery to them. She had been instantly and immensely attracted to the tall blonde haired man, and very quickly decided to marry him and bring him to The Lodge, along with his young five year old son, Tom, from his first and by then deceased wife, Jane. Marriage had never really been something she had planned for, and it certainly hadn't occurred to her that she might marry a Geratican, but she had already assumed that she would be on this world for a while at least, and it had just happened. She'd always falsely declared that she was an only child from the city of Blackdon (within Castra, five hundred miles away from Greenacres), whose parents were dead (producing fake records for them, created by herself, for official purposes), and there were no other family members. She actually felt a genuine affection for the sweet but rather meek and cowardly Colin, who when she had first visited his home, had clearly been incapable of looking after himself. He was an ideal husband for her, as she was able to take control of everything and live in exactly the way she needed to for her secret mission, and also wanted to in her personal

life (which sometimes involved being technically unfaithful, though this was her own closely guarded secret).

She was actually almost as much the boss at The Lodge with Colin and Tom, as Linda had been at The Grange with Robert and still was with Alexandra – they were the matriarchs of the Elmsbrook hamlet - though she had decided not to be so much of a disciplinarian. Again, it had never occurred to her until she came to Geratica, that she could one day be in a position where she might have possible cause to beat her own stepson, and the strength of her desire not to do so had surprised her, given that her views on disciplining children generally were broadly similar to Linda's. Up until now she had never done it. She was very fond of him too. Perhaps she had more soft maternal instincts than she thought. Fiona hoped that when he was a slightly older boy, she could use her influence at court to persuade Lady Sackville to take him on as an official trainee gardener on her estate, just outside of Greenacres.

It was useful that he was on very good personal terms with Alexandra Radcliffe, who as Robert Radcliffe's daughter was a half-mongrel, and consequently someone who she felt she needed to keep an eye on. Mongrels such as herself had always appeared to be the only people who could safely travel through the void between Geratica and Geraticai, and they were the only ones with the knowledge to construct transportation capsules - of those, usually the females. Fiona and Robert were the last known of their kind. Although she had never heard of even a half-mongrel being able to travel without being killed and causing a disruption to the planet's core, Fiona couldn't be absolutely certain that it wasn't possible, and as a bright girl Alexandra might just be able to learn the method of building a capsule, though she still thought that highly unlikely, given the delicate complexity of the procedure involved.

Fiona did not intend to give Colin any more children however and had taken the necessary steps to make it impossible.

During the course of this particular meeting, the possibility of Queen Alexandra taking a suitor was briefly discussed, but as before the queen indicated that she had no plans to do so at present. She did also make passing mention of the fact that she had a very distant younger relative who as things stood could in theory inherit the throne should she never produce any issue before she died – though it was thought to be almost certainly a scenario which would never occur, as she had every intention of doing her duty and marrying once she was ready, and was in the very best of health. (In fact it appeared, better than any of her predecessors had been known to be in at her age).

This fact was news to Fiona. Nobody had known it back on Geraticai, and it was the first time she had heard it spoken of on Geratica since she'd arrived on her mission.

"Who is this person, Ma'am?" she asked. "I must confess that this is one piece of court affairs that I was not aware of before I joined! It must obviously be a young female?"

"She is the daughter of a male cousin who is several times removed from me," replied Queen Alexandra. "Almost no one is aware of her, Fiona, as she is so far distant, so I wouldn't expect you to know about it. I can't even say whether she does herself."

"I believe she is aged twenty-one – just three years younger than Her Majesty," said Linda. "The distant male cousin is obviously somewhat older."

"Do we know where she lives?" Fiona's mind was frantically working. Even if, as it seemed, this young woman was highly unlikely ever to inherit the throne, in theory she might be somebody who needed to be quietly put out of the way, if she was to follow the orders of her secret mission from Queen Victoria on Geraticai. She needed to somehow find out her identity.

"She is living in Krindleford, where I am told that she works in a bank," replied her boss. "Due to her status she would obviously be a commoner, should it ever come to pass that she inherited the

throne, which *would* be unprecedented. But as we have always said, that is not even remotely likely. "

"But who is she?" asked Fiona, again. "Sorry, I'm just curious. I really had no idea about this young woman until you mentioned her just now!" She was trying not to show how strong her eagerness to find out was. It might make the queen and senior court administrator wonder why.

Fortunately, Linda then obliged. "Miss Phoebe Porter," she said.

"I have never met the woman," admitted Queen Alexandra. "And I don't know if I ever shall."

No. You certainly won't now, if I have anything to do with it, thought Fiona to herself. Already she was considering how to dispose of this unexpected, if small problem...

***

At lunch time, Fiona got into her car and drove over to the Records Office. There she looked up some details of this Phoebe Porter. It appeared that she lived alone. That was convenient for what she had in mind. According to the record, the dwelling was a house. She scribbled it down the address on a piece of paper. Then she put the paper away in her briefcase to refer to later at home...

***

Alexandra arrived back in Greenacres later that afternoon. Letting herself through the hamlet's security gate by swiping her card, she took out her mother's post from The Grange's letterbox, and then wheeled their dustbin through. Before the gate automatically shut behind her, Fiona came through in her car. She waved briefly, and Alexandra acknowledged her, before shooting off up the hamlet

drive, turning left outside of The Grange and down to The Lodge. Alexandra watched her go. Mrs Clark had always been a fast driver.

Reaching The Grange's front entrance, she pushed the bin up their long driveway to just outside their front door, and let herself in to the house. When she eventually reached the study, Linda had pinned a piece of paper to the noticeboard on the wall beside their desks, containing a small list of jobs for her daughter to do, in addition to her prep, before she came home. Alexandra sat down with her coffee and was soon getting down to work.

As usual, a few minutes later her mother rang to check up on what she was doing. Linda felt no shame in admitting to anybody that she did it for precisely that reason even though she did largely trust her, as well as to satisfy the pure longing to speak to the daughter who she loved more than anyone else in the world.

"Did you have a good day?" she asked.

"Yes, Mother," replied Alexandra. "The lessons went quite well, and I've got lots of prep. I've already started it, and later I'll be doing my jobs and getting the supper."

"Good. And that will be at the same time as yesterday. So, you'll be a busy girl tonight. Don't waste time. Do you understand?"

"Of course, Mother."

"I trust that the bin was emptied? Did you bring it back to the house? That was your other job for this evening."

"Yes, Mother," said Alexandra. "Just as I was coming in, Tom's stepmother drove through - in a tearing hurry as usual!"

"Hmm." Linda looked at her office clock. "Perhaps she was rushing to be home to get the dinner for Tom and his father. I hope she didn't come close to knocking you over?"

"No Mother. It was OK," her daughter assured her.

"Good," She might need to have a little word with Fiona about that, at some point. It was certainly the case too, that Fiona did not work long hours in comparison with herself. She usually left quite early, and rarely arrived much before the latest time possible of nine in the morning, by which time Linda had often already been there for an hour. It had occasionally been an issue between them. If Linda was on holiday, then Fiona had to work slightly longer. On several evenings of the week, she rather enjoyed herself drinking and gambling in Geratica's most exclusive bars and clubs, which Linda rather suspected was part of the reason why she didn't like starting earlier. After she had gone to sleep at night, it wasn't uncommon for her to be awoken around midnight by the sound of Fiona roaring past at high speed on her way back to The Lodge. Fiona was also rumoured to have a particularly healthy sex drive, so if that was to be taken into account then she couldn't be getting to sleep until the early hours of the morning.

"I've put your post on your desk again, Mother," said Alexandra.

"Thank you, darling. You're a good girl," replied Linda, reaching out and touching the photograph of Alexandra on her desk at the palace. "Right, I've got to go. I'll see you later. Now, what time do you have to get supper for?"

"A quarter to eight, Mother," said Alexandra, once more obedient.

"Excellent. Goodbye until then, sweetheart. Would you like a kiss when I get home?"

On the other line Alexandra smiled and felt her mouth water. She loved her mother's kisses.

"You know I would, Mother," she replied.

"One thing that *I* don't know though, is why I asked, darling," said Linda, smiling down the phone. "Because I can promise that I'm *going* to give you a kiss, whether you want it or not!"

"Thank you, Mother. I can't wait!" said Alexandra.

"I assure you it'll be worth it!" said her mother. "Goodbye until then, darling."

"Goodbye Mother," replied Alexandra.

Later, when she heard her mother arrive, Alexandra made a final anxious check to herself that she'd done everything asked of her and she wouldn't be in trouble. Then upon greeting Linda, her kisses did indeed prove worth waiting for.

CHAPTER 37

It had been a while since Fiona had visited Queen Victoria on Geraticai, and after the news she'd heard today, she had decided to go this evening.

Clambering out of the car, she went straight inside The Lodge. Tom had been at the Sackville estate today but was now home. On days when he went there, Colin took him in the morning, on his way to work, and he got the bus back. When he wasn't due there, Fiona still employed a nanny, Miss Candice Chaplet, to look after him during the day. A cleaner, Mrs Ivy Turner, also came in twice a week (a service which Linda didn't employ at The Grange, preferring to do the task herself – or with Alexandra, rather than pay for it to be done. She had however employed Mike Harper, a gardener and general handyman about the house, for occasional work, since losing Robert).

"Hello Tom. Have you had a good day?" she asked when she saw her stepson.

"Yes thanks, Mother," he replied.

"I shall be going out tonight, after all," continued Fiona.

"Oh. Right," said Tom. "I thought you said that you weren't?"

"A change of plan!" remarked his stepmother.

She was expecting her husband home shortly and began preparing their dinner. When it was started cooking, Fiona went to her study and shut the door. She looked up on a shelf, took down a map of Castra and spread it out on her desk. She began studying how she might reach Phoebe Porter's house by car.

Presently the smell of her cooking alerted Fiona to something she must do in the kitchen, and she hurried out.

Whilst she was away, Tom passed by the study door. To his surprise it was slightly ajar. Normally it was shut at all times. It was the one room in the house that he and his father were forbidden to enter unless she was in there and gave them permission, and when she wasn't it was always kept locked. Unable to resist his curiosity, he pushed the door further open and stepped inside.

Finishing what she had been doing in the kitchen, Fiona went back into the hall. It wasn't until then that she realised she hadn't shut the study door properly. She uttered one of the strongest Geraticaian curses under her breath and dashed to the room. She saw her stepson inside and momentarily panicked. The reason why she never allowed anyone in there without her authorisation, was because it contained some secret evidence of possible schemes which she'd considered to bring about Queen Alexandra's doom and Geratica's destruction (according to Queen Victoria of Geraticai's plan) – if and when the time was right.

"*Tom!*" she screamed, rushing in. "How dare you come in here? You know you're not allowed!"

Tom froze. "I'm sorry. I was just curious!" he protested. In fact his time there had been so brief that he had barely seen anything.

Fiona grabbed his arm and dragged him out, banging the door shut behind her this time. She took her stepson across the hall and grabbed the cane hanging from the coat stand. Stretching out her leg, she pushed Tom across her knee, pulled down his trousers and pants, and began to beat him mercilessly.

"*Don't you ever, ever, ever, ever, ever, ever do that again!*" she roared. "*If you do, I will **horse whip** you more than any other boy has ever been before! I mean it! Is that understood?*"

Tom was crying out, with tears flowing down his cheeks. "Yes Mother!" he groaned.

Fiona grunted and let go of him. She took a key from her gown pocket, went to the study door and locked it. Then she stormed back to the kitchen, shutting the door to that, too.

***

Once Colin was home, they all had dinner and Fiona confirmed that she was going out. She told them that she had some business to attend to in Greenacres and wouldn't be taking her car.

Tom listened in silence. He was in some discomfort and still couldn't quite believe what had happened earlier. It was the first time that he had ever been beaten and he didn't want it to happen again. He had never known his stepmother react so furiously to something before.

A little later, Fiona said goodbye to Colin and told him she'd be back by eleven o'clock. But before she left, she took Tom up to his bedroom.

She placed her hands on his shoulders and spoke to him. "Tom. I'm sorry about what I did just now, but I had to. You must understand. That's my most private room, and I can't allow anybody in there. Don't worry, it's nothing sinister! But I do confidential work in my study. You do understand, don't you? I hope that's the last time I cane you."

Fiona genuinely didn't want them to suddenly develop a bad relationship. She'd got used to having Tom regard her as his mother, though she obviously wasn't. He had no memory of his actual mother.

"It's alright. I know I shouldn't have been in there," replied her stepson. "I won't do it again."

"That's settled then!" smiled Fiona. "But let's keep the incident between ourselves. It'll only cause us both embarrassment. I

shouldn't have lost my temper quite like that, and I apologise. Do you promise to keep it that way?"

Tom looked at her. "Yes Mother, I promise," he said, not wanting to get into any other trouble for a while.

"Good!" replied Fiona. "Well then, I'll be off. You'll be in bed by the time I get back, so I'll see you tomorrow."

***

Fiona left The Lodge, but rather than walk down the hamlet drive in order to go out to the centre of Greenacres as she'd told Colin and Tom, she instead turned off into the wood that ran between their house and The Grange – double checking that nobody saw her. There shouldn't be any reason why her husband and stepson would look at the screen on the phone at the house, and realise that she'd never been to the security gate and left Elmsbrook.

Eventually she came to some bushes at the edge of a clearing, not far from the river. Halfway along, Fiona stretched out her arm and ran her fingers over the branches in a particular movement. Suddenly there was a flash of blue light and a cubic object was revealed that had been concealed within by a shield. It was her transportation capsule. Fiona's fingers had removed the shield by her own unique code, and the door was open. Reaching inside she pulled a lever that only she as the constructor or another mongrel could see, and the force-field was lowered. With the capsule's destination already pre-set she was immediately whisked inside and it disappeared, leaving the bush as it had been before.

A few seconds later on Geraticai, Fiona seemingly emerged from nowhere within the complex of the Royal Palace in Spanda. Behind her she ran her fingers over a spot on the top of the capsule and its shield was raised. A door now concealed the vessel in the same way that it had been by the bush in Elmsbook wood, back on Geratica.

Fiona then quickly went into the palace. All the officials of course knew her very well, and she soon reached her old office where her former deputy, Daniella Sturridge, was now working.

"My Lady!" exclaimed Daniella. "It's good to see you again."

In fact she was being less than honest. Fiona had a reputation for bullying and ruthlessness towards opponents, and many had suffered at her hands as she loyally administered Queen Victoria's business and dealt with any dissent or lawbreaking. Daniella was quite pleased for the official lady chancellor of Geraticai to be posted on a special temporary mission to Geratica (which she didn't know the precise details of), for as long as possible, so that she could do her job. But not only that – she didn't much like Fiona, personally.

"It's been some time since you were last here," added the acting lady chancellor.

"Well, there's not been a lot for me to report from Geratica," replied Fiona. She looked enquiringly at Daniella. "Is there any more news on Her Majesty's efforts to produce an heir?"

Daniella pulled a face and glanced anxiously towards the door. "No. Just between you and me, My Lady, I am starting to wonder if the prince will ever do his duty and deliver her that which she seeks."

"Don't let the queen hear you voice that opinion, Miss Sturridge!" replied her boss.

Fiona had secretly been sceptical of Queen Victoria's plan regarding the usage of the Geratican mongrel (which, in common with the people, Daniella knew nothing of), for some time, but would always be loyal to her.

"I will let Her Majesty know that you are here, My Lady," said Daniella.

Soon Fiona was with the queen in her throne room.

"The court welcomes you, Fiona," said Queen Victoria. "Please take a glass of wine with me. The length of time between your visits seems to lengthen with each one. I sometimes wonder if you are not getting a little too comfortable on Geratica, with your husband and stepson over there!"

"Thank you, Ma'am," replied Fiona. "I assure you that I remain utterly committed to the task you have assigned me to." (In fact it was quite true that life was for the most part more agreeable and prosperous for her on Geratica, and she wasn't really in any hurry to return, unless Queen Victoria *did* eventually conceive on this world, or circumstances on the other forced her to act). "But there is often little to report. However, today I have become aware of some information that was previously unknown to us. Queen Alexandra does apparently have an heir."

"*What?*" The queen nearly spilt her wine. "How can this be?"

"There should really be nothing to worry about, Ma'am," Fiona quickly assured her. "Firstly, the young woman in question is about as distant a relation to the Geratican queen as it is possible to be, and given that the latter has stated her determination to marry and give birth eventually – though still happily for us at some time in the future – it is thought extremely unlikely that the former will ever succeed to the throne. Hardly anybody seems to be even aware of the lineage, not even perhaps herself. But secondly, and more importantly, I believe that I can discreetly eliminate her from the equation fairly quickly, and then our plan will not need to change."

"Do it, Fiona," said Queen Victoria. "I *order* you to get rid of this young upstart at the earliest opportunity!"

"Of course, Ma'am. It will be my pleasure." Fiona took a sip of her wine. "Might I enquire how things are in your own Queendom?"

"The prince still continues to fail me. He rarely seems to produce any sperm whatsoever when we have intercourse, and I sometimes think that he does not find me desirable. I don't know what's wrong with the blasted mongrel. Are all Geratican men so stupid?

But anyhow, as you know I have other problems to deal with. There has continued to be occasional outbreaks of rioting on the streets from protesting workers, and now there are even some rebellions over in Plumas, that I have had to send the army in to deal with. That accursed factory manager, Vera West continues to stir up trouble. Order should be restored, but it may take time. That is my primary focus at the moment."

"I naturally wish you success, Ma'am," replied Fiona.

"I often wish that you were still here," admitted the queen. "Daniella sometimes seems a little too liberal in her attitudes for my liking. But still – you have a job to do."

Fiona continued drinking and conversing with the queen for a couple of hours before making her leave of Geraticai once more. Outside in the palace complex, she re-entered her capsule, and seconds later was standing back in Elmsbrook wood. Raising its shield so that it was concealed within the bush, she made her way back to The Lodge.

***

As Fiona reached the front of the house, she could see the light on in the mistress bedroom. Her geratis twitched and by the time she was inside and had locked the door, it was bulging thick with desire for Colin.

However, there was one last thing to attend to, before she had her pleasure. She unlocked her study door, turned on the light and locked it again behind her. Opening the safe on the wall, she took out a bottle and syringe. She had been careful not to have too much

to drink with Queen Victoria this evening, as a steady hand was required for this job.

Sitting at her desk, she carefully poured a portion of liquid from the bottle into the syringe. When it was done she locked the syringe away in her desk drawer, then put the bottle back in the safe and locked it.

Now she could go to Colin. She went out of her study and locked it, and then headed straight for the bedroom. Her husband already lying in the matrimonial bed.

"Hello darling," she said. "Mistress is back!"

"Hello Mistress!" replied Colin. Since their marriage, he had always called his wife that in the bedroom. Fiona liked him to do it as it appealed to her natural desire for sexual dominance. He didn't say it in any other circumstance. As she surveyed her husband's tall slim body and baby smooth skin, together with his blonde hair and blue eyes, she became truly turned on.

"I've been *waiting* for you!" continued Colin.

Fiona smiled wolfishly and licked her lips. Opening her bedside drawer she took out a pair of handcuffs and two pieces of rope. She marched to her husband's side of the bed and bound his wrists to the headboard with the cuffs. (They were in fact the same ones that she had used when abducting Robert Radcliffe from the wood five years earlier.) Then she did the same to his feet with the rope.

"I will be back in a moment," she said, and left for the bathroom to do her ablutions.

Colin's heart pounded with excitement. He knew what would shortly happen.

It was true. As a child he had sometimes been considered a bit of a weakling, even for a boy. As a man he had always needed a very strong woman, and had found one in Jane Ryder, his first wife and

Tom's natural mother. Traditionally it had normally been accepted that the woman was the dominant partner, and he had fallen apart when Jane, had died; as without her he couldn't cope Fiona had come into his life at precisely the right moment, and he felt that he would be equally lost without her. His relationship with Fiona was of the kind sometimes referred to in Geratican society as a husband who hid behind his wife's skirt – and he was not the only one. In truth he was one of the least brave men of his race. He knew of one or two men who were interested in the recently formed organisation, 'Male Rights Protestors' who sought a greater role in Geratican society,and some even a different relationship with women, but that was definitely not for him. He couldn't imagine how any man could possibly survive without his wife to lead and take care of him. Colin wouldn't know what to do.

He was still a delivery driver as he had been when they first met. Several drivers were women but being a man able to read semi-competently he could follow directions and deliver goods to a specific location.

His wife could dominate him, and there had been the odd occasion when he had been beaten – though Tom was not aware of it.

He could hear Fiona coming back.

"Colin! I'm coming in. Be ready for me!" came her sexy voice from outside the bedroom, and his genus ballooned inside of him. His wife could be quite a strong and aggressive lover but that excited him. Most men liked most of all to be made love to by their wives or girlfriends and he particularly did. Nothing aroused Colin more than the thought of being dominated in bed by a woman in the traditional Geratican fashion, and he regularly thought about being under Fiona during his working day.

His wife re-entered and undressed. There had always been something about her tall slim body, long dark hair and green eyes that seemed to bewitch him, and he'd fancied her more than any other woman from the moment he'd met her. Her particularly long thick geratis protruded powerfully from her vagina. Colin felt

another wave of excitement as he thought of it pounding his submissive genus.

"Dominate me, Mistress!" he said, seductively.

Fiona sat down at her dressing table and applied some lipstick. Looking through the mirror directly back at him lying in bed, she pouted her lips. Colin's genus ballooned as he imagined them all over him.

Then Fiona rose and walked to the bed. She mounted him and came down over his bound body. Her longing for sexual fulfilment was all consuming and her only thought was to satisfy it. She cast his thighs in an iron grip inside of hers, wrapped her arms around his shoulders, and stroked his hair. Fiona kissed him passionately all over and her geratis forced itself inside of her husband and began grinding over his genus. Colin began to lose control immediately as her mouth smothered his lips and their tongues touched, and she crushed him and thrust her body down violently into his, again and again. He saw the sly wolfishness in her eyes and felt her geratis expand to totally fill his vagina and throb against its walls as her arousal reached its peak. As usual he came in no time, his genus exploding. Colin screamed very loudly, and his head thrashed about on the pillow, his arms pulling against the restraints on the headboard as the powerful orgasm tore through his weak body.

A few seconds later, Fiona came too, squealing with the ecstasy that she felt as his semen trickled back through the pores of her geratis. She always knew that her husband was pleased by her when she made love to him, but whilst in the process of doing it Fiona never gave a thought to how he felt. It was all about her own desire. She was a dominant lover like her neighbour Linda at The Grange had been with her own husband, but somewhat more selfish.

As she deposited blue juice all over Colin's vagina, he gratefully felt it slip all through his veins and gasped with more pleasure.

"I love you, Mistress!" he whispered.

"I love you too, darling!" replied Fiona, with a sexiness in her voice that set her husband's heart racing once again. He knew it wouldn't be long before she recovered from her exertion and be after more of the same.

Colin was right. Fiona made love to him four more times and had two other separate orgasms in the process. As usual Colin screamed so loudly on each occasion that Fiona dryly wondered to herself whether Linda heard him over at The Grange, which gave her a wicked sense of satisfaction. She really did think it likely also, that her stepson might sometimes be awoken by the sound of his parents making love.

CHAPTER 38

Alexandra's last lesson at Charterhouse the next day was Ancient Geratican.

This was a subject that Gillian Spencer dismissed as a waste of time, openly wondering why in this day and age it was still considered relevant for schoolgirls to learn. But Alexandra still found it interesting and her mother had always told her that it was still a useful thing to be familiar with, since it formed part of the basis for the modern language used today, and could help her to understand the origins of words.

After they had been given their prep by the mistress, Alexandra packed up and went out of the building, heading for the school gates.

Just before she reached them though, Gillian and Melanie suddenly appeared and blocked her way.

"Running away to Mummy again are you, Radcliffe?" sneered Gillian.

"Mummy's girl!" scoffed Melanie.

"Yeah. And when she's here she hides away and scurries about like a little mouse!" added Gillian. She raised her hands above her head and pointed her fingers upwards in imitation of the rodent. Then she ran a couple of paces in front of Alexandra, her head looking down towards the ground.

"Mouse! That sounds quite an appropriate name for you, Radcliffe!" said Gillian. "I'm going to start calling you that from now on."

Melanie giggled. "Mouse!" she repeated and copied the action of Gillian.

"P-Please Spencer! Let me pass," begged Alexandra. "I've got to catch my train!"

"Why?" asked Gillian, in a sarcastic tone. "Is Mummy waiting for you? Will she give you the cane if you're late home?"

Alexandra went slightly red and couldn't help checking her watch anxiously. What Gillian had said wasn't entirely true. Her mother wouldn't be there when she got home. But tonight and for the rest of the week she *would* be home earlier and getting their dinner ready. That was why she hadn't needed to eat her main meal of the day at Charterhouse. But she'd still be ringing at the usual time.

If Alexandra ever did miss her usual train, then the next one was due forty-five minutes later. That would mean not being back at The Grange until after five o'clock, and she would have to explain to her mother why she was late. It wouldn't be so bad at the moment, but she was forbidden to be outside of The Grange after dusk, and the nights were gradually drawing in. Soon, getting home at that time would be breaking the rule and her mother would be continuing to call until she got an answer. Therefore, she would know and there weren't many reasons that she could give to explain why she'd out so late. Alexandra didn't want to have to tell her too much about Gillian if possible, in case she complained to Charterhouse and made things worse. Her mother would be even more annoyed if she'd been delayed for some kind of appointment due to waiting for her.

Then Gillian snatched her bag. "What have we got in here, I wonder?" she asked. "Is this where you keep your train ticket?"

She tossed it to Melanie, who then threw it back again at her new friend's beckoning. Gillian opened it, and to Alexandra's horror began to tip the contents on to the ground.

"Oh Spencer, please. Don't do that!" cried Alexandra. Her ticket, as well as her card for the security gate at Elmsbrook were in her purse that had just fallen out. She was also anxious that the library

books she'd borrowed at the beginning of the week weren't damaged.

Gillian picked up the purse and considered opening it, but then decided that she'd probably gone far enough for now. This was partly revenge for Alexandra beating her in the maths test in their very first lesson together, though she would certainly have some fun in tormenting her in the future. She knew just how to make her feel uncomfortable. But Gillian was intelligent enough to realise that even she would have to tread carefully with the daughter of the senior court administrator to Queen Alexandra. She would leave her alone sometimes – and there would be plenty of other mischief to make, as well as besting her in schoolwork.

She tossed the purse at Alexandra's feet with a smirk. "See you tomorrow, Mouse!"

Gillian turned and started walking away. Melanie was soon lapping at her heels. Alexandra quickly gathered up her stuff. She was relieved that it wasn't a windy day. Luckily the library books seemed to have survived relatively unscathed. With her bag repacked, she closed it and hurried out. She dashed around to the station and made it to the platform shortly before the train was due.

On the journey home, Alexandra very nearly sucked her thumb after what she'd just experienced, but she was trying hard to do as her mother wished. She didn't want it beaten by one of her sticks. She did find it a hard habit to break however, and for the rest of her childhood she would relapse on occasions...

***

Meanwhile at the palace, Fiona finished her work as soon as she possibly could and got in her car. However, she did not drive home. She had instructed Nanny Chaplet to stay later than normal as she had private business to attend to after work. The nanny would look

after him, and also see that he and his father were given their dinner before she came home.

Her destination was Krindleford. After an hour's drive she entered the town, and with the map that she had been looking at in her study the previous evening on the dashboard in front of her, found the way to Phoebe Porter's address. Fiona got out of the car and made a quick discreet inspection. At the moment, the house appeared to be empty. The young woman hadn't returned from work yet. She got back in the car and backed it to a location slightly further down the street on the opposite side. Then, watching intently, she settled down to wait.

After another forty-five minutes another car approached and pulled up inside the parking space of the house. An auburn-haired woman of medium height and build got out, and then went in to the house. Fiona assumed that this must be Miss Porter. The moment had come. Opening a compartment, she took out a small bag containing the syringe which she had filled up yesterday night. Then choosing a moment when nobody was about, she got out of her car, crossed the road to the house, and rang the front doorbell. The woman answered it.

"Hello. Are you Miss Phoebe Porter?" asked Fiona, smiling warmly.

"Yes," replied the woman. "And you are whom?"

"I am a member of Her Majesty's court." Fiona took out her palace security pass and flashed it before Phoebe. "If you wouldn't mind me coming in for a moment, I have something that we wish you to see." She pointed to the bag in her other hand.

Phoebe looked at it in wonderment, and then glanced back at Fiona enquiringly.

"Oh. Very well then. If it's Her Majesty's court that is asking!"

"Thank you," said Fiona, and stepped inside.

As soon as the door was closed, she reached inside the bag. "It's this!" she said.

Phoebe Porter never got a chance to see what it was. In one movement Fiona dropped the bag and gripped her shoulders, whilst lifting the syringe to her neck.

"What are you doing?" began Phoebe, before Fiona administered one jab to her neck. Immediately the young woman's eyes bulged, and her body convulsed. A few seconds later she was limp in her assailant's arms. The liquid in the syringe caused a paralysis of all the vital organs in a person's body. Fiona had concocted the potion herself since coming to Geratica, in her study at The Lodge. A minute later the woman was dead. Fiona laid her down on the hall floor, put the syringe back in the bag and stuffed it inside her coat pocket.

The next stage of her plan contained something of a gamble, but Fiona had always been one who gained a thrill from that particular activity. It wasn't apparently possible for a non-mongrel to travel through the void between their two worlds in a transportation capsule and survive the journey, but what if the person was already dead? Fiona had often thought that it might be, though there had never been any reason before to put the theory to the test. Perhaps whatever it was in the void that destroyed the person and caused an eruption in the planet's core, wouldn't react in the same way with them if they weren't alive in the first place. She would soon find out if she was correct, anyhow.

She stretched out a hand, worked her fingers in a particular motion. A transportation capsule appeared. Stepping inside, she worked the console and set a location for it to travel to on Geratica. With the course plotted, she saved the pathway. The console disappeared and she was outside of the capsule again. A force-field protected it.

Fiona bent down to her victim and hauled her to her feet. Then with Phoebe inside one of her arms, she reached inside the capsule with the other and pulled the lever to lower the force-field. She

was instantly sped away to Geraticai, with Phoebe Porter attached to her.

Shortly afterwards Fiona was on her home world and stood on a bridge over a river on the outskirts of Arista. Phoebe was still within her grip, and nothing untoward appeared to have happened. It seemed that her theory might be correct.

Fiona knew this particular spot well, and it was deserted. She quickly stepped to the edge of the bridge and tipped Phoebe Porter's lifeless body over the side. Fiona watched it hit the water below with a splash and slowly sink. If the body was found, then nobody would know who she was on Geraticai – not that it would make any difference anyhow. More importantly Phoebe would have disappeared without trace from Geratica forever and nobody could guess where she had ended up – and it wasn't possible for them to travel here, even if they ever did.

Next, Fiona used the transportation capsule to take her back to Phoebe Porter's house on Geratica. She shielded it within the banister of the stairs. Then she constructed another capsule as before and this time went to the royal palace complex on Geraticai, using the same door as previously, as a location. (You couldn't use the same capsule to travel to two different locations once a course was plotted and a pathway saved. It only took you to the original one and back – but however many times you wanted). After shielding it, she hurried inside the palace and requested another audience with Her Majesty. After informing a delighted Queen Victoria of her successful enterprise, she finally returned to Geratica, in yet another capsule.

When she arrived, Fiona was standing at the back of her car, which she had this time used as a location. Darkness had now fallen. Once again nobody had seen her appearance. She shielded the capsule within.

Then Fiona got back into her car, removed her gloves and this time she did drive home.

Whilst Fiona was carrying out her activity, Linda arrived back at Elmsbrook after work. As she drove up the hamlet drive, she passed Tom. She was shocked to see that he seemed to be moving rather gingerly. Stopping the car, she pressed a button and the passenger side window lowered.

"Tom! Are you alright?" she asked.

Tom flushed slightly. "Oh yes. That's alright, Mrs Radcliffe!" he replied.

"You look as if you're in pain!"

"In actual fact my stepmother caned me yesterday evening, Mrs Radcliffe."

Linda's eyes widened. "And you're still feeling the effects now? She must have beaten you hard!"

She reached over and opened the door. "Come on. I'll nip you round the corner to The Lodge."

"Oh no, please. I wouldn't want to put you to that trouble!" said Tom.

"For goodness sake, it's nothing of the kind!" exclaimed Linda, indignantly. "Now get in."

"OK. Thank you, Mrs Radcliffe." Tom did as she asked and closed the door.

"May I ask what you did to deserve such a punishment?" asked Linda, as she drove the short distance. "You don't have to tell me if you don't wish to, of course."

"It's a private matter, Mrs Radcliffe," Tom told her.

"Very well," said Linda, as she stopped outside of The Lodge.

"I think I'll be fine tomorrow, Mrs Radcliffe," continued Tom. "Thank you for the lift. I'll see myself in. Goodbye for now."

He opened the car door and stepped carefully out. As he closed it, he waved and shuffled up to the front door. Linda watched him go inside. She was still a little surprised. It wasn't necessarily her place to criticise another woman's punishment of her son, and she was a firm believer in very harsh discipline if necessary. She had certainly beaten Alexandra hard on occasions and felt fully justified in her actions. But never had her daughter still been in pain a day later, and as far as she was aware, Tom was rarely punished in that manner.

She drove back to The Grange and told Alexandra what she'd seen.

"Goodness only knows what he did, but Fiona must have caned him roughly!" she exclaimed. "He didn't want to say what it was – only that it was a private matter. He normally seems such a good boy!"

Alexandra was deeply shocked too. In all the years that they had grown up together, she had never known him to be beaten. In that respect at least, Tom's upbringing had been less strict than hers – though she thought his stepmother to still be quite a formidable character.

"Mrs Clark doesn't very often seem to lose her temper, Mother," she replied. "But she must have been *really* cross on this occasion. To have been beaten like that. I can't believe that he would have been so naughty!"

"Well you never know what can happen sometimes behind closed doors, darling," remarked Linda. "I think that I've punished you as severely as possible on occasion, though even that might not have

been like what Tom seems to have received yesterday. But it's not for me to judge. It's a matter for Fiona to decide upon."

"You do think he'll be alright don't you, Mother?" asked Alexandra. "He's due to go to work on the Sackville estate again on day five of this week."

"Oh yes. Don't worry about that, sweetheart," Linda assured her. "He said that he thought he'd be fine tomorrow, and I'm sure he'll be back to normal after that."

Alexandra had already decided to try and find out what had happened, the next time she saw him...

***

Fiona came back and let nanny Chaplet go home. Then she went out to a club and wined and dined. She was in high spirits after the success of her earlier exploits, and also enjoyed herself gambling at the tables and then with an escort in one of the discreet rooms at the back.

Much later she returned once again to Elmsbrook, racing up the hamlet drive to The Lodge. As usual she saw The Grange in darkness. The good Radcliffes had long since retired to bed. She was now going to do the same – though Fiona felt a sly sense of satisfaction that unlike Linda, she was about to have more sex. She was certain that Linda missed having it - and the real reason that the woman no longer had a husband to do it with, was of course due to the fact that she had secretly abducted him to Geraticai, five years earlier…

<u>PART 8</u>

CHAPTER 39

On the afternoon of 6/32/05, Alexandra called on Tom at The Lodge. She had a cup of coffee with him and Fiona in the parlour, and there did not seem to be any particular change in their overall relationship, despite what she'd heard had taken place four days ago. Tom thought of her as his mother (and would address her as such), and Alexandra knew he had always generally got on well with her. Despite that he had also always sympathised with Alexandra's slight unease about her, though he told he not to worry too much about it.

They eventually went out and went into the wood, where they had spent many hours together growing up in Elmsbrook. Tom did appear to now be completely recovered from whatever terrible beating he had suffered from his stepmother. As soon as they were clear of The Lodge and inside its entrance to the wood, Alexandra tackled him on the subject at last.

"Tom, I've been longing to ask you. What happened on day two of this week? Mother told me that Fiona beat you!"

He glanced at her. "Oh that. Well, it was nothing really. I just did something a bit foolhardy and got punished for it. All forgotten about now."

"Nothing?" exclaimed his best friend. "Come on Tom, it must have been a bit more than that! Mother said that you were noticeably looking uncomfortable as you walked – and that was a day later. Fiona must have given you a right hiding, which she never normally does. Our mothers are both particularly strong willed and traditional women, but surprisingly yours has never been quite as severe in her strictness as mine. It's always been me who's been given the cane on a few occasions - not you. But though the beatings may have hard and painful, never have I been in that kind of discomfort the next day!"

"Fiona was actually very apologetic about it afterwards," said Tom. "I think she was genuinely sorry that she'd lost her temper in a way that she hardly ever normally does."

"But what in the name of Geratica did you do?" asked Alexandra.

"I promised her that we'd keep it between ourselves," replied Tom.

"Mother told me that you'd said it was a private matter," said Alexandra. "Even from me?"

Their friendship had become so close that there wasn't a lot that they didn't confide in each other about. Although there was no one that she was nearer to than her mother, and in almost everything she was the first person that Alexandra turned to for support and guidance, when it came to certain problems that she'd experienced at Charterhouse, such as that from Sophie Brewster, she'd sometimes still found it safer to tell Tom the complete story. If things started to get very difficult with Gillian then it would most likely be the same. And whenever they talked together about internal affairs at Elmsbrook – and most especially Fiona – they both knew that what they said was also 'between themselves'.

There was always a quietness in the wood, and as they walked to their usual spot beside the river that flowed through it, the wind blew through the trees. The leaves were beginning to fall on this early autumn day. As they sat down, Tom's natural desire to tell Alexandra what had happened became stronger, and he touched her arm lightly with his hand.

"Alright. But you really must swear to me that you won't tell a single other soul! I'm breaking my promise to my stepmother, Alexandra, and I do actually love her like she was my own."

"I know that Tom, and I fully respect you for it – even if I don't always feel the same warmth for her. And *you* know how much I love Mother. But I won't tell her this if you don't want her to know, just as I didn't want her to know about Sophie – though she found

out from me in the end. And I *certainly* would never tell anybody else. You know that."

Tom took a deep breath. "I was passing Fiona's study when she was in the kitchen and it was open. She never leaves it even unlocked for a moment, whenever she's not in there, and Father and I always have to knock and wait for permission to enter if we want to see her when she is. I was so surprised that I forgot myself for a moment and couldn't resist peeking inside. I was literally only in there for a few seconds before she came back and caught me. She went absolutely wild and caned my backside *extremely* hard, more times than I could count, and screamed at me to never ever, ever go in there again. She also threatened to horse whip me more than any other boy has been before if I do! There, I've told you now."

"She did all that to you, just because you went into her study?" demanded Alexandra, in disbelief. "Goodness me, the study at The Grange is just as much for me to be in as Mother. We share it – though obviously I have to admit that her desk is the boss's! I would never interfere with that. But I'm free to go into the room whenever I need to."

"Well, you know all about rules, Alexandra," replied Tom. "You don't have to tell me that your mother punishes you for breaking them at The Grange. And at The Lodge, this is one of the rules that Fiona *is* most strict about. She says that it's her own private room where she does important and very confidential work for the court, which nobody – not even her own family - are allowed to see."

"And did you see anything?"

"No. Nothing at all, really. There might have been something on her desk. As I said just now, I was only there for the briefest period of time."

"I still find it bizarre," said Alexandra. "Mother considers the study an important place for me to be. It's rather ironic that you're not allowed in your stepmother's at all when she isn't there, whereas

when I come home from Charterhouse in the evening, I'm strictly forbidden to do my prep in any other room *but* the study - especially my bedroom - in case I get distracted from my work."

"Well, of course we boys don't go to school," said Tom. "I do remember being in there with her when I was younger, and she was teaching me the alphabet."

Alexandra wondered what Fiona did at The Lodge for Her Majesty's court, that was so important. But she knew the importance of confidentiality from things that her mother had told her about. It was always drummed into her that she must be discreet. She could understand that. Her mother didn't say all that much about what went on at the palace, but Alexandra certainly understood what she did, and that she was a very important person – the highest ranked 'commoner' in the queendom. Fiona obviously worked with her, but she wasn't mentioned much, and they never travelled to and from work together, as some might expect them to do sometimes, being neighbours. In fact, although her mother was always entirely civil and respectful whenever she was referring to Tom's stepmother, Alexandra often wondered whether they were all that close. But she had been brought up to very much respect her elders and authority, therefore it wasn't a subject that she felt was her place to get directly involved in.

Alexandra did find Fiona rather strange though, and occasionally a little over-intrusive – sometimes seeming to be excessively interested as a neighbour in what she was doing. Tom said that it was just because she cared as a friend of the family, and they were after all the only two families in the hamlet, but Alexandra wasn't always totally convinced. Her mother never seemed to have felt there was any problem in that respect either, though. Again, she was a busy woman in her job, and Alexandra didn't like to burden her with any unnecessary worry.

At the back of her mind too she was always troubled by what had happened shortly after Fiona had arrived in Elmsbrook, when her father, who couldn't swim, had seemingly fallen into the river and been swept away just a few yards from where she and Tom now

sat. He'd apparently tried to learn, but the lessons hadn't been successful.

They'd discussed the subject before. Fiona had been with her father and always said that there was nothing she could do as it had happened so fast. The current was indeed very strong when the deep water flowed through this wood, and it was apparently a very stormy day, and the ground at the riverbank was very slippery (Alexandra had only been five at the time, so she didn't remember her father that well, and certainly not the incident itself which had happened whilst she was at elementary school in the centre of Greenacres. Her mother had talked to her about it when she was older, though). Even though Alexandra could swim (as could Tom), it was one of the reasons - though not the only one - why she was forbidden to be out of The Grange after dusk. Her mother wanted to be absolutely certain that she couldn't go wandering into the wood in the dark and accidentally fall into the river herself.

Fiona had always claimed that her father wanted to walk through the wood that day with her, rather than simply go down the road to The Grange, after helping to move her furniture into The Lodge. Even if that was true, he surely wouldn't have wanted to go very near the riverbank, though. His body had never been found and the police had eventually concluded that he had indeed drowned. Her mother had accepted that he was dead. But all the same, without any conclusive evidence of a body, there was no closure to the whole sorry episode. In Alexandra's young mind it all seemed very strange, and although thinking it almost certain now that her mother was right, she still dreamed of one day seeing him again...

She brought her mind back to Tom.

"Did...did Fiona cane your bare bottom?" she asked.

Tom nodded. "She pulled my trousers and pants down, yes."

"That's something Mother has never done with me, and I'm thankful for it!" said Alexandra. "I've got very sensitive skin. It must have been awful to experience that. The rumour is that our

headmistress at Charterhouse sometimes makes girls who she canes in her office take off their skirts beforehand. I hope your mother never does horse whip you. You'll be thrashed naked like the wayward juveniles that get the punishment in the courtyard of the Royal Palace in Avermore."

"By the queen and your mother," remarked Tom.

"Hmm," Alexandra murmured in reply. It was true that it was an occasional part of her mother's duties at court. She respected her like nobody else and absorbed a lot of what she was taught by her as correct. Her mother was very much the boss of their relationship and she rarely questioned her opinions or judgements. But Alexandra was very sensitive, and this particular subject always made her squeamish – though she hadn't broached those thoughts with her mother yet.

"It was stupid of me to do it," continued Tom. "But I'm going to put the whole thing behind me now."

"Well, as long as you're sure, and you've fully recovered from the beating," said Alexandra.

"I'm alright now," confirmed Tom.

Tom had only ever seen Alexandra beaten once - when they had been younger. It was a weekend and she and Linda had been visiting the Lodge. He and Alexandra were running around the parlour in a rather excited fashion, and she had been warned by her mother to be careful. Linda had even begun to unfasten the belt from her skirt to emphasise what she intended to do if her daughter did not take heed of her instruction. This seemed to be an end to the matter and the belt had been refastened. However, they had forgotten themselves one more time and unfortunately a drink had somehow been knocked from a table by Alexandra and split on the carpet, causing a stain. Linda had lost her temper and this time removed the belt completely as she leaped up and scolded her. Alexandra was pulled across her mother's knee and given three lashes on her bottom. Tom had found out later that after returning

to the privacy of The Grange, she'd also been given the cane for misbehaving in company. The following day Alexandra had been forced to write a brief note of apology as a punishment, and marched back to The Lodge to deliver it in person to his stepmother.

Shortly afterwards they left the wood and went down the drive to the security gate of Elmsbrook. Alexandra swiped her card and opened it. Then they walked down a couple of roads until they came to a park, stopping along the way in a shop where Alexandra brought them both some sweets. She could see that Tom was clearly back to normal. At the park they sat and listened to the music being played on the bandstand, whilst they ate their sweets. Then they strolled around the grounds for about half an hour.

Whilst there, they went into an enclosed garden area. There was a lawn in the centre and a pond at the far end. Trees and hedgerows surrounded the edges and there were various park benches on the paths to the sides of the lawn. Alexandra and Tom sat down on one of them.

A girl was playing with a water pistol. She was there with her mother and younger brother who were stood by the pond. The mother was talking to another woman with her back turned. The girl was running around the garden and twice when her mother wasn't looking, took delight in firing it at people sat on the benches. When she was about to try a third time, she wasn't so fortunate. Her mother looked back and saw what she was about to do.

"Zoe!" she barked. "Don't you dare use that thing in here! I've told you before. No water pistols in a public place where people are trying to relax. Now put it away. If you fire that water at somebody, I'll do something in kind which will make your eyes water! Do you understand what I'm telling you?"

"Yes," replied the girl.

"Yes what?"

"Yes Mother," affirmed Zoe, and reaching for her handbag, put the pistol inside.

"Alright," said the woman and turned to start talking with the other again.

Alexandra exchanged a glance with Tom, as the girl moved on and was soon approaching their bench. She saw Zoe glance over in the direction of the pond, then smirk and take the pistol out again. To her disbelief, the girl then raised it and squirted another stream of water straight at her. Alexandra flinched as it caught her face, just below her right eye. Zoe began putting the pistol back in her handbag again, looking pleased with herself. Alexandra felt like she should remonstrate with her for doing this. Her mother would certainly have given the girl a blasting – even in the presence of Zoe's, who was obviously ultimately in charge of her in this situation. But she didn't really have enough nerve. She was always shy of talking to people she didn't know at the best of times. However, then there came another shout.

"How dare you, girl?"

 The mother had turned at the last moment and this time caught her daughter firing the gun. Now she was marching over. Alexandra winced. She could guess what was going to happen now.

"You disobedient girl!" she scolded. "I warned you not to do that! Right!"

She grabbed Zoe by the arm and pushed her over the knee of an outstretched leg. Then she pulled down her skirt and pants and smacked her bare bottom four times. The girl smarted from the blows. Then her mother redressed her garments.

"I'll take that," she scolded, snatching the pistol from Zoe's hand. "You'll not use it again for a week. You clearly can't be trusted to be sensible when you've got it. Now apologise to this girl, immediately!"

"I'm sorry. Miss," said the girl, humbly.

"Um…That's alright," replied Alexandra. "No harm done."

"Yes, well I'm sorry that my daughter did that to you too," said the mother.

Then another woman, of mature years, who had been sprayed by Zoe on the second bench came over.

"Your daughter's a pest!" she exclaimed. "You didn't see her blast me over there, before. And by the way, you know who the mother of this girl is, don't you? Linda Radcliffe. The senior court administrator!"

Zoe's mother reeled and momentarily looked panicked.

"You're Mrs Radcliffe's daughter? Oh, my goodness, you won't report this and get her into the court's bad books will you? Oh, I feel so ashamed. My name is Mrs Jolene Howe. Please tell her that I normally don't have any serious problems with my daughter, Zoe. She isn't really a bad girl - just a bit high spirited. Zoe's never done anything really terrible. If she did, I'd thrash her, believe me! I've got a whip. I always keep my children well disciplined."

She gave her daughter a thump on the arm.

"You foolish girl!"

Alexandra took a deep breath. She would have to say something.

"Mrs Howe, please!" begged Alexandra. "I don't want any fuss and I may not even mention it to my mother. It was nothing really! Don't worry about it."

"Are you sure?" asked Jolene.

"Yes, it's true that my mother is Mrs Linda Radcliffe. But I don't get treated any differently to anybody else, and neither does anybody get singled out for special treatment, purely for any dealings which they've had with me – whether they be good or bad!"

"Well, that's a relief then!" remarked Mrs Howe. "And I'm sorry for my daughter's behaviour towards you, Madam," she said to the woman who had complained. "Well it's nice to have met you, Miss Radcliffe. I'm going to take my daughter home now. Good day to you!"

"Good day, Mrs Howe!" replied Alexandra.

"Ben!" the woman called to her son. "Come along. We're going home. And you, Zoe, are going to hear more from me about this, when we get there. Now move!"

With that, Jolene put her hand on Zoe's shoulder and shepherded her way, somewhat roughly, with Ben following close behind. The other woman acknowledged Alexandra with a slight nod and went back to her bench.

Tom looked at Alexandra.

"Well, that was a bit of a performance!"

"Hmm," said Alexandra. "Sorry you had to see that after what happened to you the other day. This must be the week for punishments! I couldn't believe that girl disobeyed her mother like that. I wouldn't have dared do that with Mother there to possibly see. Once that Mrs Howe had done, it was obvious what was going to happen. Some children are really daring!"

"Maybe it was a bit of an over-reaction though," remarked Tom. "She was just having a bit of fun, I suppose."

"All the same, she was being a bit bothersome and it's true that a lot of people do come in here to relax and be quiet," replied

Alexandra. "And Mother would say that Zoe had been warned not to do what she did, but still went ahead, so she had to be punished. I wish that other woman over there hadn't come over and stirred things up even more, though. I don't think Mrs Howe had realised that Zoe had already used her water pistol twice, and then she found out who my mother was!"

Tom laughed.

"Do you get that a lot?"

"No, not much – thank goodness. But if people do know, there are always one or two who imagine that a good or bad word from me will get passed to Mother and they'll have some mention or other at Court, which isn't really how it works at all. And I certainly never like people to think that I get special favour in anything, just because my mother is the senior court administrator."

Soon it was time for them to leave. Whist Alexandra was out, Mike, the gardener who Linda employed at The Grange on an occasional basis, had been working under her supervision, but he'd be finished now.

Alexandra checked her watch three times during the walk back, and Tom had to jog slightly to keep up with her.

"It's alright, Alexandra," he said. "Don't worry. You'll be home in time."

"Yes, well I'd rather be safe than sorry, Tom," she replied. "You know my mother's rule. I have to be home before dusk, because afterwards it can be dangerous, and in case I have an accident or get lost. I'm not allowed out, unaccompanied by an adult, after that. She said half past four today – and I always have to be punctual."

"Of course," said Tom. He did know that on one occasion they had been out together on this day of the week, and Alexandra had been two minutes late by her mother's watch. Waiting for her at the door with the cane behind her back, Linda had not accepted any excuse

from her daughter and after closing it had immediately given her six beatings. The following weekend Alexandra had been forbidden to leave The Grange from the moment she came home from school at the end of that week, to when it was time to go back again at the start of the following one.

Fortunately, on this occasion they were in good time.

CHAPTER 40

That same afternoon at Charterhouse, Alexandra's classmates who boarded at the college were in the recreation room at Rovers House. They were shortly joined by Sophie Brewster.

"What are you doing here, Sophie?" asked Benita. "Your house is Beavers!"

"I've got every right to come in here if I want to!" protested Sophie. "There's no rule against any of us visiting each other's houses."

Benita knew that this was technically true. But she had never been particularly friendly with Sophie Brewster. Although she didn't know her all that well, what she did know she didn't much like. Everybody had seen her getting caned in the prep school assembly hall, and everybody knew what she had done to have to suffer the punishment. She was very pleased to find her in the other class, now that they were in the seniors, though less so that Gillian Spencer had now joined them instead.

"I saw that old boat moored up when I was coming over here," continued Sophie. "I wonder when somebody will take us for a trip up the lake in it?"

"Does your mother ever do that, like Mrs Moreton used to when we were in the prep school, Spencer?" asked Imelda.

"As far as I know the college's boat is communally driven by any of the mistresses qualified to do so," replied Gillian, stood with her leg bent and her foot resting against the wall. "The prep school one is actually owned by Mrs Moreton. My mother does also have a boat of her own, but it's not here – and it's a bit more plush than that one out there on the lake!"

"Could you ask her if she'll take us for a ride sometime though, Spencer?" asked Sophie.

"Well, she's not here this weekend. She spends some here and goes back home on others."

Then Gillian's face broke into a grin as she thought of an idea.

"But never mind about that. I fancy a little test drive up the river. Come with me and *I'll* take you over to the prep school and back again!"

"You?" asked Sophie. "Can you drive a boat?"

"I've taken the wheel of my mother's on several occasions!" boasted Gillian.

"You would need permission to take the one on the Charterhouse lake, naturally," pointed out Benita, calmly.

"Oh, don't worry about all that nonsense!" scoffed Gillian. "I'm the headmistress's daughter and she knows I'm quite capable. She won't mind. If any of the other mistresses see us and have a problem with it, then they can take it up with her. So, who's coming with me?"

"I will!" said Melanie, without hesitation.

But there was a pause as everybody else thought more about the proposal.

"Well, *I'm* up for the challenge," said Sophie.

"What about the rest of you?" asked Gillian.

Imelda and Rachel looked at each other.

"I suppose it might be a bit of a dare," said Imelda.

"If you're sure that you can do it, and Mrs Spencer won't mind," added Rachel.

"I'm positive," insisted Gillian. "That just leaves you, Davis. Are you in?"

Benita snorted. "Absolutely not, Spencer! You must be joking. For one thing, there's no way that you're qualified to drive that boat, so if anything happens to it, we'll all be in big trouble. But even if it doesn't, we're *bound* to be seen – and heard from the sound of the motor – and somehow, I don't think the mistresses will be very pleased."

"Don't you listen to a word I say Davis, you moron?" retorted Gillian. "My mother-"

"Your mother isn't here," Benita interrupted her. "Therefore somebody else is in charge until the weekend is over. It'll be most likely be Mrs Baldwin who'll be deciding what to do about it."

"Don't be so certain about that, Davis," said Gillian. "You like to be so sensible and all high and mighty, but you don't know as much as you think sometimes. Of course, Mouse isn't here because she's a Mummy's Girl, but if she was then we all know *she* wouldn't get involved either. She'd wet her skirt immediately and go scurrying away!"

Melanie chortled.

"Who?" asked Sophie.

"Mouse. That's what I call Radcliffe," Gillian told her.

Sophie smirked. "That's a good one, Spencer! Yeah. She'd be halfway to the library by now!"

Benita got up. "Well, you lot can do what you like. I'm not coming with you." She flounced out.

"Well, we're wasting time," urged Gillian. "If we're going to do it, we'd better do so soon, or else the light will be fading too much. All those who are coming, follow me."

She went out of the recreation room door, and after glancing at each other briefly, the rest did as she suggested.

***

Gillian took charge when they reached the boat.

"You four get in, and then I'll untie the rope."

The girls clambered aboard from the edge of the bank and sat down in the back.

Gillian unattached the boat from its mooring, and then hopped on to stand at the front.

Operating the controls, she activated the motor. Then she opened the throttle and the boat eased forward.

"All aboard!" she shouted to those behind her, as they began to move away.

The controls were a little bit stiff – much more so than she'd been used to on her mother's boat. She managed to shift the wheel slightly to steer this boat forward, but they only needed to travel in a straight line to the other end of the lake where the prep school was situated.

The girls all laughed and giggled as they went further along and could see the college campus passing by across the meadow to their left. There was more meadowland to their right. Then there was open space of grassland with trees and bushes.

After opening the throttle, Gillian had struggled to check the boat's speed and they were travelling at quite a speed of knots. The prep school soon came into view. Gillian began to pull on the brake and prepared to turn the wheel so that she could turn the boat around

before the lake's end and go back again. But like the throttle, both were proving harder than she'd expected to manoeuvre.

Imelda shifted forward.

"I say. We're coming in a bit fast, aren't we Spencer?" she observed. "You are going to turn round and take us back to the college, I hope!"

"Alright. I know what I'm doing, Thomas!" retorted Gillian, panting from the effort.

As Imelda watched her, for the first time she began to have some doubts. She rarely worried about most things, but now she was.

Mrs Moreton's small boat was moored outside of her house, just by the side of the prep school, facing in the direction of the college. As they began to approach the end of the lake, Gillian was turning the wheel and their boat was moving to the right. She needed to turn a full 180 degrees in order to return back upstream. But they were still going much too fast, and she couldn't control the boat. As she was completing the turn, they were right up beside the prep school headmistress's boat, and as they straightened up, the left side of theirs crashed into the right side of hers with a loud crunch. The impact tipped their boat over and all the girls fell into the lake with squeals and yelps.

Luckily, nobody was really hurt and being close to the bank the lake was shallow. Everybody clambered to their feet, a little shaken and wet through.

"Spencer!" Imelda spat some water out of her mouth (it tasted disgusting, she thought), "I thought you said that you knew what you were doing!"

"*Shut up, Thomas!*" snarled Gillian, rudely.

The sound of the crash had brought Roz Moreton out of her house. She rushed to the edge of the bank and stood open mouthed at

what she saw. The college's boat was beached on its side and the engine had cut out. There was a large dent in the side of her own.

"What the blazes is going on?" she cried. She looked around trying to see a mistress but couldn't find one. "Who is in charge of you?"

"I'm sorry Mrs Moreton," said Gillian. "Sophie here, and the others were keen to have a trip on the college's boat up to the end of the lake and back. I said I'd take them myself as I'd driven my mother's own vessel on occasions. But the darn thing's so unresponsive. It wasn't my fault we crashed into your boat, but I'm sorry about that!"

Roz went purple with fury. "You fool Gillian! You had no right to do anything of the kind. Only *mistresses* have the authority to drive that boat!"

She glanced at the other girls anxiously for a moment. "Are any of you hurt?"

"No, Mrs Moreton," they all replied, as they got out of the lake and stepped back on to the bank.

"Well, you're all very lucky not to have had a more serious accident," she continued, as her anger boiled over. "And just look what you've done to my boat!"

Having got over the shock of what had just happened, Sophie couldn't help sniggering. She hated Mrs Moreton for the humiliation she'd made her suffer in the prep school assembly hall, and was highly delighted that Gillian's accident had caused her boat to be damaged.

"It's not funny, Sophie!" snapped Mrs Moreton, furiously. She put her hand on her hip and rounded on the girl, pointing a finger from her other hand. "How dare you laugh under such circumstances? You've got a darn cheek! I might have known you'd be involved in something like this."

"Right!" she ordered. "Go into my house, the lot of you." She pointed the way with her finger. "I shall ring your housemistresses at once to tell them what's happened!"

***

A few minutes later Roz Moreton put down the phone in her private study, after speaking to the housemistresses in charge of the girls at the seniors. In front of her desk were Gillian, Sophie, Melanie, Imelda, and Rachel.

It had taken a few moments to sort out, as Mrs Baldwin had needed to phone the headmistress for advice on what action they were permitted to take in her absence, given that her daughter was involved. Luckily she had been at home.

"Right," asserted Mrs Moreton. "I'm going to drive you all back to the college, and deliver you to your houses where Mrs Dewhurst in your case, Sophie, and Mrs Baldwin for the rest of you, will be waiting at the door to greet you. They will take over from then onwards, and you will all have some explaining to do. Arrangements will be made to drive the boat back to the college. But let me say before we leave that I'm most disappointed in you all. As I said to Mrs Baldwin, I'm sorely tempted to involve the police after your reckless action damaged my boat, but I will refrain, and this will be kept an internal matter within Charterhouse. I'm particularly surprised at your stupidity, Imelda and Rachel. I would have expected better from you!"

Mrs Moreton reflected that if the girls had done this whilst still in the prep school, she would have been giving them all six of the best right now (Gillian and Sophie, who she thought likely to have been the ringleaders, the very best). But they were no longer under her charge now that they were in the main college, and she suspected much to her chagrin, that whilst Sophie, Imelda, Rachel, and Melanie would be disciplined, Gillian would be treated much more leniently.

She was still furious at the damage to her own boat though, and was determined that the mothers of all the girls would pay a contribution towards the cost of the repairs – and she would be so bold as to demand that Mrs Spencer be included...

***

Before the girls came back, Mrs Baldwin was on the phone to Mrs Dewhurst discussing what to do.

"I wish Mrs Spencer had put Sophie Brewster in 1F and Alexandra Radcliffe in 1H, Martha," Mrs Dewhurst was saying. "Then Brewster wouldn't be in my house!"

"Oh no, Maggie," remarked Mrs Baldwin. "Imagine what it would be like for me at Rovers House then. Gillian Spencer *and* Sophie Brewster under my responsibility!"

"Anyhow," she continued. "Normally with Elizabeth away at home, I'd say that we should take the responsibility ourselves to give them all a dressing down and cane them when they arrive back from up the river. But of course, as can often happen now, her daughter is involved, so we have to tread carefully. Blast the girl. We'd all like to beat the living daylights out of her but we're not allowed!

"Well, I've just spoken to Elizabeth on the phone. Above all else, she doesn't want news of this incident to leak out, so she is grateful to Mrs Moreton for not getting the police involved regarding her boat. She has agreed that we can simply gate the girls in their houses for the rest of the weekend, apart from meal times – Gillian included. Then the headmistress can do what she wants with them all when she returns tomorrow night, ahead of the new week."

"Agreed," said Mrs Dewhurst. "That's quite straightforward for me. But Gillian won't like that at Rovers House."

"Well that's just tough!" replied Mrs Baldwin. "Her mother's agreed to it, so if there's a problem then she can take it up with her."

Some mistresses lived in their own chambers at the college during term time. Others went back to live in regular private accommodation overnight and at weekends. There were those who did a combination of both. Mrs Spencer chose to live in the ones provided for her as headmistress most of the time and returned home to her husband on occasional weekends (though during the summer weeks she was often away on day 1 of a weekend, playing bowls for her local team in the Castra League – which involved home and away matches). Many mistresses who were single, lived in and those married and/or who might have children lived out, but there was no absolute rule. In fact, both Mrs Baldwin and Mrs Dewhurst lived at Charterhouse with their husbands during term time, in Rovers and Beavers houses, respectively. They each had children already grown up and left home. Whatever the case, there obviously had to be a certain number of mistresses there at any time during a term, in order to take responsibility for the girls under the charge of the college.

***

As they had been told to expect, Mrs Baldwin met the girls from Rovers House at the door. First they were ordered to shower and change into fresh clothes, before she shepherded them to her study upstairs.

"I cannot believe that this has happened on your first weekend at Charterhouse College!" exclaimed the housemistress. "What in the name of Divinity were you thinking of? You put yourselves in great danger by taking our boat without permission - which you were not fully capable of driving, Gillian. A couple of mistresses did see you pass the campus as you set off down the lake and informed me. We were going to have strong words with you when you got back, but then to top it all, you crashed it, causing damage

to both Miss Moreton's own boat and ours! What have you all got to say for yourselves?"

"Sophie and the others wanted a ride in the boat, Mrs Baldwin," began Gillian. "I've often taken the wheel of my mother's own boat, when we're on holiday. I knew that she wouldn't mind us taking the college's boat if I was captaining it, as she trusts me to be competent. But the stupid boat's controls don't work properly. They're too stiff!"

"*You* Gillian, are just a tad too young to be operating them," replied Mrs Baldwin, before adding sardonically, "And a competent 'captain' would not have crashed the boat!"

This time it was Imelda who tried and failed to stifle a laugh, whilst Gillian's face grew red with indignation.

"Silence!" Mrs Baldwin bellowed. "In fact, Gillian, the headmistress has decided that *all* of you should be gated here at Rovers House for the rest of the weekend, apart from meal times – and that includes you. Sophie will be under the same restriction at Beavers House. Mrs Spencer will see you all in her study when she returns to the college tomorrow night."

Gillian looked slightly surprised. "What? Me too? Are you sure about that?" she demanded. "I think perhaps you should check that you haven't misunderstood the headmistress's instruction."

"Don't be cocky with *me*, Gillian!" snapped Mrs Baldwin. "I am telling you what she has personally ordered. By all means phone her after I have finished, if you still doubt me."

Now Gillian flushed with annoyance. "As you wish," she replied, sulkily.

"What about the rest of you?" asked Mrs Baldwin. "Do you have anything to add?"

"It was a dare, Mrs Baldwin," said Imelda. "Sorry - we shouldn't have done it."

Though she hated to admit it, she was now wishing that they'd all listened to Benita.

"Sorry, Mrs Baldwin!" Rachel and Melanie echoed her.

"I think that it is Mrs Moreton who is owed the apology," observed Mrs Baldwin. "You are all very lucky that she is not involving the authorities. But for now, get out of my sight. And remember to stay in this house until Mrs Spencer summons you tomorrow evening, or you will be in even more trouble!"

**

The same thing happened to Sophie at Beavers House, with Mrs Dewhurst. She admitted that she had first mentioned the subject of the boat, but insisted that it had been Gillian's idea to take it down the lake herself, without permission. Gillian had said that she was fully capable of doing it, but had seemed to struggle with the controls and they had crashed into Mrs Moreton's boat whilst turning around to come back.

Maggie Dewhurst felt inclined to believe that this was broadly the gist of what had happened, and when she and Martha Baldwin compared notes afterwards they decided to tell Elizabeth Spencer that, when she returned. They would then hand the matter over to her to deal with as she wished.

**

All of the girls (with the exception of Gillian) went to their dormitory beds that night knowing that before the end of the

following one, they would be given a major dressing down in the headmistress's study. They also expected to be caned.

***

Meanwhile at The Grange, Alexandra went to her mother's bed. The mistress bedroom where she slept was situated directly above the front half of the parlour. This was the night of the week when they normally slept together. Since not long after her father had died it had been a routine occurrence. The bond between them had become ever stronger after his death and they had a particularly close relationship. Alexandra knew that her mother very much missed the intimacy that she had shared with him, and having her daughter there with her in the bed on just one night of the week helped fill the space that he had left. Alexandra was also aware that they were not the only ones to do it – indeed her mother had told her recently that she might be surprised at how many, and there was absolutely nothing wrong with it – but it was usually a private affair kept between two females who had especially intimate feelings for one another, often (though not always) in a situation where there was some absence of a much missed man.

Alexandra also felt a need for it. She was a girl who got anxious and nervous quite easily, and there were times when in her own bed that she woke up in the night and started worrying. When she had been small she had sometimes had nightmares, often resulting in her wetting the sheets. It was always a comfort having her mother there beside her, to snuggle up to and be held tight in her arms all night long. She soothed her and made her feel protected. But nobody else – not even Tom yet – knew that she shared a bed with her mother once a week. It *was* private, and Alexandra *really* didn't want the other girls at Charterhouse to know. She had enough taunts already about being a mummy's girl and some of them would, she knew, tease and laugh at her like never before. Gillian would have a field day if she knew the full extent of the love she received from her 'mummy' when she went home at the weekend.

Linda came into the bedroom and smiled at Alexandra lying on the same side of the bed as Robert had used to sleep on. She undressed and put her clothes away in the large wardrobe, then went into her bathroom. When she was ready for bed, Alexandra watched as she got into bed beside her and then pulled her close. Alexandra gratefully slipped her arms around her mother's waist as she was held. They exchanged kisses.

"Well, that's your first week at the Charterhouse College over with then, darling," remarked Linda. "How do you feel?"

"It's been OK, Mother," replied Alexandra. "The lessons have been quite challenging, but I've worked hard."

"I know you have sweetheart and judging by what I saw from your exercise books this morning, you've done well. I'm pleased with you." Linda kissed her daughter again and Alexandra smiled happily.

"The first week is always the worst, but now that you've been around the timetable once – apart from the first two periods of your first day – you're into the routine and it'll get easier. But for tonight my darling, you can simply relax and sleep in your mother's arms."

"Thank you, Mother. They're the best!" Alexandra kissed her mother and their grip on her tightened as the kiss was returned with interest. She murmured softly.

"A tickle monster might come for you first though!" Linda grinned in mock wickedness, and pushed her backwards. Then she began to tickle her all over, slowly at first, and then faster and faster. Alexandra giggled and squealed, and her body thrashed about uncontrollably.

"It's just as well that this is a queen-sized bed, sweetheart!" joked Linda, after she had finally relented and let her daughter regain control of herself. "I remember you almost falling out of your own when I did that to you when you were small!"

"You know how ticklish I am, Mother," replied Alexandra, smiling. "And you're still bigger than me, too."

Alexandra still had some years of growth to come, but even when reaching full maturity she would in fact still be slightly shorter than her tall mother.

"That's true," admitted Linda. "You are, and I am still! But Mother is going to hold her little daughter so tight tonight, Alexandra, my darling. You need have no worry about that!"

She moved across and wrapped her arms back around her daughter. Alexandra slipped without hesitation into Linda's embrace, her heart beating in anticipation. This was the night she looked forward to all week long – when she could be with her mother all the way through and go to sleep in her arms after their intimacy – up until now often sucking her thumb too. On all other days she was kissed goodnight in her own bed, and in a way that she liked, but on this day when she was in her mother's it was always more special.

Lying side by side, Linda and Alexandra looked into each other's eyes. Linda saw the need inside of her daughter and immediately became at her most affectionate. She kissed Alexandra's lips and her shoulder length hair brushed against her daughter's neck. Alexandra returned the kiss and then felt herself being drawn further into her mother's body as she was squeezed and given another longer kiss. She murmured contentedly and rested her head against her mother's shoulder.

Linda stroked her daughter's long blonde hair, brushing her fingers through the tips and giving Alexandra tingles. She ran them lightly down her back and over her thighs. Alexandra's sensitive skin rippled and she oozed with pleasure. Her mother's touch was always so soft and she did in a way that set her senses aflame. She looked up into her eyes and felt a message of such love and warmth that she felt more safe and protected than at any other time that week.

Then her mother shifted slightly, and held her tighter than ever, so that Alexandra's head was buried deep into her chest. Linda stroked her hair again and she felt tingles in her thighs. Her eyes closed briefly – both due to the late hour, and the ecstasy she was experiencing.

She heard her mother's voice in her ear. *"I can always make your eyes close, can't I darling?"*

Alexandra opened her eyes and saw her mother smiling at her. She smiled back.

"You make me feel so good, Mother! You know you do." She craned her neck slightly and kissed her.

Linda's loving always ended up dominating and she responded by kissing her daughter full on the lips six times, as she squeezed her tight in her arms again. They were long, warm and tender and Alexandra's heart fluttered against her mother's chest as her breath began to shorten. Linda's eyes met hers and her passion was plain for her daughter to feel. Alexandra's eyes closed again as she tingled and murmured with deep pleasure.

*"I love you with all of my heart, **my darling!**"* whispered her mother.

Alexandra's eyes opened once more and looked submissively into Linda's. She was like a baby needing all of her mother's love, and she wanted to keep gazing. The soft sound of her voice continued in Alexandra's ear, giving her a relaxing and soothing tingle, which made her feel even better.

*"Mother will hold you forever, **sweetheart!** I can hold you tighter still. Would you like me to?"*

The look in her daughter's eyes told her that she did, even before she whispered her reply hoarsely, *"Yes Mother!"*

*"Just stay in Mother's arms, and close your eyes, **my baby!**"* said Linda, as she did what she had promised.

Alexandra felt the sense of love and protection that she could only get from her mother, and she closed her eyes happily.

*"**Feel my kisses, darling!**"* whispered Linda, more lovingly than ever. *"**Keep your eyes closed and I'll kiss all your fears away. Then you can sleep!**"*

She planted a series of the softest kisses all over her daughter's face, intermingled with more whispered words. Gradually, after a couple more moments, Alexandra's senses relaxed, as the tingling in her ear from her mother's loving voice and the velvet touch of her kisses took effect. She was beginning to drift away.

*"**Goodnight, my darling!**"* whispered Linda, finally.

*"**Goodnight, Mother!**"* murmured Alexandra.

Soon she was asleep. As Linda gazed lovingly at her beloved daughter, she noted that for the first time in many weeks Alexandra's thumb wasn't in her mouth...

CHAPTER 41

At Charterhouse the following evening, the headmistress had returned and the girls involved in the boat crash on the lake were summoned to her study.

First she saw Gillian – her daughter – whilst the others waited outside.

"Well Gillian," she began. "This was certainly a surprise to me, when I got the telephone call yesterday. What happened? How did you manage to crash the thing?"

"The controls were so stiff they were barely operable." replied Gillian. "Not like ours. It's a pile of junk if you ask me!"

"The boat is quite old," admitted Elizabeth. "Charterhouse have had it for a long time. We probably should be thinking of replacing it if the budget allows us."

"Well, you might as well do that now," remarked Gillian.

"Now don't get too cheeky, girl!" said Elizabeth, holding up a hand. "You really shouldn't have done what you did. It's undeniable that you're officially far too young to be driving a boat up the lake, or anywhere else for that matter."

"I honestly didn't think you'd mind as I've driven our boat on lots of occasions," said Gillian,

"I do let you sail ours, but it's my own private vehicle, and I actually only do so when I think it's absolutely safe for you to do so and we're away from any prying eyes of the authorities," replied Elizabeth. "You've never done it without me on board. It certainly could have been a lot more serious yesterday afternoon. I'm going to give the rest of the girls six for their involvement in this, and as the one who personally drove the boat you really should get that much and more. I've considered suspensions, but you would have

to be included in that, therefore I will simply give all of you a warning. I *won't* cane you of course, but try not to do something quite like that again, Gillian! That is my official warning to you. We could have potentially had a bigger problem on our hands if dear Mrs Moreton had rung the police about what had been done to her boat. The one thing I never want is bad outside publicity, Gillian. It makes it so much more difficult for me to control situations – and to protect your interests."

"Why did you have to gate me like the others?" demanded her daughter.

"Yes, I'm sorry about that," said Elizabeth. "If I'd been here yesterday and dealt with the situation straight away then you wouldn't have been, but unfortunately I wasn't and something had to be done immediately before I returned, whilst Mrs Baldwin was deputising. As she was in temporary charge, then I could hardly argue that you should be excused even that, if you'd clearly been just as involved in the incident as the others. If you hadn't been involved, then those four girls outside would probably have been disciplined yesterday."

She smirked slightly at her daughter. "That boat is Mrs Moreton's pride and joy. She's absolutely livid!"

Privately, after being told the news, Elizabeth had wished that she'd been at the college over the weekend so that she could have seen Roz's face. She hadn't always been on the best of terms with Mrs Moreton – mainly because the prep school headmistress had refused to grant her daughter any special favours whilst under her charge. But things would be different now that Gillian was here in the main college. Perversely, Elizabeth felt a certain pleasure at what her daughter had done – though that wouldn't stop her dealing with the other girls in a firm manner.

Then she became serious again. "The other thing though, is that Mrs Moreton is demanding that all the mothers of you girls pay a contribution towards the cost of repairing her boat. She's including me in that, and I think I will have to cough up. I'm not a poor

woman, but neither am I rolling in as much money as some of the mothers of girls who come here, so I am a little cross with you about that."

"Oh," replied Gillian. "Sorry about that, Mother."

Elizabeth straightened in her chair. "Alright. Well, I'd better get this lecture and the punishments started. Now remember the agreement, Gillian. I'll allow you freedom to more or less do as you wish and no mistress will discipline you. I don't always wish to concern myself with what you might be getting up to. I'll use my influence to see that you're granted certain privileges and patronages. But in return you must do favours for me when I require them, and give me any useful information that you hear which I might use to my advantage – and hopefully yours too."

"I understand!" Gillian grinned. She had always been a particularly naughty girl, and Elizabeth had never been prepared to take any serious action against her. Instead she had always spoilt her, and now that she was responsible for her at Charterhouse, she was determined to ensure that she progressed to the very top and went on to Castra or Orpington university – even if it meant sometimes using underhand tactics and regardless of how she behaved in her classes on a daily basis.

Gillian was eventually to become Head Girl of the college, though she would ultimately be expelled under scandalous circumstances before completing her studies. Right now she was delighted at the thought of being able to be as badly behaved as she liked and to get away with the sort of things that she had been regularly disciplined for in the prep school – and more besides. No girl had been caned as many times as she had whilst she was there.

"I only wish that I could have got Radcliffe involved," she continued. "But she's a Mummy's Girl of course, so she wasn't around, and even if she had been, I bet she'd have scurried away like the little mouse that she is, as quickly as she possibly could. I still can't believe she got that perfect score in the maths test on our first day!"

"I wouldn't worry about Alexandra Radcliffe, Gillian," remarked Elizabeth. "The girl's quite bright, but you can be cleverer. She's so quiet that most people won't even know she's there unless she's forced to speak, and she'll pose no threat to you getting the things that you want. I'll be making sure that she doesn't, too. As you say, she's a Mummy's Girl, so she's only here part of the time anyhow. Day pupils can never be seriously compared with boarders in terms of quality – just as arts and humanities subjects are grossly inferior to science, mathematics and Geratican language. Granted, her 'mummy' is Linda Radcliffe, the senior court administrator to the queen, but although she's an old Charterhouse girl, she can't directly interfere in what goes on here. There'd be trouble if she tried too – and she knows it. In theory she can make a complaint like she did that time when Alexandra was in the prep school, but as far as I'm concerned she can complain all she likes – I am in charge here, not her, and that's the end of it."

Some of these assertions would come back to haunt Elizabeth later.

"Having said that," she went on, "Do be a little careful if you're giving Alexandra a hard time, Gillian. Never underestimate what her mother *might* be capable of doing. I believe she has something of a reputation at court for being a mistress tactician!"

She stood up and picked up her cane from behind the desk.

"Right. Fetch me one of those cushions from the couch over there, would you Gillian?"

Whilst her daughter went to get it, she pulled out a chair from the side of the room. Taking the cushion from Gillian she laid it on the seat of the chair.

She eyed Gillian for a second. "Now. Eight strokes for your disgraceful behaviour, my girl!"

Elizabeth beat the cushion very hard with her cane eight times, with the intention that the sound would carry out into the corridor

outside the study and be heard by the other four girls. This she hoped would create the impression that Gillian had received the cane. When she had finished, Gillian put the cushion back in its place.

"OK. Go out and send the others in as you leave, Gillian," she ordered. "You remember what I suggested that you do?"

Gillian nodded with a smirk. As she went to the door, she quickly wiped it from her mouth.

She opened the door and stepped out, making a show of rubbing her bottom. "I've just been given eight," she told the girls stood waiting in trepidation. "Mrs Spencer says that you're all to go in now."

Then she walked quickly down the corridor. She was anxious to get as far away as possible, before she burst out laughing.

***

Elizabeth was stood in front of her desk, cane in hand, with the chair still beside her.

"I can only echo what I know your house mistresses told you yesterday!" she said, sternly. "You took the college's boat without authorisation, and drove it up the lake – Gillian specifically may have done that, but you must all take some responsibility for it. It was a highly dangerous and foolhardy thing to do, as none of you are anywhere near old enough to be qualified. As it was, you crashed our boat into Mrs Moreton's causing both to be damaged, but there could have been an even more serious accident. The college is indeed fortunate that the prep school headmistress agreed not to involve the authorities – and you girls are even more so! Every one of you is in serious enough trouble already, and I am giving you all a warning that if this happens again, then the culprits

will be *suspended!*" The headmistress smacked the seat of the chair with the cane at the end of her last sentence.

"I must also tell you that Mrs Moreton has demanded that the cost of repairing her boat be met by your mothers, and letters are already in the post to your homes informing them of this and the likely amount. I will in fact be one of those contributing personally, because as most of you may know, Gillian..."

"...is the headmistress's daughter!" interrupted Imelda. Rachel sniggered, and even Sophie couldn't resist a smile.

Mrs Spencer glanced briefly at the girls in surprise and then turned her head sharply towards Imelda. "Don't be impertinent girl! You are not here to make some kind of joke. Take those smirks off your faces, all of you. I imagine that your mothers will not find this funny, especially when they find out that it will cost them money! The amounts involved should not break their personal banks, but even so you would all do well to remember that they are already paying hefty fees to send you to this most prestigious college."

Finding out that a letter had been sent home by the college, did indeed come as a bit of a blow to the girls. It meant that their mothers would know what they had done and there was likely to be trouble the next time they saw them – which might now, some of them thought, be sooner than they had been expecting, should an urgent meeting in order to deal with the matter be considered necessary. Very often, slight indiscretions could be covered up and kept from them, but that clearly wouldn't be possible on this occasion.

"We do not tolerate this sort of behaviour and you are here to be punished," continued Elizabeth. "Form a queue please girls. Sophie, I believe that it was your initial observation of the boat that prompted this affair, therefore you will be first, followed by Melanie, then Rachel, and finally Imelda."

The girls were resigned to their fate and complied with the headmistress's orders.

"Right," said Elizabeth. "First girl, step forward to the chair, lower your skirt and pants and bend over the seat. You will be given six strokes of my cane. Once you have received the last one, stand up, raise your pants and skirt again and go and stand over there." She pointed to a spot beside one of the study walls. "Then the same for the second and so forth."

Some of the girls shuddered slightly. So, the rumour was true. If a girl was caned in Mrs Spencer's study, then she was forced to take it without the protection of a skirt over her bottom.

Sophie undid the necessary and crouched over the chair. Then she gripped the legs and gritted her teeth in preparation for the beating that was about to come. She was obviously no stranger to the cane and had little fear of it – though she had never experienced it without her skirt on. The headmistress gave her six strokes which made her eyes water. It was more painful than any caning that she'd received before, but at the age she was she still had a naturally naughty streak prevalent inside of her, and as she stood up and put her skirt back in place, she was defiantly determined that it wouldn't deter her from doing something considered against the rules if she wanted to in the future.

"Next!" ordered Mrs Spencer.

Melanie felt some trepidation at being beaten on her unprotected bottom as she too hadn't been caned like that before, but otherwise she felt the same about it as Sophie. She winced through it, and groaned slightly when she walked away from the chair afterwards. She would go on to commit many more offences at Charterhouse, a couple of which would be extremely serious and result in her eventually being caned again in this study.

Rachel was the most worried. She had never been caned by Mrs Moreton in the prep school, though she had on two occasions by her mistress, Miss Rivers. She was by no means somebody who was regularly in trouble. She and Imelda had been close friends since being at the prep school and would continue to be for the rest

of their years in education. They often thought alike, though Imelda was perhaps the more dominant - and more daring. If one of them decided to do something, then the other usually followed – though Rachel now bitterly regretted the decision that they had taken yesterday. She was expecting to be summoned home quite promptly after her mother received the letter from Charterhouse, to explain herself and probably get a sound telling off and thrashing too. But it certainly wouldn't be with her skirt and pants off. Rachel audibly cried out from the strokes administered by the headmistress when it was her turn, and was virtually in tears by the time it was over.

Finally it was Imelda's turn. Being the last girl in a group about to be beaten was sometimes considered the worst position, as it meant that she had to witness all the others receiving their fate before her, allowing any feelings of tension or anxiety that she might be experiencing to build to an uncomfortable degree. But Imelda had none of those concerns. In fact her mother had sometimes caned her bare bottom when she had done something especially bad at home, so she wasn't fazed as much as the rest by the headmistress's method.

Imelda was actually quite a good natured and good humoured girl who didn't often intentionally mean any serious harm, but she liked to get her own way. She was also impulsive and sometimes found temptation too much to resist. Particularly at home she could be very naughty, especially if she thought that she wouldn't get caught (and she sometimes wasn't). At school she had been caned on a handful of occasions, but she didn't go out of her way to get into trouble, generally concentrating on her studies and leaving the blatant troublemaking to the likes of Gillian Spencer.

After all that had been said though, the matter of the cane was of little consequence to her. Never in Imelda's young life, either at home or in school, had she considered the possibility of receiving it before doing something that she knew was wrong, and being caned didn't really bother her at all. The beating, when it came, was harder than her mother had ever given her, but she still bore it with little visible discomfort or reaction – which greatly

exasperated Elizabeth who liked to see the girls who she punished broken. Even though she had been told that this girl had actually been the one to apologise on behalf of the group yesterday, she was still annoyed at the way Imelda had spoken earlier and caused the others to laugh in the middle of her lecture to them. She had to resist the urge to repeat the dosage.

"Right. Go back to your houses," said the headmistress. "I don't wish to see any of you in here under these circumstances again!"

She would in fact, see most of them again at various times.

"Yes, Mrs Spencer!" the girls replied, and hurried out, more than happy to comply with her last order.

As the door closed and Elizabeth was left alone, she put down her cane and sat behind her desk.

Confounded girls. They're all a blasted nuisance, she thought to herself.

Elizabeth Spencer had originally been a scientist, but her career had stalled and she had instead embarked upon a teaching career which had seen her becoming a science mistress at Charterhouse. The irony was that she had never been greatly fond of children – especially girls - but that was the path she had ended up following. In truth she had never been the best of mistresses either, often being too impatient with girls who struggled to understand her subject and too quick to lose her temper badly when any of them misbehaved in her lessons. She had had a reputation for sometimes being a little over-zealous with her cane in relieving her frustration and had once almost got into trouble for doing so. Despite this, Elizabeth had eventually got results and been made head of the department – she was actually the best qualified in the subject and most experienced in the field, of all the science mistresses. At the interview she'd genuinely best demonstrated her capability for running the department and dealing with the other mistresses – at least in theory.

Only a year ago she had become the headmistress. Hers had been a somewhat controversial appointment in some parts of the college – several of the mistresses, including some department heads considered her to be unsuitable for the post – but she was on good personal terms with some members of the board of governors who had ensured that she was given the position. A generous personal payment to the chairwoman had also helped.

Elizabeth did believe very strongly in traditional discipline, and there were many occasions when she felt fully justified in punishing the girls who genuinely transgressed in the college – and that most other people would agree. However, she personally disliked some of the girls who she had used to teach before becoming the headmistress. The tiresome little brats had caused her no end of headaches. In one or two cases she also had issues with their haughtily mannered mothers and one thing which she wanted to try and do, was to widen the college entrance scope slightly, so that it wasn't quite so exclusively for those who could afford the highest fees. Though sometimes a perfectly charming and agreeable woman, there was also a spiteful, vengeful, and even occasionally sadistic side to her nature when she was crossed, and now that she had the run of the college and Gillian was in the main school, she planned to engage her daughter in ploys to get the relevant girls to do things which would give her the chance to punish them. She also wanted Gillian to undermine the authority of certain mistresses by causing a lot of trouble in their classes, in order to give her the excuse to say that they were incompetent and incapable – and then get rid of them, to be replaced by ones who would not give her problems and let her run the college how she saw fit.

Gillian, who was the only child that she had from her marriage to James – currently a taxi driver – had not been planned (a fact which Elizabeth kept secret), and in fact had been conceived before the marriage – which was particularly frowned upon at the time. But once she had been born, Elizabeth had been determined that only the best would do for her in everything which was part of the reason why she'd been so badly spoilt. Also, whilst never flinching in her duty or desire to cane girls at the college for any

perceived bad behaviour, paradoxically she never felt able to apply the same measure to her own daughter in any part of life. Their family home was also in Greenacres – on the other side of town to the Radcliffes.

In most ways Elizabeth was quite conservative in her beliefs, but she had gradually become more and more passionate in some of her political convictions - most notably that men should become more prominent in Geratican society - and she had radical ideas about how to try and achieve this. These views were considered highly controversial and had set her on a collision course with many traditionalists - of which Alexandra Radcliffe's mother, Linda, was an extremely vocal member. Again she found it difficult to get along with some of these people – particularly the women - and could allow her temper to get the better of her judgement. Elizabeth Spencer's desire to have a relationship which more reflected her own views on the subject was also starting to cause problems in her marriage. James preferred to be a more traditional man. Elizabeth was in addition convinced that boys should be formally educated in the same way that girls were, and was hoping to establish a special school which would specifically do this.

She had always been sceptical of the theory that should the head of state ever not be a queen, then 'the Divine Being' would abandon Geratica and condemn her world to destruction. In fact, she was convinced that it was nonsense.

***

Benita was already in the dormitory of Rovers House when Imelda, Rachel and Melanie returned.

"What happened? Did you all get six?" she asked Imelda. "Spencer said that she got eight, as she was the one who had the idea to drive the boat."

Gillian was laid on her bunk bed, smirking inwardly to herself.

"Yes. And we had to pull down our skirts and pants, too!" replied Imelda.

Benita raised her eyebrows. "Well, I don't like to say that I told you so – but I did. I wouldn't have wished that method of punishment on you, though. Sorry to hear that." She had only ever got the cane a couple of times – on the hand. The offences had been relatively minor.

"That's alright. It didn't worry me," declared Imelda, almost boastfully. "My mother's pulled down my skirt and pants and whacked me, on more than one occasion!"

The only punishment that Imelda hoped never to suffer was a horse whipping. Her mother, Katherine Thomas, held very conservative views on crime and punishment (she had in fact been one of those who'd protested at the court's decision to abolish the death penalty. Elizabeth Spencer had been another). A year ago, together with her husband, Philip, she had taken Imelda and her younger sister, Olivia, to the royal palace in Avermore to watch a juvenile girl being horse whipped in the front courtyard by Queen Alexandra and the senior court administrator for some atrocious offence that she had committed. It was the one time that Imelda had seen Alexandra's mother.

The girl had wet herself lying face down on the stage of which the ceremony had traditionally taken place for centuries, just before getting the first of her due lashings from Queen Alexandra. Imelda had been shocked to see this, thinking only a boy could possibly be brought to do such a thing as they were the weaker sex. But her mother had assured her that such a reaction was not uncommon and that only the most utterly stupid and foolish child (which she knew Imelda was most certainly not), regardless of whether they were a girl or a boy, wouldn't feel tremendous fear before getting a flogging such as that ordered by a juvenile court. Mrs Thomas had warned her daughters that she believed neither would be any exception to experiencing such a feeling if ever she was about to

take her own riding whip to their bare skin. She had been satisfied to see their reaction to what they had witnessed generally, which had been her main intention in bringing them. She was almost sure that her youngest daughter, though appearing to be nowhere near as clever as the older one, would have the common sense not to risk putting herself in a position where she might be whipped for her actions. But she couldn't be so confident about Imelda.

Though Imelda most definitely didn't want to receive a horse whipping herself, she thought it perfectly acceptable for those sentenced by a juvenile court to be thrashed, as in her view they probably deserved it. She was already starting to inherit some of her mother's views. Imelda had never been able to imagine herself doing anything that would truly warrant more than a standard caning. She hoped that her mother would not consider this incident with the boat to be one of those things. (On this occasion she wouldn't, eventually accepting her daughter's protestations that she had only agreed to go in the boat because Gillian had assured them that the headmistress wouldn't mind, and that the accident had been entirely Gillian's fault – though she would still give her a hiding for being so stupid as to get involved, and causing her to have to put her hand in her pocket to compensate for it. However, in a few years time when Imelda was actually a young adult, her luck would run out when she finally went too far and her mother lost patience).

There was sometimes a personality clash between Katherine and Imelda Thomas, but if Imelda confided in her father he would sometimes sympathise but usually say that her mother knew best.

CHAPTER 42

The next morning, Alexandra arrived at Charterhouse for the start of a new week and went up to their form room ready for registration.

She was surprised when no sooner had she sat down at her desk, Benita came in. Normally it took a bit longer for the boarders to arrive after their breakfast in the dining hall.

"I thought I'd talk to you before the others get here," she began, immediately. "You won't believe what happened on the first day of the weekend!"

"What?" asked Alexandra.

"I don't know whether you noticed that the college's boat is missing from the lake when you arrived? That's because it's been put out of action, and we're probably going to get a new one. When we were in the recreation room of the house, your old friend Sophie Brewster came sauntering in and happened to mention that she'd seen the boat out on the lake. She wondered if someone might take us for a ride in it some time, up to the prep school and back, like Mrs Moreton used to when we were there. Mrs Spencer went home for the weekend, and Gillian – she's the headmistress's daughter you know - then had a brilliant wheeze that she could drive the boat herself up the lake to the end and back again!"

Alexandra had smiled at Benita's sarcastic definition of Gillian, but her eyes widened upon hearing what she'd just been told.

"And she did?" she enquired.

"Not half!" remarked Benita. "It was me who pointed out that even she needed permission and in any case, it was absolutely absurd to think that she could do it herself, and surely a mistress somewhere was bound to notice? Oh, she boasts. My mother often lets me take the wheel of her own private boat, and she knows I'm *competent*.

She'd be perfectly happy for me to take the college's boat up the lake myself! There's no need to ask anybody's permission and they can take it up with my mother if they've got a problem with it. I refused to have anything to do with the mad caper, but to my utter astonishment, Imelda, Rachel, Melanie, and Sophie all went with her! I couldn't believe that they could be so reckless.

"Well, what do you know? It turned out that despite all her brash words, Gillian didn't find it as easy as she'd expected. They made it down to the other end of the lake and saw the prep school, but guess what? When the *competent captain, Gillian Spencer*, turned her boat around to begin the return journey, she lost control and they crashed into the side of Mrs Moreton's which was moored outside of her house!"

Alexandra gaped. "In the name of Geratica! Were they all OK?"

"Apparently, the impact tipped the boat over and they all got a soaking in the water!" said Benita. She couldn't resist a smirk. "They were all fine though. It could have been worse, and the water was quite shallow there, not far from the bank. I must admit I couldn't help laughing when I thought of them all falling into the lake, but Mrs Moreton was truly livid at the damage to her boat – Imelda said that she'd never seen her so furious, and she even mentioned calling the police, but decided against it to keep this internal - and they were all in big trouble when she brought them back to the houses in her car - as I'd told them that they would be. It was Gillian who egged them all on, but they didn't have to follow her.

"Apart from when they ate in the dining hall, they were gated in the houses for the rest of the weekend, until Mrs Spencer returned last night. Then they were summoned to her study and from what I've heard, she rollicked them and gave them all a right good caning without their skirts on! Gillian was seen first, alone and said that she'd been given eight when she came out, and then the rest were given six, together. Some of them say that they can still feel some pain this morning! But not only that, Mrs Moreton wants the cost for repairing her boat to be contributed to by all their mothers

– which will include Mrs Spencer. The college has sent out letters to them about it, and they'll be getting them very soon. Between you and me, Alexandra, I don't think some members of our form are looking forward to the next time that they speak with their mothers – and probably not Sophie Brewster, either. Personally, I don't get the cane very often at home, but I think I might have done for this."

Alexandra thought that if she had been involved in this, to say that she wouldn't be looking forward to the next time she spoke with her mother would be the understatement of the year. In her case there was no 'might' about it – she *definitely* would have got the cane. She was very glad that she had been at home and safely out of it. It was true what Benita said. The other girls had been a bit stupid to go with Gillian – once they had they were all guilty, even if it had only been Gillian driving the boat – they'd had no authority to take it, they'd put themselves in potential danger, and they'd made it worse by causing the damage which their mothers now had to help pay to repair. The more that Alexandra considered it, she wondered if she might even have been whipped for this. Like Benita though, she did find the image of all the girls tumbling into the water quite amusing – particularly when she thought about Gillian.

Then the door opened and the girl herself came into the classroom, with Melanie close behind and Imelda and Rachel on their way.

"I thought that you bolted your breakfast down a bit fast, Davis!" snapped Gillian. "Couldn't wait to get over here to see Mouse and tell her what happened at the weekend I suppose? No doubt you're having a good gloat."

Benita simply raised her eyebrows without replying.

"Yeah, well don't you two goody goodies start getting too cocky and complacent," continued Gillian. "There'll come a time for each of you when you'll come a cropper and fall from grace. You mark my words!"

The headmistress's daughter was determined that it would happen – even if she eventually had to manipulate the circumstances. Until then she would wait.

Her mother had also subtly indicated to her that if she was ever given a plausible reason, then she would not be averse to disciplining Imelda Thomas again...

PART 9

CHAPTER 43

Phoebe Porter appeared to have vanished without trace, and was now officially missing.

In Queen Alexandra's study at the palace, the situation was being discussed.

"The police inform me that they are baffled, Ma'am," said Linda. "Miss Porter appears to have returned home from work on 3/32/05 – a week ago yesterday - but not been seen since. There is evidence that she was beginning preparations for dinner, however she is not in the house, and nobody appears to have witnessed her leave. Nor has she been at her place of work. The woman is now officially classed as a missing person. The court is obviously taking some interest in the case, given that we know she is – for the moment at least – Your Majesty's sole heir. But obviously, we have never believed that she will ever succeed to the throne."

"Indeed," replied the queen. "Well this is clearly rather disturbing news – and not least for those her know her. I hope that she is found as soon as possible, and the mystery is solved."

Fiona listened intently. She was as certain as she could be that no one had seen her enter Phoebe's house, and there was absolutely no possibility that her deceased body could be found by anybody on Geratica. It didn't matter what happened if it was found on Geraticai. Fiona was confident that the mystery would never be solved, and few people on Geratica were actually aware that the woman had a claim to the throne in any case.

"Perhaps this brings the issue of me marrying with a view to subsequently securing my successor, into greater focus," continued Queen Alexandra.

Fiona took a breath and prepared to speak. She had been thinking of a plan for the past few days, which she hoped might at least

indirectly delay any such possible marriage for the immediate future.

"Ma'am," she began, "I have been considering that subject, and specifically what will happen in the immediate aftermath of the event. I have a proposal to make. Your Majesty will obviously want a place to take her husband for the night after the reception. What I am suggesting is that we create a brand new specific location for it, in readiness for the happy event – whenever that may be."

The queen looked at her, enquiringly. This sudden idea from her court administrator was a surprise to her. But she was interested.

"Oh? And do you have anywhere particularly in mind? Tell me more."

"Certainly, Ma'am," said Fiona. "We could perhaps construct some kind of deluxe marital suite, complete with all the latest luxuries, furniture, and gadgets, as well as a well-stocked supply of fine beverages and naturally, a queen- sized bed! I recently visited the Geratica Hotel and had a sumptuous meal. I noticed that the whole of the top floor has rooms not occupied by guests. They are currently used as storage space and other such things. It is a considerable area and might be an ideal place to consider if the existing rooms could be taken out. That would obviously need to be done first, and a suite designed, which could then be built in their place."

"We may be getting a little ahead of ourselves here, Ma'am," observed Linda. "Is Your Majesty decided that she would like to spend her first night of matrimony in a public hotel? We would obviously need to ensure that there was maximum security in the building whilst you were there."

"Well it is Geratica's finest hotel, Linda," remarked Queen Alexandra. "There will inevitably always be a certain division between a monarch and her people, but at the same time I always like them to feel that I am not completely remote from them. The

idea has merit. Of course, precisely when I might have the cause to use the suite for that function is impossible to determine - nor indeed the identity of my husband!"

"It's usually me who is arguing that we don't need to rush into things without some thought, when it comes to these sort of matters, Linda," said Fiona. She was sensing that she might be making some headway over this.

"The specific matter of Her Majesty marrying is a totally separate issue from that which you are referring to!" retorted Linda.

"We could in fact ensure that there were no other guests in the hotel at the time you were there, Ma'am, if you wished for total privacy," suggested Fiona.

"Hmm. The court would need to think about that," mused the queen.

"There is another thing that could come from this, too" added Fiona. "Once the suite was built – which could take a little time – then any Geratican newlyweds who were prepared to pay the money could stay there, both before and after you had the use of it. That might be of great interest to the hotel, as it could generate considerable extra business – and the court might possibly get a share of the profits. It would be probably be quite something for any Geratican to be able to say that they spent the first night of their marriage in the same suite as their queen did – or will do!"

"I believe that you may be on to something, Fiona," said Queen Alexandra. "Very well. Let the court look into the matter and see if it can be done."

Before Fiona could reply, Linda stepped in to take charge.

"As you wish, Ma'am. The court will obviously need to carry out a cost analysis to see if all of this is affordable. If so, we will look into whether the changes to the top floor of the hotel are feasible and and assuming that is the case, endeavour to find a contractor

who can carry them out. Then we will need to find an interior designer who can draw up a plan for the proposed suite before it is constructed. Hopefully, if it can be done, there will be little or no disruption to the rest of the building whilst any work is taking place."

Fiona coughed lightly in a deliberate fashion.

"Ma'am. By 'the court,' I assume that Linda means that *she* intends to lead this project? As a matter of fact, I was rather hoping that I might take the responsibility for this myself. I am quite keen to get some more of that, and this could be done in conjunction with my role in charge of your domestic and catering staff within the palace. I am of course aware of the need for cost analysis, but I believe that I am very financially competent."

"This is a new initiative being sought by Her Majesty's court, Fiona!" countered Linda. "*I* have the responsibility for dealing with such matters."

"Technically you are of course correct, Linda," said the queen. "But actually on this occasion, I think that I might agree to Fiona's request to begin looking into it and hopefully get the process underway. You are very busy with other matters, Linda. This is after all her idea, and it might be time for her to get her teeth into something and show what she can do. You have been at court for many years now, whereas Fiona is newer, therefore I am sure that she has ambitions which she would like to fulfil, just as you certainly did when you were more junior, Linda."

"I still do, Ma'am!" asserted Linda, with a hint of indignation in her voice. "Let *no one* be in any doubt about that."

"You are quite correct, Ma'am., I do have ambitions," confirmed Fiona. "And this particular project is a major one of those."

She reflected that Queen Alexandra and Linda couldn't begin to imagine the true extent of her ambition, if her overall secret mission was to eventually be concluded successfully.

"But I do not wish to upset the feelings of the senior court administrator, or tread on her toes," she continued, not entirely truthfully. "As I have suggested before, Ma'am, perhaps an idea would be for me to take an office a short distance outside of the court administration department itself, as in my main role I do not often become very involved with the actual affairs of court business outside the palace, unlike the rest of Linda's little empire."

"No. I still think that the current system works quite well," commented Queen Alexandra. "You are her deputy after all, and if she is ever away – either on holiday or occasional extended engagements with me, then you do have the responsibility for covering Linda's position in her absence."

Linda had also privately indicated to her - in a discreet fashion – that she wanted the court administrator kept as close to her as possible, so that she could continue to indirectly keep a check on what her deputy was doing, as she performed some of the responsibility that the now senior court administrator had used to carry out herself. Fiona's presence at court would continue to be a slightly sore point for Linda, until she was forced to leave – though for entirely different reasons to any of those which the senior court administrator could have envisaged at this time - when her true identity became known. Her mission would of course ultimately not be successful and Queen Victoria of Geraicai's plan would fail. Linda's daughter would be instrumental in the cause of this failure. But that was all in the future.

"However, I do grant you the responsibility for overseeing this project, Fiona," continued the queen. "Obviously, you must ensure that it can be done within the court's budget, but otherwise, if it is possible to achieve, I will support it. This is my final decision – so let that be that."

"Very good, Ma'am, and thank you." replied Fiona. She was feeling triumphant. If she was careful, Fiona was confident that she could spin the whole process out for some time, by ensuring that

all the various stages took as long as possible. She hoped that for as long as this was going on, and Queen Alexandra really was intending to spend the first night of any possible future marriage in the suite (Fiona was now determined to ensure that she did, if she couldn't ultimately prevent her from marrying at all) then she would at least delay the wedding until its completion. This would theoretically buy Queen Victoria more valuable time to secure her longed for heir, but in practice, Fiona was becoming more and more doubtful as to whether that would ever happen under her current plan. She now thought it quite likely that she would be staying on Geratica for a while longer, and if this suite could be got up and running under her strict control, then her future here could be fairly secure for the time being, without her necessarily having to take much direct action. She didn't intend to pay too many visits to Geraticai in the near future. Life here was – for the moment at least – comfortable.

"I trust that you are in agreement Linda?" asked Queen Alexandra.

"I still believe that I could easily absorb this new responsibility into those that I have already, Ma'am," replied Linda. Inside of her, frustration was beginning to build into a wave of fury, but she did her best to conceal it. She knew from years of experience that once the queen had definitely made up her mind and declared an order, then that was the end of the matter and there was no point in any more argument. Linda strongly believed that this *should* be the case, too. The Geratican state was an absolute monarchy, and the queen's decision was final. It was just that she was used to Queen Alexandra giving orders that were broadly in line with her own opinions, and by and large they normally were – often because they were of the same mind, but sometimes because the queen was inclined to be persuaded by her most senior advisor. On rare occasions when she went against her, Linda had to accept it, but it wasn't in her nature to concede easily.

"I would appreciate it though, Fiona, if you kept me fully informed of every development." she went on. "In fact, I order you to."

"Oh yes. Of course, Linda!" replied Fiona. It was not a pledge that she had much intention of entirely keeping to, partly because she was minded to ensure that there would often be little to inform Linda of anyhow, and she couldn't care less about her order. Fiona was more delighted than she had been for a long time since she had started working at this palace. She felt that she'd got one over on Linda, who she knew would not be pleased, and Fiona always enjoyed doing that – fleeting though the moments were when it occurred.

"Excellent," declared the queen.

***

Back in the privacy of her own office, Linda fumed. She always hated it when she couldn't have absolute control over any initiative that the court proposed. Since first becoming court administrator Linda had dominated her department more than any of her predecessors - so completely that every single piece of court business was introduced and implemented in the exact way that she wanted, in conjunction with the queen. Fewer of the court's bills had been rejected by parliament under her stewardship than any of those same predecessors, too, and she ruled her 'little empire' with a rod of iron.

Fiona's arrival had at times she felt, undermined her authority, though she had been forced to accept Queen Alexandra's decision that there was a need for another court administrator and that the woman was ideal for the position. As a result, Linda had lost the day-to-day control of the palace domestic and catering staff, and although she had also been promoted to a new post of senior court administrator at the same time, and therefore retained overall responsibility, it had still rankled with her. Linda did indeed try to continue keeping her eye on things, and this in itself could cause some tension, if Fiona felt that she was 'looking over her shoulder' too much. Fiona could be quite a dominant personality herself when she wanted to be, and just occasionally there could be terse

exchanges between them in meetings with the queen, if she chose to challenge Linda's assertions and her will - in a way that had not happened before.

By no means did they disagree on everything though, and most of the time their relationship was perfectly civil, but never close (despite being neighbours). They had some similarities and shared similar tastes. However, the court administration department had grown used to their occasional 'tiffs' (as they privately referred to their quarrels, though not always knowing the cause). Sometimes these even resulted in the two women barely communicating for a short while, and they knew when to 'keep their heads down'.

In Linda's view, the proposed marital suite was very much a project that she should primarily deal with. Particularly where the court's finances were concerned, she always kept her hands firmly on the purse strings and all monetary matters were controlled by her, on behalf of Queen Alexandra – without exception. Fiona's role was supposed to be inside of the palace only, leaving her to take responsibility for all court business.

As she furiously attacked her in tray, thumping paperwork loudly across her desk, sweeping her red pen over some of it giving orders for her staff to action before putting it in the out tray, and sorting more into pending, Linda vowed that Fiona wouldn't take a single step of the process until she had personally scrutinised every possible detail beforehand.

She also intended to privately make her feelings known about this to the queen, at the earliest opportunity.

CHAPTER 44

As Alexandra was coming out of the train station in Greenacres later that day, on her way home from school, she saw a poster which attracted her attention. It was promoting a poetry reading recital, being held at Timpton House at eleven o'clock on the morning of 6/33/05 – two days from now. The woman who would be doing the reading was a young poet called Heidi Fisher, and it would be from her latest book. Children would be admitted for free.

Alexandra had read Heidi Fisher's first book and quite enjoyed it. Leaving the station and beginning her walk home, she reflected that this recital from her second might be an interesting experience. She would like to go to it. There would however be a couple of problems, which made her doubtful as to whether she could.

Timpton House was a small meeting place, just over a mile away from Elmsbrook, on the other side of Greenacres. With the obvious exception of when she had to take the train to Buckmore for school, Alexandra was not allowed to go anywhere that far away on her own, by any method. Their hamlet was in Cherrington Avenue on the far outskirts of the east side of Greenacres. The town centre was criss-crossed by four main roads, North Street, South Street, East Street, and West Street. From the centre, Elmsbrook was accessed via East Street, which was where the train station was. The boundary for Alexandra was the end of this road, on the edge of the town centre, which was a distance of almost exactly one mile. She was not to go further in any direction. South Street to the left of it and North Street to the right, were also the busiest main roads in Greenacres. Their intersection needed to be crossed in order to get to West Street, which led to the other side of the town. Alexandra had been warned several times by her mother that she was strictly forbidden to do so unless accompanied by an adult, and she never had. Whenever she and Tom were out together, they always went no further, even though Tom was under no such restriction and sometimes did when he was on his own. Timpton House was on Old Corn Road, a street leading off directly from a short way down West Street.

On some days other than the one in question, she might have been able to be driven to Timpton House by her mother, but unfortunately Alexandra knew that she was working overtime at the palace on that morning – Fiona too - and not returning until lunch time, so she wouldn't be able to. When that happened Alexandra was always given some extra housework jobs to do in her absence, so even if she could go by some other method, there would be unlikely to be time. Without question her mother would expect the tasks done in the morning and by the time she got back. Normally she would probably be seeing Tom in the afternoon, but she also knew that on this particular day he and his father were going to visit one of their relatives in Cheam, a town a few miles away. Therefore she would be alone at Elmsbrook that morning.

Heidi Fisher was still a new writer and considered mildly radical by some critics in her expressions. Alexandra had read part of her first book whilst visiting the library in town with her mother, who had, after quickly scanning the entire texts of poetry herself, consented to her borrowing it.(This confirmed to Alexandra that the woman couldn't be that much of a radical, as she already knew that most of her mother's strong views were deeply conservative and she wouldn't have tolerated her reading anything that she considered even remotely 'subversive'). All the same, she had insisted upon discussing the book with Alexandra after her daughter had read it, to make her aware of one or two points that she disagreed on, and clearly insinuating that she expected Alexandra to follow her way of thinking. Alexandra had been amazed that her mother could have such detailed knowledge of the book, after the brief look over she had given it in the library, and had openly wondered if she had been reading it herself when her daughter wasn't looking. Linda had laughed at this, and after giving her an affectionate but – to Alexandra – unexpected kiss, told her that she would never dream of doing such a thing. It was simply that she was used to quickly reading and absorbing all sorts of information in her job.

Alexandra still wasn't sure if her mother would approve of her actually buying this latest book though. She might ask her at some

point. And even if it were possible for her to go to the recital this weekend, she wondered if her mother would consider it a worthy use of her time.

She was still thinking about this when she arrived back at The Grange.

***

Later, Linda drove through the security gate of Elmsbrook and up the hamlet drive. She was still annoyed by what had happened at work earlier, and the day had been quite problematic. Her mood wasn't good. She had phoned home before leaving to tell Alexandra that she was on her way. After putting the car away in the garage for the night, she went inside The Grange.

As usual she very quickly met her daughter. They embraced and caressed. Alexandra melted in her mother's arms and Linda gave her another particularly strong kiss. There was nothing like the desire that she felt to love and protect her daughter, to make her feel a bit better, and Alexandra's pleasure in receiving it was clear for her to tell.

Soon Linda was cooking their dinner. As Alexandra joined her in the kitchen and helped with the preparation, she decided to tell her mother about the poetry recital anyhow, and that she would like to go. There was nothing to lose by trying, even if she knew that the outcome was almost certain to be negative.

"Um, Mother," she began.

"Hmm?" asked Linda, as she placed some meat in the oven.

"I saw something advertised on the way home," Alexandra continued. "There's a poetry recital being given by Heidi Fisher – you must remember her, Mother. I borrowed her first book of poetry from the library. She's just bringing out a second."

Linda's eyes glanced briefly at her daughter, before returning to her work. "Oh yes? Well of course I remember her. Why do you mention it? I assume that it means you'd like to go?"

"Well. Yes, I was thinking about it, Mother," admitted Alexandra.

"When is it then?"

"It's actually on the first day of this weekend, Mother, at eleven o'clock. At Timpton House. Children get free admittance."

Linda stopped what she was doing for a moment and turned her full attention on her daughter.

"Timpton House? Oh. Well, I think you know what my answer to that is going to be, Alexandra. I'm sorry, but you can't. I need to go into the palace that morning, so I can't take you, and you know the rule about how far you can go out on your own. That building is out of bounds. Mrs Clark is working on that morning too, so she couldn't give you a lift either, and I gather that even Mr. Clark and Tom will be away too."

Alexandra didn't particularly want to have a lift from Fiona, in any case.

"I know, Mother. But I'd really like to go and listen to one of those poetry recitals." she said.

"But not this weekend, Alexandra." replied Linda, firmly. "Apart from anything else I shall have a couple of things for you to do whilst I'm out."

"I still would like to go though, Mother," pressed Alexandra.

"I know you would, but it's out of the question on this occasion, Alexandra. I won't allow you to go over to the other side of town on your own by any means, and you *know* that you're forbidden to

cross over the main road that divides our side from theirs without an adult."

Linda took a saucepan out of one of her cupboards.

Alexandra rarely contested any of her mother's decisions and accepted her authority without very much question. Unlike some girls she knew, she had certainly never stamped her foot. Alexandra knew that her mother would never stand for much of such a thing, and it wasn't really in her nature. But just occasionally there were times when she felt a pang of resentment. She was only too well aware that many other children had greater freedom than she did – and they weren't all tearaways. Her reputation in her form class for having the strictest mother of all the girls at Charterhouse, was well founded. Most unusually, she pushed the issue again.

"Please Mother, I want to!"

It didn't take long for her to realise that she'd done it once too often.

Linda banged the saucepan onto the stove in frustration. This was all she needed after the day she'd had. Nor was she used to Alexandra challenging her. She turned to face her daughter full on, the knuckles of her hands resting on her hips.

"*Alexandra!*" she said, sternly. "Now come on! I will not have this. *I* am your mother and you will submit to my authority, and abide *my* house rules. I have told you no fewer than four times already, and after this one I won't say it again! You cannot go and that is my final word. I shouldn't need to further explain the reasons why. As it happens, I am in a bad temper tonight – though that's not to do with you. But therefore my patience will be short if you give any nonsense. I want to hear no more about this. If I do, you will be given the kitchen stick. Is that clear?"

"Yes, Mother!" replied Alexandra, becoming obedient again.

"Crystal clear?"

"Yes, Mother," Alexandra repeated.

"Good," said Linda. "Now put those vegetables that you've chopped up into this pan. Have you finished your prep?"

"Almost, Mother," said her daughter.

"Right. Lay the dining room table and then go to the study and finish it before dinner. I shall expect you to be ready when I call you to help dishing it up."

"At once, Mother!" said Alexandra, and hurried out.

With her mother in the mood that she clearly was tonight, Alexandra felt even less inclined to risk a caning for tardiness than usual. Being late to help in the preparation of, or in arriving at the table for, a meal, meant receiving the cane.

When they eventually sat down to eat, the subject was not mentioned, and Linda was keen to hear about Alexandra's lessons at Charterhouse College. What she heard was on the whole pleasing to her, and her mood lightened. She felt that her daughter was doing well.

There was no mention of the recital on the next night either. Linda was having some busy days at work at the moment, and - confident after what she had already said that the subject was closed - had put it completely out of her mind for the time being.

But it was still in her daughter's mind...

***

The following morning was the one when Alexandra knew that Heidi Fisher was to be at Timpton House.

At breakfast Linda told her daughter what she must do for housework that day. As Alexandra had expected, she instructed that it be done by lunch time when she returned.

After she had gone though, Alexandra thought on reflection that she actually hadn't been given all that much to do this morning. Next weekend she knew that her mother was planning for them to have a much busier day together. She had to do the washing for the week, clean the kitchen floor, and then, as usual, do some shopping at Judith Warwicker's grocery store across the road from Elmsbrook, but that was it. One of her regular jobs was the ironing, but that was always later in the day.

She was sure that she could get her work done quite quickly. The more that she kept thinking of the poetry recital, a slight feeling of rebelliousness came over her. She so badly wanted to go. Her mother wouldn't be phoning to tell her she was leaving work until at least shortly before one o'clock. Whilst she was in Avermore, could her mother really have any way of knowing exactly where she was when she went out of Elmsbrook? If she did her jobs fast and then left straight away, she thought that she could get to Timpton House in time for Heidi Fisher's recital and then be back at The Grange in time to receive her mother's telephone call. Alexandra thought that she would be unlucky if somebody her mother knew saw her and reported the fact back, or if she happened to ring unexpectedly whilst she was at the recital. The odds were that her mother would never find out.

Alexandra began her work, all the time running the plan through her mind. She was indeed soon finished, and then she went to the grocery store and brought what her mother wanted from her list. Once she was back at The Grange and had put the items away and her mother's change and receipts on her desk in the study, Alexandra checked her watch. Then she made her decision. She was going to go to Timpton House.

She left Elmsbrook again and made her way towards the town centre. As she reached the end of East Street, Alexandra felt a slight chill ripple through her as she thought of what she was about

to do, but then she steeled herself, and picking her moment, crossed over the road. She might as well go all the way now, she confided to herself. She had already broken one of her mother's strictest rules.

Alexandra quickly walked down West Street, and then along Old Corn Road, until finally she reached Timpton House.

There were a small number of people gathered in the small hall when she went inside. Adults were paying a fee to a woman at the door, but as a child she was waved through for free. Alexandra did appear to be the only one there without a parent. She took a seat at the back.

Eventually Heidi Fisher appeared on the stage to a round of applause from the audience. She thanked them all for coming and shortly afterwards began to read from her latest collection of poetry. Alexandra listened intently. Overall, she enjoyed it, and it was a new experience for her to be at a live performance of this medium. Previously she had been to some concerts and theatre performances with her mother, but never something like this.

Once the poet had finished there was more applause, and then some of the gathering went up to the stage to get their copy of the book personally signed by her. Alexandra took the opportunity to slip back out of the meeting hall.

She retraced her steps down Old Corn Road and along West Street. Alexandra took in the smell of beer as she passed a pub which was just opening up to begin its lunch time trading. to the end, where she needed to cross back over to the other side of Greenacres for home.

Just before she reached her place to cross, with cars passing on that side of the road, Alexandra didn't see Fiona's car travelling on the other, about to turn left into East Street. She was already on her way home from the palace.

But Fiona saw Alexandra. She was somewhat surprised to see her apparently completely alone and about to cross the road, as she knew from Linda, and also from Tom, that Alexandra had not previously been allowed to do this unaccompanied or to be over on that side of town alone, at all. She was sure that Linda wouldn't have taken her there before work this morning, as the girl would most likely have been dished out extra housework duties in her mother's absence anyhow. Perhaps the rule had been relaxed now. Or else, could the girl possibly be being a bit naughty and disobeying her mother when she was away? Fiona chuckled to herself at the thought of it being the latter.

She wondered where Alexandra had been. Once in East Street, she considered slowing down and then offering Alexandra a lift back to Elmsbrook, but then decided to leave it for now. It wasn't necessarily any business that she was interested in, but maybe she would enquire to Linda about it next week at work. Since being allowed by the queen to take the lead responsibility for the proposed marital suite, Linda had not spoken to her, but they would have to communicate once more, soon.

Alexandra arrived back at The Grange as she had planned, in good time before her mother rang to say that she was about to go out to her car and drive home. She enquired as to whether Alexandra had completed her housework, and her daughter answered in the affirmative. As far as Alexandra could possibly tell, no one knew that she had also been to the recital. She didn't realise that she had been unlucky after all...

CHAPTER 45

On 1/34/05, there was another meeting between Queen Alexandra and her two most senior court officials.

Linda had asked for a private meeting with the queen at the end of the previous week and told her respectfully of her displeasure at Fiona having been given responsibility for the marital suite project. Queen Alexandra had sympathised, but said that her decision was final and she felt that Fiona should be given the opportunity, since it was her idea. Linda had said that just because it was Fiona's idea that didn't change the fact that it should be the responsibility of herself to oversee it, but the queen was adamant that on this at least, the role would be Fiona's. She felt that the responsibility had to be led by one or other of them, as she thought *joint* responsibility would be impossible given that they were two such strong personalities. (Linda had insisted that she was the strongest and Queen Alexandra did not disagree with her). She was certain that the more junior court administrator was capable, though the queen did promise Linda that she would personally make sure that Fiona kept her fully informed of every development.

Today's meeting marked the first conversation between Linda and Fiona since last week, and Fiona confirmed that she had begun a cost analysis and promised Linda that she would inform her when she had more news.

Linda said that there still was no trace of Pheobe Porter, and that she seemed to have vanished into thin air. There were simply no leads at all. The police would keep the case open, but at the moment they had nothing to go on, and unless that changed, they privately wondered whether they would ever solve the mystery and find her. Fiona wondered to herself whether anybody had found the woman's body on Geraticai yet.

After the meeting, as Linda and Fiona went back to the department with Carol, Fiona's secretary who had taken the minutes, a few

paces behind them, Fiona tackled Linda about what she had seen at the weekend.

"I'm curious," she began. "It might not be any of my business, but where did Alexandra go at the weekend, whilst we were here working overtime in the palace?"

Linda looked at her in puzzlement. "Where did she *go*? Oh...yes. To Judith Warwicker's grocery store. She often goes there on an errand for me to buy some supplies, once a week, and she did that day. That would have been it, I expect. Why do you ask?"

"Oh no. She was some way away from Mrs Warwicker's store when I saw her on my way back to The Lodge," remarked Fiona. "I passed her in my car. It was about ten past midday."

"What do you mean? *Where* did you see her?" demanded Linda. "Is there something that you're trying to tell me, Fiona? If so, then out with it please!"

"It was actually at the end of West Street," said Fiona. "I was just about to turn off from North Street into East Street, and I assume that she was about to cross over the road and walk back to The Grange in the same direction. I didn't realise that she was now allowed to do that, and go over to the other side of Greenacres on her own."

"What? No, she isn't!" exclaimed Linda.

Fiona forced herself to keep a straight face. So her suspicions had been correct. Alexandra had been up to something she shouldn't, behind her mother's back!

"Oh! I'm terribly sorry, Linda," she lied. "I didn't mean to drop Alexandra in it."

For what it was worth, as far as Fiona was concerned, Alexandra was utterly under the thumb of her mother, who was far too overprotective of her daughter. Linda dominated Alexandra's life

so strictly and completely that everything she did was totally controlled by her. It wasn't surprising that the girl might rebel on an occasion. Linda was lucky that she had such a mild mannered, placid daughter – though Fiona did acknowledge that the two of them loved each other deeply. Alexandra's sometimes timid nature meant that she often didn't like to stray too far away. Some other children might give Mrs Radcliffe a few more problems if she was their mother. But that was up to her, and Fiona didn't really care what happened between Linda and Alexandra in their personal relationship.

"Yes. Well, thank you for that Fiona," replied Linda, as they went through the door to the administration department. "I shall make enquiries about this tonight. See you later."

She hurried into her office and the door closed behind her. As she prepared herself a cup of coffee from her machine, she frantically gathered her thoughts.

Fiona couldn't be entirely making up what she claimed to have seen. It was obviously to do with that wretched poetry recital! The naughty girl must have defied her and gone to listen to it. She might need to ask some searching questions of Alexandra later to be sure of exactly what had happened, but it seemed too much of a coincidence given how much she had almost begged to be allowed to go, for there to be any other reason for her being where Fiona had indicated – and the time would fit too. She had probably got back to Elmsbrook at around half past twelve - well before she would have been expecting her mother's call to say that she was on her way home. Linda felt a kind of fury that she seldom experienced towards her daughter. Alexandra appeared to have been blatantly disobedient on at least two counts. Tonight she would get a beating for doing this – there could be no question about that.

Looking back with hindsight, Linda thought she should have realised that it might not have been the end of the matter for Alexandra after their conversation about the issue the previous week. Perhaps if before leaving for work on the day of this recital,

she'd given Alexandra a strong warning not to consider going, and mentioned the cane, then her daughter might have thought twice about it. But it actually hadn't been in her mind at the time, and she still couldn't believe that Alexandra had dared to defy her in this way. The fact that she had done so, and broken her rules, shocked and angered her. Her daughter really was normally a very well behaved girl – it was a while since she'd taken a stick to her, and longer still since she'd been forced to use the cane – and she was very rarely disobedient, but she clearly had been on this occasion, and had obviously felt that she could get away with it. Alexandra would find out her mistake very soon, her mother determined, as she slapped her cup and saucer down on the desk and sat down. Linda didn't think that Alexandra would have done this if she had felt that her actions would certainly be discovered, but even so she had underestimated her daughter's will. Well, now Alexandra would find her mother's own will vigorously reasserted...

***

At half past four that afternoon, the phone rang at The Grange. Alexandra was in the kitchen, just making a first cup of coffee for herself after coming home. She picked up the extension from there.

"Hello, Mother," she said.

"Hello, Alexandra," said Linda, without some of her usual warmth. "Have you just got in?"

She was wondering if Fiona might have told Tom that she'd seen Alexandra at the end of West Street on her own, and about to cross back over to their side of town unaccompanied. As he knew that she wasn't allowed to do this, he would probably try to warn her that she'd been spotted.

"Yes, Mother," replied Alexandra. "I'm just making myself a drink, and then I shall get straight on with my prep in the study."

"Good," said Linda. "So, there've been no other callers? And you've seen no one from The Lodge?"

"No, Mother. As you said. I've just got home. Are you expecting Mrs Clark?"

"Not necessarily. I'm just checking."

Without any further delay, Linda began quizzing Alexandra, now assuming that she currently had the advantage of knowing what her daughter didn't yet.

"Alexandra. Can you find the receipt for the groceries that you brought from Judith at the weekend for me, please?"

"Of course, Mother. Hold on."

Alexandra went out and down the passages to the study, then found her mother's accounts book in a tray on her desk. She kept all of her household receipts inside of it, beside the latest page. The one she was referring to was on the top. Alexandra picked up that room's extension.

"I've got it, Mother," she said.

"What time was it issued?" asked Linda.

"Ten past ten, Mother." replied Alexandra.

"Right." That confirmed to Linda that her daughter had been to the store more than two hours before Fiona had said that she'd seen her on West Street.

"And I presume that you brought the groceries straight back to The Grange, after you brought them?"

"Yes, Mother. Why? Is there a problem with the receipt that Judith gave me?"

"No. It's fine. Whilst I was working at the palace, I know that you were busy at The Grange. You did all of the jobs that I asked of you, didn't you?"

"Yes, Mother," replied Alexandra, a little surprised by this question. "You know I did."

"Therefore, apart from when you had to go to the store, I wouldn't think that you had the time to go out anywhere."

"No, Mother. I was here all the time."

Alexandra hoped that her mother couldn't tell that she was lying, over the phone. Linda now knew that if what Fiona had told her was correct then that was exactly what her daughter was doing now. In fact she believed that it would have been quite possible for Alexandra to have done the housework jobs that she'd given her, and still found the time to go out somewhere else if she'd wanted to.

"So, when I get home, if I check the film from the security gate camera, I obviously won't see you leaving Elmsbrook again, nor coming back in at - let us say - around half past twelve?"

"What?" An alarm bell suddenly went off in Alexandra's head, and she battled to keep the unease from her voice. "The security gate film, Mother? But… but that was two days ago! Can you look back and see who's come and gone?"

"Oh yes. Of course. Did you think that it simply showed the live picture, and then it was gone, Alexandra? No. It records the images and stores them for a period. I can look back to the time when I was away at the palace."

"Oh. No, I didn't know that, Mother."

A cold shiver ran right through Alexandra. Her mother was going to see that she'd gone out. And somehow, from her rather cool demeanour on the phone today, and the way she'd been questioned, Alexandra could tell that that her mother already somehow knew

that she had – why else would she want to suddenly check the security gate film? Half past twelve was indeed roughly the time that she'd got back from the recital. She would have to confess that she had gone out again, but if she pretended that it was to somewhere else on their side of town, then hopefully she would still be able to keep the whole story from her.

"Actually Mother, I did go out at one point, but..."

Linda pounced.

"Yes, Alexandra, I rather suspected that. You were seen by Mrs Clark as she drove past on the other side of the road, on her way home. She told me this morning." Then the coolness in her voice hardened. "*And* my girl, I think that I know where you went. Because Mrs Clark saw you at the end of West Street at a quarter past twelve, appearing to be about to cross over to East Street! You went to hear Heidi Fisher, didn't you? Come on. It's time to be completely honest now. Did you, or didn't you? Why else would you have been there at that time, given your whining to me about letting you go to the recital last week? Or were Mrs Clark's eyes deceiving her? If you try to lie about this and then I find out that the truth is indeed what I believe, then you will only get yourself into more trouble!"

Alexandra felt another shiver. She'd been caught.

"It is true, Mother," she admitted, weakly. "I'm very sorry. But I was just so frustrated that I couldn't go..."

"Don't try to make excuses Alexandra!" barked Linda. "You have been a *very* naughty girl! Right! Now I've got to get to parliament pronto – I'm already now behind schedule. Listen to me. You will get all of your prep done by the time I get home, which will probably be between quarter to and eight o'clock. Tonight, I shall get the supper instead of you, *after* we have talked about this. You might do well to think about what I am likely to say, and the actions that will be taken. Meet me in the study when I return. Be ready for me, Alexandra!"

There was a click as Linda hung up, without even waiting for her daughter to reply, or to say goodbye.

Alexandra trembled. She was going to be roasted alive for certain, and when she looked behind her mother's desk, she saw the instrument of one of the actions she believed her mother would take. So, it had been Fiona who had seen her! Now Alexandra guessed the reason why her mother had asked whether anybody from The Lodge had contacted her. Had Fiona told Tom? She considered phoning him, but his stepmother would almost certainly answer, and it would feel a bit awkward having to speak to her, just at the moment. She didn't like using the device at the best of times.

Alexandra sat down at her desk and began her prep, concentrating as best she could, though not truly being able to take her mind off what she knew was surely to occur later.

***

In fact, her mother arrived not long after the usual time for this night of the week. Alexandra's hand moved towards her mouth as she heard the car outside, and she gulped as the front door opened and closed. When she knew that she was about to be told off and given punishment, she was extremely frightened of her mother.

Whilst driving home, Linda had come to the conclusion that she must punish her daughter particularly severely after what she had done. She walked down the passage and hung her coat in the cloakroom. Alexandra felt another shiver run right through her as she heard the footsteps. Then the door opened and her mother entered the study. She looked with trepidation at her, but Linda didn't acknowledge her. She went straight to her desk, put her jacket on the back of her chair, and rolled up her blouse sleeves.

The first thing she did was press a button on the study phone. The screen attached which showed an image of anybody who was at the security gate when they pressed The Grange's intercom button, came to life. Linda operated a dial, and Alexandra saw the screen flickering. Then her mother turned and spoke.

"Right. Here you are, Alexandra. The evidence! Look at the screen."

Her daughter stood and stepped around so that she could view it properly.

"I can see that you went to Judith's store and came back again. But then according to the time on the film, you left again at half past ten, and returned at – well goodness me – half past twelve!"

Linda pressed the button again, and the screen went blank. She sat down on her chair. Then she picked up her cane hanging behind her desk with one hand, grabbed Alexandra roughly by the arm to face her with the other, and finally exploded, her voice raised and her tone so sharp that it cut through her daughter like a knife,

"I cannot believe that you did this! I told you no less than *five* times that you were not permitted to go to the poetry recital, yet still you dared to defy me! That is bad enough, but what you did in order to disobey me makes it even worse. You knew why you weren't allowed. I will not let you go further than the end of East Road on your own and that's the end of it. After that everything is out of bounds. But you went further! Timpton House is on the other side of town, and you are most strictly forbidden to cross the main road on your own to reach it. But you *did* cross it! You have broken *two* very strict house rules! I do not care if you *wanted* to go to Timpton House. You could not, as no adult could accompany you. Furthermore, you abused my trust in you when I went out and left you alone for the morning, and then when I phoned earlier today after finding out about this, you clearly tried to lie, thinking that you could deceive me!"

Suddenly Linda pulled her daughter downwards, and Alexandra found herself across her mother's knees. She gave a small squeal of fear as she anticipated what was about to happen.

"You, naughty, disobedient girl!" shouted Linda, striking Alexandra's bottom with her cane. Alexandra yelped.

"I will *not* be lied to or deceived!" Alexandra winced as she felt another blow.

"You will *not* go out of bounds!" Linda caned her daughter again, and Alexandra cried out.

"You will *not* cross over North or South Road!" Linda caned her harder still, and Alexandra squealed again. As she began to cry uncontrollably, her mother pulled her back upright.

"Now then, Alexandra. "I've given you four strokes out of a standard dosage of six. But don't start thinking that you're being let off lightly. Far from it! I want to make very sure that you never forget this punishment, and that you are never persuaded to disregard such important rules again. Come with me."

Linda yanked on her daughter's arm and pulled her behind, as she went out of the study and down the passage. Still sobbing, Alexandra was taken upstairs to her mother's bedroom. They crossed the room to the dressing table. Linda opened the bottom drawer and took something out.

Alexandra's body twitched when she saw what it was.

"No, Mother! Not the whip!" she begged. Then her stammer briefly returned. "P-Please. I won't do anything like this again. I p-promise!"

"Alexandra. Be quiet and listen to me," ordered Linda. "I am going to give you three lashings of this on your bottom, but fully dressed – not on your naked skin. They will not be anywhere near as hard as I could make them, and three lashings is considerably less than

the number that many of the naughtiest children might expect to receive of the whip. In their case it would also be from head to toe, back and front. By no means could this be conceived as a true horse whipping; more of a semi one. I merely think that you deserve to at least get a small flavour of it – which I hope might deter you from such seriously bad behaviour in the future. You are in no position to protest after what you have done. Now just be a brave girl, and try to bear your punishment well."

Linda pushed her daughter down onto the bed stomach first. Alexandra's legs were shaking uncontrollably. Although the whip – her mother's riding crop - had always been threatened as the ultimate punishment, it had always been very much in the background. There was an understanding that it would only be used in the most extreme of circumstances. It never had been, and the only times in Alexandra's life that she had even seen it were when her mother went hunting. A riding crop was shorter than the horse whips used at the palace for wayward juveniles, but it was a horse whip nevertheless and some Geratican mothers possessed one, whether they were horsewomen or not.

Linda wasn't surprised to see Alexandra's fear. She'd been expecting it. She wrapped an arm tight around her daughter's waist as she lay faced down on the bed.

"I'll hold you," she said.

Then with her other arm she brought the whip down. Alexandra tried to do as her mother told her and bear it as best she could. Even though the first lashing was apparently mild, she still flinched from its sting. After the second, she couldn't help but utter a short involuntary squeal. Her mother's method was always to make the final stroke of the punishment the hardest, so that this would be the one she remembered longest, and when it came, though her mother had insisted it wouldn't be that harsh, Alexandra still screamed as she felt the painful sensation run through her buttocks and make the whole of the lower part of her body shudder.

Linda's arm had never left Alexandra's waist and with each lashing she had in fact intensified her grip. Now she put down the whip and with both arms squeezed her daughter even tighter to help comfort her as she wept again. Then she lifted her off the bed and set her on her feet. Taking a handkerchief from her skirt pocket, she dabbed Alexandra's eyes.

"Alright. Well, that's over with, at least," she remarked. "I hope that you'll learn a lesson from it."

"Yes, Mother," replied Alexandra, still sobbing slightly.

"Right," continued Linda, her voice becoming strict and assertive again. "I trust that you finished your prep before I came home, as you were ordered?"

"Of course, Mother. In plenty of time," said Alexandra, obediently.

"Good. Well then it's time I got the supper. Go and set the table for me. Whilst we eat, I shall tell you the rest of your punishment. And then when we're finished and cleared away, you will go straight to bed. What do you say, Alexandra?"

"Yes Mother!" replied Alexandra.

She hurried out of the bedroom. Linda put the whip back in the drawer and then left herself for the kitchen.

***

Alexandra was still sniffing slightly as she laid the table for her mother in the dining room. She was still feeling discomfort from the beatings too. From bitter experience she knew that this would continue for a little while yet, and the whipping had been excruciatingly painful.

Linda continued to scold her daughter as they ate their supper.

"It particularly annoys me that you presumably did this because you thought that you would get away with it. Well, you've found out today that you never can be sure of that, Alexandra. You were unlucky perhaps that Mrs Clark usually leaves work earlier than me and happened to see you when she drove past, at the very moment when you reached the end of West Street. And you also now know that the security camera film history can be checked. I might not necessarily have had reason to look back to that morning if Mrs Clark hadn't alerted me to what she'd witnessed, but it proves to you that it can be done if the need arises, Alexandra. I should have thought to strongly warn you not to consider going to the recital before I left, I suppose, given that you'd made such an unusual fuss about it two days earlier, but it never crossed my mind that you might – especially after I had set out the position so clearly.

"That main road has a lot of traffic passing down it, Alexandra. Crossing over it needs a lot of care. It may be that I'm old fashioned, and that a lot of other children of your age can do that as a matter of course, but I'm afraid that I still feel that you're a bit too young to, without an adult. Maybe you managed it this time, and I suppose you think that proves that you can do it alone, but on the other hand, you may simply have been lucky. You still could have had an accident. The rule is there for your protection, Alexandra, and I am very cross that you suddenly chose to disregard it for your own purposes, just as you also broke the rule about going beyond the end of East Road. I simply will not have you going more than a mile away from here on your own. I like to know exactly where you are and that you're close to home. The further away you go, then if you were to get lost, or something was to happen to you, the greater the chance would be of you getting into danger, and I might not be able to find you. Or you might end up going to somewhere that I would not want you to be. Greenacres is one of the nicest towns in the whole of Geratica, but even this town has its rougher areas! Above all else, Alexandra, you must never go somewhere as far as Timpton House without me knowing.

"I am not telling you all of this as a matter for debate tonight. Do you understand what I mean by that, Alexandra?"

"Yes Mother," said Alexandra. She was sitting gingerly on her chair, whilst she ate and listened.

"What do I mean then?"

Alexandra tensed as her mother put her on the spot.

"Well. That what you're telling me is the rule of your skirt in this house, and that I mustn't question it, Mother," she replied.

"Correct," said Linda. "And I shall say this once, and once only. If you *ever* so blatantly disregard my rules again, as seriously as you did two days ago, then I *will* give you a proper horse whipping, Alexandra!"

Without waiting for any reply, she carried straight on.

"Now I will tell you what I have decided is going to happen this week. Firstly, you are going to behave impeccably and work your hardest both here and at school. I will look at the work you do at Charterhouse each day. I shall be even stricter than usual, and you will obey every rule and follow every instruction to the letter. If you transgress in any way whatsoever, you will be punished with the cane."

Alexandra had finished her supper, and now she swallowed hard.

"Yes, Mother," she said.

"Then, on the first day of this coming weekend, you will be gated at The Grange. You will not see Tom all day. Nor will you have the time to, in any case. You are going to clean this house from top to bottom, entirely by yourself, under my supervision. I was planning for us to do it together. But now, after your disobedience last weekend - when you presumably made sure to get your work done quickly so that you do something that you shouldn't have,

alone - you will do exactly what I tell you to do, *alone*, whilst I watch. If you don't work hard enough, or you don't do it properly then again you will be caned. Is that clear?"

"Crystal clear, Mother."

"Perhaps I should have made sure that you had more to do last weekend," said Linda. "Then you wouldn't have had the time to defy my order of last week!

"I shall ask Mrs Clark tomorrow to tell Tom that you won't be seeing him on the first day of this weekend.

"Well, I don't think that there's anything more to talk about this evening. I haven't given you much opportunity to speak since I've been home tonight, but that was deliberate. I shall talk to you about this incident again directly at the weekend, after your period of punishment is over, but until then you know what you must do, and how you must behave.

"Right. We'll wash up and then you will go to bed!"

"Of course, Mother," replied Alexandra.

***

Alexandra lay in bed. When she had left Charterhouse, she'd felt that it had been quite a good day. It was incredible how it had turned so bad. Of all the people who could have found her out, she might have known that it would be Tom's stepmother. The woman did seem to have a keen interest in her sometimes.

Linda came in to say goodnight. She crossed to the bed and sat down beside her daughter. Alexandra realised that they hadn't kissed all evening, and she wondered if her mother wouldn't bother tonight after what she'd discovered today. But then Linda leant

over and gently stroked her hair the way she liked it and smiled softly.

"Now don't start worrying that I don't love you anymore, my darling!" she said. "That will never happen. I always will!"

She planted a soft kiss on Alexandra's lips which her daughter returned.

"I love you darling. Goodnight and sweet dreams. See you tomorrow." Linda wrapped her arms around her daughter's neck and kissed her again.

Alexandra clutched at her mother's hand. "I still love you too, Mother!" she said, and kissed her.

Linda kissed Alexandra once more.

"Goodnight, darling!"

"Goodnight, Mother!"

Linda got up, switched off the light and went out, locking the door behind her,

Alexandra shifted her position in the bed. She could still feel the sting of the whip, though it should be gone by the morning. This was the worst punishment that she had ever received from her mother. Thankfully though, the whipping had not been quite as terrible as she'd first anticipated. She was grateful that her mother had spared her the worst of the traditional punishment. And even at the moment when she'd felt it necessary for her to experience the whip, her mother had still at the same time ensured that she felt a sense of protection by holding her. Alexandra wasn't a strong girl, and deep inside of her mind she knew how much she needed her mother, even though she was still frustrated that she hadn't been given the freedom to go to the poetry recital on her own. Despite what she had been through that night, Alexandra felt an even

deeper respect for her. She was determined that over the next week she would be the very good girl that her mother demanded.

What she had experienced of the whip was bad enough though. Alexandra also knew with even greater certainty than before, that she would never be able to face a truly authentic horse whipping. (Fortunately, she never would have to).

CHAPTER 46

In the car the next morning, as Linda dropped Alexandra off at the train station, she made sure to give her daughter a final reminder of what she'd said the night before.

"Right, now don't forget what I told you yesterday, my girl. It shouldn't need repeating. I shall be closely scrutinising you each evening this week to check that you've been a model pupil at Charterhouse, and tonight I will be checking that you've done all that I've asked you to do when you get home."

"Yes, Mother," replied Alexandra. Going out of her way to show maximum obedience she added, "I know that I was extremely naughty last weekend, but I'm going to be a very good girl this week."

"I hope so," said Linda. "I shall decide for myself about that at the end of your punishment period."

They embraced and kissed as usual and said goodbye. Outside of the car, Alexandra waved goodbye to her mother. Instead of waving back though, Linda pointed her finger sternly at her daughter. When Alexandra looked into her mother's eyes, she read a warning message of such severity that she shuddered to her core and felt a tiny light dampness in her pants as she emitted a drop of urine. As her mother drove away, Alexandra turned and hurried towards her platform. There was nobody in the world who she loved more, but equally there was nobody who she feared more when she crossed her- including all of the strictest mistresses that she'd encountered in her school career so far. Alexandra shivered in the cold autumn air and pulled her scarf around her tighter as she walked through the early morning mist.

***

At Charterhouse, Alexandra prepared herself in the form room, before the boarders arrived. On some mornings, throughout her time at the college she had occasionally been teased by some of the girls, jokingly suggesting that they bet she'd been caned at home the previous night, as they knew how strict her mother was reputed to be. Usually she hadn't, but today if anybody said it then they'd be right – and then some. But Alexandra had no intention of making this information public, if she could help it.

All day long, Alexandra plunged herself into her studies with vigorous intensity. She was relieved that Gillian, for the moment at least, seemed to be leaving her largely alone.

In fact, Gillian's attentions were to become diverted elsewhere today. There was a third year girl called Lauren Payne, who was one of a number that her mother had asked her to keep a close watch on. She was a girl who had irked the headmistress whilst a first year at Charterhouse, when Mrs Spencer had still been a science mistress – and head of the department. Elizabeth Spencer had been less than impressed with a lot of the girl's work and had marked her down considerably. On one occasion she had written a negative comment about a particular theory that she believed Lauren had got wrong in her prep. During a school holiday, the girl's mother, Miriam Payne, had seen it and taken exception.

During a visit to Charterhouse a short time later to discuss her daughter's overall progress, Mrs Payne had requested from the headmistress a separate meeting with Mrs Spencer. During it, she had remonstrated with the science mistress, telling her that she considered the comment unjustified and that it was herself who was in error. This had considerably annoyed Elizabeth, and she had insisted that the opposite was true. The conversation had grown quite heated, and they had parted without agreement. It had appeared that Mrs Payne was a research chemist, so Elizabeth had been forced to admit that she clearly had some scientific knowledge, and as a result she had been more measured in her dealings with Lauren after that, realising that the girl's blasted mother might be looking over her shoulder. Elizabeth personally considered the Paynes to be aptly named. It had not pleased her

either, to recently learn that another one, Becky, had just started at Charterhouse Preparatory School, and was hoping to follow in her sister's footsteps.

But even so, Elizabeth had never forgotten the episode, and had been outraged at what she had seen as a challenge to her scientific expertise. She was itching for an opportunity to put them in their place.

During morning break time, Lauren was sat in the recreation room of Rovers House, talking with a friend of hers, Denise Redwood. Gillian was in the background, observing the whole gathering of girls. During the course of her conversation, Lauren happened to encroach upon the subject of the headmistress.

"Let's face it," she said. "We all know that the woman's a cow! She'd love to give the whole school a caning all at once if she could! And she's not as great a scientist as she likes to think either. My mother says that if she's one of Geratica's great experts then the Divine Being is a man!"

Both girls hooted with laughter at this, as did some others who had been listening.

Gillian also heard it. She was not so amused, strongly believing that her mother was definitely one of Geratica's leading scientists. She also knew the task given to her. Slipping quietly out of the room, her first thought was to immediately go to the headmistress's study and report what she'd heard. But then she had another, and smirked to herself.

She went out of Rovers House towards the exercise yard. On the way, she slipped into a classroom and stole a piece of chalk from the blackboard.

Once Gillian reached the yard, she was pleased to see that there was nobody about, and when she peered through the window of the assembly hall it was empty. Going to a wall she wrote, "MRS SPENCER IS A COW," with the chalk, in huge letters. Satisfied

that her handiwork wouldn't be identifiable as her own writing, she threw the chalk into a bin and then did hurry to find her mother.

***

"She said what?" cried Elizabeth, jumping up from behind the desk in her study. Gillian had quoted Lauren Payne's comments to her in their entirety. "The cheeky little brat! And it's her mother who's the upstart scientist. What right has *she* got to question *me*?"

"I know," said Gillian. "You might also want to look out at the exercise yard wall!"

"What?" asked her mother. Bustling out of the room she found the nearest window from where she could gain a vantage point. Her eyes widened and her jaw dropped when she saw the writing.

"How dare..." she began, but then looked at her daughter's smirking face. She wondered if Gillian had done it herself, after hearing what Lauren had said. Elizabeth didn't want to know. But she now had enough evidence to provide her with an excuse to punish the Payne girl for her impertinence.

"Well done, Gillian," she said. "I shall find out what her next period is and go to personally confront her! You will get a rise in your weekly allowance for this."

Her daughter grinned.

***

Mrs Willis had just begun her third year 'A' stream mathematics lesson. Suddenly there was a knock on the door and the headmistress burst in. All of the girls immediately rose.

"I'm sorry to interrupt your class, Mrs Willis, but I must speak with one of your girls, Lauren Payne."

Elizabeth glanced around until she saw her.

"Lauren Payne!" she boomed. "What is the meaning of that remark written on the exercise yard wall?"

Lauren looked at her in bemusement. "What remark, Mrs Spencer? I've no idea what you mean."

"Don't give me that!" replied the headmistress. "Gillian Spencer overheard you referring to me as a cow in the recreation room at Rovers House at break time, and now the very same comment has been chalked on the wall of the exercise yard."

She turned to Denise, sat at the desk opposite Lauren's.

"Miss Redwood! Can you confirm that Lauren made this remark at break time?"

Denise paused, not wishing to get her friend into trouble. "Um..."

"Come on! Out with it, girl!" pressed Elizabeth, impatiently. "Gillian heard Lauren say it, and I believe her. There's no sense in denying it to protect Miss Payne. If you lie, then you will feel my cane on your backside!"

Denise looked at Lauren desperately, and then back at the headmistress. "Well, yes she did, Mrs Spencer, but..."

"I admit that I did say that, and I'm sorry to have been rude, Mrs Spencer," said Lauren. "But I swear that I never wrote it on the exercise yard wall! I came straight to this classroom, directly after break time."

"That's true she did, Mrs Spencer," confirmed Denise.

"I'm sorry but I don't believe you, Lauren," said Elizabeth. "I think that you chalked that remark on the wall before the end of break time. Report to me in my study after lunch. That is my final word!"

She glanced at the mathematics mistress. "Sorry to have disturbed your class, Mrs Willis. Please continue."

With that she went out, closing the door behind her.

Lauren looked aghast, and Mrs Willis took a moment to recover from what had just happened too. She found it surprising that Lauren would actually write a comment like that on a wall and didn't entirely trust anything that Gillian said. But when the headmistress's daughter was involved, there wasn't much anybody could do about it.

Finally, she addressed her class.

"Alright 3A1, let us return to where we were..."

***

After the lesson, Lauren and Denise hurried to the exercise yard. There they saw the comment on the wall.

"Someone's framed me!" cried Lauren.

"And I bet I can guess who it was," said Denise. "You've got to be so careful with the headmistress's daughter in the room, listening to everything."

"There's no point in trying to tell Mrs Spencer that we think it was Gillian though," added Lauren. "She'll never have anybody suggesting that, and I'll only be in even more trouble. I'll just have to take what's likely coming for me and put up with it."

Once she'd finished her lunch in the dining hall, Lauren reported with some trepidation to Mrs Spencer's study, as instructed. Despite strongly protesting her innocence again, she found herself receiving six strokes of the cane on her bare bottom.

***

Even before Alexandra had passed through the gates of Charterhouse later, she turned her thoughts to her duties at home. She did feel a certain guilt about what she'd done, and she really wanted to make up for it and please her mother. The warning that she'd received earlier was also dominant in her mind.

Shortly after arriving at The Grange, she received a phone call which – as expected – vigorously checked up upon her. Having satisfied her mother, Alexandra was relieved that their conversation was of a more usual nature compared to the day before.

Later, when she was immersed in her prep, the phone rang again making her jump. Her mother always answered the phone when she was there. When she wasn't, there weren't usually many calls, but if there ever were, then Alexandra was always nervous of taking them. On the whole, the only times she used the phone were to speak to Tom at The Lodge, and that wasn't very often.

She sighed and went over to look at the number on the display screen. To her relief it turned out to be The Lodge on this occasion. It would either be Fiona or Tom. Alexandra hoped that it would be Tom. She picked up the receiver.

"Hello?"

"Alexandra!" said Tom.

"Oh. Hello Tom!" replied Alexandra, happily. "Thanks for calling. I'm glad that you have actually."

"What's happened?" he asked. "My mother's told me that *your* mother says you can't see me on the first day of this weekend. She says that she thinks you might have done something wrong and are being punished for it!"

"Is Fiona around?" asked Alexandra, anxiously. "It'll be easier to talk if she's not listening."

Tom glanced about. He did see her seemingly hovering about a little by the kitchen door, but then she disappeared inside. The door was still open, and he considered going and shutting it, but he didn't like to do that.

"It's alright. She's in the kitchen," he replied.

"Good," said Alexandra.

Over at The Lodge, Fiona did strain her ears to try and pick up any kind of information that she could from Tom's end. Linda hadn't told her anything specific about what the normally good and obedient Alexandra had been doing last weekend, but it was clear that whatever it was had got her into serious trouble at home. She had assumed that it would when she'd told Linda, and now she longed to know the details. She suspected that Linda didn't intend to tell her anything more.

"I can't spend long talking," continued Alexandra. "I've got to get on with my prep and have supper ready for Mother when she gets home, plus a couple of other things, or I'll be for it. Mother is going to be *really* strict this week because it's true, I got a terrible telling off last night for something that I did last weekend."

"Why? What did you do?"

"I went beyond the end of East Street, and crossed over to West Street on my own. There's a poet called Heidi Fisher. She was giving a poetry recital at Timpton House on Old Corn Road, and I wanted to go and listen to it. But it was the same morning that both

of our mothers were working at the palace and you and your father were away, therefore there was no one who could have taken me, and you know that I'm not allowed to go as far as that or cross over the road to the other side of town without an adult. I had some housework to do, and also had to go to Mrs Warwicker's store.

"I knew that Mother wouldn't let me go, but I still asked her, and she actually got cross with me for keeping on about it and told me very firmly that I couldn't. I should have listened, but I so much wanted to go that when Mother didn't really give me all that many jobs to do that morning, I thought that I could probably get them done quite quickly and then still have time to go over to Timpton House and back again, before Mother rang to tell me that she was on her way home. I'm not normally anywhere near so daring, but I really didn't think that Mother could find out if I went - so I did!

"I did manage to get back home in plenty of time, and I truly thought that I'd got away with it – until your stepmother opened her big mouth!"

Tom frowned. "Fiona? But she was at work at the palace wasn't she?"

"Well you know that she usually leaves earlier than Mother. And apparently, what I didn't know until last evening was that just as I was coming back to the end of West Street, she was coming down North Street in her car and about to turn into East Street."

"And she saw you?"

"Of course. Fiona doesn't miss a thing! She obviously knew that Mother forbids me to be where I was on my own, and therefore guessed that I must have broken her rule to do it, *and* that I must have crossed North Road. She simply went home and didn't say anything at the time, but then at work yesterday she told Mother.

"Mother rang me after I got home from Charterhouse yesterday and to cut a long story short, before telling me what she'd found out, she asked me some questions and trapped me into lying that I

hadn't been anywhere other than to Mrs Warwicker's store. Then she told me that she could look at the recorded film from Elmsbrook's security gate to confirm it. I didn't know that she could do that. I panicked slightly, but I thought that if I told her I actually had gone out, but to somewhere other than the other side of town, then I could still get away with it. But of course, Mother then revealed what Fiona had told her and I was forced to confess the truth.

"When she got home from work, Mother checked the gate film and showed me the evidence. As you can imagine, she hit the roof about it all and I got my worst ever punishment. I was beaten four times with the cane – and then I got three strokes of the whip, which I've never had before."

Tom gasped. "The whip? Your mother gave you a horse whipping?"

"Well, no not really. I was fully clothed and it *was* only three strokes across my bottom, which Mother assured me beforehand was less than standard and that they would be nowhere near as hard as she *could* make them. They were hard enough for me, though! The sting was unbearable, and I don't mind admitting to you in confidence, Tom, that I screamed at the end. The only thing that did help was that even as Mother was whipping me, she also wrapped her arm around me and held me tight, which gave me some comfort. I never want to have to receive a full horse whipping!

"After that, over supper Mother told me that I was gated at The Grange on the day that Fiona told you about, and I'm forbidden to see you. I've got to clean the whole house whilst she supervises. And I've got to be on my very best behaviour and work especially hard both at Charterhouse and at The Grange between today and then. I've been warned *extremely* seriously that I'll be in more trouble if I transgress even a small amount.

"So there you have it, Tom. I admit, I wish now that I'd simply accepted what Mother told me last week and forgotten about the recital."

"I don't like to speak out of turn against your mother, Alexandra," said Tom. "But maybe it's time that you were allowed to cross over that road. I've been allowed to for…well, I'm not sure if there ever was a specific rule over it, actually – but anyhow, I don't know anybody else of our age who wouldn't be."

"Hmm, well. Mother's made it quite clear that she still doesn't think that I'm old enough, Tom," replied Alexandra. "And I don't think that she'll be changing her opinion any time soon! Nor does she feel that it's safe for her to allow me more than a mile away from Elmsbrook."

"But you clearly didn't have a problem crossing the road at the weekend!" declared Tom.

"She thinks that might have been partly down to me just being lucky."

Alexandra heard Tom scoff to himself.

"The rule is the rule, and you know Mother's line on that," she said. "If I disobey her rule then I get punished. These were very strict ones and in her view I blatantly disregarded them, and mainly because I could get away doing it without being caught, therefore I had to be punished severely. I very rarely disobey Mother. I really do respect her judgement, and she was quite right that I definitely wouldn't have gone to the recital if I'd thought that there was a likelihood of me being found out! I've been bought up to respect authority and I shouldn't have gone against my mother's orders. I'm sorry and I'm going to really be good, work hard and make it up to her."

"I like to think that I've been brought up to respect authority, too," remarked Tom.

He wondered if there was anybody other than Alexandra who loved their mother so deeply and was as respectful and loyal to her, when she had such a strict and some might say domineering and controlling hold over them. Alexandra was expected to do as she was told and there was rarely any other option but to do so without getting into trouble. For all that though, Tom knew that there was an extraordinary amount of love and affection felt by the two of them for each other. He was beginning to sense that there was a deep and remarkable bond between them. He also very much liked and respected Mrs Radcliffe, despite her formidable reputation – which was quite deserved. Alexandra was a very shy and sometimes rather nervous girl who he felt seemed to need her mother's dominance to protect her.

"We both respect authority," agreed Alexandra.

Then she checked her watch anxiously "Look, Tom. I'd better be getting on. If Mother finds out that I've been gossiping for a long time she'll go mad! I don't dare cross her this week. She means what she says, Tom, she'll..."

"It's alright, I understand, Alexandra!" laughed Tom. "She'll horsewhip you on the courtyard of The Grange, if you talk any longer!"

"It's no laughing matter, Tom!" said Alexandra.

"No. I know it's not," replied Tom. "Sorry. And you know that I do like and respect your mother too."

"In actual fact I was thinking more about the stick," continued Alexandra.

Tom could sense Alexandra's agitation. In his mind he could see her becoming nervous that she wasn't going to manage to get everything done that she'd been instructed to do, and thinking of the punishment that she might get if that was the case. He had seen it before, sometimes when she was anxious not to get home late to The Grange after they'd been out together. He knew that she feared

a telling off and punishment from her mother more than almost anything else in the world.

"Well, I've got to go too, as I think our dinner will soon be ready," he said.

"Just before you do though, Tom, what I was going to ask was if you could return me a favour?"

"What's that?"

"Well, remember when you got beaten by Fiona?" asked Alexandra. "I swore that I wouldn't tell anybody what it was actually for, as you'd promised her that it would be kept between yourselves. If Mother hasn't told her why I was over on the other side of Greenacres, then could you promise me not to tell her yourself? There's no need for Fiona to know. It's really a private affair between Mother and I - though of course I don't mind you knowing. If Mother does eventually decide to tell her, well that can't be helped."

"Fair enough," replied Tom. "I understand. Not a word from me. I promise."

"Oh, thank you, Tom!" said Alexandra, smiling. "Well let's say goodbye then we'll talk again soon. But sorry that I can't see you for our usual meeting this weekend."

After they'd hung up, Fiona appeared again briefly in the hall.

"I wasn't eavesdropping, but I couldn't help overhearing some of what you were saying, Tom. Do I gather that Alexandra got a horse whipping from her mother for crossing a road?"

"She did get a small dose of the whip, yes, but she actually said it wasn't a true horse whipping, as she was fully clothed, and her mother only lashed her reasonably lightly on her bottom three times," replied her stepson. He felt that there was reason to put her right about that, at least.

Fiona could contain herself no longer. "What exactly was she doing there in the first place?"

"She doesn't want me to talk about it, Mother," said Tom.

He saw his stepmother's jaw tighten.

"Oh, come on, Tom. You can tell me!" she urged.

"Sorry, Mother, I've promised. And you know that she's my best friend. If I make a promise to her, then it means as much to me as one that I make to you."

Tom knew that he had actually broken his own promise to his stepmother when he had confided in Alexandra, but he was determined that she would never know that.

Fiona's eyes flashed for a split second, as she realised her stepson's meaning, and that she was beaten.

"Oh, very well!" she snapped, and turned and began flouncing back towards the kitchen. "Dinner's nearly ready. Go and get your father from the parlour and come and sit to the table!"

Until recently usage of the phone at The Lodge had been almost exclusively hers. Perhaps now she would consider getting another extension fitted, so that she could eavesdrop on any conversations that interested her...

CHAPTER 47

When 1F went to their second period of the next day, geography, they found as they were allowed into the classroom by their mistress, Mrs Whitelaw, that there was another woman who they didn't know already there.

"This is Mrs Haskins, 1F," explained the mistress. "She is a member of the Charterhouse board of governors and is here in an observatory capacity only. You need not concern yourselves with her. You will most likely not realise that she is there. But please do say good morning to her."

"Good morning, Mrs Haskins!" the girls said, together.

Mrs Haskins smiled thinly and nodded in acknowledgement.

Alexandra wondered *why* a member of the Charterhouse board of governors was observing their geography class. She thought it likely that the rest of the girls were probably thinking the same thing. After the brief pause that followed, she was surprised that Gillian, who was normally much bolder than the others, did not ask.

During the course of the lesson, Mrs Whitelaw struggled to keep order. The main culprit was Gillian, who persistently disrupted the class. In what was now a common theme at the college, the mistress wanted to take action against the girl, but felt her hands tied by the constraints laid down by the headmistress.

Mrs Haskins sat quietly in the corner of the room, making careful notes about what she had witnessed...

***

After the lesson was over, with the girls going off for morning break time, Mrs Haskins went to see the headmistress.

"Well Elizabeth," she said, "I think I am able to draw the conclusion you seek, based on the events of the lesson that I just assessed."

"That Sue Whitelaw is unable to control a class with the necessary skill that would be expected from a head of department?" asked the headmistress.

"Yes. I'll make a report for the board to that effect, and then I'm sure that the chair will agree that it isn't appropriate for this particular mistress to be selected for interview."

"Excellent!" beamed Elizabeth.

She was delighted. The position of the head of geography had become vacant and Sue Whitelaw, a mistress who had been at Charterhouse for three years was thought to be a strong candidate to fill it. Unfortunately though, she had fallen out with Mrs Spencer rather badly and the headmistress was determined to do whatever it took to stop her. She was due to be conducting interviews alongside the chair of the board next week, and had arranged for this impromptu assessment of her teaching ability to be carried out today by another board member. Both of the women were allies of hers, and she hoped that the report Mrs Haskins wrote would give her a legitimate reason to reject Sue's application. Gillian had been under her mother's instruction to create as many problems for the mistress as possible during the lesson...

***

By now Mrs Moreton had reached an agreement with the mothers of the girls involved in the damage to her boat for a contribution from all of them towards the repairs. They were somewhat aggrieved though, and their daughters did find themselves being taken to task over the issue in much the way that they had been anticipating.

A new boat had been ordered by Charterhouse College.

CHAPTER 48

On the morning of 6/34/05, Alexandra awoke early.

Since being given her punishment at the beginning of the week she had made every effort to behave impeccably. Her mother had indeed been at her strictest each evening, and been most exacting in her scrutinising of Alexandra's day at Charterhouse and of her work, but she appeared to have been satisfied.

But today was the main day of Alexandra's period of punishment, and she knew that her mother's eyes would be fully upon her as she worked around the house.

As they finished breakfast, Linda began to set the tone for the day.

"Right, Alexandra. It's a cold day, but you are going to be busier than you have ever been before, so I can assure you that you will soon warm up! You will do everything that I say immediately, without question, and in exactly the way that I expect it. Do you wish to feel the cane across your bottom?"

"No, Mother," replied Alexandra.

Unusually the said instrument had been removed from where it normally hung in the study and was lying across the breakfast room table.

"Well then remember my words," said Linda.

"I will, Mother," said her daughter. "I'm going to work very hard today. I promise." Alexandra was feeling almost as scared of her mother now, as when she'd been about to receive the initial punishment.

"You certainly are. I shall make sure of it!" asserted Linda. "Sleeves up and pinafore on. And you can begin now, by washing up the breakfast things."

"Yes, Mother," obeyed Alexandra, and immediately got up and began clearing away the table.

Not only did she have to wash up, but dry up too. After that Linda began directing her daughter. Alexandra did the washing and cleaned, dusted, scrubbed and vacuumed all over the house, according to her mother's orders. Whilst she worked, Linda watched her like a hawk. One of her hands was on her hip and the other always held the cane. Shaking slightly with nerves, Alexandra began to appreciate what her mother had meant about warming up and did her best to remain calm under the pressure that she was deliberately putting her through. Once or twice, Alexandra feared that she might incur her mother's wrath and be punished further, but although the commands were strict and stern she was fortunately not seriously rebuked. There was a break for coffee at mid morning, which Linda made and at lunch time when her mother prepared a snack, after which Alexandra had to wash and dry up again before continuing.

Finally, later in the afternoon, Linda told her daughter to begin some preparations for their dinner that night, whilst she went to the grocery store.

Judith was surprised to be seeing Linda at that time and not Alexandra earlier as was usual, and asked whether Alexandra was unwell. Linda assured Judith that her daughter was fine, but that she would not be going out today. Mrs Warwicker decided not to enquire as to the exact reason why.

On the way back, Linda picked up the post - and the Geratican Times newspaper which she had delivered to her at the weekend - from their letterbox. The Lodge had some post too, so she went up and around the hamlet drive to that house. Fiona's car was in their driveway, but rather than ringing the doorbell and meeting her, Linda simply put the post through their door. She didn't really want to speak to Fiona today – and in any case it was time to be getting back to Alexandra.

At The Grange later, Linda and Alexandra had dinner. Linda confirmed that her daughter's period of punishment was over, but said that they would speak about it presently. Once they had finished, Linda washed up as normal and Alexandra dried, and then she did her ironing duties.

Eventually Linda made them both a cup of coffee and Alexandra went to the parlour.

"Alexandra, close the door and keep the heat in when the fire is on!" her mother lightly scolded when she brought the coffee in on a tray. "How many times do I have to tell you? Anybody would think that you were you born in a barn!"

"Sorry, Mother!" Alexandra got up and shut the door, whilst her mother set the tray down.

Linda poured herself a glass of port, and sat down on the sofa beside her daughter. With some after dinner mints on the table in front of them, she laid a hand lightly on Alexandra's arm.

"Alright then, darling, let's get one thing out of the way without any further ado," she began. "Mother thinks that you've been a good girl since the second day of this week, and that you've done a very good job today. She is pleased with you. Well done, darling. You may now have a kiss!"

She slipped her arms around her daughter's shoulders and Alexandra craned her neck to receive the kiss. As Linda smothered her lips and gave her what she had been longing to ever since breakfast, she saw a look of both pleasure and relief.

"But now we must have another chat about what happened the other day," continued Linda. "I was taken aback that you would disobey me in quite such a manner, I can tell you Alexandra – and to break those rules in particular made it especially shocking. You are normally an exceptionally good girl, who I am immensely proud of. I couldn't believe it when Mrs Clark told me what she'd seen! I haven't told her any specific details about what you were

doing there, and it isn't my intention to discuss the matter further with her."

"I asked Tom not to say anything more to her as well, when he rang the other evening before you got home, Mother," replied Alexandra.

"Right," said Linda, with a slight nod. "Well, on the night that I gave you your punishment, I acknowledged that I hadn't given you much of a chance to say anything once you'd admitted what you'd done. But now you may. Clearly, I underestimated the strength of your will to go to Heidi Fisher's poetry recital. Tell me how you feel, darling."

She took her daughter's hand, and squeezed it from the outside in encouragement. Alexandra looked at her.

"I did want to go, Mother. I thought that it would be an interesting experience. I obviously knew that I wasn't allowed to go that far or to cross over North Road on my own, but it does frustrate me sometimes. I really didn't find it a problem and Tom is allowed to do it."

"If Tom was my son, then he would be bound by the same rules that you are, Alexandra!" said Linda, sharply. "It's up to his stepmother what she allows him to do."

She sighed. "To be honest I didn't think that you would have the nerve to defy me. And perhaps the one positive thing that I can take from this is that it might demonstrate you had the confidence to do it. But I will not have you breaking house rules and behaving in such a way, to prove that to me. You also attempted to lie to me before you realised the full extent of what I already knew, which made it even worse. If I'd known what you'd done on this day of last week, then you would most likely not have slept with me that night!" Linda jabbed her daughter in the chest with her finger. "I trust that you've learnt your lesson, and you realise what will happen if you do something like this again?"

"Yes Mother," replied Alexandra. "I'll be given a full horse whipping."

"Correct. And despite what happened last weekend, I'm still fairly confident that you'll never give me cause to do that, Alexandra. You aren't a naughty girl by nature, and I hope and believe that the small, light demonstration of the whip on your fully clothed bottom will be enough to make it even more of a deterrent for you than it already is."

Alexandra reflected that although she had always known of the threat of her mother's horse whip and dreaded the thought of receiving it, that particular punishment had never crossed her mind when she had done this, therefore she wondered if it was truly a deterrent. But she decided that this was not the time to be expressing such an opinion to her mother.

"In fact, maybe it is going to be time at some point in the near future to think about relaxing these boundary rules. But after what you've just done, I'm certainly not going to alter them at present. You aren't going to benefit from this disobedience, simply because you've managed to come to no harm on this occasion."

"No. Of course not, Mother," said Alexandra.

"But we shall see what happens. You must understand though, sweetheart that you are all I've got, and I want to protect and guide you. Now, I know that I run a strict regime, but you are allowed some leeway to express yourself and tell me if there's something you want to do, as you did last week. There are limits as to how far I will let you go in challenging the authority of my skirt though, which might be tighter than some other mothers of girls of your age, and you must at least respect my opinion and *always* accept my decision as the way something must be, once I have clearly stated that it is final. I am your mother and I *do* know best, Alexandra. I am in charge, I give the orders and expect you to be compliant. You mostly are, but have considerably disobeyed me this time. Do not do so again!"

"No Mother. I won't. I promise," replied Alexandra.

"I might have considered letting you buy Heidi Fisher's latest book or even given it to you as a present for the Festival of Divinity, but under the present circumstances I'm afraid that book is prohibited until further notice, Alexandra. Do I make myself clear? If you dare try and go behind my back to disobey me again in order to obtain it, and I find out – which I will – then you'll be caned. Maybe we'll review the situation after the Festival."

"That's crystal clear, Mother."

"Good," said Linda. "And on the week after next you have your tests at Charterhouse to sit, so next week I want your mind to be totally focused on revising for them. It's very important that you do as well as you can in them, Alexandra. You're more than capable of getting in to the 'A' stream."

"Yes Mother."

Linda finished her coffee and took another sip of port. "Alright. Lecture over. The subject is now closed, and we'll move on. Come here, darling!"

She wrapped her daughter up in her arms and gave her another big kiss. Alexandra returned it and was kissed four more times as her mother ran fingers lightly through her hair and brushed the tips.

"Ooh Mother. You're making me tingle!" she exclaimed.

Linda smiled. "Lots more tingles to come for you tonight, darling" she said, softly.

She felt her daughter's heartbeat quicken. This night of the week was always the one when Alexandra was quickest up to bed, because it was her mother's...

***

On the same day that this was happening at The Grange, Miriam Payne received a letter from Lauren at Charterhouse, telling her all about what had happened that week. She strongly denied having written the rude statement on the exercise yard wall and insisted that it had been somebody else.

Mrs Payne could not believe that her daughter would have done such a thing either and was furious at the conclusion that the headmistress appeared to have jumped to. She immediately rattled off an official letter of complaint to the chair of the board of governors about Mrs Spencer's actions.

CHAPTER 49

"This is outrageous! Things are getting out of hand!" exclaimed Mrs Willis. "We must do something soon."

"*Getting* out of hand, Jayne?" remarked Sue Whitelaw, "I'd say that things have been out of hand here ever since that blasted Spencer woman took over as headmistress last autumn!"

"I agree," said Norah Nettleton, the head of Geratican language at Charterhouse. "But we really should at least try to take some action."

The three mistresses were meeting in secret in Mrs Nettleton's office at the end of the day's official curriculum on 1/35/05.

"And you propose to write a letter to the chair of the governors?" asked Sue. "Don't get me wrong, nobody would like to bring that woman down a peg or two more than me. She had absolutely no right to spring that inspection on me last week, and it was obviously just a set up. I was fuming, and of course 'the headmistress's daughter' ensured that I got given the maximum amount of trouble whilst not being able to do a thing about it! That's the reason why I didn't get an interview for the head position in my department. But we must tread carefully. If she thinks that we're going to rock the boat too much, we could end up making things even worse."

"Rocking the boat might be an unfortunate turn of phrase just at the moment, after what happened to ours the other weekend!" said Jayne.

"We'll do it anonymously," explained Norah. "If we all decide together what we'd like to say, then I'll draft it and type it up. But our names will not be revealed. There is a board meeting being held here on day three of this week, so I'll make sure that the chair receives it in time for that. Sue has been treated disgracefully, and we cannot let it go without some sort of fight. But we all know of

other things that have gone on – especially since the arrival of Gillian Spencer."

"Well, it's worth a try, obviously," said Mrs Willis. "But to be honest, I'm not sure if it'll make much of a difference. Mrs Spencer's got most of that board in her pocket. She can more or less do what she likes here, just as in turn Spencer Junior does the same in her lessons!"

"Let's give it a try, though," said Mrs Whitelaw. "I could never forgive myself if I didn't make a fuss about what's just happened to me at least."

"Right," asserted Mrs Nettleton, reaching for her pen. "Then let's begin..."

***

At 10.00 am on 3/35/05, the board meeting took place.

"Moving on to the next item on the agenda, ladies," said the chairwoman, Mavis Baverstock. "The headmistress."

She pressed a button beside her on the conference table.

"Is Mrs Spencer there, Janine?"

"Yes. She's ready for you now," replied her secretary.

"Good. Send her in please."

The door opened and the headmistress walked in.

"Take a seat please, Elizabeth," said Mavis. "I'm sure that this won't take long."

"Thank you, Chair," replied Elizabeth.

"We've received a couple of communications which we just need to quickly discuss," continued Mavis. "Firstly, a Mrs Miriam Payne, is alleging that you falsely accused her daughter, Lauren – one of our third year pupils – of writing an offensive message on the exercise yard wall. Secondly, I've been sent a letter from three mistresses who say that they wish to remain anonymous, making various wild claims, but lastly that you deliberately arranged for a negative assessment to be made of one of the geography mistresses, Sue Whitehall to be conducted by my fellow board member, Edna Haskins, in order to discredit her teaching ability in class and thus deny her an interview for the vacant head of department position. If you wish I can show you a copy of each of the letters."

"Thank you, Chair" said Elizabeth, taking them from Mavis's hand. She quickly looked at them.

"As to the first letter, I have met Miriam Payne previously, when I was still a science mistress. She took offence at something I had written on her daughter's prep, asserting that I was wrong. I was not and I am afraid that the woman is quite deranged! *She* is wrong over this. My daughter, Gillian, clearly overheard Lauren in the Rovers House recreation room making the very same remark that was shortly afterwards chalked on the exercise yard wall. I trust her judgement over this. It was obviously Lauren Payne who wrote it.

"With regards to this other letter from these three mistresses who do not wish to reveal themselves to us, I say that firstly if they wish to make such an allegation, they should be women about it and have the courage to say it openly to my face, and that secondly, I will run this college as I see fit. Nothing improper has taken place and if I decide to have an impromptu check on a mistress's teaching skills to keep her on her toes, then it is none of their business. This assessment of Mrs Whitehall certainly was not done in order to provide some sort of excuse not to select her for an interview for the position of head of department!"

The chairwoman nodded. She knew that this was exactly why the assessment had been carried out, but there was an agreement between the headmistress and a majority of the board of governors that Mrs Spencer could conduct affairs at the college as she wanted – without too many questions asked. Mavis was indeed very grateful for the payment that Elizabeth had slipped to her upon being appointed.

"It does seem rather a coincidence though, does it not?" asked one board member, Sonia Eastman.

"A coincidence it may seem to some, but a coincidence is all that it is!" snapped Elizabeth.

"Hmm, well I think what you've said is broadly in line with what I thought the true position was," said Mavis. "I think – if the rest of the board are in agreement – that we can dismiss these allegations forthwith."

None of the other members said anything. Mavis smiled at Elizabeth.

"I think that will be all, Mrs Spencer!" she said.

"Thank you, Chair!" replied Elizabeth.

She got up and left the boardroom. Things were going quite well so far this term. She felt secure in her position, knowing that she had rock solid backing from the board of governors. She wondered who precisely the three mistresses were though. She had some ideas, but she would probably not be able to prove anything...

CHAPTER 50

Throughout the next week, the girls of 1F and 1H at Charterhouse sat their tests to determine who would be in the 'A' and 'B' streams from week 38 onwards.

Alexandra knew the significance of the tests. Linda had gone to great lengths to ensure that her daughter was well prepared for them. She felt light waves of nervousness wash over her as they began. But she was a natural student and wanted to do well for herself, as well as for her future at the college and to please her mother.

In fact, Alexandra often found that when lessons were like this, they were more comfortable to her. Once a test began, she could soon become absorbed in it and in truth she was by now quite confident in her ability to perform in the discipline. She didn't have to worry about speaking during the class. Taking tests and exams was one thing that she knew she was good at. Alexandra wasn't as naturally competitive as some females of her race, but if she was aware of her capability in beating the other girls and if she came top of the class then she did feel a sense of pride.

***

During week 37 the girls gradually started to get their results. Alexandra and Gillian mostly shared out the top positions in 1F. To Gillian's frustration, Alexandra was first in mathematics, though it was partly tempered by the fact that she herself managed the same feat in her favourite subject of science. Imelda was annoyed with herself as only a careless mistake had stopped her from beating Benita in Geratican language. On 4/37/05, the 'A' and 'B' stream members were officially announced. In fact it turned out that all but one member of 1F had made it to the 'A' stream. That one was Melanie. From 1H, Emma Thatcher became the last member, and everybody else was put into the 'B' stream. The 'A'

stream class would subsequently contain the same members throughout the years to come, up until they took their Certificate of Geratica examinations.

***

Linda was immensely pleased and proud of her daughter when she heard the news, and she treated Alexandra to an evening in a box at a theatre in Avermore on 6/38/05, travelling there and back by train. The start of the Festival of Divinity was only just over a week away, and the town was richly decorated with coloured lights and bunting – as was Greenacres, including of course the hamlet of Elmsbrook and at The Grange and The Lodge.

As was traditional the Festival of Divinity officially began on day 1 of week 40. The official story paying tribute to the Divine Being was performed by members of the community, involving both adults and children and accompanied by singing from choristers. Linda performed her usual role as one of the narrators. Along with other local dignitaries she also made a brief speech and traditional festive songs were sung, led by the choristers.

CHAPTER 51

Geratica Winter 5006

ON 5/2/06, Linda celebrated her fortieth birthday. At the palace she was taken out to lunch by all her staff in the court

administration department, and at The Grange Alexandra baked her a special cake.

PART 10

CHAPTER 52

Geratica Spring 5007

At The Grange Linda was hosting a small dinner party. The guest of honour was to be Queen Alexandra of Geratica.

Linda told her daughter that she naturally expected her to help with the preparation of the meal. She asked her for any thoughts with regards to courses. Alexandra, keen to demonstrate to her mother what she'd been learning in cookery lessons at Charterhouse, suggested a particular new dish which they'd recently prepared in a lesson for the starter. She believed that their dinner guests would enjoy it just as much as her contemporaries had at the college. However, Linda wasn't keen and felt that another more traditional one would go better with her planned main course.

Alexandra was slightly disappointed and tried delicately to convince her mother to change her mind, as she felt that her own combination would work just as well. But after several minutes of debate, Linda quite literally put her foot down, very lightly pressing the sole of her shoe over Alexandra's toe and looking her in the eye.

"Now Alexandra, we've discussed the options together, but you know that I make the final decisions. I'm clear that my way is best and that's the way it will be. I trust that's understood and there'll be no more argument?"

Her daughter looked back at her.

"Um, er, yes Mother," she replied in resignation.

On the night, the queen was sat at the head of the dining room table, with Linda to her right. Alexandra sat beside her mother. Fiona was opposite her, but the other guests were women who she hadn't met before. (It was a formal gathering, with family members

not invited, however as hostess, Linda was making an exception for her daughter, to enable her to be part of the gathering, rather than stay in the breakfast room with the queen's lady-in-waiting and her bodyguards). Alexandra had spent most of the time before the dinner, in the kitchen helping her mother to prepare it, which she was quite happy about, as she didn't feel comfortable socialising with the guests.

During the meal she sat quietly listening to the conversations. Most of the talk centred around current affairs and political matters and Alexandra understood the general thread of the discussion, but she didn't feel ready to contribute anything herself yet – she found the prospect so overwhelming and daunting, and wondered if she would ever have enough confidence to do so. A couple of people made general enquiries of her which she answered politely and with deference, in the manner that her mother had brought her up to behave in social occasions. Linda held her daughter's hand beneath the table for protection throughout most of the dinner when they weren't eating. Alexandra hadn't yet begun to drink alcohol, so she was just drinking water.

After they had all finished their dessert course, Linda invited them to adjourn to the parlour for after dinner drinks. This she intended to be a landmark moment for her daughter. As the women relaxed with their beverages, and some smoked and played cards (including Linda herself, who smoked cigars socially), Alexandra was to play the piano in the background. She was becoming quite proficient in the art, and her mother hoped that her confidence could be boosted by knowing that she was capable of performing behind the scenes in a small gathering. Linda held dinner parties from time to time and she thought that this could become a regular occurrence. Alexandra had been worried by the suggestion, but her mother had gradually encouraged her to give it a go. And what better party to begin with than one with the queen as guest of honour, she had said. Alexandra had expressed a hope that she might start with slightly less exalted company but Linda had insisted, and her daughter had agreed with some trepidation.

Seated at the piano she took a deep breath and began to play. She started off with something from her favourite Geratican composer, Philippa Barrington. There was a light round of applause. Gradually as she continued, she found that with the women concentrating on their social activities, she was able to play without feeling the pressure of anybody closely observing her performance, though she still tried to be at her best and didn't think that she made any significant mistakes.

At the end of the evening, before the queen left, she congratulated Alexandra on her ability and told her how much she had enjoyed listening to her. Alexandra was relieved and honoured to receive her praise and thanked her very much. Linda was also delighted that her faith in her daughter had been justified, and it was decided that Alexandra would take on this role at any dinner party in the future...

As it happened, at a later dinner party at The Grange, with a different main course, Alexandra's starter was cooked and everybody thoroughly enjoyed it...

CHAPTER 53

Geratica Summer 5007

One evening, Linda and Fiona both attended a dinner at the Sackville estate. Alexandra joined her mother and Fiona brought Tom with her too. Colin stayed at home. Fiona explained that she thought that somebody should remain to hold the fort at Elmsbrook, though truthfully most of the guests were not surprised at his absence, as he rarely came to social gatherings. There were four other guests who Alexandra didn't know.

Being very shy Alexandra always kept quiet in such company and Linda held her hand under the table. She was in any case very sure to be on her best behaviour. Her mother had warned of what would happen when they got home, if she wasn't. As Alexandra listened to the women talking politics, she was doubtful if even when she was older she could ever find the courage to join in and contribute. The company of a group of typically strong assertive Geratican women was still rather daunting to her.

After the meal, when the adults retired to the parlour for some card games, Lady Sackville suggested that Tom show Alexandra the estate, as he worked there part time. Linda and Fiona both agreed, though Linda urged her daughter to be careful.

Tom took Alexandra outside. Eventually as they ventured around the side of the mansion house, they came across a door with no handle which looked as if it was designed to blend in with the wall and not be noticed. It was only Alexandra's sharp eyes which did do so. Tom gave it a push and to their surprise it opened. Beyond, there seemed to be a narrow passageway. Tom stepped inside.

"Tom, I'm not sure if we should go down there,' cautioned Alexandra. 'It might be private. You know what Mother said. I'll be in a lot of trouble later, if she finds out that I've been somewhere I shouldn't."

"Well you stay here and I'll take a look then," replied Tom.

"Alright," said Alexandra. 'But don't be too long.'

Tom set off, and she waited, anxiously looking around in case somebody should come and tell them off.

Soon afterwards, Tom returned.

"Don't worry," he said, grinning. "The passage just leads to another door with no handle like this one, which opens onto a corridor inside. There's nothing else. Come through and close this door behind you. Then we can go back in through the other one."

Alexandra glanced around for a final time and then followed Tom, closing the door as he suggested. The passage was quite long, but as Tom had said, quite empty. Although there were several cobwebs. When they reached the end there was the other door.

"You know, I think that this must be a secret passageway,' she remarked, looking back. Judging by the dust and cobwebs, I doubt if anybody's been along here for some time."

"Well I never," replied Tom. "I wonder what it was used for?"

"Perhaps it was for if somebody wanted to escape unnoticed for any reason." said Alexandra. "You're definitely sure that this door opens?"

"Yes," confirmed Tom, "I checked it just now."

He demonstrated by pushing the door and the corridor inside was revealed. When they went through, Alexandra noted that this door also blended into the interior wall and seemed to be designed in such a way that it wouldn't be noticed.

"Tom," said Alexandra, as he closed the door after them, 'If this *is* a secret passageway, then let's keep the fact that we found it to ourselves. I still think that perhaps we weren't supposed to.'

"Alright then," replied Tom, smiling. "If you like."

They continued exploring until later being reunited with their mothers.

Little did Alexandra and Tom know then that the passageway would be used again in just over three years' time, and Alexandra's knowledge of it would be of crucial importance in bringing to an end a major incident at the estate.

CHAPTER 54

In the autumn Linda took Alexandra back to the Sackville Estate.

Linda was an accomplished horsewoman and had the hiring of Chestnut, one of Lady Sackville's mares from her stables, which she rode on hunting expeditions. She'd now decided that it was high time her daughter learnt the art of equestrianism and was today going to give Alexandra a lesson in the basics.

She had special permission to use one of the paddocks on the estate and had brought her horse out. Beside the mare stood a male pony, Casper, which Alexandra was going to practice on. One of Lady Sackville's grooms, Pamela, was also present.

Alexandra was worried. She didn't like the look of horses at all and couldn't disguise her trepidation as her mother encouraged her to fondle the pony's head, in order to gain his trust.

"For Geratica's sake girl, he won't bite!" exclaimed Linda.

As much as she loved her daughter, not for the first time Linda fought to control her impatience. Alexandra was extremely timid, and it never ceased to amaze her how she – who had never been nervous of anything in her life and always been supremely confident – could have sired a girl who was so much her opposite in that regard. Perhaps she'd inherited part of it from her father.

That's easy for you to say, Mother! thought Alexandra. *You're a natural with horses. I'm not so sure.*

Linda reached down and took her hand. Then she spoke in a kindlier fashion.

"Just try and relax, darling. Otherwise, you'll worry the stallion. Come on. You can do it."

"I'll try, Mother," replied Alexandra.

"Good girl. Right, now we'll begin. First you must mount. Listen carefully and watch me demonstrate with Chestnut. Hold the reins in the left hand along with part of the horse's mane. Then put the ball of your left foot in the left stirrup and your right hand on the saddle cantle. You next use the right leg to push up, while your hands balance the body weight over the horse. Step up to a standing position, with your right leg hanging next to your left. Swing your right leg up and over the horse's rump, being careful not to accidentally kick them on the way. Sit down in the saddle as gently as possible. Adjust your stirrups to the proper length. Put your right foot in the other stirrup. Remember to centre the ball of your foot on the stirrup, not your toe or heel."

Having shown the procedure, Linda now dismounted.

"Right, now let's see you have a try. I'll be stood here to hold Casper and help you up, as it's your first time."

Alexandra had been watching intently, knowing that her mother would be cross if she didn't pay proper attention. Gingerly she began the process and with support from Linda, after a few seconds she was at least sat on the pony.

Then Linda began to teach her daughter how to move Casper forward at a trot and then stop. After some difficulty, Alexandra did successfully advance, but she found it extremely hard to being the pony to a halt.

"You must assert yourself with the animal, Alexandra!" declared Linda. "You must show it who is in charge and make it follow your lead."

Alexandra didn't feel she'd ever shown any person that she was in charge before, let alone an animal. Even Tom. With a couple of orders from her mother and help from Pamela, the pony at last became still.

As Linda's lesson continued, the pony now moved to a gentle canter around the paddock. The general motion and the way Casper seemed to raise his forelegs every time she tried to stop, made Alexandra alarmed. Gradually her fear grew worse and worse, and she cried out in panic, terrified that she might fall, despite her mother's efforts to calm her. Eventually Linda managed to stop the animal and helped Alexandra back down on to the ground.

"Oh Mother," said Alexandra, pushing herself against her mother's body as she held her tight. "Please. I don't ever want to ride a horse! And I need to go to the lavatory!"

Linda was quite capable of judging natural or potential prowess in horsewomanship, and although it could obviously be attained with practice, she had to admit there could be no doubt that her daughter had no aptitude for the art at all, and indeed was terrified of such animals. Although she generally liked to encourage her to do things which she considered important or would help her to become as ladylike as possible – and to instruct her in the way she thought best – Linda nevertheless knew when not to push something too far and destroy Alexandra's already fragile confidence completely. Unless her daughter had a radical change of mind, there would be no more riding lessons.

***

A week later there was a shooting contest at the Sackville estate. Both Linda and Fiona were taking part. Alexandra was loading for her mother, whist Lucy Worthington, now Chief Administration Officer at Her Majesty's Court was doing so for Fiona. Three other ladies joined Lady Sackville to make up a party of six.

Tom was also there as a spectator, though his father was not. Linda had quietly warned Alexandra, just for the sake of clarity, that if she misbehaved in such exalted company as that which they'd be

mixing in that afternoon, then she'd have the belt taken to her, there and then.

"I won't, Mother," Alexandra had promised.

"Now remember what I've you, Alexandra," said Linda, before the contest began. "As soon as I empty one shotgun, you take it and hand me the next, which you've loaded, ready for me to fire."

"Yes Mother," replied Alexandra.

As they got underway, Alexandra found that this was a discipline she was much more capable of performing than that of riding a horse. Then she had to control the animal and show it who was in charge. But in this her mother was in the lead and she was assisting – which was much more the arrangement she was used to and generally preferred. Alexandra quite enjoyed her task.

What nobody present knew, was that Fiona had been trained in shooting by the Geraticaian Court and was a crack shot. Today, as it happened, she was in particularly good form and downed more birds than anybody else.

Linda was second. She never liked being bested by Fiona and felt a twinge of frustration – though she kept it hidden and congratulated her afterwards. Fiona lapped up the praise for her performance which she received. Linda did secretly vow to get her revenge – which she would in time.

CHAPTER 55

Geratica Summer 5008

Another activity which Linda encouraged Alexandra to get involved in was Crown Green Bowling, which had been growing in popularity amongst some Geraticans in recent times, adapted from the game that had originally been picked up from the planet Earth. There would eventually be a private green built at the royal palace in Avermore.

For several years now Linda had been the captain of Greenacres Town bowling club. Whilst showing Alexandra how to play the game on the lawn, in the back garden of The Grange over the previous summer, teaching her the correct stance and delivery and how to read the green, she had noticed that her daughter appeared to have some talent. In fact on an occasion when they had played a game together, Alexandra had beaten her. (Alexandra had been secretly amused by her mother's barely concealed annoyance at this, and it had reinforced her realisation that she was a very competitive woman).

Another thing which had made Alexandra smile, was what her mother had said, when once demonstrating a particular shot. "Now, in the words of all skilled players, I'll have one practice go at it. But if it works, it counts!" It did work. "But seriously though, darling," she added, "Don't think that you'd be getting practice goes in a competitive league game."

On one occasion whilst practising out on the lawn with her mother's set of bowls, with Linda inside the house, Alexandra had momentarily lost technique in her delivery. One of the bowls flew wildly from her hand and came to rest with a crash against a side of the greenhouse, smashing part of the glass. Linda had come rushing out at the sound. It was clearly an accident and luckily no serious harm was done to any of the plants in the greenhouse, but even so she'd been extremely cross with her daughter's carelessness,

and at the damage. Alexandra apologised wholeheartedly to her, but she was still scolded severely, before being marched back inside to the kitchen and given three beatings to her hand from the stick. A small amount was also deducted from her monthly allowance, towards paying for the cost of t.

However, later Linda had arranged for her daughter to meet the president of the club, and after a brief demonstration of her skills it had been agreed that Alexandra would partner her mother in the Castra League Division One team the next year, replacing her existing one who was retiring and moving away. There would though, be two games which she would miss, due to the necessity of her revising for her end of year exams. On these occasions a reserve would stand in.

Alexandra had been considerably nervous when she made her debut, and despite her ability, took a little time to get used to the pressure of the match play. But with her mother there beside her, she began to settle down, and began to gradually develop into one of the team's best players. She enjoyed the atmosphere, with the quiet applause at a good shot coming from a small group of spectators, and the women at the side of the green updating the scoreboard. Linda had also instructed her daughter on the etiquette of the game and the importance of respecting the referee. She had warned Alexandra that she would take her belt to her on the spot, should there ever be any misbehaviour on the green. It was noticed by most of the players that the junior Radcliffe was very quiet and shy, rarely straying far from her mother (whose presence she was always mindful of), and generally doing as she was told.

As far as their general approach to games, there was little doubt that the senior Radcliffe was the boss with regards to tactics.

The local rivals to Greenacres Town were Greenacres All-Comers, based in the other side of town, and towards the end of the summer, with Greenacres Town at the top of the table, they went to visit the All-Comers for an away derby match. They had already beaten them at home early in the summer, and Greenacres All-Comers had not had quite such a good season as their rivals. They now

needed to win this match to keep their hopes alive of winning the league title this year.

Alexandra felt an additional pressure when these two teams met, as the All-Comers were captained by none other than her headmistress at Charterhouse, Elizabeth Spencer.

On a typically warm day, with the musty smell of summer in the air, the first game of the match when all eight members of the team played as a group against the other team, was won by Greenacres Town, making the score 1-0 to them. Alexandra scored the most points of all the players. Then after lunch, the four pairs games began. Alexandra had been relieved during their home match that she and her mother had not been drawn against Mrs Spencer and her partner Rose Harman, but this time their names were the last to be drawn out of the hat, meaning that they would play the final game. Alexandra hoped that the match might be over by that time, so that the game would be a 'dead rubber' and not matter.

Greenacres Town moved to within one game of victory when they won the first pairs game for 2-0. However, Elizabeth roused her team to fight back, and to Alexandra's growing dismay the next two games were won by the All-Comers, though they were close affairs. It would indeed all come down to the deciding game.

As Elizabeth and Rose shook hands with Linda and Alexandra before the start, the Charterhouse headmistress attempted to unnerve her pupil.

"Well, I must say that I've been looking forward to this!" she exclaimed with a broad smile. "You might have the potential to be a good player, Miss Radcliffe. But this is where the big girls really show what they're made of!"

Linda was not pleased with this comment. She had only just recently managed to gain a seat on the Charterhouse board of governors (with greater difficulty than she'd anticipated which had also disgruntled her).

"Don't take any notice of that, darling!" she said quietly in her daughter's ear as they prepared to begin. "She's just trying to intimidate you. You're at least as good, if not better than anyone else here. Now remember what I've always told you. Just concentrate on your own bowls as they come, maintain your technique and don't worry about anything else."

The game was another close contest. At 17-17, Elizabeth and Rose had three winning shots – one of her own the nearest, closely flanked by two of Rose's - with only Alexandra's last bowl to come. Elizabeth was confident that all three shots were banked, and they were about to move to within a shot of winning this vital match for their club. But summoning up some determination from within her, perhaps strengthened by wanting to dispel the slight that she had been given by her headmistress before the start, Alexandra sent her bowl down the green and finding a path, with perfect line and length it drew Elizabeth's shot away and nestled against the jack, giving them the winning shot instead for 18-17. Mrs Spencer's smile abruptly left her face and Alexandra distinctly thought that she heard her headmistress mutter a swear word.

Linda was beside herself with delight. "Well done, Alexandra!" she said, quietly. "Now we'll see how big Mrs Spencer really is!"

The Radcliffes moved further clear at the next end by taking another shot. It was now 19-17, and they needed just another two to win. Alexandra could see beads of sweat dripping from Elizabeth's forehead, and she was forced to mop her brow. She and Rose rallied at the next end taking a shot at and making the score 19-18. But in the next, Linda managed to force one of Rose's bowls off the green and finished by taking the winning shot and with this they moved to 20-18. This proved to be the killing trust and in the next end Alexandra secured their final shot to win the game 21-18 and the match for Greenacres Town 3-2.

In the end, as everybody shook hands, Elizabeth took the defeat with apparent good grace.

"Well done, Alexandra. I have to admit that you are a highly skilled player. I thought that we more or less had the match at that end when you stole the shot from us with your last bowl!"

"Thank you, Mrs Spencer," replied Alexandra, politely. "You played well, also."

Elizabeth's gracious words placated Linda a little. But inside, Elizabeth was still fuming that she and Rose had let near victory slip from their grasp, and that of all people it had been one of her blasted girls from Charterhouse who had taken it from them. Not just any girl either, but Mrs Radcliffe's daughter, which made it an even more bitter pill to swallow. She vowed that this defeat would one day be avenged in some way.

***

The following weekend, Greenacres Town secured the League Division One title in Alexandra's first year with the team, making Linda the proudest mother in Geratica that summer.

CHAPTER 56

Geratica Autumn 5008

Linda was sat in the car during her lunch break in Avermore, eating her sandwiches. She was parked in a quiet street about a mile away from the palace. In the passenger seat was a man also eating some sandwiches – James Spencer.

"So, how are things with your daughter at Charterhouse then?" she asked.

"Well, I don't hear all that much about her from her mother, but I think she's doing well – particularly in the subjects that interest her," replied James. "I imagine that she's a bit of a handful in her behaviour, though! I leave those kind of issues to Elizabeth, and I think that on that at least, my wife prefers it that way. She's Gillian's headmistress too, after all. If I knew everything she got up to, then I suppose I might not be entirely comfortable. How about yours?"

"Alexandra is certainly a good girl at school, I'm happy to say," said Linda. "She knows that there will be more trouble at home if not, and I do keep a check on her. And she's also very academically gifted. I'm confident that she'll pass the Certificate of Geratica next summer and go on to study for the advanced level. She's a very studious girl and she also takes quite an interest in current affairs. There was recently a trip to see Her Majesty in a session of parliament for the girls in her form class and I know that she was delighted to come – obviously she saw me working behind her too - and then afterwards when the others had gone back, she came over to my little empire and was shown the records room at the end of the corridor.

"She clearly lacks confidence for a girl, to a degree that I will admit has occasionally concerned me, but she is getting there,

though it can be a bit up and down. I'm not sure where she gets it from – certainly not from me – but maybe she's inherited some of her father's genes. She truly hates using the telephone, but I am trying to encourage her to make the odd call for me. I do believe that in her own way she can achieve a lot, but I need to support and guide her."

"Elizabeth was telling me that there was a story in the Greenacres Observer a couple of weeks ago, which said that two young local girls had been messing about during the summer holiday, ringing household doorbells and then running away before the owners answered," said James.

"Yes, I read that too," replied Linda. "They were eventually caught by a passing policewoman - who gave them a biff on their bottoms with her truncheon - and received a warning in the presence of their parents. Their mothers also personally caned them later of course, but no further action was deemed necessary. I made sure that Alexandra's attention was drawn to the article and warned her of the consequences should I ever find out that she had dared to get involved in such behaviour. I was given an assurance by my daughter that she would not."

(Alexandra had heard another story however, in Judith Warwicker's grocery store, that the same thing was happening in a street nearby, though it wasn't known who precisely was doing it. She couldn't help but wonder if perhaps Gillian was involved).

"She's shown a talent for bowls," remarked James.

"Yes, well obviously I was delighted about that. I could immediately tell that she was a natural at the game when she started playing it with me on the lawn at The Grange. For Greenacres Town to win the First Division League title this summer in the first season that she partnered me in the team was a joy. She plays the piano very well too, and she was persuaded to do it to entertain the guests at some of my dinner parties at The Grange – including when Queen Alexandra visited, a year and a

half ago now. Of course, that was just before you started with us at the palace."

James had become chauffeur to Queen Alexandra in the summer of 5007. When Linda had first seen his name as an applicant for the position, she had actually been quite dismayed as she realised who his wife was. (She had on occasions seen him spectating at bowls matches against Greenacres All-Comers, when he was supporting his wife, but there'd never been any need for them to be introduced then and it had been some time ago). However, when she had interviewed him alone in the administration department meeting room, two things had happened.

Firstly, she had found him to be a most amiable person, who was very much the kind of man that she liked. Slowly but surely there was a growing movement developing for greater male rights and she understood that there was even now a formal group calling itself the 'Male Rights Protestors.' Linda totally disagreed with their views though they were entitled to them, and she was determined that no man with that particular persuasion would ever work in the royal palace of Geratica – especially not the chauffeur to the queen. But Mr. Spencer appeared to be much more traditional in his thoughts than his outspoken wife.

Secondly, she had almost immediately experienced the strongest sexual arousal that she had felt in the almost seven years since losing her husband. He was similar in stature and with his dark hair he really did remind her of Robert. Linda had found him so attractive that once she had decided to appoint him and he had agreed, she had found that she was unable to fully remove him from her mind, even after finishing work for the day and returning home. Whilst washing up, her thoughts occasionally drifted towards carnal desire.

James was actually the first male chauffeur that the court of Geratica had ever employed to serve its monarch, and some in the palace had been surprised that Mrs Radcliffe of all people would employ one. But he had proved to be an excellent choice and Queen Alexandra was very happy with him. It was also the case

that in recent times more men had started to drive, though it would normally still be the lady of the house who would take the responsibility domestically. Robert had never done it. Some women still rather regarded the activity as their preserve though and were prone to making disparaging remarks about male drivers.

Linda had got to know James quite well whilst preparing for the queen's official engagements and in the royal car during the journeys to them. She was gradually becoming quite fond of him and had recently started to ask him out to lunch with her on occasions. Due to the fact that he was a married man – and to Elizabeth Spencer too – she always made sure to be very discreet, which was why at the moment they always travelled to this spot in her car where they could talk. So far Linda was not aware that there was any serious gossip going on about them within the palace walls.

She *was* aware that there were problems in Elizabeth and James' marriage, and that he was not very happy (that was one of the reasons why he'd eventually stopped being at the bowls matches). Linda did harbour the occasional thought that maybe she could make him happy, but she wasn't going to break up their marriage for them. She wasn't going to suggest an affair, despite the fact that she longed to make love to a man again and liking James very much as she did, he would be the man she would ideally choose to take to bed. But Linda wasn't sure if James would, when it came to it, ever leave his wife – or indeed if Elizabeth would ever let him go – so she had to move slowly.

She still of course loved Robert, and kept a picture of him in a locket given to her by her mother on her fourteenth birthday. Linda generally wore it discreetly about her person, but would occasionally allow it to be visible.

"The one thing that didn't go so well was when I tried to give her a basic horse-riding lesson one weekend last autumn at the Sackville estate," she continued. "She was found a pony to ride, but she was clearly so terrified that I had to abandon it. I've not made any more attempts since. I really don't think that she's going to be much of a

horsewoman! She won't be accompanying me on any hunting expeditions, I fear. She did seem to be more happy assisting me with shooting as a loader, though, again at the Sackville estate. Fiona Clark was shooing also and her stepson, Tom, who works at the estate part time was there as well."

"Hmm. Gillian sometimes loads for Elizabeth too," remarked James.

"Your wife and I don't tend to meet very much at such events," said Linda. "I don't think that you'll take offence James, when I tell you that I tend to avoid a social occasion if I know that Elizabeth will be there!"

"No. You're right. I won't Linda!" he confirmed.

"And how are things in that respect?" asked Linda.

"Still about the same," replied James. "You know that Elizabeth wants me to be more of the kind of modern man that she sees as the future for Geratica."

"*She* may see that as the future, but it will never happen for as long as *I* have anything to do with it!" growled Linda. "Women are naturally born to lead on our world and the men to be subservient. That is how the Divine Being created us in our minds at the core of the planet and we have no right to change it, no matter what these radical hotheads say! Your wife is supposed to be intelligent. I can't understand why she's so supportive of such tosh!"

"She says it's precisely because she's a scientist that she does," said James. "She's all for going down to the core and investigating. Because we know that Geraticai was somehow formed as a parallel world, but many people aren't sure why or how, she'd like to try and find out and at the same time see if it's possible to find a way of altering the make-up of our minds so that men are able to become more naturally prominent in society."

"Yes, well our scientists are constantly monitoring the core," replied Linda. "That's how we're able to form a judgement on the situation as we see it at the moment. But it would be far too dangerous and reckless to actually go down there yet, until we know a lot more about what we might have to deal with when we do. And if we ever do, then it will only be to try and fix the problem of Geraticai, assuming that we can without harming Geratica in the process. But we will do nothing to alter the basic and natural make-up of Geratican – and probably Geraticaian – women and men."

"Hmm," said James. "Anyhow, I don't like this kind of new relationship. She's changing the terms of our marriage contract somewhat. When we married, our agreement was more traditional, in that the running of the house was to be her affair. And yet now she has me dealing with some of the money matters myself and even paying a bill on an occasion. In fact, I don't much care for answering phones myself, but Elizabeth likes to suggest that it's not just the responsibility of the lady of the house."

"Well, it's not my place to interfere," remarked Linda, "But I'm strongly of the opinion that the terms of a marriage contract, once agreed and signed, should on both sides be abided by forever."

James coughed lightly. "She even now prefers me to go on top when we make love – and that feels most unnatural to me too!"

Linda pulled a face. She had met very few women in her entire life who, if the subject was ever discussed, said that they didn't have sex in the standard position of on top, partly because of the way their organs were designed, and because sexual activity was generated by the female's arousal – which was why most women naturally took the lead. Women were stronger sexually than men. It could be done another way, but it was surely not so pleasurable for either sex - and Linda had never been in any doubt when she made love to a man that it was the greatest pleasure possible. When Robert had been alive, she had not been able to get enough of it, and she always liked to lead and be in total control of everything she did. It was such a strange idea to her that a woman would want

a man to be on top that the thought actually occurred to her that Elizabeth Spencer might be a bit 'kinky' but she kept it to herself.

"I don't doubt it, James!" she exclaimed. "When Robert was alive, I can assure you that he was always beneath me every night and even some mornings too. And if I say so myself, I kept him very satisfied!"

Linda's geratis became erect both at that memory and of what she'd like to do to James in the future, if she ever got the opportunity. At the same time James's genus inflated as he imagined a woman making love to him in the old fashioned way – and it was Linda who was stirring up the thoughts in his mind. For a couple of moments after they had finished eating their sandwiches they each sat feeling intense sexual arousal at the other, but not wishing to let it be too well known at this stage. They were not lovers, but they were fast developing a deep friendship...

CHAPTER 57

After returning to her office, Linda had a comparatively short afternoon and at 3.30 pm she finished for the week, got in the car and drove away. But her immediate destination was not Greenacres. Instead she headed towards Buckmore and Charterhouse College. It wasn't very often that she did it, but tonight she was picking Alexandra up and driving her home.

At 4.00 pm she arrived and drove up the road towards the school gates. Alexandra was waiting just outside. Linda waved and stopped the car, and her daughter opened the door and got in.

"Hello darling!" said Linda, warmly, reaching out to embrace her.

"Hello Mother!" replied Alexandra, and they kissed.

"Have you had a good day?" asked Linda. "And you've been a good girl?"

"Yes Mother, I have. And I've worked hard. How was yours?"

"Oh, fairly routine, sweetheart, for day 5 of the week. Well now it's the weekend, and you've got the special treat of having me drive you home!"

Linda dropped the handbrake and they moved off. It wasn't long before she was giving Alexandra her views upon various things which were currently happening on Geratica. Her daughter listened quietly and attentively, occasionally indicating her agreement when necessary. As the car swept away from Buckmore, Alexandra was taken through streets that she didn't normally see when she was on her usual train journey home. Lights were coming on as the end of the day approached, and most of the traffic was made up of people on their way home from work for the weekend.

Then her mother reached the open road and they sped through the late afternoon light. Alexandra looked out of the window and saw fields and trees. The leaves had fallen and now the branches were bare.

Up above as the night drew in, she could see Geratica's two moons and the stars. Alexandra and her mother had always been interested observers of the night sky, with a telescope set up in the loft at The Grange.

Eventually she saw a road sign with Greenacres on it, with an arrow pointing the direction. Shortly afterwards her mother swung the car down a road and their hometown came into view. By just after 4.30 pm they reached Elmsbrook and Linda swiped her card to operate the security gate. It opened and she drove them up the hamlet drive and then down their own to The Grange. They were home at last.

***

Meanwhile on the other side of Greenacres, James also went home. This weekend his wife would be there too and going back to Charterhouse on the eve of the new week.

Late in the evening as Elizabeth read a scientific book which had just been published, her husband was sat beside her. Bedtime was approaching and he found himself actually thinking about Linda, and what he dreamed of her doing to him. James's genus started to balloon. However, he was a loyal man and he did still feel some duty to his wife. Instinctively he stretched out his hand and ran his finger over Elizabeth's crotch. He felt her geratis through her skirt and began to slowly stroke it. Elizabeth had always loved it when he did that, and tonight proved no exception. Her geratis hardened immediately and she shuddered, dropping the book on the floor in the process.

Wildly excited she looked at James and studied him. She sensed that this might be a moment when both of them wanted sex – something that was slowly becoming less common between them – and she decided to make the most of it.

"Take me to bed, James!" she said, seductively and held out her hand for him to take.

James took a deep breath. He had really hoped that she would take him. He stood up shyly and took Elizabeth's hand. They went up the stairs, Elizabeth turning the parlour light off as they left.

In the bedroom, Elizabeth got into her side of the bed and lay on her back.

"Make love to me, darling!" she cooed softly, stretching herself out and opening her legs.

James winced. "Oh Elizabeth! Couldn't we do it in the old traditional way again, just for once?"

"Oh nonsense, James! You know that I won't have talk of 'the traditional way' when it comes to the relationship between a man and a woman in this house. Don't be such a weed James. You can do it. Now come here!"

She held out her arms. With a heavy heart, James got into bed beside his wife and laid on top of her. Elizabeth's eager geratis immediately shot up into his vagina and found his genus. He kissed her lips and ran his fingers through her hair, then began to work his way over her body. Elizabeth's desire made her geratis thicken so much that it soon filled James's vagina and throbbed against its walls. James did still find his wife attractive, but somehow, having to make love in this position made things more difficult for him and the appeal was cooling. He couldn't really naturally summon up enough passion. His genus was only moderately inflated.

Elizabeth grew impatient. "Come on. *Dominate me, man!*" she urged.

Her geratis thrust upwards against James's genus as her desire began to reach its peak. James gripped her tight and kissed her mouth, feeling Elizabeth's tongue slip inside his own. They licked together, and James's arousal increased slightly. But still his genus was not responding to his wife's geratis in quite the way that she wanted or that he needed in order to orgasm.

He closed his eyes and thought of Linda. He imagined her making love to him. If he was in her bed now instead of Elizabeth's...It was a naughty thought but though he tried to put it out of his mind, he couldn't. And he found Linda gorgeously attractive. Now James finally did become truly aroused. It was his wife's geratis thrusting up against his now ballooning genus, but it was Linda who was turning him on. Suddenly he gave a groan as his genus exploded and he came, sending his sperm through the pores of Elizabeth's geratis. Seconds later Elizabeth had an orgasm too, moaning as she sprayed James's vagina walls with blue sticky fluid. He felt some nourishment in his veins.

Soon afterwards James rolled off Elizabeth. They had made love – though neither were entirely satisfied with the results. Unlike most Geratican partners – particularly the women - they did not seek any further activity in this regard that night, and instead went straight to sleep.

CHAPTER 58

The following evening, Alexandra assisted her mother in cooking their dinner at The Grange. Under Linda's strict tutoring she was learning to become quite proficient, though not, Alexandra was still certain, in her mother's class. As she was laying the dining room table ready for their dinner, she was surprised when her mother told her to set two wine glasses out. Linda always had a couple of tall and stout bottles of red with her meal on this night, and after they had dished up and Alexandra was sat at the table, she noticed that her mother had an extra bottle.

"Right then, darling," she said, as she unscrewed the top of one. "See what you think of this."

She poured some of the wine into the glass in front of her daughter.

Alexandra gaped. "Am I to be allowed to drink alcohol now, Mother?"

Linda smiled. "Well since I've just invited you to taste some, then I think the answer to that must be in the affirmative, sweetheart! Don't look so surprised. You're some way past your thirteenth birthday now, and most Geratican females begin to get familiar with it around then. Strictly in moderation though, at this stage. I shall teach you how to handle your drink!"

Her daughter took a breath and lifted the glass to her lips. Linda watched her reaction as she tasted the red wine for the first time.

"Well?" she asked. "What *do* you think?"

"Hmm," replied Alexandra. "It tastes nice, Mother!"

She took another slightly larger sip.

"I thought you'd say that," said Linda. "The idea is that you drink it with your meal as you eat, darling!"

"Oh! Yes, Mother. Sorry!"

Linda chuckled. "That's alright sweetheart. There aren't many women who don't like it, in my estimation. And you're approaching the age when you will officially become one. It's less than three years away now, which won't take long. You'll be taking your Certificate of Geratica exams next summer, and then I hope that you'll be going on to the advanced stage with a view to a university place after that."

"Yes Mother."

There was a pause as they ate, before Linda continued.

"I've now decided that you've reached a certain stage in your childhood, darling. You're a very well-behaved girl, you work hard, and I think that you're gradually developing in the way that you should in order to become a young woman. You're not one of the more confident or strongest of females in our race, and you still perhaps have a little way to go, but you've had some significant landmarks, notably in the way that you performed in the bowls matches over the summer, when we won the league – thanks to a not inconsiderable input from you – and you're now feeling able to entertain the guests on the piano in the background, when we have dinner parties.

"It's time I think to redraw the boundaries slightly. I'm no longer going to have sticks in the various rooms of the house. I don't think that they're needed any more. They will be officially retired. I believe that you know, respect and accept the rules of my house and that you understand the reasons for them. From today also, I am lifting the ban on you crossing over North or South Road without an adult, and you may travel beyond a mile away from The Grange on your own."

"Oh. Thank you, Mother," said Alexandra. She hadn't been expecting this tonight, either.

"I won't put any specific restrictions on exactly where you can go, but I do want to make it clear though Alexandra, that the other rules still apply. You are to always make sure that you're within The Grange after dusk. The cane will still be behind my desk in the study, even if there are no longer any sticks. And you have seen where I keep the whip!"

"Of course, Mother," replied Alexandra, obediently. "I promise not to break the rules. I haven't for a long time now!"

"No, you haven't, sweetheart. I know," agreed Linda. She didn't believe that her daughter would now.

They never discussed the incident that Alexandra had been given a semi-whipping for, though eventually Linda had allowed Alexandra to buy the book that Heidi Thomas had been promoting. It was on the bookshelf in her bedroom.

"You are still going to need me to guide you through the rest of your childhood, and I suspect beyond it sometimes too," she went on. "I shall instruct you in what to do, especially when – as is sometimes the case – you aren't sure of yourself. You and I will be a partnership. We will always discuss everything together and both of us express views. But obviously, as your mother I am the senior partner and you the junior. Therefore, I am the boss and will decide what is best for you. If you feel particularly strongly about something and we should reach an impasse, then I will do my best to accommodate you – though I don't think that such a situation will arise very often between us. When we do things together as we often will, then I think that it will probably only be natural and easier for you to defer to me in making a final decision – at least until you're older and are more fully capable and confident in yourself. Does that all sound reasonable to you?"

"It does, Mother. Thank you," replied Alexandra.

"Good," said Linda. "I won't stop you from putting your foot down exactly, but..."

"I will do it if I really feel the need to, but your foot will naturally be stronger, Mother!" said Alexandra, smiling.

Linda nodded and smiled back. She shifted her foot underneath the table and pressed it against her daughter's. Alexandra pressed on it lightly, before her mother responded by pushing down slightly harder on her own.

"Would you like a drop more wine?" asked Linda. "I see that you've already finished your first glass!"

"Ooh. Yes, thank you, Mother!" exclaimed Alexandra. "It is *very* nice, I have to say!"

Linda opened the second bottle and poured another amount into her daughter's glass, before giving herself a third.

"As I said, you'll be drinking in moderation to start off with, darling. You will doubtless realise that you aren't being served as much as me, but in time, as you get older I'm sure that we'll be consuming equal measures! Also, I don't want you to start thinking that you might be able to explore the delights of the drinks cabinet, should you be here on your own!"

She pointed to the cabinet by the wall.

"Your grandmother once made that mistake, but I too learnt from it in more ways than one, and I'm not about to make the same mistake with my own daughter! That cabinet will still be kept locked, and the key held by me. It will only be opened, and you will only drink here at The Grange, in my presence."

Alexandra stared at her mother for a few seconds, before she started to guess what she meant, and then she couldn't stop herself from giggling.

"Mother! Are you saying that..."

"Yes sweetheart," Linda anticipated her question. "One evening when your grandmother and grandfather were out, I decided that - as I knew plenty about Geratican alcoholic beverages - I would take the opportunity to sample some of them for myself. I certainly did enjoy what I tasted, and I drank more and more. Eventually when your grandparents returned, they found me blotto on the sofa! Grandmother had to put me to bed, and boy was I in trouble when I'd sobered up the following morning! I was only just a little older than you are now, and Grandmother considered what I'd done to have been grossly irresponsible and she caned me for it. She was right of course, in that I could have made myself even more ill or had some kind of accident falling over, and not been found by your grandparents until it was too late, but what made her most cross was that I drank all of her best port! The amount that she needed to replenish her supply was deducted from my allowance!"

Alexandra's giggles became a laugh.

"I'm sorry Mother!" she said, wiping the water from her eyes. "But you do sometimes tell me some good stories from your childhood, and that's a classic!"

"I thought that you'd like it," admitted Linda, as she waited for Alexandra to recover. She was in a good mood tonight, and happy to have some fun with her daughter. "Try not to give yourself indigestion, darling! One of the things that you can often suffer from when you're first learning to drink properly is hiccups. Take a couple of deep breaths!"

Alexandra did so.

"I'm sorry, Mother. I think that I'm alright now!"

Linda smiled and took her hand.

"That's alright. But that story does give you an insight into the perils of drinking too much before you're ready, and of not knowing as much as you might think about what you're actually

consuming. I mixed a lot of things which you shouldn't that evening!"

"Don't worry, Mother. I already realise that I don't know much about the subject, and I need you to teach me about it," Alexandra assured her. "Would you also cane me if I did what you did?"

"Well, you wouldn't be able to do it sweetheart, for the reason that I explained," remarked Linda. "But maybe now that I've got you started, then I wouldn't be quite so harsh – though that doesn't't mean that I want you to deliberately get yourself drunk, nor to get into the habit of it!"

"No. Of course not, Mother!" said Alexandra.

"And not a word of that story is to be passed on to your classmates at Charterhouse, is that clear?" asked Linda. "I've no doubt that they'd be just as amused as you were to know that the senior court administrator of Geratica once did that and got smashed out of her mind on her mother's sofa, and let's be honest, Geratican girls have been getting drunk whilst experimenting with alcohol for as long as it's been around – and even the odd boy too – though men cannot naturally drink as much as we women can, anyhow...have I said something to further amuse you, darling?"

Alexandra was giggling again.

"Smashed out of her mind! I never thought that I'd hear you use that expression, Mother!"

"Stoned, smashed, blotto! They all amount to the same thing. Drunk!" observed Linda. "Drunk as a Lady, even. What I was going to say was, let's please observe the rule of discretion in any information that we impart. Alright, I'll admit that I'm joking sightly, and it obviously wouldn't be the end of the world if anybody else knew, but I do like to keep our more intimate family affairs and any slightly embarrassing secrets private – partly to protect you, darling."

"I know Mother, and I do understand," said Alexandra. "Does that include Tom on this occasion?" She'd been very much looking forward to repeating the story to Tom. They shared the same sense of humour, and she was certain that he'd find it hilarious.

Linda looked at her daughter. She knew that Alexandra and Tom had become very close, growing up together as the only two children in their small hamlet, and she didn't mind at all. She was very fond of Tom. Her daughter couldn't have a better person to be a best friend. Linda was very much aware that they talked a great deal about what went on in their lives and the things that they heard.

"As long as it doesn't leave Elmsbrook," she replied. "Remember the watchword, Alexandra. Discretion."

"Yes Mother. Of course."

A few minutes later they were eating their dessert and Alexandra had another drop of wine. She had lost count of the number of glasses that her mother had drunk. Geratican women had a very high alcohol consumption level.

"Was Grandmother very strict, Mother?" she asked. "I'm not sure if it's my place to ask, but given what you've told me tonight - were you caned a lot?"

Linda smiled. "I don't mind you asking darling! I would say that your grandmother was about as strict as the average mother of my generation, which by today's standards might I suppose mean quite a lot – though I never thought much about it at the time. I was caned at least as many times by her as you have been by me – slightly more probably – but I certainly got into a lot more trouble than you ever have done through my temper. I used to stamp my foot a great deal as a young girl, when I didn't get my way, which earned me a few beatings when I went too far – and yes, I disobeyed her on occasions. I can't remember many of the reasons why now, though I'm certain that I learnt from the punishment. If you're wondering if I was ever whipped, then the answer is yes –

once – for going into Grandmother's car unsupervised, and then whilst I was pretending to drive it, letting the handbrake off so that the car jolted forward and crashed into the garage door, causing damage to both that and the car. Do *not* follow my example over this, Alexandra!"

"No Mother!" Alexandra didn't think it likely that she would ever be in the driver's seat of her mother's car. She had never really felt any desire to copy her mother in that area, though she knew that some other girls did. Most Geratican women drove, and Alexandra supposed that she probably would too eventually, but she wasn't eager for it to happen.

"When I look at old photographs of Grandmother, I must say that she sometimes looked quite stern," she continued.

"Well, I suppose a rather formal appearance and the style of clothing in those days made it appear so," replied Linda. "Also, your grandmother and grandfather were relatively senior in age when they had me. Grandmother was forty-eight at the time and Grandfather fifty. In my youth, many things were still more formal than they are for a lot of society now. As girls – and the boys too of course – we had to call any woman in authority Madam – including our school mistresses and even our mothers. You would always call your boss at work, Madam. Even today, I like my staff to still refer to me as Mrs Radcliffe. I'm old fashioned in that regard and very traditional – as you well know, Alexandra – and I like respect to be shown to those in authority. Girls at school and others at work were always referred to by their surnames. And if you think that discipline is strict now, you should have seen how things were when I was a small girl. You probably noticed that she had her cane under her arm. Mothers often carried them about, so that they were always at hand, even when they went out with their children. I remember it being lodged in the pushchair when your grandmother took me with her when she shopped."

"Oh. I must admit that I didn't realise it was as rigid as that, Mother!" exclaimed Alexandra.

"You children of today don't know you're born!" replied Linda. "The whip could still be used in schools, for the gravest of offences. Even the horse whippings at the royal palace were more severe."

"Even more than now, Mother?" exclaimed her daughter. "Then they must have been horrendous!"

"Well, the juveniles learnt their lesson," remarked Linda.

"Was that definitely the case for all of them though, Mother? Did none of them ever commit any further offences?"

"In some cases they must have done, yes obviously. But most I'm sure were deterred by the thought of more lashes from the queen and her court administrator."

"I must admit, Mother, that horse whippings trouble me. I'm not just talking about the thought of receiving one at the palace, either."

Linda eyed her. "Trouble you? What do you mean?"

Alexandra took a deep breath. This was still a subject that she'd never really expressed a view on to her mother.

"I think that it's an awful thing to inflict upon someone whatever they've done, Mother. And most children like me would never dream of doing anything so horrendous that a court would consider that we should be punished in such a way. The ones who would, probably never think about getting the horse whip before they commit a serious offence, anyhow. A lot of them take the attitude that they'll just make sure that they aren't caught, rather than be deterred."

"Do you know, in fact I hear some echoes of my own arguments when Her Majesty's court abolished the death penalty, a decade ago now," said Linda. "But I won't necessarily draw a parallel between the two subjects. We aren't talking about the taking of a

life here. A horse whipping has always been the traditional punishment for the most atrocious behaviour of juveniles, and you well know Alexandra that I am a staunch supporter of the old ways in most areas of life. Children *should* be – and I believe *are* – frightened of the lash on their bare skin!"

"Most, but maybe not all, Mother," countered Alexandra. She generally accepted what her mother thought, and as she got older was developing broadly similar conservative – albeit sometimes slightly more liberal – views. They rarely had exchanges of opinion, and for Alexandra, on the whole, what her mother said went. But this was something that she felt unusually passionate about.

"I've observed a lot of this in some of the girls who get caned the most at Charterhouse," she added. "Once the worst offenders get used to receiving the punishment, they think they're very hard and trendy amongst their peers and are almost deliberately doing things to get given it again. Most girls get it once or twice, but it often tends to be the same ones who keep getting punished repeatedly – often to compete with others as to who can get the most. And also, I suspect that rather than be deterred by it, there are some wayward juveniles who simply become resentful of how they've been treated and vow to become even more rebellious and defiant."

"Alexandra, I hope you aren't going to start becoming influenced by radical opinion!" remarked Linda, sternly. "I will not tolerate that from someone within my own house *and* the daughter of a woman in my position at the palace. As you well know, it is a small part of my duties to carry out such punishments on juveniles when a juvenile court sentences them, together with the monarch."

Despite the happy and jovial mood during their meal, Alexandra could hear the faint trace of annoyance in her mother's voice. She always by instinct tried to placate her as much as possible.

"No Mother, of course not. I agree that most of those views are wrong – and sometimes even dangerous. But this-"

"In any case darling, I am quite convinced that you will never end up being horse whipped at the palace, so I don't know why you're so bothered about it," interrupted Linda.

"It doesn't stop me being bothered by the thought of others having to suffer the ordeal though, Mother," replied Alexandra.

"Well, that's very laudable I'm sure, but they must still be punished," said Linda. "Those children should have thought about the whip before they misbehaved, but if they didn't then receiving it teaches them a lesson which they would be wise to learn."

"But they don't always learn it, do they, Mother?" replied Alexandra.

"If they are sensible and have enough intelligence, then they will,' retorted Linda.

"What about the ones who don't, Mother?" persisted Alexandra.

"Then they will be thrashed even harder the next time!" snapped Linda. "And that's my final word which is what goes, so there's an end to it. But if that's how you truly feel about this whole thing, Alexandra, then we'll agree to disagree."

Then she smiled, reached out and touched her daughter's arm. "Don't worry though, darling," she continued. "As you become a woman then I'm sure that you'll come around to my way of thinking."

"Yes Mother," replied Alexandra. She was sure her mother meant that she *expected* her to follow towards her viewpoint. But on this, she wasn't certain that she could.

CHAPTER 59

After their meal, Linda took Alexandra to the parlour for coffee and mints. As usual, both of them took their coffee black. For the first time Linda also poured her daughter a glass of port.

It wasn't long before Alexandra confirmed that she enjoyed this very much also.

A little later on, she was in her mother's bed. Alexandra snuggled up to her and they kissed. She felt the familiar tingles as Linda squeezed her tight and stroked her hair. Her mother's fingers ran lightly over her skin. She sighed with pleasure.

"Ooh Mother!" she gasped. "I can't imagine anything better than the way you make me feel on this night of every week. It's fantastic!"

Linda smiled. She hoped that one day when her daughter was an adult and with the right man, Alexandra would experience something ten times better than she could give her as a mother. On the other hand, there was a way that she as a woman could give even more pleasure to her daughter. Alexandra had entered the final stages of her childhood. She was probably ready for it.

Suddenly a huge wave of affection and desire came over Linda. She pulled Alexandra up against her again.

"You know my darling, your clever mother knows a few tricks that *could* make her daughter feel even better than she can imagine!"

Alexandra looked suddenly puzzled, and her eyes gazed enquiringly into her mother's.

In one movement Linda rolled her daughter onto her back and laid flat on top of her. Alexandra gave a small cry of surprise.

"It's alright, sweetheart. Now you just relax and leave everything to me," soothed her mother. "Just lay back and I'll love you!"

She wrapped her arms around Alexandra's shoulders, smoothed her hair and kissed her lips. Alexandra felt Linda's strong thighs squeeze her legs inside of them. The feeling of her mother's body covering her was something she had never experienced before, and it was wonderful. The smell of Linda's perfume filled Alexandra's nostrils. She oozed. Then she heard her mother's voice whisper softly into her ear.

*"I'll cover you in kisses and run my fingers all over your body, **my darling!** I know that you'll like that!"*

Alexandra's heart beat fast with excitement. Her mother kissed her lips again several times whilst she stroked her long blonde hair through to the tips. Then Linda's kisses moved down her daughter's neck, across her neck, and all over her chest to her stomach, with her fingers tracing a similar path, before continuing as she gently massaged Alexandra's thighs. Alexandra felt tingles like never before and she murmured in huge satisfaction.

Her mother's kisses travelled back up her body to her lips once more, and she felt herself being engulfed in the embrace of her arms and legs. Underneath her body, as she was held tight and kissed, Alexandra was in ecstasy and she sighed heavily.

Linda stopped kissing for a brief moment to give her daughter a short rest.

"Oh Mother, that was incredible!" breathed Alexandra. *"I never thought anything could feel so good!"*

Linda smiled again and moved close to her.

*"I've got much more loving left yet, and I'm going to give it **all** to you now, sweetheart! You just cling to me whilst I squeeze and kiss you to ecstasy! Go on. Slip your arms around my waist like normal. I'll take control."*

Alexandra's heart raced as she did so, and she looked wonderingly into her mother's eyes. How could she possibly feel any better than this?

Linda discerned the thought from Alexandra's eyes immediately. She couldn't wait any longer. She was a highly passionate and affectionate woman. Linda wanted to shower her daughter with so much loving that she truly would feel like never before, and herself experience the ecstasy that she always loved in giving it – just as she had used to when making love to Robert.

"Look into my eyes, darling!" she whispered, and kissed Alexandra's lips. Then she wrapped her arms tight around her daughter and locked her thighs inside of her own.

*"I love you **my darling**! I'll look after you always!"* said Linda, softly. *"I'm going to take you to ecstasy. I'll keep you safe. I'm going to give you all my love!"*

Then she began to passionately kiss her daughter. Alexandra's lips parted slightly, and Linda gently slipped her tongue inside of her mouth and licked her daughter's ever so softly. Alexandra experienced a brand new tingle and she exhaled heavily.

*"I'm going to give you all my love, **darling**!"* whispered Linda again, in between her kisses.

Alexandra felt her mother's hot breath over her face and her tall body smothering her as she held on to it. Somehow she did feel as if she was being taken on a journey.

*"**All** my loving for my darling!"*

Gradually Alexandra felt all of her senses being overwhelmed. As she continued to gaze into Linda's eyes, her mother squeezed her more than ever before and her fingers gently stroked part of her skin. Now everything she saw, felt, smelt, heard, and tasted was her mother. She felt herself dominated, having completely

surrendered control, yet trusting her mother totally – the way she always truly like it to be.

Linda's loving was reaching a climax, and her breathing was heavy. She thrust herself deep into her daughter's chest, as she held and kissed her. She was sighing with pleasure too now as she revelled in her own ecstasy. Alexandra felt as if she was right inside of her body. As each thrust seemed to come down deeper and deeper, she finally began to lose control.

Suddenly Alexandra felt the strangest sensation. She seemed to be floating above the bed inside the safety of her mother's firm embrace. She murmured in the deepest ecstasy she had ever felt and every part of her tingled. Then her breath shortened and her heart began to pound in her chest as her excitement and pleasure reached their zenith. The room started spinning around, lights flashed before her eyes and she saw stars. She gave a moan and clutched at her mother's body. Knowing that she had taken her daughter to the limit she could receive, and having reached the outer edges of her own energy in taking her there, Linda stopped and rolled off Alexandra.

Side by side they lay panting after the exertion for a moment. Then Linda leant over to look at Alexandra. Her breath was only just returning to normal. She slipped her arms around her smiling, and pulled her close to her body.

*"Did you enjoy that **my darling?**"* she asked, softly.

"Yes Mother, Thank you," Alexandra breathed back. Her eyes immediately closed, and Linda knew she was almost asleep. After the alcohol that she'd drunk for the first time that evening, followed by the sensation she'd experienced just now, it had never been going to take long tonight. Her mother gently eased her back on to the pillow on her side of the bed.

*"Goodnight, **my darling!**"* she whispered into her daughter's ear.

"*Goodnight, Mother!*" replied Alexandra, before finally drifting away...

***

The next morning, Alexandra awoke to the smell of cooking. As she opened her eyes, she glanced over to the other side of the bed and realised that her mother was already up and preparing breakfast downstairs in the kitchen. It had become a weekly treat for her on the morning after her night in this bedroom to be able to lie in until her mother had cooked it and then eat it with her in bed. They usually had a leisurely start to this morning, and there was always some more intimacy between too, before they got up for the day.

Alexandra stretched and relaxed. It was always very quiet in the hamlet. Somewhere outside she could hear the faint sound of car travelling along a road.

The bed was fitted with a special table that could be pulled across. She sat up, reached out and pulled one half of it over from her side of the bed, then moved over to the other side and did the same, before joining them together.

Thinking about intimacy made Alexandra immediately reflect on what had happened last night. She still wasn't quite sure what exactly had happened, although she did know that she had loved every minute of it.

It was still in her mind when her mother appeared at the door with a tray.

"Ah, good morning, darling," said Linda. "Breakfast is served. I was just wondering to myself as I came up the stairs whether I was going to have to actually wake you up before we ate it this week!"

"Good morning, Mother," replied Alexandra.

Linda set the tray down on the table, took off her dressing gown, and got into bed. After a first morning kiss, they took their plates and began to tuck in.

"Mmm. Mother this is delicious. Your cooking is the best!" exclaimed Alexandra.

Linda beamed. No matter how many times her daughter complimented her cooking – which she did regularly, and always seemed to devour everything that was put in front of her with great enthusiasm – she still loved to hear it. She was in any case very proud of her culinary skills.

"Thank you sweetheart!" she replied, leaning over and pecking Alexandra on the forehead as she ate.

Then Alexandra's thoughts returned to where they'd been when her mother had arrived with the breakfast.

"Mother? What you did last night. It was...it was...incredible!"

"I was fairly confident that you'd like it., darling," replied Linda. "I can assure you that it was my pleasure. I very much enjoyed doing it!"

"Um, Mother..." Alexandra made an effort to continue, trying to find the right words. What exactly..? I mean was that..? Well, no of course it couldn't have been, but what..?"

Linda chuckled. "Are you trying to ask if we committed some kind of sexual intercourse last night, Alexandra? Of course not! A bright girl of your age will know from her science lessons, if nothing else, that two Geraticans of the same sex cannot have intercourse, whether they be mother and daughter, father and son, or otherwise. It is biologically impossible. The act of intimacy that we indulged in was indeed similar to making love, but I promise you at the climax of sex something far greater happens and passes between a woman and a man. But that's a matter for another time.

And you know that you aren't legally allowed to participate in that kind of union until you are sixteen, Alexandra!"

Alexandra saw her mother's head tilt slightly in the direction of the chest of drawers where, to her cost, she knew where the horse whip was kept. She had never before thought about sex, but she was fairly certain that if she ever *was* caught having, or found out to have had sex before she was sixteen, then it was something that she would receive a full thrashing for.

"Yes Mother. I definitely do," she confirmed.

"As for exactly what it was last night, there isn't really any real technical term for it. It's an extension of our previous level of intimacy which as I've discussed with you before is perfectly legitimate and does go on in strict privacy, in certain circumstances, between women. I suppose really it's whatever you make of it. How would you describe what you felt at the end, darling?"

Alexandra considered, as she came towards the end of her last piece of bacon.

"Well. I think I'd say that it felt like you'd taken me over, Mother! All of my senses seemed to be dominated. The truth is that the room span around, and I saw stars. I even felt as if I was floating over the bed in your arms! You were in complete control. I was absolutely breathless by the end!"

"I know sweetheart, and that was when I knew that it was time to stop," replied Linda. "I said that I'd take you to ecstasy, and I believe that I did. But that was your limit and it could be dangerous to go any further. I was losing mine too in loving you, darling. I like feeling like I'm in full flight, which matches your analogy. I know what you mean about seeing stars! It's true that I was in control, so I suppose that 'taking you over' could be a fair enough description."

As they munched their toast and drank cups of black coffee which Linda had poured from the pot, Alexandra thought more about

what this could mean for future nights that she spent in her mother's bed.

"Mother?" she asked.

"Hmm?"

"If we both enjoyed what happened last night...and there's nothing wrong with it...could...could..."

"Could we do it again, I suspect is what you're trying to ask, am I right, darling?"

"Er. Well yes. That was rather what was on my mind, Mother!" said Alexandra.

"You sometimes babble when you're nervous of asking something, Alexandra, but you really have no need to be so over this. The answer is unquestionably yes!"

Alexandra felt her heartbeat quicken as excitement built up inside. Then she began to think of something else.

"Mother? Your loving is always so strong, and you know how much I do like it when you hold and kiss me. I need it so much and it helps me. It was truly wonderful being beneath you. It felt very natural to me..."

"Good. I'm glad about that," interjected Linda, before she got any further. "Because that's the way I'm planning for it to generally be in the future! Me to you, darling – the way it always has been. I'm your mother and as well as being the boss of the partnership you'll always get plenty of affection from me. It really should only be natural for me to do the 'taking over' as you put it. I've always told you that for every kiss you give back to me, I'll give you plenty more! I love you more than anyone else in the world and I want to give it all to you, sweetheart. You know that I love nothing more than to take you in my arms and have you ready and waiting to receive! Don't resist me darling!"

Alexandra couldn't imagine why any girl would want to resist a mother who could make her feel like last night. She thought she was quite the luckiest one in the world.

She smiled happily. "Oh thank you, Mother! I *was* wondering about whether it would usually be like last night between us in the future. I can't wait for next weekend!"

Now it was Linda's turn to smile. She reached out and took the empty cup that Alexandra was holding from her. After placing it on the table she turned and stroked her daughter's hair.

"Who said anything about waiting for next weekend, *sweetheart*!" she asked.

Linda saw Alexandra's eyes widen with delight and her excitement was self-evident. She slipped her arms around her daughter's neck and pushed her gently back on to the pillow on her side of the bed...

***

Elizabeth Spencer lay naked on a four-poster bed, prostrate on her back. The bed was in the middle of an open field.

In the distance, marching down from a hill were a group of a dozen men. The men were all big, strong and muscular, and were naked to the waist. Beneath the waist they wore skirts.

Once the men got to the bottom of the hill, they began to march across the field to Elizabeth. As she observed their physiques and saw them all wearing the item of clothing which most signified power on Geratica, Elizabeth felt a flush of excitement and her geratis went hard. She stretched out on the bed, her arms by her sides. When the men reached the bed, she opened her legs and pouted seductively.

The first man took off his skirt, went over to the bed and mounted Elizabeth. He laid down and made love to her passionately, ravishing her in the way that she fantasised. One by one the others did the same...

Suddenly Elizabeth found herself awake. It had all been a dream, and she was disappointed - though not altogether surprised. She wondered if there ever could be a Geratican man who would live up to her fantasies and naturally break away from the traditional male sexual role.

The dream had been intensely erotic though, and now Elizabeth was extremely sexually aroused. She reached down and touched her geratis. Her thighs twitched.

With her other hand she reached over to touch her husband lying next to her in the bed.

"James, are you awake?"

"Hmm?" asked James, sleepily.

"Come over to my side of the bed, darling!" said Elizabeth, in the sexiest voice that she could muster.

James had his back to her, and his heart sank as he heard the words and realised his wife's desire. He was a traditional Geratican man and he therefore felt that it was his duty to have sex with his wife whenever she wanted it. The problem was that increasingly he really didn't *want* to have it with her.

He turned over to face Elizabeth, still feeling half asleep. "What time is it?"

"Time enough for you to ravish me!" replied his wife, and with both arms she pulled him down over her. James grunted.

He began his task, but James was not a natural ravisher, and this time the sex was even less successful than before. Elizabeth

eventually agreed to compromise, and they did it side by side. She had a small orgasm, but James didn't come at all.

CHAPTER 60

The following weekend, after meeting Tom and going into the wood, Alexandra had permission from her mother to invite him to The Grange for the rest of the afternoon.

She told him of the story her mother had told, about when she'd once got "smashed out of her mind," experimenting with alcohol after being left alone in Alexandra's grandmother's parlour – including that she'd apparently drunk all of the best port and been docked money from her allowance to pay for its replacement. As Alexandra had anticipated he roared with laughter.

"Don't forget that we must always be discreet about these things, though Tom!" said Alexandra, as she too giggled. "Remember Mother's golden rule."

"Of course. Not a word!" replied Tom.

They spent some time listening to some music on Alexandra's machine. Geratica's scanning techniques had enabled them to pick up activity on the far away planet of Earth and they had adapted and incorporated quite a lot of the culture that they liked into their own. Alexandra was greatly interested in their music, amongst many other things, and her mother had given her a music machine which enabled her to scan for and record music from there, for her tenth birthday. As a result she was now developing quite an extensive collection of it. She liked quite a wide range from classical through to 'pop music' – the latter of which there was not very much of on Geratica. Tom often enjoyed what she played to him, and her mother was always a keen listener too. Of course Alexandra also greatly admired and liked Geratica's own classical music heritage which was also prominent in her collection, and none more so than that of her favourite composer, Philippa Barrington.

CHAPTER 61

Having established herself as Headmistress of Charterhouse College and with her husband now the personal chauffeur to Queen Alexandra, Elizabeth Spencer had decided to hold a small dinner party at their home. Such things were not Elizabeth's natural forte, and the affair would be by no means lavish.

She sent out invitations to an exclusive group of society ladies – including at Her Majesty's court - and told those who were married that they were welcome to bring their husbands too. To her pleasure, Queen Alexandra honoured her by accepting, but Linda Radcliffe apologised and said that she must decline as she and her daughter would be away on an excursion that weekend. This news did not displease Elizabeth either. However, Fiona was able to, though she wouldn't be bringing Colin. In the end the guests joining Elizabeth and James were the queen, Fiona and two other women with their husbands. James would also be driving Queen Alexandra from the Royal Palace and back again.

On the night, with Queen Alexandra's lady-in-waiting and her bodyguards having their own meal in the kitchen, the party were eating their main course in the dining room.

"I congratulate you, Elizabeth," said the queen. "This is the first time that I've had the pleasure of your hospitality, and I must say that this meat is delicious."

"Thank you. Ma'am."

Elizabeth wasn't generally of an anxious disposition, but tonight was a big occasion for her and she had been feeling some nerves. Although Linda Radcliffe wasn't here tonight, her dinner parties were much acclaimed and both she and Fiona were renowned for their culinary skills. Now Elizabeth smiled and relaxed.

The conversation gradually turned to affairs of the day. Fiona, looking glamorous as ever in a long flowing black gown, was

enjoying in Linda's absence, being able to more dominate the table. Eventually she spoke to Elizabeth.

"I hear that you're setting up a special school for boys, Mrs Spencer."

"That's correct, Mrs Clark," replied Elizabeth. "In fact, I'm hoping to establish a couple."

"I know that you don't have a son," continued Fiona, "but I have a stepson. I've personally given him some tuition on the basics. I believe that's quire sufficient for anything which he might do as a man. Isn't this new school of yours going to be rather a waste of money?"

Elizabeth felt her blood rising, but did her best to remain cool. She wanted tonight to be a success. Although a number of women in Geratican society intensely annoyed her with their traditionalist views on gender rights and equality, and she was determined to bring about change, Elizabeth nevertheless recognised the need to gain her place amongst them, as part of the establishment.

"I see no reason why boys shouldn't have just the same education as girls," she remarked. "I happen to believe that a good education should be the right of anybody, regardless of their gender."

This was the first time that Fiona had met Elizabeth. She knew of her views and was enjoying the opportunity to bait her.

"I'm all for giving boys as good an education as is necessary for them," she replied. "But of course, you're a supporter of greater male rights, aren't you? My goodness, if Linda Radcliffe were here…"

"Alright Fiona," intervened Queen Alexandra. "Let's not get too deeply drawn into political issues tonight, and instead try and enjoy ourselves."

"Of course, Ma'am," replied Fiona. "My apologies."

As the subject of conversation changed, James felt relieved. His wife's tongue could be acidic when her temper was roused. He didn't want ant embarrassing scenes in front of the queen – his boss.

After the meal, everybody moved into the parlour.

"If anybody would like to dance, then I'll put some music on," announced Elizabeth, walking over to the machine.

She knew that dancing was one thing which didn't feature so much at Mrs Radcliffe's parties. Linda didn't consider herself very good at performing the art (a rare modest admission, so it seemed), and therefore wasn't terribly keen to indulge the practice at her own house.

The three married women danced with their husbands, before swapping partners. However, as the activity continued, Queen Alexandra and Fiona gradually danced with all of the men too. There being five women and only three men, two women at a time dropped out.

Fiona admired the features of James. By the time she'd danced with the other men as well, her geratis was highly aroused. Colin was going to get a molesting when she got back home tonight.

Afterwards the women played cards and Fiona suggested playing for money. When she won, Elizabeth noticed how hungrily she collected her cash.

At the end of the evening, Fiona spoke quietly to her.

"Without us discussing the topic of male rights specifically, would I be right in thinking, you were actually quite pleased that Linda was unable to make it here today? Just between you and me?"

Elizabeth looked at her.

"So long as it *is* just between you and me, then yes, perhaps I wasn't greatly disappointed at her declining my invitation."

Fiona smiled.

"In fact, nor was I... just between you and me!"

With that she left. Elizabeth took note of what she'd seen and heard from her, for future reference.

***

Upon arriving home however, the rest of Fiona's evening did not go quite as she'd planned. She was suddenly struck down by a great sickness and far from being full of desire to make love to her husband, (as Colin had fully expected), instead spent most of the night being ill in the bathroom.

By the beginning of the following week, she was better. It soon transpired that none of the other guests at the dinner party had been ill. However, at the Royal Palace, Fiona told everybody about her sickness and insisted that Elizabeth Spencer's cooking was to blame for it. Linda for once felt that Elizabeth was probably being unfairly maligned. If had been Elizabeth's cooking – or anything to do with the food - then others would likely have been ill too. (Although she still couldn't help but be a little amused). Fiona had probably just picked up a bug of some kind.

It didn't take long for the news to spread around certain social circles and eventually Elizabeth herself got to hear of Fiona's claim. She was furious. She'd managed to keep her temper under control with the woman at the dinner table. But now it spilled over. From her desk in the headmistress's study at Charterhouse College, she rang the palace and demanded Fiona's secretary put her directly through to the court administrator.

"How dare you make such an outrageous allegation?" she fumed. "Nobody else was ill. You just most likely picked up a bug from somewhere. You've no proof that your *brief* illness had any connection whatsoever with my dinner party – and certainly not my cooking! I know your game. You're just trying to cast a foul slur upon me, so that nobody will accept any more dinner party invitations from me. You bitch!"

"Oh, I see," countered Fiona. "So, it was pure coincidence that I became ill just a few minutes after leaving your dinner party, was it? I just so happened to pick up a bug at the same time. What rubbish! And how dare *you* disturb me at work over this? I'm very busy you know!"

Elizabeth eventually angrily put her phone down. If some hoity-toity biddies in Geratican society were prepared to believe Fiona Clark's story, then that was up to them. But she didn't think many people would.

Meanwhile in her office, Fiona smirked. It was of course quite possible that Elizabeth Spencer's cooking hadn't played the slightest part in causing her illness (though if it was a bug, then she must have caught it from somewhere). However, she always delighted in causing mischief…

PART 11

CHAPTER 62

Geratica Winter 5009

On 01/04/09, after dinner in the dining hall at Charterhouse, the boarders from Rovers House had come back and were now in the prep room.

At the insistence of the headmistress, her daughter was now head of House.

The girls were often supervised by one of the most senior pupils whilst they did their nightly prep, and today it was a sixth year called Natalie Throbisher.

"Alright, settle down now girls, and make a start," she said as she sat at the front of the room, to get on with her own prep. "You know that you've got between now and half past eight when you go to your dormitory for the night to do it."

They all opened their books at the prep room desks and began working.

"Mouse is probably already tucked up in bed!" sneered Gillian quietly to the others, a few minutes later, and Melanie chuckled.

"What was that?" asked Natalie, looking up.

"Nothing," replied Gillian.

Natalie returned to her own studies. She knew who this girl was and usually tried to ignore the things that she said.

"Shut up, Spencer!" hissed Benita. She was tired of hearing her constantly make snide comments about Alexandra and taunt her.

"Why? What's it to you, Davis?" asked Gillian.

"Because Alexandra's a thoroughly decent girl, Spencer," replied Benita. "She doesn't deserve to be so bad mouthed all the time – especially by you."

"She's so quiet that I doubt anybody in this college really knows what she's *really* like," said Gillian, cheekily. "You know what they say. Sometimes it's the quiet ones who are the worst!"

"No one could be worse than you, Spencer! She's very shy, that's all. At least she always shows some respect."

"Watch it, Davis!" snarled Gillian. "What do you mean, 'especially by me,' anyhow? Why single me out as the worst?"

Benita snorted and she let some of her true feelings come to the fore.

"I should have thought that was obvious to someone who is supposedly so intelligent as you! Or is that just what the headmistress wants everybody to think?" She saw Gillian's eyes widen and her teeth begin to set into a glare, but she didn't stop. "It's because you pick on Alexandra and say things that you wouldn't to some of the rest of us, because you know that she won't fight back. You're a nasty, bullying conniving, manipulative, petty minded bitch! You get away with murder in this place, simply because, *"you're the headmistress's daughter!"*"

Benita said the last words in a sarcastic impression of Gillian, who now completely lost her temper.

"How dare you, Davis! You'll pay for that!" she shouted, as she leapt up from her desk with an ink pot in her hand.

"Hey! What's going on?" demanded Natalie.

Gillian stepped across to Benita's desk and flicked ink from the open bottle onto her prep. Natalie sprang out of her chair.

Benita was furious. "You absolute cow!" she yelled, and getting up, slapped Gillian across the face.

"No! Stop that! That's enough!" said Natalie, but in vain.

Gillian recovered and punched Benita full in the face, before Benita returned it. More angry than ever before, Gillian sent back two rapid blows in quick succession which sent Benita reeling. She stumbled backwards over her desk and it crashed on to the floor, smashing another ink pot and sending books and writing implements flying.

Imelda and Rachel were out of their chairs now and holding Gillian by the arms to restrain her.

"Spencer stop being such an idiot!" exclaimed Imelda.

Natalie rushed to help Benita up. "Are you alright?" she asked, in concern.

"Yeah. It's alright, I'll be fine," grunted Benita. She was a little dazed, but otherwise she wasn't hurt.

"What in the name of Geratica is going on!" asked a voice. When everybody looked they saw Mrs Baldwin at the door. "Natalie? You're supposed to be supervising here. What's happened? I heard an awful lot of noise and came down. Judging by what I see in this this room, it's just as well!"

"I'm sorry, Mrs Baldwin," said Natalie. "These two girls seem to have had some kind of disagreement, which unfortunately turned rather violent before I could intervene to stop it!"

Martha Baldwin cursed to herself. Gillian Spencer again! She checked Benita's face. She had a couple of bruises just below the eyes, one of which looked like it might turn black.

"You'd better go and be examined by the nurse straight away, girl," she ordered. "Then both of you will see Mrs Spencer!"

CHAPTER 63

"Fighting in the prep room! I don't know what standards are coming to in this college."

Elizabeth Spencer was sat behind the desk in her study. Gillian and Benita were stood in front of it.

"Gillian started it, Mrs Spencer," protested Benita. "She flicked a bottle of ink all over my prep!"

"But you did strike the first blow. You will admit that, I hope? Gillian has already given me an explanation."

Benita pulled a face. "Well, yes, Mrs Spencer. But after heavy provocation!"

"Provocation?" spluttered Gillian, "I was the one who got provoked!"

"Yes, well I'm not interested in what this petty squabble was about," said Elizabeth. "Though I understand that you suggested Gillian to be unfairly treating Alexandra Radcliffe. That is completely untrue and you will desist from making such outrageous remarks. Do I make myself clear, girl?"

Benita caught the trace of a smirk on Gillian's face. She well knew that being "the headmistress's daughter," the cow's comments and actions regarding anybody, let alone Alexandra, would be overlooked.

"Yes, Mrs Spencer," she said, reluctantly.

"Right. I will now of course take some action over this." remarked Elizabeth. "Gillian, please leave us. I shall deal with you in a moment."

"Of course, Mrs Spencer," replied Gillian.

Before Benita could see her smile slyly again, she quickly went out of the room.

The headmistress got up and moved a chair from the side of the study to the centre.

"Approach the chair, lower your skirt and bend over the seat," she ordered.

Somehow, Benita had always suspected that this would happen one day. She'd made an enemy of Gillian Spencer by standing up to her, which in turn was bound to make her unpopular with Mrs Spencer, who in four and a half years as headmistress had allegedly caned more girls in her study than any other over a similar period of time. She steeled herself and did as she was bidden. Elizabeth beat her bottom six times. Benita gritted her teeth and gave a light groan at the end as the discomfort reached its peak. Satisfied, Elizabeth told her to stand up, and pull her skirt back up.

"Now go to your dormitory immediately, and don't ever behave like that again!" she said. "Send Gillian in here, on your way out."

"Yes, Mrs Spencer," obeyed Benita, and left.

A few seconds later the door opened again and Gillian strode in.

"You caned her then?" she observed.

"Yes. And it was about time that girl got her comeuppance!" remarked Elizabeth. "But Gillian. Be careful not to go too far in what you say about Alexandra Radcliffe. I agree with you that she's a mouse, and I still maintain that she should pose no threat to my – to *your* ambitions here. But let's try and make sure that she doesn't report too much back to her mother. It was most unfortunate – not to say darned annoying – that she did eventually manage to gain a seat on the board of governors. The chair couldn't prevent it any longer. As you know, I have some differences with her, and I would be only too pleased to cane the confounded

woman's daughter should I ever get the chance, but particularly in her case it must be seen to be entirely just, so let's be patient and not get too concerned about it."

"Yeah, alright. I'll be careful," said Gillian.

"We can make something of this, though," continued Elizabeth. "The tuckshop are looking for someone new to take over the running of it during morning break and after the end of the official curriculum for the day. I believe that Benita Davis is interested, but again you know that I was rather hoping you might be able to do it. It'll be a good thing for you to have on your C.V. After this, I could probably put an end to Benita's chances. Have you thought any more about it?"

Gillian had done. In fact, she could think of a few other ways that she could turn such a position to her advantage too.

"I have, Mother," she replied. "I'd like to do it."

"Alright then," said Elizabeth, feeling pleased with her daughter's decision. "I'll knock some heads together and you should get put into the position shortly."

CHAPTER 64

The next day at morning registration, Alexandra was shocked to see Benita sporting a black eye. As they went to their first lesson, domestic science, she commented on it to her.

"Goodness me, that's a shiner! How in the name of Geratica did you get that?"

"Gillian and I had a fight in the prep room last night," explained Benita.

"A fight?" exclaimed Alexandra, "What about?"

"Well actually it was mainly inspired by an argument over the way Gillian treats you sometimes," said Benita. "Though it did go slightly broader than that, too."

She told Alexandra everything.

"So, I think that now makes you the only girl in our form class who's still not got a beating from Mrs Spencer in her study!" remarked Benita, dryly.

"Thanks for sticking up for me," said Alexandra. "Though I wish that you weren't caned for it. Sorry about that!"

"Oh, don't worry," Benita reassured her. "It's obvious to all of us that if you get on the wrong side of the headmistress's daughter, then you also get into the headmistress's bad books."

Alexandra wondered with trepidation if she'd be next...

***

When the bell rang for break time, Alexandra was surprised and alarmed when Gillian told her that Mrs Spencer wanted to see her in her study.

Making her way there apprehensively, thoughts began to form wildly in her mind. Had she inadvertently done something wrong which the headmistress would now punish her for too, as well as Benita? She couldn't think of anything. But it was quite unusual for a girl to be summoned to Mrs Spencer's study unless they were in trouble. Apart from her daughter she rarely socialised with any of them and in fact Alexandra got the distinct impression that she didn't like her pupils all that much.

However, when she arrived, the headmistress appeared to greet her warmly and even offered her a quick cup of coffee.

"I want to tell you that Charterhouse is very pleased to have you as one of its pupils, Alexandra!" she declared. "You are doing very well and are most popular. Everybody likes and respects you."

"Oh. Thank you, Mrs Spencer," replied Alexandra. "I'm pleased and proud to be here, also."

She was surprised at this sudden outpouring of praise from the headmistress and wondered if it was truly sincere. She thought that perhaps after last night's fracas in the prep room, Mrs Spencer wanted to keep her 'sweet' and try to ensure that she didn't go home and tell her mother everything that Gillian said both to her when she was there, and about her when she was away. The headmistress would have surmised that Benita might have passed on the details of her row with Gillian, this morning.

Alexandra was of course correct.

"Keep up the good work, girl," said Elizabeth.

***

It was confirmed later that day, that Gillian would be running the tuck shop from now on. Benita was neither pleased nor surprised.

CHAPTER 65

Geratica Spring 5009

It was late afternoon on 7/13/09 at Charterhouse, some of the boarders were returning from a field trip in Buckmore. Imelda and Rachel were amongst them.

Imelda had something carefully concealed in her bag. When she and Rachel got back to Rivers House and were in the dormitory, she took it out.

In her hands was a top shelf – or 'women's – magazine. Imelda was interested and excited at its reputation and had taken the opportunity to nip into a newsagent's store and buy a copy. The magazine was not approved of by the college, and in fact Mrs Spencer had declared it banned material. This had only made Imelda want to read it even more.

Sitting on the edge of the bed she looked at the front cover. It was dominated by a naked man in a very provocative but submissive sexual position. Imelda felt stirrings of sexual desire build up within her loins – something that had been happening with increasing strength for some time now. At the beginning of this term, she had boasted to the other girls, that during the holiday she had spied on her mother making love to her father. Imelda had already concluded that it didn't look terribly difficult to do and was confident she would be most capable of copying her mother when the opportunity finally arrived.

Rachel had known that Imelda was buying the magazine and now she joined her on the bed. Together they looked inside. There were similar pictures to the one on the cover, as well as some rather erotic short stories. Imelda and Rachel smiled and chuckled softly to each other as their geratises became aroused.

"What are you two giggling at over there?" asked Benita.

"Come and see for yourself," invited Imelda. 'It'll be worth it, believe me! And any of the rest of you, too."

Benita left her area of the dormitory and came over. She glanced at what the other two were reading.

"Oh, in the name of Geratica!" she snorted. "What do you want to read rubbish like that for? I thought that you were supposed to be intelligent? And don't let Mrs Baldwin, or Gillian see it. They'll report it straight to Mrs Spencer! You know that she's banned material such as that from Charterhouse. Even the college library has strict controls on any erotic literature."

Now other Rovers House girls were beginning to crowd around to see what all the fuss was about.

"Yes, well Gillian isn't here at the moment," remarked Imelda. 'She's on a canoeing course up the road in Pilkington. Melanie too. They won't be back until later. And as for Baldwin, if you're going to be so snooty about this, why don't you at least keep a lookout for her for her?"

"I don't take orders from you!" snapped Benita. But all the same she decided that it might not be a bad idea. "Oh, alright then. Just this once."

She went and opened the dormitory door a fraction and scanned the passage outside. There was no one there or on the stairs leading up to the ground floor level.

The girls gathered around Imelda's bed were all at the age where they were beginning to become aware of their sexual desires. Some of them got an erection for the first time as the magazine was passed around.

"I'm letting you all know, here and now," declared Imelda, "that no man will be safe, once I've come of age. Mothers will have to lock up all of their sons!"

The others chortled. Though in the future her reputation would sometimes be exaggerated, few of them imagined then quite how accurate Imelda's prediction would prove to be.

Soon afterwards it was dinner time in the school dining room, and later the lights went out in the dormitory for the night.

Imelda was restless as she lay in her bed thinking about what she'd seen and read. She was particularly aroused and experiencing extremely strong sexual yearnings. Reaching out to her bedside table, she quietly opened a drawer and took out a torch. Then Imelda brought out the magazine from under her pillow and switching on the torch began to discreetly gaze at the erotic pictures, taking care to shield the glow as much as possible so as not to awaken or alert the other girls.

Her geratis became harder and more extended from her vagina than ever before, and as she lay on her stomach it pressed against the sheet. Imelda exhaled softly and instinctively reached down and stroked it with her finger. Her thighs tingled and she stroked them too. She imagined kissing, touching and making love to all the gorgeous men that she saw, and saliva dripped from her mouth as she licked her lips hungrily. In ecstasy she pushed herself deeper into the bed, and a shooting sensation in her geratis made her shiver all over. Imelda gasped and let out a small cry.

Imelda's mind was made up. She liked this feeling like nothing else and she wanted the full experience. As soon as she could she was going to find herself a boyfriend – probably after leaving Charterhouse – and, immediately upon becoming allowed, make love to him.

***

In Elizabeth's private study at her chambers, the phone rang. It was Jennie Seacombe, the owner of the newsagent's store that Imelda had visited that afternoon.

Jennie was a friend of Elizabeth's, and a board member at Charterhouse. She told her that a girl she believed to be from the college had come into the shop and brought a top shelf magazine. She knew that the headmistress strongly disapproved of such publications.

Elizabeth was outraged. She immediately phoned Maggie Dewhurst and Martha Baldwin. Martha was in her chambers at Rovers House, preparing to go to bed, and she cursed when the phone rang.

"Blasted filth!" spat Elizabeth, after she had recounted the news to the Rovers housemistress. "I won't have any girl bringing things like that into *my* college. See to it that the dormitory is thoroughly searched. I want that magazine found and destroyed. The guilty girl must then be sent to me."

"Do you mean right now?" asked Martha, wearily. "The girls are now in bed after 'lights out' and I was about to retire myself."

"Oh no," said Elizabeth. "It can wait until tomorrow, when the regular daily inspection takes place after assembly. But I want it to be more vigorous than normal, and not to finish until this thing is uncovered. I've instructed Maggie to do the same at Beavers House."

"Very well," replied Martha. "Of course it could be that the girl who brought the magazine, simply discarded it in a bin somewhere before coming back into the college grounds."

"Possibly," agreed Elizabeth. "But I have my doubts about that. My instincts tell me that it's here somewhere."

***

And so, after assembly the next morning, with the girls in the exercise yard before the start of lessons at the start of a new week, the inspections began at Rovers and Beavers houses.

Normally the housemistresses simply checked that the girls had made their beds properly and made a quick observation of their bedside tables and sleeping areas. However, today they were opening every drawer, and checking under all of the beds.

As she checked Imelda's bed, Mrs Baldwin immediately noticed three spots of blue staining the sheet, which were likely to have come from an erect geratis and looked quite recent. This wasn't necessarily unusual amongst girls of her age. They were beginning to develop sexually and Martha was never surprised to see evidence of their arousal. All the same, in view of what she was supposed to be looking for this morning, it did make her consider just what exactly had made Imelda so excited. She looked on the bedside table and started opening the drawers. Martha didn't really like doing this, as it meant looking at the girls' private things, but she had a job to do. Gradually she worked her way to the bottom of the chest. In this drawer she rummaged through the contents until finally she found a magazine matching the description given to her by Elizabeth.

Taking a heavy breath Mrs Baldwin took the sheet off Imelda's bed, and with that and the magazine went out of the dormitory to the headmistress's study.

***

Halfway through the double period of ancient Geratican that started the week, Mrs Baldwin came in.

"I'm sorry Miss Trimble," she said to the mistress. "But if I could just interrupt for one moment please? Imelda Thomas. Mrs

Spencer wishes to see you in her study at break time. Please go there immediately after the bell rings for it. That's all. Carry on Miss Trimble."

Mrs Baldwin left, and a murmur went around the classroom.

"Alright, settle down now girls!" said the mistress.

When she got an opportunity Benita spoke quietly to Imelda.

"I'll bet that they've discovered your erotic magazine. I said that you ought to be careful in case anyone saw it!"

"Oh no," denied Imelda. "I hid it deep inside my bottom drawer. Mrs Baldwin would never have been bothering to look in there during the daily inspection."

"Unless someone tipped her off," remarked Benita.

Imelda pulled a face at her.

"You didn't sneak on me, did you?"

"No, of course I didn't!" retorted Benita, indignantly. "I would never do that."

Although Imelda had been certain that the magazine wouldn't be found, she privately had to admit that it did seem a bit of a coincidence that the headmistress now wanted to see her. She couldn't think of anything other logical reason for it and she swore to herself. Imelda looked across at Gillian, but she actually seemed surprised too.

At break time, Benita explained to an enquiring Alexandra what she thought the reason was for Imelda's summons to Mrs Spencer's study.

Inside Mrs Spencer's study, Imelda immediately saw Mrs Baldwin holding the top shelf magazine that she'd brought the day before

and the sheet from her bed. Any hopes that she'd had for this meeting being about another matter quickly evaporated, and she swore to herself again. She was told to stand before the headmistress's desk and made to listen to her lecturing.

"I was told yesterday night by the owner of one of the newsagent's store, in a particular part of Buckmore, that a girl from this college had brought a copy of this disgusting publication," Elizabeth was saying. "She also happens to be a member of the college's board of governors. You were, I believe, on a field trip in that area of the town yesterday. This morning this dirty magazine was found in the bottom drawer of your bedside table. You also appear to have stained your bed sheet, presumably after becoming rather too over excited by the explicit material! Do you admit that you purchased this magazine and brought it into Charterhouse? Or at least if it wasn't you, then someone else on that field trip did?"

"Er, well yes I do admit that, Mrs Spencer," confirmed Imelda. There was no point in denying it she thought, and for all of her faults she wasn't a girl who liked to get another into trouble through no fault of their own. Imelda was honest to that degree. "But it isn't a *dirty* magazine!"

"I say that it is, and anything like that is banned from this college!" exclaimed Elizabeth. "Darn it you foul girl, are you that depraved? Using images of men in this way purely for the sexual gratification of women is a degradation of the male sex!"

"It's just a bit of fun, Mrs Spencer," remarked Imelda.

"A bit of fun? Rubbish! For a girl in this college to think like that about a publication such as this is disgraceful. It just goes to prove that we need greater rights for men, and for boys to be educated in the same way as girls are. I'm sure that *they* would prove far more sensible! I hope that as you get older you will understand. You are not yet a mature woman, Imelda – despite what you might think. Magazines like this are targeted at them. Girls of your age should not be reading them – and as far as I'm concerned you should never *ever* read them, even as an adult."

Elizabeth turned to Martha. "Give me the magazine please, Mrs Baldwin."

Martha did so and Elizabeth held it up, looking squarely at Imelda. Then she slowly ripped it to pieces.

"That's how we deal with any of this sort of filth here," she declared. "OK leave us Mrs Baldwin. Take that dirty sheet to be cleaned and burn this paper!"

As Martha went out, the headmistress fetched a chair and placed it in the centre of her study.

"You will of course be punished for this," said Elizabeth. "Approach the chair, lower your skirt and bend over the seat."

"Yes Mrs Spencer," obeyed Imelda. She didn't consider that she'd done anything wrong, nor did she think this was justified, but she'd been resigned to her fate since realising that her magazine had been found.

Elizabeth picked up her cane eagerly. Not only did she hate this sort of material and despise the women who read it, she had waited a long time for an opportunity to beat this impudent girl again. She caned her six times on her bare bottom. The strokes were particularly vigorous, and Imelda felt such discomfort that by the end she was forced to moan softly. Triumphant that she had at last got such a reaction from Imelda, the headmistress told her to stand up and put her skirt back on.

"Don't let me catch you with any more of this rubbish," she ordered. "Or you'll get another six. Now get out of my sight!"

Imelda did so, willingly. Her mind was made up once again. She would obey Mrs Spencer – but only insofar that she wouldn't let the headmistress catch her. Imelda saw no reason why she shouldn't read or view what she wanted and wasn't going to let

anybody stop her. She would make sure not to buy anything like this from that newsagent again, though.

She and Rachel had considered becoming intimate together, in order to be able to stimulate the feeling of loving or being loved by someone, even though it would never nor could be a sexual one, but although they were very close, they did not really have that exceptional bond.

***

Later, everybody wanted to know what had happened. Everybody but Gillian, however, who had already got the details from her mother.

"If Mrs Baldwin or Gillian doesn't report you to Mrs Spencer, then one of her cronies will!" remarked Imelda, ruefully, after she'd explained everything to them. It also slightly exasperated her that once again the cool and sensible Benita was able to say she'd told her so, after warning her of the possibility of being found out the previous evening.

That night in the dormitory, Gillian approached Imelda, discreetly.

"I've heard about what you brought yesterday, and I know that it got discovered this morning," she said. "I'd have liked to have seen it if I'd been here. You should get some more."

Imelda was surprised and slightly suspicious.

"Get some more? You mean you'll then be able to tell your mother, and land me in more trouble!"

"Not necessarily," said Gillian, slyly. "I won't say a word to the headmistress – as long as I get first peek. That's the deal, Thomas. Take it or leave it. If you bring any more erotic material into Charterhouse, let me be the first to see it."

"Why can't you buy your own material?" asked Imelda.

"That's none of your business, Thomas!" snarled Gillian. "Just be aware of how it is. If you want to bring that sort of stuff into the college, then give me a first viewing. I can give you my word that I'll be a very keen observer! I don't necessarily share all of my mother's views on this particular subject. But otherwise, I *will* report you to the headmistress."

Eventually Imelda agreed...

CHAPTER 66

Geratica Summer 5009

At the Royal Palace, Linda checked the clock on the main office wall of 'her little empire'. At precisely 9.00 am, as the clock tower in the capital struck the hour, she picked up a rule and red pen and drew a red line underneath the name of the last woman to sign the registration book indicating that they had arrived and were present for work. This was the latest time that any member of the palace staff was permitted to start. Once the line was drawn anybody who signed in after that was officially late, and Linda demanded an explanation for it.

Fiona's name was not on the list. She was supposed to be having a meeting with Linda, starting at this very moment. The senior court administrator cursed to herself. This wasn't the first time that her deputy had failed to be punctual.

Most of Linda's staff were always hard working and obedient to the rules under her iron rod rule, though since she had first become court administrator two women had received verbal warnings. Another had been given a written one following a suspension, after she had been caught deliberately taking her phone off the hook in order to avoid getting calls.

As she was beginning to walk towards the door and back to her own office, Fiona swept in and raced to the registration book. She scribbled her signature beneath the red line.

"You are late, Mrs Clark!" declared Linda. "I drew the red line just a moment ago. I trust that you have a very good reason for it?"

"I realise that, Mrs Radcliffe, and I apologise for my tardiness," replied Fiona. "I had a particularly heavy session in the bedroom last night. I was late arising. We women with men can get so carried away indulging our pleasures sometimes!"

There were titters from some of the court administration department staff.

"Alright, that's enough of that!" asserted Linda. "Get on with your work." She didn't approve of such bawdy humour in the office and Fiona's usage of it so flippantly, often irked her.

"Oh, I'm sorry Mrs Radcliffe. I didn't mean to be insensitive to your own position in regard to that," added Fiona.

This annoyed Linda even more. It seemed as if her deputy was having the cheek to deliberately make a crude remark at her expense, after just infringing upon the court's code of conduct. She certainly did miss having sex, and no doubt some of the women in her department suspected it. But any other woman in the same 'position' would feel the same, Linda was certain of that.

"I'm joking, of course!" continued Fiona. "The honest reason for my being late, is that I was stuck in traffic."

"Yes. Well, whatever the reason, we won't discuss it here." said Linda. "We were due for a meeting in my office, starting at nine o'clock. Let us go and begin."

Once they were there, Linda made a cup of coffee for them both, and spoke frankly.

"Fiona, please refrain from making such smutty jokes in the office. You do have a very responsible position here. And for that reason also, you should be more mindful of your timekeeping. You've been late on occasions before. If it continues, then I shall have to issue you with a formal warning. Nobody else seems to have experienced any problems, when travelling in this morning."

"I probably left home the latest," admitted Fiona.

And you'll probably be going *back* home the earliest too, thought Linda. This was an issue that they had discussed previously,

though she had to acknowledge that Fiona was correct when she asserted that she always performed her daily responsibilities during the time when she was at the palace. But she often only did the bare minimum number of hours required of her. Linda also believed that the court administrator had been gambling at one of her regular haunts last night.

"Well from now onwards, make sure that you set out in good time, so that there's no danger of you being late," she replied. "We did have a meeting planned which we're now behind schedule on."

"I'm sorry, Linda," said Fiona. "I promise that it won't happen again."

"Hmm," remarked Linda. "I hope not."

"Well, *I'm* ready," declared Fiona.

The main topic of the meeting was the situation regarding the Queen Alexandra Marital Suite.

"Just what is the current position?" demanded Linda. "Things do seem to be progressing rather slowly."

"The layout of the suite is designed," replied Fiona. "All that remains is for a contractor to be found who can begin its construction on the top floor of the Geratica hotel."

"I see. And when will that be? I trust that you are already looking for tenders?"

"There are a couple of options. I will need to study them in detail before I make a decision, and then I will obviously inform Her Majesty and yourself. Once we are all agreed, then the work can begin."

"Well just ensure that you make it a priority, Fiona," said Linda. "This autumn it will be four years since this the idea of this suite was first suggested. Her Majesty's court is usually prompt in

implementing its plans once they're decided upon, and the queen will want to start to see some concrete results, soon."

"Everything is in hand, Linda," said Fiona, with a smile which she hoped looked reassuring. "Do not worry!"

"Hmm," murmured Linda. She wanted to say that if it had been left to her to get the necessary work done to construct the suite, then it would probably be completed by now and ready to be opened. She was surprised that, given it had been Fiona's own original suggestion, and that her deputy had seemed so keen to prove herself in performing the task (upon which Queen Alexandra had based her own decision to grant her wish), that Fiona was not pushing the issue rather harder. It still rankled with her that she had not been allowed to take full responsibility for it herself. But she held her tongue.

Fiona was of course procrastinating as much as she could. The latest news that she had from Geratcai was that the situation was little changed. The mongrel Robert had still not done his duty as Prince Edward, and Queen Victoria still faced unrest amongst some of her industrial workers.

There was a rebellion in Plumas, involving that region's mayor, Fran Topham and several members of its council. The queen ordered her troops in, but the rebels refused to surrender and locked themselves away in the main council building. They were in there for several days and eventually the army began cutting off supplies to the building. Queen Victoria sailed over to personally take charge of the operation. She allowed no concessions whatsoever to be made unless the rebels agreed to wholeheartedly agree to her terms - and the situation became a siege. Gradually after several more days, the people inside the building began to starve. Eventually in desperation, some of them came out in a dishevelled state and surrendered. They were taken away to Arista, capital of Spanda, with most never seen again, including Fran Topham, who the queen officially denounced as a traitor. She then sent her army into the council building to massacre all those left

inside, and an entirely new band of her loyalist workers replaced them.

CHAPTER 67

That summer at Charterhouse, Alexandra was due to sit her Certificate of Geratica examinations.

Weeks before, she began revising and Linda implemented a rigorous routine for her to follow during the weekends at The Grange. It left her with little free time and she was unable to see Tom as much as she normally would have liked.

She worked at her desk in her mother's study. Sometimes Linda was there with her. On occasions she was out of the house and Alexandra was left with strict instructions to use her time wisely. She was forbidden to go out and meet Tom.

Needing to gain at least a pass in six or more of the ten subjects – which had to include mathematics and Geratican language - in the end, Alexandra passed with top grades in every examination. She was obviously delighted and Linda was overjoyed, and as a treat, took her daughter out to see a classical music concert in Avermore, followed by dinner in an exclusive restaurant.

All of the 'A' stream also got the certificate, and of those in the 'B' stream, even Melanie Patterson was one who did also. One who failed was Sophie Brewster, who now left the college.

Greenacres Town again won the Division One Crown Green Bowling Championship, despite Alexandra once again having to miss certain games whilst preparing for and taking her Certificate.

For her fourteenth birthday, Alexandra was given a diamond necklace by her mother. She was delighted with it.

In late summer, Linda took Alexandra on holiday to Bourneville, on the coast of Castra, where they stayed in a hotel for a fortnight. By now Alexandra had stayed in several of Geratica's most splendid, and she enjoyed plenty of fine food and drink. Alexandra and her mother had a double room with a spectacular view of the

seafront. They could observe the fishing boats sailing in and out of the harbour and people on the jetty with their nets.

Alexandra had been 'taken over' by her mother in bed many more times since it had fist happened the previous autumn, and on the usual day of the week it occurred again at the hotel. In many ways their bond had become even closer as a result of that activity.

Alexandra took her music machine with her, and one of the songs that she played for her mother was *'If Not For You'* by the Earth twentieth century singer, *Olivia Newton John*. Alexandra felt that it contained words which summed up some of the feelings which she had for her. Linda was overwhelmed by affection for her daughter at this, and gave her all the love that she had.

CHAPTER 68

Geratica Festival of Divinity 5009

One of the features of the Festival of Divinity at The Grange was a series of logic games played between Linda and Alexandra each night. The first took place on the night of Divinity Day itself – the first day of the New Year, and they continued each night until the seventh day of the second week of the Festival – 7/1/10.

It had been a tradition they had started four years ago, and Linda had won each time, though Alexandra was steadily improving and could give her a good match. Last year's series had gone to the deciding night, and it was to go to the wire again this time, with Alexandra leading 1-0, 2-1, and 3-2. But then after levelling once again at 3-3, her mother once again won a close decider.

The series was always a battle of wills and Linda was always immensely satisfied after her victories. But this year she generously declared that her daughter had played better than ever before.

"One day darling, perhaps you will defeat me," she said. "One day!"

"Yes, Mother," replied Alexandra, "One day!"

Alexandra wasn't nearly as competitive as some women of her race, and certainly not as much as her mother, but she *was* determined to at last beat her mother in this. She knew now that she was capable, and their epic annual struggles were always hugely enjoyable. They both looked forward to them.

Next year Alexandra, after another great contest with much friendly exchange of friendly fighting banter and despite her mother's fiercest determination to prevent it, would finally achieve

her ambition, again in a final night decider. It would not be the only time she won, either...

PART 12

CHAPTER 69

Geratica Winter 5010

At Charterhouse on the morning of 1/3/10, Mrs Spencer addressed the girls during assembly as usual.

She used most of the time to lecture the girls on the injustices that she claimed men were suffering in society. Some of the mistresses were privately uncomfortable about it, feeling that she was slightly entering into politics, and this was neither the place nor the appropriate audience for it. Many of the girls wished that she would finish and let them get on with the day, too.

Hidden inside of her skirt, Elizabeth's geratis became aroused as she spoke. Her passion for the subject, combined with the thought of the kind of traits men could have, if the gender balance between the two sexes was altered in the way she'd like, often stirred such a reaction within her.

Afterwards, Alexandra was in her Geratican Literature lesson for the first period of the day. Soon after it began, Mrs Baldwin came in and spoke to the mistress, Mrs Ripley. Then she came over.

"Alexandra, could you just come outside for a moment?" she asked, quietly. "Don't worry. You haven't done anything wrong!"

"Yes, Mrs Baldwin," replied Alexandra, surprised. She left her place at the workbench and followed the Rovers house mistress out.

"Sorry, Alexandra. I don't want you to miss much of your lesson, so I won't keep you long," remarked Mrs Baldwin. "But I have a favour to ask of you. You'll have gathered that Gillian is ill. Poor girl. It appears that she has the measles all over her face and parts of her body!"

Martha Baldwin found herself hoping for a brief moment that they would spread all over Miss Spencer, before rapidly pulling herself together.

"Now unfortunately, as Gillian will be confined to her bed for a few days, this means that we need somebody to step in and look after the tuck shop accounts. Gillian deals with them all, normally. We really need somebody with fine mathematical skills. I can think of nobody better qualified that you, Alexandra! I was wondering if I could persuade you to do it – just for a short while, hopefully?"

Alexandra looked at her in alarm. She'd never yet thought of having a role at Charterhouse that might give her some responsibility. It wasn't something that she'd naturally seek.

"Me, Mrs Baldwin?" she asked. "Um…but I could never serve the girls over the counter. I'd be terrified!"

"It's alright, you wouldn't have to do any of that, Alexandra," replied Mrs Baldwin. "You don't necessarily need to actually be in there at break time, but later – perhaps in your lunch hour – you would check over the figures and the money, just to make sure that everything is OK. It would be a great help."

Alexandra considered. That didn't sound so bad. She was certainly confident that she could deal with simple accounts. Her mother had meticulously trained her in that regard, ready for when she was a woman with her own household to manage. In any case she was an obedient girl and if a mistress, let alone the housemistress asked her to something then she didn't feel able to decline.

"Very well. I will Mrs Baldwin," she replied.

"Oh, that's great!" declared Martha with a broad smile. "I don't know if you were planning to visit there and buy something this morning, but if at break time today you wouldn't mind going along, and then one of the other girls can show you where the accounts books are in the room behind the shop. Thank you very much,

Alexandra. It's much appreciated. I'll let you go back to your lesson."

She turned and hurried away.

And so, at morning break time that was what Alexandra did, then at lunch time after finishing her meal, she went to the tuck shop to study the accounts, letting herself in with a special temporary key that she'd been given.

***

It was only the next day though, that Alexandra began to notice that something wasn't quite right. There appeared to be some discrepancies between the figures and cash machine print outs in the accounts book, and the amount of money that the shop had. They seemed to go back some way too. There were older accounts books, but she couldn't check those as Gillian had locked them away in a cabinet and the key was with her. She checked everything very carefully, but was becoming quite certain. Gillian was fiddling the books – though in quite a subtle way which many people might not notice. But Alexandra calculated that she must have pocketed for herself quite a bit of money over the previous year, since taking over the running of the tuck shop.

Alexandra thought about what to do. In theory she should obviously inform Mrs Baldwin. But it was always something of a risk, telling on the headmistress's daughter. Gillian would be furious and even then, it was likely that nothing would be done about it. Alexandra was however becoming a bit more confident in herself, and Benita's actions last year had helped a little. When she was with her, she did feel some protection. And although Gillian still took opportunities to cause her trouble, she did seem to be wary of Benita. Also, now that they were studying for the Advanced Certificate of Geratica, Alexandra and Gillian were not (as they had been previously for Certificate of Geratica) always in the same classes. The girls were allowed to drop two subjects

(though mathematics, Geratican language and science were compulsory). Gillian had chosen artistic studies and music; Alexandra, artistic studies and ancient Geratican. Therefore, due to having selected different 'options', there was some divergence in their lesson timetables.

Just like Gillian, Alexandra and Benita were mathematically gifted. Benita had begun to recognise Alexandra's great knowledge of many other subjects as well, and wasn't averse to asking for her help before morning registration began, if there'd been something she'd been struggling with in her prep the previous night.

Now that they were Advanced Geratican Certificate girls at Charterhouse, the boarders also no longer slept in the dormitory with the other girls, but each had their own private chambers within their houses.

Alexandra wondered whether to say nothing. But she also thought about how it might look if this was later discovered and somebody *did* decide to take some action and they suspected that she must have known about it. She could be implicated too.

The following morning at morning break time, Alexandra took the accounts books from the tuck shop and went to see her house mistress. She told her what she'd discovered and what she suspected.

Mrs Baldwin went pale, and for a moment Alexandra wondered if she'd done the right thing. But respecting Alexandra Radcliffe's intelligence very highly, in common with most of the mistresses at Charterhouse, Martha spent a few minutes poring over the figures herself. There could be no denying it. Alexandra was right. In the name of Divinity, what were they going to do about this? The headmistress's daughter was 'untouchable' and her integrity not to be questioned. Yet here was rock solid evidence that she had committed a serious offence. Any other girl would be at the very least suspended for it. The darned girl was sailing very close to the wind.

The housemistress winced. Gillian Spencer would be the death of her! She reflected that perhaps it wasn't such a good idea to give the responsibility of handling the tuck shop money entirely to a girl in the school, but normally the girls of Gillian's age who they chose to perform the task were mature and trustworthy enough. They had never had a problem in the past. But of course on this occasion, the headmistress herself had chosen her own daughter and there had been nothing anybody could do about it. She was undeniably capable, but equally, clearly corrupt.

"Are you alright, Mrs Baldwin?" asked Alexandra, just as at that moment the bell rang for the first period after break.

"Yes, yes," replied Martha. "You did the right thing in informing me of what you suspect, Alexandra. Well done. Leave it with me, and I'll speak with the headmistress. You'd best be getting along to your next lesson now."

"Very good, Mrs Baldwin," said Alexandra. Although she hadn't said it, she believed that her house mistress – who was after all also the head of the mathematics department at Charterhouse – thought the same as she did.

CHAPTER 70

Martha went to see Elizabeth with the accounts books and delicately told her what Alexandra had discovered. She showed her the figures and as gently as possible gave her own honest opinion.

"I'm sorry, Elizabeth. I don't want to accuse your daughter of anything, and there may be some other explanation," she concluded. "But the figures are there for us all to see, and nothing can change the way they make the position look."

The headmistress pursed her lips. "See to it that the figures in this book are amended, so that at least they don't show that there's less cash in the tuck shop than we have accounted for. I shall go and speak with Gillian, myself. I'm sure that there's been some kind of mistake." She held up a finger. "But let me be clear. Whatever happens, my daughter remains in place there. When she's recovered from her illness, then she will return."

"Very well," said Mrs Baldwin. She was effectively being asked to massage the figures to ensure that the headmistress's daughter wasn't accused of theft. Still, it didn't surprise her. She was sure that Elizabeth wouldn't make Gillian pay the money back either.

***

Elizabeth immediately raced to her daughter, and finally Gillian was made aware of everything that had been happening since she'd fallen ill.

"Radcliffe got drafted in to help look after the accounts?" she exclaimed. "Baldwin should have informed me first!"

"*Mrs* Baldwin to you, Gillian!" remarked Elizabeth, sharply. "And of course she didn't have to inform you. Don't overreach yourself. In any case you're unwell. Well, whatever it was that you were

doing, you presumably have done quite well out of it, but I'm afraid that Alexandra has found you out, and now your housemistress knows, so you must stop. I'm seeing to it that the worst of the offence will be covered up, and you can return as normal once you're fully recovered. Keep what you've gained, but no more fiddling the books. Do you hear me?"

"Yes, Mother," replied Gillian, sullenly. She was determined that she would make Alexandra pay for snitching on her though, no matter what.

***

After the lunch time meal in the dining hall, Mrs Baldwin asked Alexandra to come back to Rovers House with her. They went to her study and the housemistress closed the door firmly.

"I shall hang on to these books until tomorrow," she explained. "I've spoken with Mrs Spencer and she has apparently asked Gillian about the figures and she believes that there has been some kind of misunderstanding. I reserve my judgement, Alexandra. Take that to mean what you will, but don't go speculating about it beyond the walls of this study, hmm?"

Alexandra looked at her. She assumed that her housemistress meant that she didn't believe there had been any misunderstanding and that Gillian was guilty of fraud. But she didn't want to say so directly and was advising her to do the same.

"Of course not, Mrs Baldwin," she replied.

"The headmistress hopes that Gillian will be well enough to return to her lessons next week, and she will be resuming her role at the tuck shop as normal," continued Martha. "Therefore, you'll be relieved of the responsibility then, Alexandra. Mrs Spencer assures me she is certain that the accounts will balance from now on."

"Very well. That's fine, Mrs Baldwin," said Alexandra.

***

Once Alexandra had been given the accounts books back from the housemistress the next day, it didn't take her long to see that they were not the same ones she had left with her. These books had someone else's writing in them, which Alexandra thought she recognised as Mrs Baldwin's. Checking the amount of cash at the tuck shop she found that the accounts now balanced. She was certain that the transactions recorded were not necessarily genuine, however. It was obvious that the college were trying to ensure that any future audit conducted would not uncover the fact that the headmistress's daughter had been fiddling the accounts to line her own pocket. Gillian would be back next week and Alexandra assumed that no further action would be taken after that.

In the back of her mind though, she did still wonder whether Gillian would take further action against *her*.

***

On 1/4/10, Alexandra's mind was proved right.

As she was making her way along a quiet part of the college grounds towards the gates at the end of the day, Gillian suddenly appeared. Beside her were a couple of burly girls who Alexandra didn't know.

"Not so fast, Mouse!" snarled Gillian. She walked up close in front of Alexandra, whilst the others went behind her.

"So, you were clever enough to uncover my little scheme, were you?" she sneered. "Baldwin would bring *you* in to check the

accounts. I might have known! But you grassed on me you little snitch, didn't you?"

"I...I," Alexandra floundered.

"*I...I...I!*" said Gillian, mockingly. "St...st...stammering again are we? Yes, you did! But you're never going to do this again, do you understand?"

"Yes Spencer," replied Alexandra.

"Let's make sure!"

Gillian glanced about quickly and seeing that there was nobody in sight gave a nod to her friends. As each of them took hold of one of Alexandra's arms, forcing her to drop her school bag, Gillian delivered a hard punch to her stomach. Alexandra gasped and momentarily struggled for breath. The two big girls let her go and she collapsed to her knees, winded.

"Well I'm back now," Gillian continued. "I have to be legitimate, but *you and I* are going to come to *an arrangement!* You'll pay for what you did, Mouse – quite literally! From now onwards you're barred from the tuck shop. But you'll still give me your money. Whatever your mummy gives you out of your allowance each week to buy something from the shop, you'll hand straight to me at break time. Do that, and I might just leave you alone sometimes. But if you don't, you'll get another thumping just like that one. So, do we have an agreement? Or shall I thump you again?"

She nodded once more, and the other girls hoisted Alexandra back to her feet.

"No! No, Spencer!" cried Alexandra desperately. Her breath was slowly returning to normal, but her heart suddenly quickened again in fear. "I agree. I'll pay you!"

"Good," said Gillian. "But just remember what I've said. See you tomorrow, Mouse. Go home and hide behind your mother's skirt!"

With that the threesome went away. Alexandra picked up her bag and walked as quickly as possible out of Charterhouse.

On the train home she collected her thoughts, sucking the finger of her glove. She didn't do that very much now, but after what had just happened, she felt the need of some comfort. There was no one else in her carriage at the moment, anyhow.

Alexandra didn't want to tell her mother what Gillian had done to her on the way out of the college, or that she'd been forced to agree to pay the headmistress's daughter her tuck shop money. She still worried that her mother would complain to Charterhouse about it - in fact Alexandra thought it highly likely, especially as she was on the board of governors. That could make life very difficult for her, each day at school. Alexandra talked to her mother extensively about most things, but not so much about Gillian. She only said marginally more about her to Tom. Alexandra would feel a little guilty about her mother giving her money intended for her to spend at the tuck shop which would instead be going directly to Gillian, but that couldn't be helped at the moment. Fortunately the shop didn't issue receipts to the girls after they had brought what they wanted, therefore back at home she would only need to enter the amount she paid to Gillian alongside an item that she knew the rough price of, in her personal account book. Her mother wouldn't realise when she checked her accounts that the item was in fact fictitious.

As the train puffed along through a tunnel, Alexandra began to long for her mother to hold her. When she was in her arms and when she was beneath her, she felt completely safe and protected. Nobody – not even Gillian Spencer – could harm her there.

Alexandra realised that some of the girls at Charterhouse did indeed think, as they grew older and got to know her, that she preferred to hide behind her mother's skirt, rather than wear her own. In truth it was also that at home, her mother's skirt dominated.

CHAPTER 71

The next afternoon, Gillian Spencer played truant from Charterhouse, skipping her double period of history. There was no fear in her mind that she might be punished for doing so. She went to the centre of Buckmore where in a public convenience, she changed out of her school uniform into more casual dress. Then she entered a massage parlour.

Gillian was becoming more sexually aware than many of her contemporaries, and she wanted to explore her desires. She was a confident, precocious and naughty girl, which made for a lethal combination in this regard.

The parlour was fronted by a striptease club. Gillian paid for a ticket at the door. Even in mid-afternoon there were three women seated in the audience, intently watching as a man performed on the stage, moving seductively to sexily themed music as he slowly undressed. They were all clearly highly aroused and two of them had even pulled their skirts down to their knees and were stroking their erect geratises. The other belched, and Gillian caught a waft of alcohol from her breath. She had clearly had a skinful.

None of the women noticed Gillian's arrival as she sat down behind them, so transfixed were they on the man, who was now naked. Her own geratis went rock hard and was extended further from her vagina than ever before, as she looked on, and then thought about what she had come here to do.

Abruptly, one of the women with her skirt down got up and hastily fastened it back to her waist. The huge bulge of her erection formed a visible shape inside of it. Then she hurried to a door at the back of the room and went through. Realising where that must lead to, after a moment Gillian got up and followed.

On the other side of the door, she walked down a short corridor and reached a desk. The woman was being taken down another corridor by a girl. There were four open doors, two on each side,

and the girl invited the woman to see inside each one. Eventually the woman indicated a preference and she was taken inside by the girl.

"Can I help you, Madam?" asked a second girl at the desk.

"I wish to see one of your boys," said Gillian, trying to keep the overwhelming excitement that she felt from being too obvious in her voice.

"Of course," replied the girl. She looked Gillian over and smiled. "You are quite young. If this should be your first time with a man, would you prefer him to take the lead? I mean that either sexual position can be catered for."

The girl had seen many women pass through the parlour to have sex with an escort. The vast majority simply wanted it in the traditional and most overwhelmingly popular Geratican fashion. Very occasionally there might be a request for a man on top – perhaps one in every hundred.

"No, no. That's alright. I like to be on top," said Gillian. She wasn't prepared to admit that she was a virgin, and certainly not publicly that she was underage, but she *was* very sure of how she wanted to have sex.

Gillian paid the girl another sum of money. Her mother gave her a handsome weekly allowance and she had indeed made quite a bit from her tuck shop scam before being discovered, but all the same she had now made a dent in her savings. It would be worth it though, she was convinced.

The girl now took Gillian down the same corridor as the woman before her. She looked through three of the doors and in each of them saw a naked man lying seductively on a bed. The only door that was closed was the one where the woman had gone. At the moment when she passed the door, Gillian heard the unmistakable sound of her having an orgasm.

In one of the rooms there was a slim dark-haired man of medium height that Gillian found particularly attractive.

"This one please," she said.

"Very well – and an excellent choice!" replied the girl. "David, this young lady, Gillian, wishes to have sex with you in the standard fashion."

She glanced back at Gillian before she left the room.

"Have a pleasurable hour."

As the door closed Gillian's heart raced and her geratis was aroused like never before.

David turned so that he rested on his elbow and smiled slyly at her.

"Hello Gillian, darling!" he said huskily. "And how old are you, then?"

"Never you mind about that!" replied Gillian. She was already half undressed. "I've taken the necessary precautions."

David chuckled. Gillian could tell that he suspected she wasn't yet legally old enough to be having consensual sexual intercourse, but she didn't care about that now, and she knew that once you were behind closed doors here, nobody asked too many questions, and everybody was discreet. All she wanted was to lose her virginity and be able to boast that she was a woman.

"Have me then, darling!" encouraged David, sexily, as he saw her erect geratis throbbing out from her vagina. His eyes fixed seductively on her in a 'come to bed' fashion.

In no time at all, Gillian had climbed on to the bed and he pulled her down on top of him. David stretched out and pouted his lips. He reached up and stroked her hair. Then his fingers slipped lightly down her back and over her buttocks and legs. When a Geratican

woman was sexually aroused her powerful thighs were particularly sensitive, and Gillian exhaled heavily with pleasure. She smelt his scent and it aroused her even more. His hand briefly moved downwards to her crotch and touched her geratis. She gasped. David was an expert in seducing women in this parlour, and he had never met one yet who wasn't turned on by his technique and could resist making love to a man when he offered himself to her on a plate. Gillian, still not quite a woman but a highly confident virgin girl, was even easier to seduce and she smiled wolfishly. This was how she had always fantasised of a man behaving towards her when she finally had sex. She could contain herself no longer and hungrily ravished David, as her geratis slipped inside his vagina and felt a man's genus for the first time. Gillian was so over excited that her geratis immediately expanded to fill him completely and as it throbbed against his walls and thrust down across his genus, she came first. The orgasm was far stronger than Gillian had anticipated, and she screamed loudly. Then David's genus exploded, and he came too. As she felt his semen trickling through the pores of her geratis, Gillian felt tingles all over, like never before.

At first, she felt embarrassed that she'd reacted in such a way. Gillian had always arrogantly thought that screaming was for boys. But as she lay recovering, she began to realise that it was probably just a natural reaction to this, and it had after all been her first time. So, she had done it at last! And she definitely wanted to do so again.

By the end of her hour-long session, she had made love to a man three times.

***

Afterwards, Gillian went back to the desk and asked to speak to the manager, saying that she had a business proposition for her. There was considerable surprise at this, but eventually the manager, Nina Sellars, agreed to see Gillian in her office.

Back in Charterhouse, Gillian couldn't resist boasting to the other girls about her sexual achievements at the parlour. She also informed her mother that whilst out on a trip within Buckmore she had become friendly with a couple of young men who it turned out were actors. They were offering to come to her chambers and give 'drama lessons' to any girl who was interested. Initially it would be for one day a week, but maybe two if it proved popular. But they didn't want any publicity about it, and therefore requested it to be kept confidential.

Elizabeth paid no attention whatsoever to anything to do with the arts and didn't know one actor from another. She was surprised that her daughter was so interested in helping the pair, but thought it a pleasant gesture which might make her popular with the rest of the college. She gave her blessing and told Gillian to take sole responsibility for them as her personal guests. Elizabeth would discover to her cost later, that she had been deceived – and the price to be paid would be heavy for both she and her daughter.

Gillian then began to tell the rest of the girls about the secret 'unofficial' arrangement she had made and asked if they were interested. Most were not and this included Alexandra, Benita, Imelda (though the latter did give it some consideration), Rachel and Emma. In fact, many told her what she could do with her offer. But as Gillian had predicted she did manage to find a small number were, including Melanie who was unable to contain her excitement.

The first visit of the 'actors' to Charterhouse took place on day 5 of that week.

***

At around the same time, Gillian was also holding secret card games for money in her chambers, attended by a small number of

girls, flouting the college's strict laws against gambling in the process.

CHAPTER 72

On the afternoon of 7/4/10, Alexandra was with her mother in Greenacres Crematorium. They were visiting the plot that contained the ashes of her grandmother and grandfather. A tombstone denoted their names, when they had been born and when they had died.

They placed some fresh flowers in the plot, and then strolled around the rest of the grounds looking respectfully at other tombstones of those now departed from Geratica. As she walked, clinging to her mother's waist, with Linda's arm around her shoulders, in the quiet surroundings of the graveyard, Alexandra (as she often did when they came here) found herself reading the details of the people who lived sometimes long ago, thinking of what they might have been like, the lives that they led and the stories they could probably tell if ever it was possible to come back. There was no real belief of an afterlife on Geratica, or any religion or god, and it was thought to be the same on the parallel world of Geraticai. Everybody knew that their world had somehow been created by the Divine Being who was the core of their planet – a live female sex whose presence they could all feel faintly in their minds.

Alexandra studied how old the people were when they died. In the future more would join them in the same crematorium. She could hear the wind in the trees and birds flying about above. Whenever she visited a graveyard, she was always reminded of the Earth twentieth century pop song '*In A Country Churchyard (Let Your Love Shine On)'* by *Chris de Burgh*.

She continued to be deep in thought. Gradually she became aware of a voice speaking to her.

"...They're very pretty aren't they?"

Alexandra blinked and turned her head.

"Sorry Mother, I was miles away!" she replied. "What were you saying?"

"For goodness sake, Alexandra!" exclaimed Linda. "Haven't you been listening to a word that I've told you? I hope you don't daydream like that in your lessons at Charterhouse!"

"No Mother. I don't, I promise!" said Alexandra.

Linda wagged a finger gently at her.

"You *will* listen to me when I'm talking to you, daughter. Pay attention, or you might miss something important. I say things for your own good, a lot of the time. Do you understand?"

"Oh yes, Mother!" replied Alexandra, quickly, her heart fluttering slightly. "I'm sorry Mother, I was just admiring the beautiful surroundings."

Then Linda smiled and pulled her close.

"Yes, they are lovely. In fact, what I was saying darling, is that the plots in this area are some of the oldest and that the groundsmen have clearly done a good job in building a very pretty rose garden to commemorate the deceased. Very tasteful. Would you agree?"

"Oh yes, definitely Mother," replied Alexandra. "The flowers are definitely extremely pretty."

"It's alright. I can understand how your attention might have wandered in this case, sweetheart," continued Linda. "It was something relatively minor, but you must make an effort to concentrate at all times. That applies in all situations and it's also impolite to have appeared not to have listened to somebody. And as your mother, I *will* be listened to, taken notice of and obeyed as appropriate. I believe that I make myself clear."

"Crystal clear, Mother," confirmed Alexandra.

"Good girl," said Linda.

They sat down on a bench for a few minutes, enjoying the peace and quiet. Alexandra smuggled up to her mother.

 Then after paying a last visit to Alexandra's grandparents' plot, they went back to the car and Linda drove them back to The Grange.

CHAPTER 73

Geratica Spring 5010

At the Royal Palace, Queen Alexandra was holding a meeting with Linda and Fiona. High on the agenda was the new marital suite still to be completed in the Geratica Hotel.

"I have to agree with Linda that this does seem to be taking an extraordinarily long time!" remarked the queen. "It's now four and a half years since you first mooted this idea, Fiona. Surely my suite must be ready soon?"

"It will, Ma'am, I assure you," replied her court administrator. "There have been some last minute queries over the layout plans, but the contractor should be able to go ahead and complete the job shortly."

"Good. I'm glad to hear it," said Queen Alexandra.

"I should think so too!" added Linda.

"But Your Majesty still has no definite idea as to when she might have need for the suite, does she?" asked Fiona.

"No," confirmed the queen. "But it still will be a relief when it is at least open for use by my subjects, should they so choose."

Fiona knew that she couldn't hold off completing this operation for much longer. Back over on Geraticai she understood that the situation was *still* no different regarding the prince. Dr. Bethany Peters, the queen's chief royal physician, had said privately that although the operation had been a success physically, and his body had accepted the DNA of the Geratican mongrel, and that he appeared fertile, she could find no way of guaranteeing that he would deliver a child to the queen, and she suspected that maybe he couldn't – whether it be due to an unforeseen side effect of the

operation, or any other reason. Queen Victoria was growing more and more bad tempered with each day that passed.

Linda looked at the clock on Queen Alexandra's study wall. She was going to be having lunch with James Spencer. They had recently started going to a fish and chip shop together, a couple of miles away, where there were tables to sit and eat at. Linda often dined on fine delicacies, but she did enjoy this type of food too – and especially in the company of James. They were growing ever closer and Linda was beginning to feel that she loved him. He was clearly unhappy in his marriage to Elizabeth, and she was hoping that she might one day be able to persuade him to leave her. But she was moving cautiously, and so far she didn't think that he was minded to do it.

***

Meanwhile at Charterhouse, Elizabeth received some disappointing news. Linda Radcliffe, though she did not attend every meeting, was a forceful member of the board of governors. She had clashed with Mavis Baverstock who had given the headmistress such strong support, over her style of chairmanship and managed to get her voted out. Sonia Eastman had been elected in her place and replaced two old members with new ones. The backing that Elizabeth had previously enjoyed as headmistress of Charterhouse was no longer as overwhelming.

She had however now managed to set up a couple of very small special schools where boys could be educated – though it still remained the official policy of the court that formal education was only necessary for girls.

Elizabeth was also beginning to become suspicious of Linda's relationship with her husband. She knew that as the queen's chauffeur, James spent some time with the senior court administrator, both at the palace and when travelling to her official engagements. Rumour had it that the pair got on rather well.

Linda had, as yet, not made any direct mention of James to Alexandra. She and her daughter had an especially close relationship at The Grange which she wanted to preserve, and at the moment although she wanted him very badly, she wasn't sure if he ever would leave his wife. Linda was quietly planning, but it would need to be done delicately and with her daughter's feelings considered. It might never happen, but she was a woman accustomed to getting what she wanted eventually, even if it took time – though Linda's patience was far from inexhaustible. (Alexandra actually often had greater reserves of that). She wasn't going to wait forever before taking the initiative and making a move. In fact, many of the girls at Charterhouse knew that James Spencer was the queen's chauffeur, as the headmistress's daughter had boasted about the fact on many occasions.

Alexandra's friendship with Tom was seemingly beginning to develop into something more, though she was still coming to terms with the situation in her mind. Alone in Elmsbrook wood they had once or twice held hands and Alexandra had experienced her first erection. She thought that Tom probably felt the same way about her as she did about him, but she was too shy and hadn't yet enough confidence to take the initiative on it in the way that some other Geratican girls did. It wasn't a subject that she felt yet ready to discuss with her mother. Alexandra wondered if she would think her too young to be embarking upon a relationship. She would be sixteen – the Geratican age of consent – in the summer of next year. Alexandra had no intention of doing anything improper whilst she was still a girl, but she was certain that if she ever did and her mother found out (somehow she felt that she would), then she would be in a lot of trouble.

Linda had considered what their close friendship could potentially lead to, but at this stage considered it unlikely that there would be any imminent change in their relationship.

Gillian had found that she and her small gang of friends who wanted to see the escort boys in her chambers – often twice a week - would need to generate more cash if they were to continue, as

their allowances wouldn't stretch much further. In fact, it was now usually just herself and Melanie. She was now beginning to encourage Melanie to assist her in visiting shops and stores at dinner times and some weekends, to steal goods which they could then bring back to Charterhouse and sell on to the other girls there at greatly inflated prices – in order to keep being able to pay for their pleasures. Gillian still asked everybody in her form whether they were interested in coming to the 'drama lessons' but invariably it remained only Melanie who answered in the affirmative.

***

Fiona had decided that she had better pay another visit to Geraticai. They were becoming fewer and farther in between. In the late afternoon of 7/12/10. she made her way through the wood to her transportation capsule. A moment later she had vanished...

VOLUME 3

The events of the third volume in this book begin the year after the end of the second chronicle in the original 'Geratica' series...

PART 13

CHAPTER 74

Geratica Summer 5024

Queen Alexandra of Geratica was now in her Silver Jubilee year. Linda Radcliffe who at the end of 5023 had retired as Geratica's first ever prime minister after ten years, had been specially appointed to oversee the events that would commemorate and celebrate the milestone, largely due to her previously close working relationship with the queen as firstly court administrator and then senior court administrator at the Royal Palace.

The queen had visited every town in every region of Geratica, to cheering crowds. Her royal car was of course driven by her chauffeur, James Radcliffe, husband of Linda since 5013. All over the world there were street celebrations, and shops and stores sold numerous Jubilee souvenir items.

Queen Saphron of Geraticai was now paying a State Visit, and she and Queen Alexandra went on a hunting expedition together, in the countryside surrounding the royal palace in Avermore. They were accompanied by senior dignitaries from both queendoms.

Today, both royal families were appearing on the balcony of the royal palace together with a mass of adulating crowds stretching far beyond the gates. There was Queen Alexandra, her consort, Prince George, and her two children, Princess Mary – the heir to the Geratican throne – and Prince Charles. Representing Geraticai were Queen Saphron, her consort, Prince Gordon, and her only child, son and heir to the Geraticaian throne, Henry. Also with them was Linda, and completing the group was the girl who the previous year the retiring prime minister had called 'The Most Special Geratican Of All' her daughter, the ever popular Alexandra Radcliffe, now approaching her twenty ninth birthday.

After a few moments the party withdrew from the balcony and back into the palace, on their way to a sumptuous lunch in the state

dining room, prepared in honour of Queen Alexandra. James would be there, along with Tom Radcliffe – Alexandra's husband.

Alexandra followed Linda down the corridor to the hall. On the way she saw a portrait of her mother hanging on a wall, painted in honour of her contribution to Geratican state affairs, both as Senior Court Administrator at the palace and as Prime Minister. Alexandra thought how bold and assertive looking the picture portrayed her to be, looking confidently at the observer, with her hands resting on her hips – which reflected her personality.

Linda and Alexandra walked though into the state dining room together. But as they did so, something strange happened. There was a sudden flash of white light and they felt as if they were being transported away...

CHAPTER 75

Domain of the Time Guardians of Geratica and Geraticai

When the light faded, they were in a large room with plain white walls. A table with two chairs was at the centre. Beyond that there was what appeared to be some kind of circular globe, with fleeting images of people swirling around within.

"Where are we?" exclaimed Linda.

"Well, it certainly doesn't look like the state dining room, Mother," replied Alexandra. "Unless they've radically changed it since I last visited the palace!"

"I think that's quite obvious, darling," said Linda. "I was there only earlier on this morning, overseeing the final preparations for the lunch. But we were certainly walking into it. So how in the name of Geratica have we ended up here – wherever this is?"

She looked behind them.

"The door is no longer there, either!"

"Welcome, Linda and Alexandra Radcliffe!" said a voice suddenly, making them both jump. At the far end of the room the image of a woman had appeared on a screen. On her head was a silver crown.

"Who are you?" demanded Linda, still naturally taking the lead role in the partnership with her daughter. "Where the blazes are we?"

"Do not be alarmed," said the woman. "I will do my best to explain. Please both of you, take a seat at the table."

"Thank you," replied Linda. As they sat down facing the woman, with Alexandra to the left of her mother, a cup of black coffee appeared before each of them, with a biscuit in the saucer.

"Some refreshment for you," remarked the woman. "Don't worry, it's perfectly safe! This isn't some kind of trap. But we aware of all that there is to know about you. If you relax and listen, then I will tell you about us."

Linda and Alexandra glanced at each other. "Go on. We are listening," confirmed Linda.

"You are in what we call the Domain of the Time Guardians of Geratica and Geraticai," began the woman. "My name is Lady Tara. You may find this difficult to comprehend, but you have both been removed from space and time – temporarily we hope."

Linda and Alexandra looked at each other again in astonishment.

"Then where exactly are we?" asked Alexandra.

"In a place on the very edge of space," replied Lady Tara. "But if I may continue? In your present time stream, it is the year 5024 on Geratica and 3974 on Geraticai. Many centuries in your future, an elite group of people, comprising both Geraticans and Geraticaians became experts in the field of time. We began to develop certain unique and extensive powers and gradually started to evolve away from the rest of our race. Eventually we established a secret domain here and became time guardians. We set up a Council of Guardians and undertook to observe and preserve the natural time of both worlds for the rest of their natural existence, which as you know will be until the mistress herself ceases to be. We no longer took physical form beyond the image that you see on this screen now, and have never left this domain, though with our minds we have sometimes travelled backwards and forwards through time to observe and maintain the balance. That's how we know all about you, and the great contribution that you have made to Geratican history – plus some of your particular tastes, hence the black

coffees and biscuits! We are not immortal, but we have mastered the art of extensively elongating our lives.

"For years we had no problems, but unfortunately a small fanatical faction has emerged within the council who seek to change the order of the timeline. They wish to create one new world by melding all of time together and mixing it up. But this will mean that Geratica and Geraticai and all of their people will no longer exist, and their correct future timelines will not occur."

"What?" gasped Alexandra. "You've got to stop them, Lady Tara!"

"I can't believe it Lady Tara. They've no right to do that!" said Linda. "But there must be something that you can do. I'm sure that the mistress would have the power to prevent it."

"The fanatics believe that they are strong enough to overcome her," said Lady Tara. "We cannot say for certain. Our domain probably has similarities with hers, but we are a slightly different entity. I had better now explain to you how they will attempt to implement the time meld. There is a specific method. It cannot be done directly by guardians alone, without assistance from an agent. They have taken a Geraticaian out of space and time in the same way as you were by us. This woman will, with the fanatical faction's protection, be able to survive the time meld unchanged, and then have the opportunity to rule over the new world. She will also be allowed to take three people from her own time with her. But everybody else will cease to exist. You will have noticed the globe in front of you. Those images that you see swirling about are all of the people on Geratica and Geratiai from your own time, who will no longer exist after the meld. This woman will be shown a similar globe in her own time and asked to select three people who will also be saved. They will presumably be those that she knows best or is closest to.

"However, once the faction have begun the process, it will take thirty minutes to fully implement, therefore there will be a period when the woman and her companions will be in a void before finding themselves on the new world. That gives the rest of the

guardians some time to try and stop this, and this is why you two have been taken out of your own time stream by us. We want to send you to follow where the others have gone. You will be able to select two others to take with you also, to help counterbalance the situation, but it will not be possible for any more to go. Once you are sent, then we believe that the two time streams will meet in some form – we cannot predict what that may be – and on your arrival, your task will be to find the Geraticaian woman and her companions and stop them. Again, we do not know exactly what you will have to do in order to achieve this, but there will be an encounter of some kind. We think it likely that the fanatics will have anticipated our response and will probably warn your opposite number to expect to meet you. If you are successful, then everybody concerned should return to their own time streams and remember nothing of what happened. The future of Geratica and Geraticai will continue unchanged. But if you are not...”

At that moment there was the sound of a bell pinging.

“Ah,” said Lady Tara.”We are about to be joined!”

Beside her, another screen came to life and the image of a man appeared. Linda's mouth dropped open. Not only did he also have a silver crown on his head. He was wearing a skirt.

“This is Lord Anthony, ladies,” announced Lady Tara.

“Good afternoon Linda and Alexandra Radcliffe,” said the lord.

“Good afternoon, Lord Anthony,” replied Alexandra.

Linda was still recovering from her shock. Lady Tara smiled.

“Are you surprised to see Lord Anthony wearing the traditional garment that represents authority on Geratica, Linda?”

Alexandra was chuckling too at her mother's reaction.

Linda coughed lightly. "Well yes, I must admit that I am, Lady Tara. I never thought that I would live to see the day when..." She broke off with a slight shake of her head.

"Men became much more represented in many areas of Geratican life after your time in office, Linda," said the lady. "By the time of the formation of the council of guardians, there had even been three male prime ministers and four kings! Some men – though perhaps still a minority - began to see no reason why they should not wear the skirt from time to time. It must be admitted though that not many women decided to wear trousers! But of course, though you were a staunch traditionalist on this subject, the government under your premiership did in fact begin the process of greater gender equality in Geratican society!"

"This is true," acknowledged Linda.

"Lady Tara, we have news regarding the fanatical faction," said Lord Anthony. "Their Geraticaian agent has selected her companions. They will be starting the time meld very soon."

"Who is this Geraticaian agent, and what year is she living in?" asked Alexandra.

"She is somebody who you will already both be very familiar with," said Lord Anthony. "The mongrel, Fiona, from the Geraticaian year 3960."

"Fiona?" Linda nearly dropped her coffee cup. "I don't believe it! I thought that we must have seen the last of her ten years ago. But she keeps on being resurrected! Will we ever be free of her?"

"Don't forget that this is Fiona from several years in your past though, Linda," remarked Lady Tara. "*We* and *you* know what eventually happened to her, but that is still to come."

"The Geraticaian year 3960," said Alexandra, thoughtfully. "Let me see. That makes the corresponding year on Geratica 5010. She was still living in Elmsbrook then, and we didn't find out that she

was a Geraticaian spy until the end of the next year. It was when Father was still being held on Geraticai and their Queen Victoria was plotting to try and be rid of Geratica as a parallel world and for it to become the one true planet. The male rights issue was starting to come to a boil too."

"You are of course correct, Alexandra," said Lord Anthony. "We believe that year may have been chosen by the fanatics as the decade or so that followed it was quite a pivotal time in history for the relationship between Geratica and Geraticai. Even very many years later, the fact that Geraticai was initially just a parallel imitation of Geratica rankles with a small minority of its inhabitants who still feel that it is the poor relation. That is at least part of this faction's motivation for doing this. In fact Fiona was taken out of her time stream at the very moment that she was embarking upon a secret trip back to Geraticai in her transportation capsule. The companions that she has chosen are, from Geraticai, Queen Victoria, and from Geratica, her husband Colin and stepson Tom."

"Tom!" cried Alexandra. "Oh, my goodness!"

"Will the two of you go?" asked Lady Tara. "We have the means to send you in the same path that Fiona travels in. The fate of both Geratica and Geraticai will be in your hands after that."

"Well, I suppose when you put it like that, then we have little choice!" said Linda. "That's all very well though. But how are we supposed to decide what to do when we get to this place, if we don't even know anything about the situation we'll be facing beforehand?"

"I am afraid that we can do no more," said Lady Tara. "Once you are there, you will need to find the way to defeat the fanatics' plan yourselves. But the council has every confidence that if any people can do it then you two women can."

"What will happen to the guardians if we do fail?" asked Alexandra.

"If the fanatics succeed then they will become the sole guardians and the rest of us on the council will die," said Lady Tara. "So, you see we have every reason to hope that they don't!"

"One last thing," she added. "As this is a fight between two rival factions of the council, then you may find that there are certain unknown characters who will be trying to stop you. It will be exactly the same for the other side."

Alexandra raised her eyebrows.

"That sounds ominous!" she said, with trepidation. "What would happen if somebody were to die in the void, but Mother and I are still successful in our mission? Would the person still return to their own time stream as before, or would they truly be gone?"

"Whatever may happen to any of you there, if the two of you succeed then everything will return to normal back in your own time streams," the lady assured her.

Suddenly the top of the globe in front of Linda and Alexandra glowed red, and then the number 30 appeared in black digits.

"The time meld has been started!" declared Lord Anthony. "That is a timer. The number denotes the number of minutes left until implementation. There is no time to lose. If you agree to do this, then you must now select two companions to take with you. Then we will send you after Fiona's party, and you will have until the timer reaches zero to stop them."

Linda thought quickly and taking her daughter's hand, looked into her eyes. They both silently agreed that although this situation they now found themselves in was indeed bizarre, these two 'time guardians' did seem genuine. They nodded to each other as they made their decision with Linda. as always, taking the initiative.

"Very well we accept the task," she said. "Logic would seem to suggest that as Fiona has taken Queen Victoria from her time, then

we should take Queen Alexandra from 5024. The other who we wish to select from our time stream is Tom."

"Of course," said Lord Anthony.

"That means that there will be two Toms, though!" pointed out Alexandra. "I take it that is possible in this unknown place?"

"Yes," confirmed the lord. "Each of them are from different time streams. They exist in both globes."

Now a blue glow appeared from within the circular globe and a few seconds later, Queen Alexandra and Tom stood in the room.

"You must now leave," said Lady Tara. "We sincerely wish you good luck and hope that you succeed. Farewell!"

Then a beam of white light flashes from the ceiling and sweeps the foursome away...

CHAPTER 76

In another part of the domain, in an identical room, the images of two guardians making up the fanatical faction of the council were on the screens. On the globe before them they watched their own timer beginning to tick down.

"Our agent and her companions are gone, but as we suspected the other guardians have sent others from a different time to try and interfere with our plans," said one, Lady Evelyn.

"They will not succeed," asserted the other, Lord Peter. "But for now, we can only wait."

CHAPTER 77

Linda and Alexandra found themselves standing in a rose garden. Beside them were Queen Alexandra and Tom.

"What's going on?" demanded the queen, as she glanced around. "How did we get here? And where are we?"

The Radcliffe women did their best to explain what they understood to have happened and why they were all there.

"This must be the strangest event to have happened in our world yet!" exclaimed Tom. "I thought that when the copy Fiona took over the minds of the people on Geratica and Geraticai, and declared herself Empress of the Geraticaian Empire was the limit. But this..."

"Well, if we're successful then none of us will ever actually know about it," said Linda.

"I must admit that I thought I'd done my bit for Geratica – and Geraticai," declared Alexandra. "But it appears that we must fight one last battle."

"That scoundrel, Fiona!" said Queen Alexandra. "I know it's not entirely her own doing, but even so. She keeps turning up. Well we'd better get on with this and return everything to normal."

They quickly looked about the garden. Alexandra reached the wall at the end. There was a gate in the middle. Opening it, she peered cautiously out. There was a lawn beyond, and a short distance away there lay what appeared to be some kind of building.

"Mother!" she called. "Come over here and look."

Linda walked over.

"What do you think Mother?" asked Alexandra. "It looks like a castle."

"I don't know, but I would suggest that whatever our destiny is here, it may well be going to take place there," replied Linda. " And yes, I agree. It is unmistakably a castle. We'd better get over there quickly. Time will be ticking on."

"Ma'am, if you would like to follow us," she said to Queen Alexandra who was making her way to the wall, "I think that we know where we should be going. Tom! Come with us."

"Lead on please, Linda!" replied the queen.

They set off quickly across the lawn. As they approached the castle, they could see an entrance, and they walked across a small courtyard to a back door...

***

On the front side of the castle, Fiona, Queen Victoria, Colin, and the Tom from Geratica 5010 had arrived at the edge of a moat.

Due to what the time guardians had told her, she suspected that this place was not yet the desired new world, but rather the void in which they needed to win some sort of confrontation with people from another time before they could get there.

 They walked around he moat and made their way towards the front entrance of the castle.

When they reached the door, there appeared to be a bell, but when Fiona pressed it, a screen above came to life. First it indicated that there was twenty minutes to go before implementation, and then a mathematical formula appeared. Then there was a woman's automated voice.

"Entry to this castle is restricted. Solve this mathematical equation, and it will reveal a code to you. Enter it in the space provided, and the door will open."

The equation flashed up upon the screen with box and keypad underneath.

"You'd best deal with that, dear," said Colin to his wife. "You know about figures."

"Yes, do it Fiona!" ordered Queen Victoria. Her official lady chancellor (Daniella Sturridge was still officially only 'acting' in the position) had informed her of their purpose on this strange void upon their arrival, and she was now greatly excited. This could solve all of her problems. If Fiona succeeded in her mission and became ruler of the new world, then the queen had already demanded that she step aside for her. Then she would finally be the monarch of one queendom with no other parallel world existing. Fiona had agreed.

"I still don't quite understand all of this," said Tom. "Why aren't Alexandra and her mother here as well? And who is this woman with us?"

"Once we have established the new world, then the Radcliffes will join us," Fiona lied to her stepson. "The woman with us is a friend of mine." After she had explained to the queen what they were doing here, they had agreed that she would tell a slightly different story to her Geratican family. Colin and Tom still didn't yet know that Fiona was actually from Geraticai.

She began to work out the equation in her head...

***

Meanwhile at the other entrance, the party from 5024 heard the same message two minutes later. Working together, Linda and Alexandra too began to solve the equation.

All of a sudden there came a terrible screeching from somewhere in the distance. Everybody jumped.

"What was that?" asked Alexandra.

The sound came again, only this time it appeared to be nearer.

"Remember what Lady Tara said?" replied Linda. "That there might be certain unknown characters trying to stop us. Perhaps this is one of them. And it doesn't sound terribly friendly! Let's get this code cracked quickly and go inside the castle!"

They hurriedly continued. Then there was another screech and something appeared overhead.

It was a huge black bird.

"What in the name of Divinity is that?" gasped Queen Alexandra. "I've never seen anything like it!"

The bird surveyed them, sensing their smell. It was hungry and was tempted to swoop down and devour the group. But then it suddenly sensed another even stronger smell, coming from the other side of the castle. Unable to resist its allure, the bird left and flew over the top of the castle to investigate...

***

The bird saw Fiona and her band of companions. Its existence and purpose was linked to the creation of the void. This group were trying to manipulate time in order to create a new world and the bird's natural instinct was to prevent that. Their stronger scent, in

comparison with the other people, alerted it to the danger, and its hunger increased.

Just as Fiona was finding the answer to the equation, the bird swooped and began to descend. They all looked up in alarm.

"That doesn't look very friendly!" remarked Fiona.

"Hurry up, Fiona!" screamed Queen Victoria, as Colin and Tom also cried out in alarm. She felt as if the bird was coming right for her, alone. A slight wetness trickled into her pants beneath her skirts. She squealed, turned about and started to run away.

"I have the code!" shouted Fiona, as she began to furiously enter it in the box on the screen.

At this, the queen rallied and just managed to recover her composure a little, stopping and retracing her steps. As the bird came down and was almost upon them, she drew her knife and slashed out wildly. She caught the bird on its left wing, and it screamed in pain, recoiling slightly. Then just before Fiona entered the final part of the code, Victoria took the gun she was carrying from her hip and swung round to take aim at the bird. Firing one shot, she caught it square on the temple. With one more terrible screech, it fell to the ground just a few paces in front of them, dead.

Fiona quickly finished entering the code. To her relief the screen indicated that it was accepted, and the door swung open.

"Follow me, everybody!" she said, and they went inside. Queen Victoria breathed deeply. She hoped that nobody noticed that the Geraticaian monarch had just wet herself in fear, and – as she secretly felt - momentarily betrayed such cowardice.

They walked across a lobby. On the other side there was a lift. Beside it was another screen indicating a timer. There was now thirteen minutes until implementation.

Fiona pressed the button on the wall to call the lift. It immediately opened and they all stepped inside. The doors closed, and they were taken up...

***

By the back door, Linda and Alexandra had worked out the code, just a moment after Fiona. They were caching up. Alexandra entered it and the door opened.

When they walked into the castle, they were in a hallway with passages leading off from it in all directions. To their right was a stone staircase. On the pillar at the foot of the stairs was another screen. This timer also indicated that there were thirteen minutes to go.

"Which way now?" asked Tom.

"Well, as this staircase has a timer on it, then perhaps we should go up the stairs?" suggested Alexandra.

"I agree," said Linda.

"It seems logical," remarked Queen Alexandra.

"Right. Here we go, then, Ma'am" declared Linda, and made to lead the way up.

"Alexandra!" called a voice, suddenly. "Wait!"

Whirling around, Alexandra was astonished to see Gillian Spencer coming out of one of the passages. It was the Gillian from 5010, and behind her was Elizabeth Spencer from the same time. They wore their respective Charterhouse College uniforms.

"Gillian! How in the name of Geratica did you get here?" she asked, incredulously.

"We aren't sure," said Gillian. "We just suddenly found ourselves here and have been walking about these corridors ever since."

"Don't go up those stairs, though!" warned Elizabeth.

"Why not? It seems fairly likely that's where we need to go," said Linda.

"No. It's too dangerous. We've already tried to go up there," replied Gillian.

Alexandra frowned. "The time guardians specifically told us that nobody besides those people we selected, and Fiona's choices, could come to the void. So, I ask again. How can you be here? Also, whenever we were at Charterhouse, you never addressed me by my proper name. It was always Mouse! I don't think that you're real. This is some kind of decoy to stop us from going up the stairs."

"We were warned to expect something like this," said Linda. "If it's so dangerous, then what did you encounter when you tried earlier?"

Elizabeth and Gillian looked at each other. "Don't go up!" they both insisted, together.

Alexandra eye them, thoughtfully. An idea came to her. Turning to the foot of the staircase, she trod upon the first step.

"No!" shouted Gillian.

Alexandra looked back, before taking another. Elizabeth and Gillian glanced at each other for one final time, and then they slowly faded away.

"Well I never!" exclaimed Queen Alexandra.

"Alexandra is quite right. They were simply images, designed to trick us," said Linda. "But they're gone now. I think it's obvious that we need to go up this staircase. And time is running out. Let's proceed!"

The other three followed her, racing up the steps...

CHAPTER 78

Fiona stepped out of the lift, with her companions behind her. They were in a chamber which was empty except for a circular black panelled console in the middle. She led everybody across and studied it with Queen Victoria.

At the same time the other group reached the top of the staircase. They found themselves at a doorway which led into the other end of the chamber. When Linda saw Fiona, she quickly motioned to those with her to stop and they hid themselves behind the entrance.

At the front of the console Fiona saw another timer, now indicating twelve minutes to go before implementation, and a single red button beneath it. With a glance towards the queen, she reached down and pressed it.

All of a sudden, there was a flash of white light, which made everybody instinctively shield their eyes and an aged looking woman appeared, standing at the centre atop of the console. She wore a crown of gold, and in her hand was a staff.

"I am The Keeper of All Time!" announced the woman, in a loud, clear voice. "This castle represents my position, and as such I am its keeper too. Please identify yourself!"

"I am Fiona Clark, from Geratica, Keeper," Fiona lied. "These people are my husband, my stepson, and a close friend of mine. The guardians of Geratican and Geraticaian time are implementing a time meld which will create a new world. I have been assigned and sent to rule over it when the process is completed."

"I know why you are here," said the keeper. "I also know that there are others who have been sent to this place to prevent it. I must hear from them."

"I know not of whom you speak," declared Fiona.

"Well, let us enlighten you then, Fiona!" shouted Linda, stepping forward into the chamber. Alexandra was quickly at her shoulder, followed closely by her husband and the Geratican queen. They swept towards the console.

Fiona studied them carefully. Even though this was Linda some fourteen years ahead of her own time, she still couldn't fail to recognise her – nor the others.

"Linda and Alexandra Radcliffe!" she exclaimed. "Somehow I just knew that it would be you that the other guardians would send. It was almost fate!"

"Keeper," said Linda, "I am indeed Linda Radcliffe, and this is my daughter, Alexandra. With me are Queen Alexandra of Geratica, and my daughter's husband, Tom. In our time, the year is 5024. We must prevent this time meld, as it will mean the end of life for both Geratica and Geraticai, and all of their inhabitants!"

"Linda Radcliffe?" enquired Queen Victoria. "I seem to recall your name from somewhere."

"This is the wife of the mongrel, Robert," Fiona told her.

"And this close friend of Fiona's is actually none other than Queen Victoria of Geraticai, Keeper," responded Linda. "Fiona is a Geraticaiian spy working upon her behalf on Geratica, though in 5010, nobody there yet knew it. It was she who abducted my first husband to Geraticai!"

"What?" said Colin and the Tom from 5010 together, in incomprehension.

"We on Geratica in 5024, know all about what you did to him, Your Majesty," continued Linda. Although she had seen and listened to her at the chasm, when the mistress had first appeared, this was the first time that she had really been able to talk to the woman whose scheming had caused her so many years of grief. "But the plan hasn't quite worked out, has it?"

"Keeper, Geratican history has always wrongly stated that Geraticai was created as a parallel world to Geratica," asserted Queen Victoria, ignoring Linda. "It is the other way round. Geraticai is the one true planet, and Geratica an inferior copy! This melding of time will ensure that one – and only one - world can be created. Once it is, I intend to reign there as Queen."

"We shall see about that," replied the keeper. "I shall have to make a judgement. How do I know that all you say is the truth?"

"It is not, Keeper!" said Queen Alexandra, furiously. "Victoria, you are talking nonsense!

"Address me by my full title, woman!" retorted the Geraticaian queen, "I am Queen Victoria of Geraticai, and you are merely a puppet queen!"

"Keeper. Geratica was created by a being who calls herself the mistress, though historically we always referred to her as the Divine Being," said Linda. "Geratcai was created accidentally when she developed a fault in her brain. That is simply both an historic and a scientific fact. People born on one world were automatically linked to someone on the other at birth through their minds – though they never knew them. It was eventually put right, and in the end the two worlds and their inhabitants did become entirely separate, but that all happens in the years ahead of Geratica 5010 and Geraticai 3960. In fact, *my* brain has been enhanced to be able to link up to the mistress, and it also turned out that mine is almost identical to hers, which is extremely rare! I know not if anybody previously linked to me had a similar mind. I believe that the time guardians in your domain have developed some powers that are similar to the mistress's, keeper. If you search my brain, then I assure you that you will find what I say to be true."

The keeper regarded her. At the same time as she spoke, Linda was attempting to establish some kind of contact with the mistress. Although they were out of space and time and she didn't know for

sure if it was possible, it was worth a try in order to help fully convince the keeper to support their faction of the time guardians over the radicals. For that, Linda suspected was what they were required to do here. If the timer reached zero before they could persuade her, then the time meld would be implemented.

Queen Victoria faced Linda. "Your mongrel husband is a totally useless man. He is utterly failing to do his duty!" She wasn't quite sure how, but she sensed that this Linda Radcliffe now knew the truth of what had happened.

"Robert was my first husband, and he is now dead, Ma'am" replied Linda. "As in fact are you! But happily, he eventually escaped, aided by our own daughter. I see no reason why I shouldn't tell you the future, since if this time meld is prevented then none of us will remember any of this when we return to our own times. I'm sorry to have to inform you that your life will end within the next two years, Ma'am. But you were a nasty, scheming, bullying tyrant, that Geraticai has never since missed!"

"How dare you blaspheme like that, woman!" seethed Queen Victoria. "I shall kill you for making such ridiculous comments about the Geraticaian monarch!"

She drew her knife from within her layers of skirts and marched boldly forward.

"Victoria don't be a fool!" exclaimed Queen Alexandra, quickly stepping into her path. She grabbed at the Geraticaian queen's wrist and grappled with her.

"Stop woman!" bellowed the keeper. "There will be no bloodshed in this place!"

She raised her staff and pointed it. A red barrier appeared between Queen Victoria and Linda. The queen kicked against it with her foot and found it impenetrable. She snarled angrily.

"I will find out more about this being called the mistress," said the keeper. Linda felt the sensation of her mind being searched.

Alexandra looked across at the Tom from 5010.

"Tom, listen to me! You must help us to stop your stepmother. If this faction of the time guardians succeed in implementing this meld and she creates a new world, then you will never see me again. Nobody except Fiona and those she's chosen can survive. The rest of us will die. Look at the man who stands beside me. Surely you recognise him? He's you in fourteen years' time, Tom, and soon I will propose a relationship with you. Eventually we will marry. But none of that can happen if Mother and I cannot prevent this time meld!"

"Alexandra is right, Tom," said Linda. "We must persuade the Keeper of All Time that we have the right to continue living, and that the other time guardians should prevail and allow our existing worlds to survive. The fanatical faction must be stopped, and we have to convince the keeper that they are mad, and that Queen Victoria of Geraticai and your stepmother have malicious intent."

"My stepmother told me that you'd follow once she'd established the new world," replied Tom.

"She's lying, Tom," said Alexandra. "You can't trust her. You *mustn't*. You know I always had my misgivings about her, and they'll turn out to be well founded. You heard what Mother said about her just now. She'll soon be discovered to be a Geraticaian spy!"

The 5024 Tom took a pace forward.

"It's true, Tom. I'm you. And in 5018, Alexandra will be your wife! Come over to our side and join us." He stretched out his arm. "You too, Father!"

"How can it be possible for you both to be here at the same time though?" asked Colin.

"I know it seems difficult to believe, but you are, Mr. Clark," insisted Alexandra. "The time guardians made it possible. Tom, please. Come and join us." She now held out her hand.

"Come Father!" urged the Tom next to her.

Tom looked at his father and they nodded. Slowly they inched across the short distance to the other group.

Fiona darted towards them. She was starting to feel concerned.

"Take no notice of them. They're trying to trick you!" she begged, and yanking hold of their arms tried to pull them back. But Alexandra and Tom rushed to help.

"Let them go!" cried Alexandra, and for a moment there was a scuffle.

"Stop interfering you, pesky girl!" growled Fiona.

"I'm not a girl anymore. I'm a woman!" retorted Alexandra, and with all the strength she could muster pushed Tom's stepmother away. Fiona stumbled backwards – straight into Queen Alexandra's arms.

"The biggest mistake I ever made was making you one of my court administrators!" remarked the queen of Geratica. "I'm sick and tired of you." Then she struck Fiona's shoulder hard with her fist (in the exact same spot that Fiona had once struck Robert with a truncheon, when she'd abducted him from Geratica). Fiona slumped to the chamber floor, stunned.

Meanwhile, Linda was beginning to discern the mistress's presence within her mind, though there was no communication. Perhaps her hunch had been correct. The keeper was continuing to scan her.

Alexandra and her mother both anxiously looked at the timer. It now registered three minutes. They only had that long before the

time meld would be complete, and a new world created at the expense of Geratica and Geraticai.

Queen Victoria was becoming impatient. "Keeper!" she shouted. "Please allow this new world to be created. I want to create unity at last. I alone shall be Queen of it, and I vow to be the greatest ever!"

The keeper took one last look at Linda and Alexandra, and then to Fiona lying on the chamber floor.

"No!" she cried, suddenly.

"What?" exclaimed Queen Victoria. "*Yes!*" She stamped her foot.

"This shall not be!" asserted the keeper. "I am familiar with this mistress's kind. She was noble in creating the world of Geratica, and Geraticai was indeed formed in parallel by accident, though it is now freely independent. No time guardians have the right to deny either one its existence, and those sent to my castle by the rest to prevent this time meld have displayed admirable qualities in persuading the woman Fiona's husband and stepson to join them. Fiona and the Geraticaian queen are motivated by greed and their lust for power!"

She banged her staff on the console. "Time guardians Lord Peter and Lady Evelyn be gone, I say, and let all the Geraticans and Geraticaians return to their worlds in their own time streams. They will remember nothing of this. Lord Peter and Lady Evelyn be banished *forever!*"

The Keeper of All Time banged her staff again, this time far harder. There was another huge flash of white light and the chamber span round and round...

***

In the domain of the time guardians of Geratica and Geraticai, the images of Lord Peter and Lady Evelyn were still on their screens, as they awaited the result of their attempted time meld. Now they saw Queen Victoria, Colin and Tom (5010) reappear and slip back inside their globe.

"The time meld has failed," observed Lord Peter.

Then both time guardians felt their lives draining away, their images fading from the screens as they died. The room exploded and was jettisoned from the domain...

***

At the same time, Queen Alexandra and Tom (5024) returned to the room where Lady Tara and Lord Anthony waited. The time guardians watched from their screens as they too went back inside their globe.

"The time meld has not been implemented," confirmed Lord Anthony. "We have been successful."

"Thanks to Linda and Alexandra Radcliffe, with their companions," remarked Lady Tara. "It is well. Now all can return to normal...

***

On Geraticai in 3960 (Geratica in 5010), Fiona stepped out of her transportation capsule and made her way through the complex of the royal palace in Arista, Spanda. She was on her way to meet Queen Victoria...

***

On Geratica in 5024, Linda and Alexandra walked into the state dining room of the Royal Palace in Avermore, Castra, and took their seats at the long table beside James and Tom, ready to enjoy the lunch prepared in honour of Queen Alexandra, to mark her silver jubilee...

THE END

AUTHOR'S NOTE

At the end of the original *'Geratica'* series, I said that the story was now completed. I did also say, however, that it was possible I might return to it.

I felt that there were enough previous events referred to in the series, to call for another which would principally serve as a prequel, but with a twist at the end which would link it to first the present and then the future.

It has been a pleasure to write for these characters again, and I hope that you have felt the same way in reading about them. If you have read all of the original books and now this, then I thank you, and sincerely hope that you have enjoyed the journey...

Anne Hampton
April 2017